"You saved my life. I desire now to wipe away the debt I owe you. So I will make my submission to you." Lady Margaret's voice had sunk, but it vibrated with her pride.

"I want more than that," Simon said.

"You seek my life?" she asked.

"Thy life, aye. All of thee." Suddenly he bent forward, and kissed her, full on her red lips. "I want thy hand in marriage."

She sprang away, trembling and shaken, pressing her hands to her hot cheeks. "For what do ye take me? Think I would wed an English boor?" She spat the words at him and her bosom heaved.

"I think that thou wilt wed me, madame. What I want, I take."

"Ye take not me! Mordieu, are ye mad? Wed me? I am Margaret of Belrémy!"

"Thou art my prisoner."

Fawcett Crest Books
by Georgette Heyer:

THE MASQUERADERS   23253 $1.75

THE TALISMAN RING   23675 $1.75

COUSIN KATE   23723 $1.75

Buy them at your local bookstore or use this handy coupon for ordering.

This offer expires July 1, 1981   8999

SIMON
the
COLDHEART

Georgette Heyer

FAWCETT CREST • NEW YORK

TO
THE MEMORY OF
MY FATHER—
THIS,
HIS FAVOURITE

Foreword

This is not 'a new Georgette Heyer', alas. A glance at the fly leaf will show that it was first published in 1925 when my mother was in her early twenties. Nevertheless, many of her readers will not have seen it before. With the exception of a female living in California who, for reasons which were somewhat obscurely expressed, considered that all her works should be publicly burned by the hangman, my mother was her own sternest critic, and many years ago had stated that there were some five or six titles which she never wished to see reprinted. This is one of them. After her death in 1974 I was persuaded to read the book once more, and soon came to the conclusion that, in this instance at all events, her judgment had been too harsh. The style of the book may not be that of a mature writer nor the scholarship profound, but it is easy to detect in it a quick eye for historical detail and an ability to paint a scene from another age which were to become the hallmarks of her later works. It is to be hoped that these qualities, added to the scores of requests for the book that she, her family, and her publisher have received over the years, will excuse such filial disobedience.

December 1977   R.G.R.

PART ONE

I

How he came to Fulk of Montlice

He came walking from Bedford into Cambridge one May morning when the sun was still young and the dew scarce gone from the grass. His worldly possessions he carried on his back in an old knapsack; his short jerkin was stained and torn, and there were holes in his long hose. On his square head and drawn over his brow he wore a frayed cap set jauntily, with a heron's feather pointing skywards. He carried a quarter-staff, and stepped out right manfully, scanning the flat fen-land from beneath his thick brows, his young mouth dogged, his sombre eyes coldly calculating. Of years he numbered fourteen, but his shoulders had a breadth beyond his age, and his thighs a thickness of muscle that gave him the appearance of a grown man dwarfed. Nor was the face below the clubbed fair hair that of a child, for in the low brow lay strength, and about the straight mouth purpose. There was little boyishness in the eyes, but a frowning look, and at the back, lurking in the green-blue depths, a watchful gleam that was never absent.

One spoke to him on the road, a pedlar tramping south, and gave him good-day. He answered in a crisp, deep voice, and smiled, showing a row of strong white teeth.

"Whither goest thou, younker?" the pedlar asked him idly.

"To my goal, fellow," Simon retorted, and passed on. The pedlar called after him for his haughtiness, but he paid no heed. He was never one to waste words.

So at length he came to Montlice, which was his goal, and stood for a moment before the drawbridge, surveying the rugged castle. A man-at-arms, lounging on the bridge, hailed him good-naturedly.

"What want ye, boy? This is the lion's den."

The glimmer of a smile came to light the darkness of Simon's eyes.

"I seek the lion," he said, and walked forward across the bridge.

The man laughed at him, barring his passage.

"Ho-ho! Ye seek the lion, eh? He would make but one mouthful of you, my fine sprig."

Simon looked up into his face, jutting brows lowering, eyes agleam.

"I seek my Lord the Earl," he said. "Out of the way, sirrah!"

At that the man clapped his hands to his sides, shaken with herculean laughter. Having recovered somewhat he achieved a clumsy bow.

"My lord is from home," he said, mocking Simon.

"You lie!" Simon answered quickly. "My lord will know how to punish a lying servant. Let me pass!" He awaited no permission, but slipped by, eel-like, and was gone across the bridge in a flash. Out of sight he paused, not hesitating, but seeming to debate within himself. He looked thoughtfully at the great gateway, standing wide with soldiers lounging there, and his lips tightened. He went swiftly through, light-footed and sure, and attracted but little notice. One of the men stopped his task to shout a surprised question after him, and Simon answered briefly over his shoulder: "On my lord's business!" The man laughed, thinking him some scullion's child, and turned back to his companion. Simon went on up the winding slope to the castle door and was there met by a group of men-at-arms who denied him ingress.

"To the scullions' entrance, babe!" one told him, and the muscles about his mouth stood out in anger. He kept his ground, not a whit afraid.

"I must see my lord," he answered, and only that.

"Wherefore, pup?" the man asked him, and when he would not answer, sought to hustle him roughly away.

But Simon wriggled from under his hands, and springing to one side, brought his heavy quarterstaff

9

down athwart the man's shoulders with so much force that, great man though he was, the soldier staggered.

Matters then would have gone ill with Simon but for the appearance of a boy, a little younger than himself, who came strolling towards them, followed by two liver-coloured hounds. He was dark, and magnificently clad, and he carried himself with an air of languid arrogance.

"Holà there!" he called, and the soldiers fell away from Simon, leaving him to stand alone, arms folded and head turned to survey the newcomer.

The boy came up gracefully, looking at Simon with a questioning lift to his brows.

"What is this?" he asked. "Who are you who strike our men?"

Simon stepped forward.

"So please you, sir, I seek my Lord the Earl."

One of the men, he whom Simon had dealt that lusty blow, started to speak, but was hushed by an imperious gesture from the boy. He smiled at Simon with a mixture of friendliness and hauteur.

"I am Alan of Montlice," he said. "What want you of my father?"

Simon doffed his cap, showing his thick, straight hair clubbed across his brow and at the nape of his brown neck. He bowed awkwardly.

"I want employment, sir," he replied. "These men deny me entrance."

Alan of Montlice hesitated.

"My father stands in no need—" he began, then paused, fingering his dark curls. "There is that in you that I like," he said frankly. "Come within."

Simon bowed again, but he gave no thanks, only standing aside for the young Montlice to pass through the doorway. And as Alan went by, he shot him an upward look, keen as steel, appraising him as it were. That was a trick which in after years had the effect of disconcerting his foes most mightily. Alan did not see the glance, but swept into the castle whistling through his teeth. Across the great stone hall he led Simon to an archway over which hung a leathern curtain, nail-studded. Before he pulled it back he spoke again to Simon, in a whisper.

"Ye will speak my lord fair," he cautioned. "He is not so douce."

The flickering smile touched Simon's lips.

"Fulk the Lion," he said. "I know."

"He is to be feared," Alan said, breathless.

Simon looked scorn.

"I fear no man."

At that Alan opened wide his brown eyes and giggled a little.

"Ye do not know my lord," he said, and pulled the curtain aside.

They entered a fair room carpeted with rushes and hung with all manner of paintings, biblical and historical. A table stood in the middle, and although it was now past eight o'clock in the forenoon, the remains of my lord's breakfast still stood upon it: a chine of salt-beef, a broken manchett, and a tankard of ale. In a great chair beside the table, leaning back at his ease, sat Fulk of Montlice, a giant of a man, deep-chested and magnificently proportioned, as fair as his son was dark, with a crisp, golden beard, whose point came forward belligerently. One of his hands was tucked in the belt of his long gown, the other lay on the table, massive and hairy. Alan ran forward and fell to his knees.

"Sir, here is a boy who would speak with thee."

My lord's heavy, light-lashed eyelids lifted and his small blue eyes travelled slowly from his son to Simon.

"Shouldst know that I do not speak with every vagrant whelp who is presumptuous," he said, a rumbling note of annoyance in his voice. "Away with you, sirrah!"

Simon stepped to the table, cap in hand.

"I am no vagrant, good my lord. Nor will I be so miscalled."

Alan stayed on his knees, affrighted at such temerity, but my Lord of Montlice laughed.

"Good lack, what then are you, springald?"

"I hope one day to be a man, my lord, even as you,"

11

Simon answered. "That is my ambition, sir, and so I come to seek employment with you."

Montlice flung back his head and laughed again.

"For that you beard the lion in his den, eh? I will eat you for my dinner, cockerel."

"So said they at the gate, my lord, but you will find me of more use alive than eaten."

"Shall I so? And what canst do? Wind silks for womenfolk?"

"That and other things, my lord," Simon answered coolly.

"Soso! What then? Tend my hounds, or are they too strong for your management?"

At that Simon curled his lip in disdain.

"There does not live the beast I will not tame, my lord."

My lord's eyes were now a-twinkle. He clapped the table jovially.

"By the Rood, I like thy spirit, my young spring-chicken! Canst take a buffet?"

"Ay, and give one."

My lord cast him a quizzical look.

"As thou didst to my man without?"

If he expected Simon to show discomfiture he was disappointed, for Simon only nodded. My lord laughed.

"Impudence! Why camest thou to the great door? Know ye not the scullions' entrance at the back?"

"I have never approached my goal through the back door, my lord, nor ever will. I march straight."

"It seems so indeed," said my lord. "Well, what dost thou want of me?"

"I would carry your lance and squire you, sir."

Montlice snapped his fingers, jeering.

"Thou sit a horse! A flea on a camel!"

The thick brows drew closer together and a little colour stole into Simon's cheeks.

"I shall grow, my lord."

"Nay, nay. Art too small. What are thy years?"

"Fourteen, sir."

"A babe, forsooth! Get thee gone, babe; I've no need of squires."

Simon stood still.

"Your page, then, till I am grown to your liking."

"God's my life, methinks thou art over-bold, babe, I do not take peasants for my pages."

"I am no peasant."

"Ho-ho! What then?"

"As gentle as yourself, my lord."

"By Our Lady! What art called?"

"Simon, my lord."

"Well, it's a name. What else?"

Simon lifted his shoulders, half-impatiently.

"I call myself Beauvallet, sir."

My lord pursed his full lips.

"It hath a ring," he nodded. "What is thy real name, sirrah?"

"I have none."

"Tush! Your father's name!"

Simon did not answer for a moment, but at last he shrugged again, and looked up.

"Geoffrey of Malvellet," he answered.

"Holy Virgin! I should have known that face! Art Malvallet's bastard then?"

"So my mother told me, my lord."

"Who is she? Does she live?"

"She is dead these four years, sir. She was one Jehanne, of Malvallet's household. That is nothing."

Montlice sank back again.

"Ay, ay. But what proof have you?"

"A ring, my lord. Little enough."

"Show me."

Simon put his hands up to his neck and drew a riband from his breast from which hung a golden ring. Montlice looked at it long and curiously.

"How came she by this?"

"I never asked, my lord. It matters not to me whether I am Malvallet's son or another's. I am what I choose to be."

"Here's a philosophy!" Montlice became aware of his son, still kneeling, and waved him to his feet. "What thinkest thou, Alan? Here is one of the Malvallet brood."

Alan leaned carelessly against the table.

"Malvallet is no friend of ours, sir, but I like this boy."

"He hath courage. Tell me, babe, where hast been since thy mother died?"

"I had a home with her brother, sir, a wood-cutter."

"Well, and then?"

"I wearied of it, my lord, and I came here."

"Why not to thy father, bantam?"

Simon jerked his shoulder again.

"Him I have seen, my lord."

Montlice rumbled forth a laugh.

"And liked not his looks?"

"Well enough, sir, but you also had I seen, and of both have I heard."

"God's Body, do I so take thy fancy?"

"Men call you the Lion, my lord, and think it harder to enter your service than that of Malvallet."

My lord puffed out his cheeks.

"Ay, so is it. Ye like the harder task, babe?"

Simon considered.

"It is more worth the doing, my lord," he replied.

My lord looked him over.

"Art a strange lad. Having forced thy way into my stronghold, thou'lt not leave it?"

"I will not."

"I am no easy master," Montlice warned him.

"I would not serve any such."

"Ye think to earn knighthood with me?"

Simon glanced up.

"What I become will be of mine own making, sir. I ask no favours."

"Then I like thee the better for it. Shalt be page to my son till I find thee fitter occupation. And that to spite Malvallet, look you. Art satisfied?"

Simon knelt.

"Ay, my lord. And I will serve you faithfully and well, that there shall be no gratitude to weigh me down."

Montlice smote him on the shoulder, delighted.

"Spoken like a sage, my little fish! Well, get thee gone. Alan, take him, and see to it that he is clothed and fed."

And thus it was that Simon came to Fulk of Montlice.

14

II

How he grew to manhood

From page to Alan, he became page to my lord himself, and was decked out in Montlice red and gold. Very brave he looked in the short red tunic worked with gold and caught in at the waist by a leathern belt. His hose were gold, his shoon red, and red was the cap that sat a thought rakishly on his fair head. His duties were many and arduous, nor did my lord spare him any fatigue or exertion. He slept on a hard pallet across Fulk's threshold, rose early and went late to bed. It was part of his duty to wait upon my lord and his lady at dinner, and every morning at ten Simon took his stand on the dais beside my lord's chair, attending to his wants or standing immobile the while my lord and his guests ate and drank their fill. He was at three people's beck and call: my lord, his lady, and young Alan, and he spent his time running from one to the other.

He grew apace in height and breadth and strength until there were few who could throw him in a wrestling match; few who could shoot an arrow farther or more precisely, be it at butt, prick or rover; and few who could stand beneath his mighty buffet. Yet for the most part he was gentle enough, if stern, and it was only when his cold anger was aroused that the caged lion within him sprang to life and swept all before it. And when that happened there came that light to his eyes which could make the hardiest evildoer cringe and the most arrogant squire cry mercy, even before Simon's iron hands had touched him.

Blows he received a-many, whenever my lord chanced to be in an ill-humour, which was often, but they never disturbed his cold composure, nor awakened any feeling of resentment in his breast. From Fulk he bore blows in an acquiescent mood that yet held no meekness nor humility, but woebetide the squire or serf who crossed his path belligerently inclined! When he still was page, my lord's squire, Lancelot of the Black Isle, commanded him loftily, and when Simon paid no heed to his orders, dealt him a buffet that should have felled him to the ground. Simon staggered under it, but recovered, and gave back blow for blow with so much force behind his steel wrist that Lancelot, full five years his senior, went tumbling head over heels and was sore and bruised for days after. When Fulk heard the tale he made Simon squire in Lancelot's room, and swore that there was more of himself in Simon than in his own son.

But it was seldom that Simon fell foul of his peers. His very calmness of temper compelled respect, and for that he was every inch a man, men liked him and were eager to call him friend. Friendship he never courted, caring nothing for man's opinion of himself, nor seemed he to have an ounce of affection in him, save it were for Fulk of Montlice, or Alan, whom he regarded with a mixture of contempt and liking. His father he saw a-many times, but it is doubtful whether Geoffrey of Malvallet noticed him. Once indeed at Bedford in the court of law, whither Simon had gone in Fulk's wake to settle a dispute over some land between Montlice and Malvallet, Geoffrey, glancing idly round, surprised an intent stare from his enemy's page, who sat with his chin in his hand, calmly and keenly scrutinizing him. Geoffrey looked him over haughtily, but when his eyes met Simon's and encountered that strangely disconcerting gleam he turned his head away quickly, a tinge of colour in his cheeks. Simon continued to survey him, not from any wish to annoy, but simply because he was interested, and wished to see what manner of man was his sire. He was not ill-pleased with what he saw, but neither was he enthusiastic. Geoffrey was a tall man, and slim, fastidious in his dress and appointments, soft-spoken, and proud—so said Montlice—as Lucifer himself. His close-cropped hair was grizzled now, but his eyes were like Simon's in colour, and as deep set. His eyebrows too were thick and straight, but his mouth was gentle and full-lipped, which Simon's was not, and his brow was not so rugged. He had one son, Geoffrey, who was just two years older than Simon, and whom Simon had never seen.

Between Alan and Simon positions were very soon reversed. It was Alan who gave devoted love and obedience; Simon received, and could return naught but a tolerant protection. They played together often, but in every sport Simon was an easy victor save when the game was of a gentle kind. At bowls and closh Alan could beat him, but when they played at balloon ball, Alan ruefully declared that he was no match for Simon, who played with his naked hand and struck the great leather ball with such deadly accuracy and strength that Alan was fain to dodge it instead of returning it. At archery he was even less skilled, and Simon watched his efforts to bend the bow with a contemptuous, rather amused air, which incensed young Alan so that he shot his arrow still more wide of the mark than ever. Simon tried to teach him the sport of the quarterstaff, and wielded his own staff moderately enough, in deference to Alan's tender years. But Alan, although he was not lacking in courage, disliked such rude and rough play, and would not engage with Simon. He liked to go out chasing or hawking, and he showed an aptitude for pretty and quick sword-play. Tourneys were not so much to his taste, and rather than enter into any of these pastimes would he sit at home, strumming upon his harp and weaving fanciful songs to his many lady-loves. He would paint, too, and make poesies, for all the world like some troubadour of a century ago. With the ladies he was ever a favourite, and by the time he was fifteen he was for ever paying court to some dame or another, greatly to Simon's disgust.

"Hast thou never loved?" he asked Simon once, plaintively.

They were sitting together in a room high up in one

17

of the turrets, Alan playing his harp, and Simon fashioning a new string to his great bow.

Simon did not raise his eyes from his task, but his lips curled disdainfully.

"Oh, love, love! Art for ever prating of this love. What is it?"

Alan played a soft chord or two, bending his handsome head a little to one side. His dark eyes glowed, and he smiled.

"Dost thou not know? Is there no maid who stirs thy heart?"

"I know of none," Simon answered shortly.

Alan put his harp away and crossed his shapely legs. He was wearing a tunic of peacock-blue velvet with long sleeves, lined with gold, that touched the ground. There was a jewel in his left ear, and a ring on his finger, while the belt that drew in his tunic at the waist was of wrought gold, studded with gems. He formed a striking contrast to Simon, who was clad in a long robe of crimson, with high boots on his feet and no ornament on all his dress. He still wore his hair clubbed at neck and brow, although it was now customary to display a close-cropped head. He was sixteen at the time, and already stood six foot in height, with mighty thews and sinews, a broad back down which the muscles rolled and rippled, and a pair of arms that were bear-like in their strength. Beside Alan's slim figure he seemed a very giant.

Alan watched him for a moment, still smiling.

"My sisters are not so ill-looking," he remarked, a laugh in his eyes. "Elaine is perhaps more comely than Joan."

"Is she?" Simon said, still intent on his task.

"Which dost thou like the best, Simon?" Alan asked softly.

"I know not. I have never thought." He glanced up, a sudden smile flashing across his face. "Dost suggest that one of them should stir my heart?"

"They do not? Ye feel not the smallest pulse-leap in their presence?"

Simon stretched his new string experimentally.

"A pulse-leap," he said slowly. "What folly! My pulse

18

leaps when I have sent an arrow home, or when I have thrown my man, or when a hawk has swooped upon its prey."

Alan sighed.

"Simon, Simon, is there no softness in thee at all? Dost love no one?"

"I tell thee I know not what it is, this Love. It stirs me not! I think it is nothing save the sick-fancy of a maudlin youth."

Alan laughed at that.

"Thy tongue stings, Simon."

"If it might sting thee to more manly pastimes than this moaning of love, 'twere to some purpose."

"But it will not. Love is all. One day thou'lt find that I speak sooth."

"I wonder!" Simon retorted.

Again Alan sighed.

"Simon, what hast thou in place of a heart? Is it a block of granite that ye carry in your breast? Is no one anything to you? Am I nothing? Is my lord nothing? There is no love in you for either of us?"

Simon laid his bow down, and began to polish an arrow.

"Art like a whining babe, Alan," he rebuked his friend. "What shouldst thou be but my lords, thou and Montlice?"

Alan stretched out his hands.

"That is not what I would be to thee!" he cried. "I give you Love, and what dost thou give me in return? Hast a single spark of affection for me, Simon?"

Simon selected another arrow, and passed his hand over its broad feather almost lovingly. He looked thoughtfully at Alan, so that the boy sprang up, flushing.

"Thou carest more for that arrow than for me!"

"That is folly," Simon answered coolly. "How can I tell thee what my feelings are when I do not know myself?"

"Couldst thou leave Montlice today without one pang of regret?" demanded Alan.

"Nay," Simon said. "But one day I shall. For the present I bide, for I want some years to full manhood.

19

And I am happy here, if that is what thou wouldst know. Between thee and me is friendship, and between my Lord Fulk and me is understanding. A truce to this silly woman's talk."

Alan sat down again, twanging his harp discordantly.

"Thou art so strange, Simon, and so cold. I wonder why I do so love thee?"

"Because thou art weak," Simon replied curtly, "and because thou takest delight in such fondlings."

"Maybe," Alan shrugged. "Thou at least art not weak."

"Nay," Simon said placidly. "I am not weak, neither am I strange. See if thou canst bend that bow, Alan."

Alan glanced at it casually.

"I know I cannot."

"Shouldst practise then. Thou wouldst please my lord."

"Certes, I do not want to please him. I was not fashioned for these irksome sports. 'Tis thou who shouldst try to please him, for 'tis thou whom he loves."

Simon balanced a broad feathered arrow on his forefinger.

"Good lack, what has my lord to do with love? There is little enough of that in his heart."

"So ye think!" retorted Alan. "I know that he watches thee fondly. Perchance he will knight thee soon."

"I have done naught to deserve it," replied Simon shortly.

"Natheless, he will do it, I think. He might even give thee one of my sisters in marriage if thou didst wish it, Simon."

"I am not like to. There is no place for women in my life, and no liking for women in my breast."

"Why, what will be thy life?" asked Alan.

Then at last a gleam shone in Simon's eyes, cold yet eager.

"My life will be"—he paused—"what I choose to make it."

"And what is that?"

"I will tell thee one day," Simon said, with a rare touch of humour. Then he gathered up his arrows and went away, treading heavily yet noiselessly, like some great animal.

True it was that Fulk cared for him more than for his own son. The lion-spirit was not in Alan, and between him and his father was less and less understanding as the years passed by. Fulk's jovial roughness, his energetic ways, his frequent law-suits, wearied and disgusted Alan, and in the same way Alan's fastidious temper and more cultured tastes became the subject for Fulk's jeers and sighs. In place of his son Fulk turned to Simon and took him wherever he went, sparing him no exertion nor hardship, but watching his squire's iron equanimity with an appreciative, almost admiring eye. Thus, bit by bit, grew up between the two an odd understanding and affection, never spoken of, but there at the root of their attitude towards each other. Fulk wanted not servility nor maudlin love, and from Simon he got neither. Strength was the straight road to his heart, and fearlessness: Simon had both. They were not always at one, and sometimes a quarrel would crop up when neither would give way an inch, when Fulk stormed and raged like a wounded buffalo, and when Simon stood rock-like, unshaken by anything Fulk might do to him, icy anger in his strange eyes, inflexible obstinacy about his mouth, and his brows forming a straight line across his hawk-nose.

"What I have I hold!" Fulk roared at him once, pointing to the device on his shield.

"I have not, but still I hold," Simon retorted.

Fulk's eyes showed red a moment, and a fleck of foam was on his pointing beard.

"God's Wounds!" he barked. "Am I to be braved by you, mongrel-whelp? It will be the whip for you, or a dungeon-cell!"

"And still I shall hold," Simon answered him, folding his arms across his great chest.

"By Death, I will tame you, wild-cat!" Fulk cried, and drew back his fist to strike. But even as he would have done so, he checked himself, and the red went out of his eyes. A grin came, and a rumbling laugh.

" 'I have not, but still I hold,' " he repeated. "Ho-ho!

'I have not, but—' Ho-ho!" Chuckling, he smote Simon on the shoulder, a friendly blow which would have crumpled an ordinary stripling to the ground. He became indulgent, even coaxing. "Come lad! Thou'lt do as I bid thee!"

Coaxing left Simon as unmoved as the late storm. He shook his fair head stubbornly.

"Nay, I go mine own road in this."

The red light showed again.

"Dare ye defy me?" roared Fulk, and closed his huge hand on Simon's shoulder. "I can snap thy puny body as a reed!"

Simon shot him that upward, rapier-glance.

"I dare all," he said.

The grip on his shoulder tightened until little rivulets of pain ran down from it across his chest. He did not so much as wince, but held Fulk's look steadily. Slowly the grip relaxed.

"Ay, ye dare," Fulk said. "I am of a mind to break thee over my knee."

"That is as may be," Simon answered. "But still I shall hold."

At that Fulk broke into a great laugh, and released him.

"Oh, go thine own road, cub, so ye do not take it into thy hot head to hold me!"

Simon looked him over, frowning.

"That I think I cannot do," he said. "I am not sure."

Whereat Fulk laughed the more and liked him the better.

When his seventeenth birthday came Simon was already a man in build and cool sagacity. In face he had changed hardly at all, save that his forehead was more rugged, the thick brows jutting further over the deep-set eyes of green-blue, and that his mouth had lost its youthful curve together with any softness that it might once have had. He smiled but rarely, nor ever laughed out as did my Lord of Montlice. If he laughed it was a short, dry sound, somewhat sardonic in tone, and quickly gone, but when he smiled there were two ways he had of doing it; one when he was crossed, that one more terrible than his frown, the other when he

22

was in smiling humour, a singularly sweet smile, this, with a hint of boyishness at the back of it.

Fulk knew him for a soldier born, and a leader of men. If a disturbance arose in the Earl's vast household it was Simon who quenched it when the fussy, incompetent Marshal had failed, and the Steward threatened in vain. The guards, inactive and fractious, would quarrel among themselves, and, heated by too much sack, come to blows and noisy, perilous fights. It needed but for Simon to come upon them with his soft tread and his cold composure to cause the brawlers to fall apart, great men though they were, and stand sheepishly before him, answering his crisp, stern questions with a meekness they did not show to John the Marshal. Boy as he was, Simon could reduce the most drunken roysterer to a state of penitent humility. He had but to use that upward glance of his and all insubordination was at an end. This he very soon discovered, and came to use the disconcerting look more than ever. There was something compelling in his appearance, an elusive air of rulership and haughtiness, and a suggestion of a hidden force that was invincible. Montlice recognized this as the Malvallet in him, and chuckled to himself, watching. He set Simon to rule his guards, and observed his ruthless methods with amusement. He would not throw the garment of his protection about his squire, wondering how he would maintain his position alone. Simon wanted no protection and found no difficulty in maintaining his position. At first, when he interfered in some quarrel, he met with insolence and threatened blows. That lasted for a very little time. Men found that insolence moved him to an icy-anger that was to be dreaded, and if it came to blows there would be broken ribs, or dislocated jaws for those whom Simon's fist struck. Therefore it swiftly ceased to come to blows. If it was a question of judgment or arbitration men found Simon relentlessly, mercilessly just, and because of this justice, no complaints of him were carried to my Lord Fulk.

With all his harshness and cold demeanour Simon was liked and trusted. The grumblers dwindled in number, for Simon had short shrift for any such. His code was a queer one, and men found his advice puzzling. But when they had slowly unravelled his line of thought they found it good, and this because it was his own code.

A guard met him once on the battlements and unfolded a tale of woe. One of his companions had a spite against him and plagued away his life. On this day the man had slyly tripped him up with his spear, so that he was burning to be avenged. What would Simon do for him?

"Naught," Simon answered curtly. "Fight thine own battle."

"Yet, sir, if I strike this man as he deserves, you will come upon us and have us shut up for brawling, or maybe whipped."

"But ye will have struck him," Simon said, and walked on, leaving his man to think it over.

Presently the man came to him again.

"Sir, if I punish mine enemy and there be something of a brawl, we shall both be punished by you."

Simon nodded indifferently.

"But if I strike him hard enough, methinks he will not again plague me."

"That is so," Simon said.

"I think I will strike him," decided the man, and straightway went to do so.

There was indeed something of a brawl, and as a consequence Simon had them both under lock and key for twenty-four hours. But neither bore him any ill-will, nor was there another complaint lodged on the matter. Simon knew his men, and his method of ruling was his own, rude as were those men, and as rough. He was master, and not one of them thought to dispute the fact.

Fulk, watching from afar, smote his thigh and laughed triumphantly.

"The boy is a man," he said, hugely delighted. "And was there ever such another?"

III

How he went with Fulk to Shrewsbury

At the time of Simon's seventeenth birthday, affairs in Wales and the North of England had reached something approaching a crisis. It was in the year 1403, when Bolinbroke had sat upon the throne for four years, and his son, Henry of Monmouth, had held the reins of government in Wales, unassisted, for some months only. Although he was but sixteen years of age, the Prince had already led a punitive expedition into North Wales, and considerably harried the rebel, Owen Glyndourdy. But now Percy, the redoubtable Hotspur, had, with his father, the Earl of Northumberland, and his uncle, the Earl of Worcester, raised his standard in the North against the King, and was on the point of marching to join Glyndourdy in Wales.

It was in July that these state affairs first affected Montlice, although for some time past Fulk, ever-ready for war, had chafed and fretted in his fair land, debating whether he should take his men to join the Prince on the Marches or no. His uncertainty rendered him irritable to all who crossed his path; only Simon understood the reason of this irritability, and he gave no sign that he understood. But although he said little, he too was watching affairs, and under his habitual placidity was a glowing desire to be gone from quiet Montlice to Shrewsbury where lay the Prince of Wales with his insufficient army and his insufficient supplies.

One rode hot-haste through Cambridge, early in the month, and came to Montlice, covered with dust, dropping with fatigue, upon a jaded horse whose sides were flecked with foam, and whose slender legs trembled when at last he was checked before the bridge of the castle of Montlice.

"In the King's Name!" he cried to those who would have questioned him, and passed over the bridge and up the winding path to the castle at a stumbling trot. At the great door he was met by Simon, coming forth to target practice. "In the King's Name!" he said again, and slipped wearily to the ground. "My lord the Earl is within, young sir?"

"Ay." Simon beckoned to one of the guards who came to the tired horse's head. "Take yon beast to the stables, William, and see to it that he is well cared for. Come within, sir." He led the King's Messenger through the great, central hall where the scullions were clearing away the remains of dinner, to the room where he himself had first come to Fulk. The same leathern curtain hung across the doorway, and Simon pulled it back, stepping aside for the Messenger to enter.

"My lord," he said calmly, "one comes from the King." Then, seeing the man safely within, he let fall the curtain and went out again to his target practice.

When at length he returned he found the Messenger departed and Fulk roaring for his squire. Even before he had set foot across the threshold of the castle he could hear his lord bellowing his name from the hall. He went in unhurriedly, and found that Fulk was standing at the foot of the winding stairway, vainly calling him. Alan sat in a great chair by the empty fireplace, and Simon saw at once that he was perturbed and a little nervous.

"You called, my lord?" Simon said, walking forward across the stone floor.

Fulk wheeled about.

"So thou art here! And where hast been, cub? I have shouted myself hoarse, thou hapless fool!"

Simon propped his bow up against the wall.

"I have been shooting without, sir. What is your pleasure?"

"Shooting without, forsooth!" roared Fulk. Then of a sudden his wrath died down. "Well, well, we shall have need of it belike. Come thou hither, Simon lad."

26

Simon came to the table, and Fulk handed him a sheet of parchment. Simon read it through slowly, the while my lord puffed and blew, and stamped his feet, for all the world like some curbed-in battle-horse.

"Well," Simon said at last. "So we go to war." He gave the King's writ back to Fulk and frowned. "We can make ready in the space of three days," he added tranquilly.

Fulk laughed, stuffing the parchment into his belt.

"Thou cold little fish! Is it nothing that the King has sent for me to join him at Shrewsbury?"

"Nay, it is a great thing," answered Simon, "but I shall not be in a heat because of it. That is foolish."

"Holy Virgin, why?" demanded Fulk.

"There will be more done, and that expeditiously, if a head is kept firm upon one's shoulders."

"Wise boy!" Fulk shook with laughter. "Eh, but one would think thou hadst been in a dozen campaigns! Sit thee down, my Simon, that I may confer with thee. See our Alan there. The lad's in a ferment! Never fret, Alan, I'll not take thee along with me."

Alan flushed at the taunt.

"Indeed, sir, and that is my place! Dost say I shall not ride forth with thee?" he cried.

"A pretty captain wouldst thou make!" jeered Fulk. "Paling at every sound, weary ere ever the day is begun! Thou'lt stay with the womenfolk. 'Twill be more to thy taste, methinks."

Up sprang Alan in a rage.

"It is not to be borne!" he cried. "I have as much courage as thou, and I say it is my right to go with thee!"

"And I say thou art a very babe," Fulk replied. "It is Simon I will take." Then as Alan looked as though he would fly at him, he spoke more gently, pleased at his son's fury. "Nay, nay, Alan, calm thyself. I did not mean to taunt thee. Art too young for a hard campaign, but shalt rule here in my stead."

"I tell thee—"

Fulk brought his fist down on the table so that the boards almost cracked beneath it.

"Hold thy tongue! What I have said I have said. Sit thee down again!"

Alan went sulkily to his chair and sank into it. Satisfied that he was silenced for the time, Fulk turned to Simon.

"Look you, Simon, there are six score men-at-arms I can muster, and eight score archers, under Francis of Dalley. There is John the Marshal, and Vincent, my captain. No puny force that, lad! And thou shalt ride with me and taste the joys of war. Does the prospect please thee?"

"Very well," Simon said, with the glimmer of a smile. "Which way do we go?"

For over an hour they discussed the various routes, until Alan began to yawn and fidget.

"It is through Northampton and Warwick I will go!" declared Fulk obstinately.

"And thereby waste time," said Simon. "It is through Lutterworth and Tamworth, or Lichfield, we must go."

"I say I will not! Who can tell in what state are the roads that way, foolish boy?"

"The Messenger came through Lichfield, sir," remarked Alan languidly. "He made no complaint."

"Well, I will think on it," growled Fulk. "Hotspur is marching towards Chester, so we must e'en take the speediest road." He heaved himself out of his chair. "And now to tell my lady," he said, and tugged ruefully at his beard. For my lady, gentle though she was, was the only being before whom Fulk bent the knee of his headstrong obstinacy. He went heavily up the stairs now to her bower, leaving Alan and Simon alone.

Alan bent down, fondling one of the hounds.

"Thou hast the luck, Simon," he said.

"Thou dost not want to go," Simon answered. "What are wars to thee?"

"How can I tell when I have never taken part in one?"

"Ye quibble," Simon said harshly. "Wilt be happier here with thy lady-loves."

Alan said nothing for a while, still stroking his hound. At length he sat back in his chair.

"Needs must I win my spurs one day," he said. "Why not now?"

"Time enough," Simon replied. "This will mean forced marches over rough ground. Thou wouldst be weary ere thou hadst come to Shrewsbury."

Alan looked wistfully up at him.

"And—and thou who art but one year my senior—art made of iron."

"Hadst thou led the life I have led since my birth thou also wouldst be of sterner stuff."

"Or dead," Alan said, smiling.

"Ay, perhaps. Where went the Messenger from here?"

"To Grayman, and from thence to the Baron of Shirley. He was at Malvallet two days ago. The King calls for his loyal servants. I wonder, shall we vanquish Percy?"

"God willing," Simon answered.

"God willing indeed. Right must triumph."

"In that case," said Simon drily, "Hotspur is like to win."

Alan opened his eyes wide.

"Simon! The King—the King—is the King!"

"So too was Richard," Simon reminded him.

Alan digested this.

"And—and so thou dost not believe that—that right must win?"

"Not I!" Simon laughed shortly. "Might and generalship will win. What else?"

Alan hesitated.

"Simon, I fear me 'tis as Father Peter says," he remarked gravely.

Simon cast him an inquiring glance.

"What says our worthy priest?"

"That thou art thought godless in thy spirit."

Simon laughed again, and this time the sardonic note sounded strongly.

"When said he this, Alan? Do I not attend Mass, and go I not to Confession?"

"Ay—but—sometimes thou dost say things. . . . Father Peter spoke to my lord of you."

Simon was smiling now, so that his eyes were almost slits.

"And what answered my lord?"

"Oh, my father said: 'Let be, Simon is very well.'"

"Ay, so I think. Set thy mind at rest, Alan, I am no heretic."

Alan started up, shocked.

"Simon, I meant not that! Nor did Father Peter."

"What a heat over naught!" Simon jeered. "What if thou hadst meant it? Yet I do not think I look a Lollard."

"Oh, no, no!" Alan cried, and wondered to hear Simon laugh again.

Three days later Fulk left Montlice with his following, and started on the arduous march to Shrewsbury. And rough ground as much of it was they arrived at that town at the end of the week, one day before the King himself, who was hastening there to throw his army between the oncoming Hotspur and the Prince.

Some sprinkling of men Fulk lost on the march, but his casualties were few, so that he remarked with unwonted philosophy that if the weaklings would all fall out before they came to Shrewsbury, so much the better. Now that he was in action his irritability left him, and he surprised Simon by his good humour, and his patience in cheering on his men. His joviality was infectious, and it was a light-spirited little army that halted before the gates of Shrewsbury at the end of that weary week. They were welcomed royally, and quartered well, and within an hour of their coming the Prince of Wales sent to bid my lord wait on him at once. So Fulk sallied forth, accompanied only by his squire, and made all haste to Henry's court. It was there, while waiting for Fulk to emerge from his audience, that Simon first met his half-brother, Geoffrey of Malvallet.

Geoffrey had arrived not twenty-four hours before Montlice, leading his men in place of his father who was sick at home. Simon recognized him at once from his likeness to Malvallet.

Geoffrey was sauntering through the great hall. He lounged past Simon, and glancing casually over his shoulder to see who it was, was startled to find that he was the object of a directly piercing stare, cast upward at him from under heavy brows. He paused on his way, and returned that stare from his superior two inches in height.

He was a handsome young man, some nineteen years of age, dark as Simon was fair, but with the same projecting forehead and green-blue eyes. But where Simon's eyes were cold, Geoffrey's sparkled; and where Simon's mouth was hard, Geoffrey's had a softer curve of laughter. It curved now in unveiled amusement, and his eyes twinkled merrily.

"What's to do, young cockalorum?" he asked. "Whence that haughty frown? My complexion likes you not, perchance?"

Simon came forward, and as he came Geoffrey saw the red and gold device on his surcoat. His smile faded, and he half shrugged his shoulders.

"Ha, one of the Montlice brood!" he said, and would have turned on his heel.

"Nay," Simon said. "Though I would as lief be that as aught else."

Malvallet paused, and looked him over.

"And what are you, Master Deep-Voice!"

"I think I am Nobody, Sir Geoffrey."

"Why so do I!" Malvallet mocked him. "And being Nobody, see ye cast me not another such glance as I surprised today, for it may be that I am hot of temper."

Simon smiled then, not a whit angered.

"It may also be that I am strong of arm," he said.

"Well, see ye cross not my path again," Malvallet answered. "I am not so puny, I give you warning." He strode on, leaving Simon to look after him with a curious glint in his eyes, not unfriendly.

Then Fulk came out in rare good spirits, and bore his squire back to their quarters, making him ride beside him instead of a few paces behind.

"By my troth, Simon," he said energetically, "that boy is a man, with all a man's brain and courage!"

Simon turned his head.

"The Prince, my lord?"

"Ay, young Henry of Monmouth. He is one year thy junior, but by God, he is three years thy senior as well! And thou art no babe."

Simon bent to pass his hand thoughtfully down his horse's neck.

"What thinks he, sir? Can we hold against Hotspur?"

Fulk shot him a sidelong glance, and pursed his small mouth.

"Who shall say, Simon? It is said that Hotspur is fourteen hundred strong. And he hath Douglas with him, and Worcester, with Glyndourdy like to join him ere we can engage. Word is brought that he is little over a day's march from here. We are a handful, and if help comes not we can but hold the town."

"The while Glyndourdy joins him. H'm! Where lies the King this night?"

"I know not. If he comes before Hotspur all may be well. But . . ."

"What manner of man is this Henry of Bolinbroke?" asked Simon. "Is he one to allow another to forestall him?"

"Nay, by the Rood! Henry is a man, even as his son."

"Then I doubt not he will be with us before Percy," said Simon placidly. "Whate'er befall, it will be an interesting combat."

"It is like to be bloody enough to satisfy even thy savage heart," Fulk grunted. He shifted a little in his saddle. "Malvallet is here."

"I know."

"Hast seen him then? 'Tis not thy father, but his first-born. Thy father lies sick of a fever."

"Doth he so? I have spoken with Geoffrey of Malvallet. While ye were with his Highness."

"Spoken with him?" Fulk turned to look at him. "What said he? Why didst thou accost him, pray?"

"I did not. I but looked, and my look misliked him. Wherefore he gave me warning that I should not again cross his path."

Fulk laughed.

"That swift glance of thine, eh, Simon? So Malvallet called thee to book? And what dost thou think of him?"

"He seems a man," Simon answered, and then relapsed into a silence which was not broken until they came back to their lodging.

A little after noon on the following day Simon sallied forth from his quarters and went afoot through the packed town towards the battlements. The streets were thronged with soldiers, both of high estate and low, so that Simon's progress was necessarily slow. But at length he came to the battlements, on the east side of Shrewsbury, and entered into conversation with some of the men-at-arms stationed there. He was permitted, presently, to mount the battlements, and stood behind the parapet, looking out across the country. The breeze stirred his fair hair, and whipped his surcoat about his legs. He leaned his hands on the low wall; closely scanning the surrounding country. Thus he stood, motionless, until an officer came up to him.

"Well, young sir, and what seest thou?" he asked, rather amused.

"I do not know," Simon answered. "Presently I will tell you."

The officer shaded his eyes from the sun, looking out from under his hand to where Simon gazed.

"There is naught, Sir Sharp-eyes. No sign of life of Hotspur or of our King. For the one God be praised, and for the other God pity us. Ye came with Montlice?"

"Ay." Still Simon stared at the distant horizon, his eyes narrowed and keen.

The officer laughed at him.

"Do ye think to take my place in spying out the approach of men?" he inquired.

"Mine eyes are sharper than most," Simon replied. "See yonder!" He stretched out his arm, pointing to the south-east.

The officer screwed up his face against the sun's rays, blinking rapidly.

"What is it? I see naught."

"Look more to the right. There, coming over the brow of the hill. Something moves. Do ye see it not?"

The man leaned forward, again shading his eyes.

"Naught," he said uneasily. "Art sure, Sir Squire?"

Simon's gaze did not waver.

"Ay, I am sure. Something is coming over yonder hill, for I can see movement, and ever and anon there is a glistening like a tiny star. That is the sun on armour."

The officer turned to hail one of his men.

"Godfrey! Come hither! Ye have sharp eyes. What can ye see yonder?"

The archer stared at the far-away hills for a long time in silence.

"A clump of trees, my captain," he ventured at last.

"Nay, not that. Coming over the brow, more to the right."

"I see naught, sir. Ah!"

"Well, what?"

"Little enough, sir, or perhaps mine eyes deceived me. Methought I saw a twinkling. There again!"

Captain Lenoir turned again to Simon.

"Mayhap ye are right, sir. But I'll sound no alarm till we see more plainly. If what ye see is indeed an army it is twenty miles distant, or more. If it is Hotspur, we—"

At last Simon turned.

"Hotspur? What folly is this? Hotspur will come from the north, from Chester. What I see is the King's army."

"It may be." Paul Lenoir looked out again, and in a moment gave a start. "I saw a flash! Yet another!"

"Ye will see them more and more as the army comes over the hill," Simon remarked.

Lenoir sat down upon the parapet.

"I would give something for thine eyes, sir. May I not know thy name? I am called Paul of Lenoir."

"I am Simon of Beauvallet." He too sat down on the parapet, and for a long time they stayed thus, saying little, but ever watching the twinkling line that was slowly growing. And at last Paul of Lenoir rose and gave orders for the trumpeters to blare forth the great news that the King's army was approaching. Then Simon left him, and went back to his lord's side.

The town was of a sudden in a ferment, the streets more crowded than ever, some men cheering, others asking excited questions, others gloomily prophesying that it was Percy and not the King who had made a cunning detour in order to bewilder them. One and all rushed to the walls to verify the joyous tidings, and Simon's progress was even slower than it had been before.

He came upon Fulk, who was conferring with his marshal, and would have passed him silently had not Fulk called after him.

"Ha, Simon! Where hast been? Is the King indeed approaching?"

Simon paused.

"Ay, my lord. He is over twenty miles from here, but he brings a fair army as I should judge."

"Saw ye the approach then?"

"I have been with one Lenoir upon the battlements and espied the army by the glittering of armour in the sun."

"I dare swear thou wert the first to do so, my lynx-eyed Simon!"

"Ay, but one saw them not long after me. They will be at the gates soon after dusk, for they are marching swiftly."

He proved to be right, for not long after sundown an advance guard from the army galloped up to the gates to tell, officially, of the King's coming in full force. The gates were opened, and the young Prince of Wales rode out to stand there in readiness to receive his father. Henry came at last, and publicly embraced his son. Then he rode into the town beside him, while the excited inhabitants who lined the streets cheered till they were hoarse, flinging flowers before him, and scuffling among themselves to obtain a better view.

Within an hour a council was summoned from which Fulk did not return until well into the night, when Simon lay sleeping peacefully and dreamlessly upon his hard pallet.

They had hardly risen next morning when my lord's page came flying in with the news that Percy had appeared before the walls, and at sight of the royal banner, withdrawn his men, some thought to one place, some to another.

Fulk summoned his squire to him, and made all

haste to the court, which they found packed with the various captains and generals. The King held another council, and when Fulk at last rejoined Simon his eyes were kindling with the lust for battle, and his mouth smiled grimly.

"We are to march forth, God be thanked!" he told Simon. "Glyndourdy is not come, so the King will pit his strength against Percy. Stafford is to lead the van, the King takes the right wing, and the Prince the left. We are to go with the Prince. Malvallet also. Malvallet is the Prince's friend," he added. "I did not know. He is very like thee in face, Simon."

"Save that he is dark. Do we enrol ourselves under the Prince's standard?"

"Ay, at once. Summon me John the Marshal and Vincent, lad, and see to it that thou bearest thyself in readiness within the hour. I will carry my great cross-hilted sword, and the old lance."

Simon nodded and went quickly away to carry out his orders. In an hour he was fully equipped, riding behind his lord, and after what seemed to be a marvellously short time, the army was marched out of the town, fourteen to fifteen hundred strong, north to Hayteley-hill, whereon Hotspur had drawn up his army.

"God's my life!" muttered Fulk. "This is a pretty place for fighting!"

Simon surveyed the ground coolly, and frowned a little. Along the foot of the hill were a number of ponds, and in front of them grew thick rows of peas. Behind these obstructions were the rebels ensconced.

There was a long, long wait, during which the horses stamped and fidgeted restlessly, and the men murmured among themselves. Then from the royal lines went forth a herald to treat with Percy. Another wait followed, and the herald returned, accompanied by a man clad all in armour and mounted on a fine horse, with his squire behind him.

"Worcester," said Fulk. "Are we to treat, then?"

No one had an answer for him, and he sat silent, waiting. To Simon it seemed hours before the Earl returned to the rebel lines, and after that was still another long pause. Evidently Hotspur refused to accept the terms laid before him, for there was a stir in the enemy's lines, and word came down the King's army that the King was about to give the order to "advance banner." It was now long past noon, and from the impatient, chafing men came something of a cheer, and cries of "St George for England! St George, St George!"

Fulk settled himself more firmly in his saddle, curbing his horse's sidling movements.

"Is thy blood fired, Simon?" he asked, smiling from beneath his helmet.

Simon's eyes looked out, cool and watchful as ever.

"Ay," he said shortly. "Does Stafford charge?"

Fulk nodded.

"God help him, yes! I mislike the look of yon army, Simon. Hotspur is no novice in battle, but there is some talk of a prophecy concerning him that says he will fall today. Keep at my back as far as thou art able, and do not lose thy head. Hey, we are moving—and so are they!"

After that there was no time for conversation. Through the hampering growth of peas charged the van, led by Stafford, and to meet him came Hotspur, thundering down the hill with spears levelled, and from either wing the archers shooting. Suddenly the air seemed thick with flying arrows, and alive with cries and the clash of arms. Among the ponds and beyond them the vans of the two armies engaged, and for a while nothing could be seen save a medley of soldiers fighting together in growing disorder.

A shout went up from Hotspur's lines, and one cried from beside Simon: "Stafford is down, and they are through!"

An order ran down the Prince's flank, and in a moment they were in action, galloping forward to charge the enemy's right wing.

In a minute they seemed to be in the midst of a storm of flying arrows. One whistled past Simon's head, but he only laughed, and spurred on, trampling peas underfoot, and hacking through. A cry came to his ears, taken up by many voices: "The Prince is wounded! The Prince is wounded!" The ranks wavered and fell back irresolute, appalled by the flood of arrows. One rode up to the Prince who had plucked the arrow from out his cheek, and was stanching the blood. He seemed to remonstrate, to try to force Henry away. But the Prince shook him off, and rose in his stirrups, waving his sword. His clear, young voice was wafted back to the serried lines.

"Onward, onward!" he shouted. "Follow me!" He set spur to his horse and charged forward. "St George, St George for us!" he cried.

Others followed his example. Montlice and Malvallet galloped forward side by side with Simon a little to the fore.

"Follow the Prince!" roared Fulk. "The Prince and Victory!"

A rumble went through the lines: "The Prince, the Prince!" There was a sudden surge forward, as the King's men charged up the hill after that heroic, flying figure. Some fell into the disastrous ponds, some stumbled in the entangling pea-rows, but the bulk kept on till they had overtaken their leader. Then onward still to meet the enemy's right flank. Like some heavy thunderbolt they fell upon it, and carried on, as it were, by their own impetus, they rolled it back and back, hacking and hewing before and beside them, until they had enclosed it between themselves and the King's division.

Far away to the right Simon could see Fulk, swept from him by the tide of men, wielding his sword like one possessed; and nearer to him was Malvallet, cut off from the main body of the fight and hard-pressed by Percy's men, yet holding his own nobly. From his own tight-packed corner Simon saw Malvallet's horse go down, and Malvallet spring clear. A man on foot caught at his own horse's rein, but before he could strike Simon had bent forward and slashed him across his unvisored face. Then he broke free, and cut himself a way to where Malvallet fought. Down he came upon the group at a full gallop, and ere the rebels could turn to see what it was that fell upon them so suddenly like a bolt from the blue, he had struck. His huge sword with all his iron strength behind it descended on one hapless shoulder where it joined his victim's neck, and cleaved through the sheltering armour as though it had been so much cardboard. As the man fell, soundless, Simon came to Malvallet's side, and sprang to earth. His sword swept a circle before them, and with his free hand he thrust the horse's bridle into Malvallet's hand.

"Up, up!" he cried, and sprang forward, lithe as a panther, to bring one man to earth by a single stroke so nicely measured, with so much skill and brute force behind it, that his two-edged sword split the helm on which it fell, and also its wearer's crown. He leaped back again as Malvallet shook the reins clear of his arm.

"At my back!" Geoffrey gasped, and swept his sword up suddenly to intercept a deadly blow at his neck.

"Fool!" Simon answered in a fury. He caught his horse as it would have bolted past him, and setting his feet squarely, forced it back upon its haunches. From the saddle-holster he snatched his treasured bow which not all Fulk's remonstrances had induced him to leave behind. Down he went on his knee, seeing that Malvallet could still stand alone, and calmly fitted an arrow to the bow. Calmly, too, he took aim, and bent that mighty weapon. The arrow sang forth, but so sure was Simon of his skill, equal, Fulk said, to that of the best bowman in all Cheshire, that he paused not to see it hit its mark. One after another he fitted arrows to his bow, and shot them among the dwindling group about Malvallet, until a sound behind him warned of danger. Up he sprang, cat-like, and in a flash exchanged bow for sword. And with this he did so much good work that when Malvallet came to guard his back, he had killed a man outright, and dealt three others some shattering blows.

"I am with thee!" Malvallet called from behind, but Simon needed no encouragement. Not for nothing had he trained his muscles throughout the years he had been at Montlice. His arm seemed tireless, his eye unwavering.

Then the body of the fight swept down upon them, and they were all but lost in its writhing masses. Free of his assailants, Simon caught at a horse's bridle. He had lost his shield and his bow, but with his sword he did battle against the mounted man. Then, once more, Malvallet was with him, himself mounted on a stray horse, and helmed again. He charged down upon Simon's foe, lance poised in readiness, and as the unknown rider would have cut Simon to earth, caught him fairly in the ribs with such force that the man, taken unawares, was toppled backwards out of his saddle, and the wind knocked out of him.

"Up, lad!" Malvallet cried. "Art hurt?"

Simon swung himself on to the frightened animal's back, and there in the heat of battle, smiled his tranquil smile, still calm and unruffled.

"A scratch or two. Take no heed of me, Geoffrey of Malvallet."

"That will I!" Geoffrey retorted. "Stay by me—nobody!"

Again they were enveloped in a swirling mass, and with it swept onward, their horses flank to flank, themselves hacking a path before them. Once Fulk drew near, puffing and blowing, his eyes gleaming red through his visor, then he too was swept onward and away.

To Simon the battle seemed interminable, but although his arm was weary and he had to change his sword to his left hand, he lost not one jot of his grim enjoyment. He fought on beside Malvallet, silent for the most part, his lips set in a hard, tight line, and his strange eyes glowing.

"Canst see Hotspur?" panted Geoffrey once. "Methought I heard a shout."

Even as he spoke it came again, caught up by many voices: "Hotspur has fallen! Hotspur is dead! Hurrah for St George of England!"

"He is down," said Simon, "and they waver."

Waver they did, and from that moment the zest seemed to go from the rebel army. The fighting became less arduous, but it was not until dusk fell that the battle ceased. And when at last the end came and his tired arm could be still, Simon sat quiet for a moment on his jaded horse, surveying the terrible field inscrutably, with little pity in his glance, but an expression of detached interest.

Geoffrey of Malvallet watched him for a moment in the half-light, and presently spoke to him.

"Art a very hardy youngster," he remarked. "What think you of it all?" With a wave of his gauntleted hand he embraced the battlefield.

Simon made answer without turning his head.

"It is disorderly," he said reflectively. "Methinks I will aid them to tidy it."

Malvallet realized that he was of a mind to assist in carrying away the wounded.

"Not so fast, not so fast! Is that all ye think?"

Simon threw him a fleeting glance.

"It has been a fair day," he said. "I would we might have another."

Malvallet laughed at him.

"Thou cold-blooded tiger-cub! Thou hast no compassion for these wounded and these dead?"

"One must die," Simon answered. "And I would deem this a good death. Why should I pity them?"

"Yet thou wouldst go tend the wounded," Malvallet reminded him.

"So they may fight again," Simon said. "I would help them, but I would not pity them, for that is foolish."

Malvallet laughed again, wonderingly.

"Good lack, art made of ice! I'll not have thee aid the wounded now. Art hurt thyself."

Simon cast a casual glance at his arm, round which, through the shattered plates, he had twisted a scarf.

"Hurt? I? That is but a scratch, Sir Geoffrey. And thyself?"

"Well enough," Malvallet replied. "This is not my first fight. I have been with the Prince here until a few months ago."

"I pray God 'twill not be my last fight," Simon said.

"Or mine. I had thought from thy bearing that an hundred campaigns had seen thee."

"Nay. But mine is fighting blood."

Malvallet eyed him curiously.

"Is it? From what stock dost thou spring, I wonder? Methinks I have seen thy like before."

Simon gave his short laugh.

"Look in thy mirror, Geoffrey of Malvallet."

Malvallet nodded, not surprised.

"It struck me that that was so a while back when thou didst come to my rescue. For which I thank thee, brother." He held out his mailed hand, and Simon gripped it, flushing slightly. They rode slowly on, down the hill.

"Thy name?" Geoffrey asked presently.

"Simon—of Beauvallet."

Geoffrey laughed.

"Oh, well done, Simon! I would thou wert not with Montlice. My father would take thee to himself were I to ask it."

"Nay."

"There is hatred in thy heart for him? Desire for vengeance, maybe?"

Simon turned his head.

"Why should I hate him?"

"Because of thy namelessness! Thy—thy mother?"

"A name will I make for myself. My mother chose her own road, and if she was not happy at least I never heard of it. She is dead. All that is nothing."

"Thou art the strangest lad ever I saw!" Malvallet exclaimed. "Art squire, then, to Montlice?"

"Ay. One day I shall call no man save the King my master, but for the present I owe allegiance to Montlice. I wonder, is he here, or did he fall?" He looked round keenly, but in the fading light could not see his lord, nor distinguish one man from Montlice.

"If he is killed, what comes to thee?" asked Malvallet. "Wilt join my train?"

"Nay, I must lead our men back to Montlice. If Fulk is dead, then do I owe allegiance to Alan, his son. But I do not think he is dead."

A rider came up with them, sitting very upright in his saddle. From under the shade of his protecting helm Simon saw a pair of shrewd, youthful eyes shining above the bandage that crossed the young man's face. Malvallet lifted his lance in salute, and the stripling reined in his horse to walk beside them.

"Oh, bravely done, Malvallet, and you, sir! Bravely done indeed! I saw thee yonder, Geoffrey, when thou wert hard-pressed, and I saw thy companion go valiantly to aid thee. Is all well with thee?"

"I took no hurt, Highness, thanks be to Simon of Beauvallet here. I grieve to see you wounded, sir."

"Why, it is naught!" Henry said merrily. "They made a deal of pother over it, but it irks me not." He stretched his arms. "Ah, but this has been a glorious day!"

"Why, so Simon thinks, Highness, and wishes we might enjoy yet another like it."

Henry bent forward to smile at Simon across Malvallet.

"That's the spirit I love," he said. "Whose man are you, Simon of Beauvallet?"

"I serve Montlice, Highness," Simon answered.

"Montlice? I saw him fall a while since. They bore him away, but I do not think he is dead."

"He would be hard to kill, sir," Simon said. "I must go seek him, with your permission."

Henry nodded pleasantly.

"Ay, do not wait on my coming. I would speak with Geoffrey. But I shall not forget you or your valour this day."

Simon bowed.

"Your Highness is very kind, sir."

Malvallet held out his hand yet again.

"We shall meet again, Simon."

Simon gripped his outstretched hand.

"As foes, Malvallet, once I am at Montlice again."

"Nay, nay," Geoffrey answered. "I shall see thee in Shrewsbury. Remember I am in thy debt!"

Simon smiled, and released his hand.

"As I will bear no man gratitude so let no man be grateful unto me, Malvallet. Mayhap we shall fight again one day, side by side. Who knows?"

"Then it is farewell for the present, Simon?"

"Ay, Geoffrey. But one day we shall meet again as equals."

"See thou forgettest me not!" Malvallet called after

him, and watched him ride away towards the rear-guard where they were tending the wounded.

"That is a passing strange man, Geoffrey," the young Prince remarked. "Who is he? He is very like thee, save that he is fair where thou art dark."

"He calls himself Beauvallet, sir, and is my half-brother. I met him for the first time on this campaign. He saved my life a while back, as your Highness saw."

Henry nodded.

"Ay, 'twas bravely done. Shall I have my father knight him?"

"Ah, if your Highness would! Indeed, he deserves it on this day's work alone."

Henry looked after the now distant figure thoughtfully.

"There is that in him that pleases," he said. "But he is very cold. Perhaps he will be a great man one day. I would fain call him friend, methinks."

IV

How he was knighted, and how he had speech with his father

He did not find his lord anywhere on the battlefield, but he was in no way perturbed. Back he rode to Shrewsbury, to Fulk's lodging, and there he found Montlice, stretched upon a bed, and swearing mightily, whiles a leech dressed the wound in his shoulder. Simon clanked in, a grim figure in dusty, blood-stained armour that in one or two places had been shattered by some lusty blows. The face that looked out from under the peak of his helm was tired and drawn, but his green-blue eyes were as calm as ever, as if he had not seen more horrors today than in all his young life.

At sight of him a look of relief swept over Fulk's countenance.

"Ah, God be thanked!" he rumbled. "I might have known thou'dst be hard to kill."

"As I knew of thee," Simon said. He beckoned to my lord's page. "Unlace me, Francis."

Montlice nodded.

"Ay, ay, unlace him, boy. Art whole, Simon?"

"Save for a scratch," Simon answered. "Gently, Francis, with mine arm. How deep goes your wound, my lord?"

Fulk growled.

"A nothing, a nothing——Hey, thou clumsy wretch, have a care!" he roared as the leech handled him. "I saw thee by Malvallet, Simon. What madness seized thee?"

"None," said Simon briefly. With his ungauntleted hand he unstrapped his helm and cast it on to the table. "When left you the field, sir?"

"I fell," Fulk replied angrily, "and they bore me away, a million curses be upon them! I left it not of mine own will! They were wavering. What came of it?"

"They are in full flight," Simon said. Free of his armour he stretched himself, and heaved a sigh of relief. "God's my life, I am weary! Give me leave, sir, I would sleep."

"Wait!" Fulk ordered. "Thine arm?"

Simon untwisted the bloody scarf, revealing a great gash that at once began to bleed again. Fulk pushed the leech away from him.

"Go tend my squire, good surgeon. I shall do very well." He waited in silence while the leech washed and bandaged Simon's wound. Then he nodded.

"Go thou, Simon, and rest. I will see thee anon."

Simon went out and to his own tiny room. There he flung himself down upon his hard bed, and slept almost at once. He did not wake until past eight on the following day, and then he made all haste to dress himself and wait upon his lord. He found Fulk breakfasting, despite the late hour, his shoulder neatly bandaged and himself seemingly not very much the worse for wear. He grunted when he saw Simon, and waved him to a seat at his own table. Simon, unimpressed by the honour, sat down and disposed of a tankard of ale. He then drew a platter towards him and proceeded to make a hearty meal. Neither he nor Fulk spoke until they had satisfied their hunger. At length my lord pushed back his chair, and wiping his fingers on the coarse cloth, looked across at his squire.

"Thomas of Worcester and the Scottish Earl were taken," he remarked.

Simon nodded, and there the conversation ended. Fulk went out presently, accompanied by his page, and Simon spent the morning polishing his sword and armour. Fulk did not return for dinner, which he took at Court, but soon after three in the afternoon he rolled in.

"Hark ye, Simon," he puffed, "the King goes to make some dozen knights." He looked narrowly at Simon as he spoke, but Simon displayed no interest. He was cleaning my lord's shield, and his whole attention seemed centred upon it.

"With my good will he will make thee knight," Fulk said.

Simon's busy hands grew still. He shot an upward glance at Montlice.

"Ye jest, my lord."

"Nay. The Prince remarked thy courage on the field and hath recommended thee for knighthood."

For a minute Simon sat silent, staring before him. He drew a deep breath of wonderment, and looked again at Montlice.

"And thy—good will, sir?"

"Well, well," Fulk said. "I should have recommended thee myself. Shalt have thy knighthood, lad, an thou'lt stay yet a while with me."

"As your squire, my lord?" he asked.

Fulk laid a clumsy hand on his shoulder.

"As my son if thou wilt, Simon. Art too young to fare forth alone. When Alan is older shalt go forth with him. Till then stay thou with me, and grow yet taller."

Simon pondered it for a time.

"But what will you have me do, lord? It seems that I am no longer necessary to you, and I'll not stay idle at Montlice."

"Shalt command my men in Vincent's room, who fell yesterday, God rest his soul! I will pay thee a good wage so thou mayst have money against thy later needs."

Simon pondered again, his eyes on the distant hills. He brought them back presently to rest on his lord, and smiled.

"It is a fair offer," he said.

"Thy hand on it!" Fulk answered promptly, and held out his great paw. Simon gripped it until the veins along the back of his hand stood out blue and thick. So he accepted Fulk as his liege lord.

The ceremony of knighting took place on the following day. Besides Simon were twelve other men, so that he made the thirteenth, a happening that Fulk regarded as inauspicious until Simon told him that thirteen was a number that brought him good luck. Fulk attended him to Court, and kept an anxious yet proud eye upon him during the rite.

Simon was the last to kneel before the King, and as he bent the knee he saw Malvallet standing amongst a group behind the Prince. Geoffrey smiled at him and made a little saluting movement with his hand.

At the King's last words to him: "Rise, Sir Simon of Beauvallet," Simon came to his feet. The rest of the ceremony passed in a kind of haze. When it was over he found that Geoffrey was at his side with the Prince. Simon bowed.

"I have heard yet more of your doings, Sir Simon," Henry said, twinkling. "Paul of Lenoir tells a tale of your lynx-eyes."

"That was nothing, lord," Simon answered. "Mine eyes are sharp, and I can see in darkness." He looked at Geoffrey for a moment. "So thou hast paid thy debt to me, Malvallet."

"No, no!" Malvallet cried. "This is none of my making, though glad I am to see you knighted. Tell him, sir, that 'tis your Highness' own contriving!"

47

"Ay, that is so," nodded Henry. "Geoffrey had naught to say in the matter."

"And so the debt remains unpaid," Malvallet said. "Now at least, Simon, thou'lt quit Montlice."

"Nay," Simon answered. "I remain with him yet another year or two."

At this point the Prince stepped aside to speak with one who passed. Geoffrey spoke lower, jerking his head towards the young Henry.

"Why dost thou not take service under him? He is a good master."

"One day I will," Simon answered. "For the nonce there are reasons why I should stay at Montlice. And Fulk has my word."

"Then it is useless for me to say more," Geoffrey shrugged. "It irks me to see thee with our life-long foe." Then, as Fulk came towards them, he clasped Simon's hand for a moment. "I could love thee, Simon. Forget it not."

"What did the fellow want with thee?" grumbled Fulk, when Malvallet was out of earshot. "Why must thou make a friend of mine enemy?"

"I make friends where I will," Simon said curtly.

"Nay, that thou shalt not! Mine enemy is thine, I'll have thee know!"

Simon looked at him thoughtfully.

"Not so. Yet this do I owe to you, that I will not call Malvallet friend while I remain under your roof."

They left Shrewsbury with the King, two days later, and went south with him until they had to branch off to reach Cambridge. Fulk's losses had been few, and in place of Vincent was Simon, who proved himself to be so thoroughly equal to his task that Fulk remarked that Vincent's death was more of a blessing than a curse.

And so they arrived at Montlice, early in August, after an absence of nearly a month. They rode up the castle-slope to find Alan awaiting them, with my lady at his side, and her two daughters behind her.

Fulk dropped heavily from the saddle and enfolded his frail wife in an elephantine embrace. The two girls hung back shyly, but he kissed them both heartily, and his son.

"Well, well, well!" he puffed. "So here ye see me, safe and sound, sweetling, with naught to show for my fighting save a scratch upon the shoulder."

"For which I thank God with all my heart!" said my lady devoutly. "I have been in an agony of dread, my dear lord, for thy sake."

"A pack of rebels cannot slay Montlice," he answered. "Simon is safe, as thou seest, but Vincent is gone."

"Ah, poor Vincent!" she cried, but held out her hand to Simon. "I rejoice to see thee again, Simon of Beauvallet. Ye took no harm?"

Simon knelt to kiss her hand.

"None, lady, that is worth the telling. I trust I do see you well?"

She smiled.

"Well enough, now that I have my lord again."

Fulk put his hand on her shoulder.

"There is news for thee, Eleanor. Our Simon is my squire no longer."

She was puzzled, and looked inquiringly at Simon, who had risen to his feet. It was Alan whose quick instinct divined the truth. He ran forward and caught Simon's hand.

"Hast been knighted! Simon, Simon, is't true indeed?"

"Ay, knighted he is," said Fulk, "and by the King's own hand, for his exceeding great valour on the field. I present thee Sir Simon of Beauvallet, my lady."

Then the Countess out of the sweetness of her nature, made Simon mightily uncomfortable. Overcoming her slight timidity of him, she stepped forward and laid her hands in his. Simon, flushing, bent, and received a kiss upon his rugged brow.

Fulk laughed, clapping his hands to his sides.

"Now art thou honoured indeed, lad! My lady, is there refreshment within? I could drain a well, and Simon too, I'll swear."

" 'Tis laid out against your coming, my lord," she answered. "Come within, and Simon also."

Simon stepped back.

"I give ye thanks, lady, but I must first see to my men."

"Ay, ay, there speaks the general," chuckled Fulk, and watched him walk away towards the waiting column of men.

From that day onwards Simon ranked with Alan in my lord's household. He sat at table with the family, far above the salt, and he was given a squire of his own and a page. A fair chamber was allotted to him, and in addition to all this he received a round sum each month as wage for his services. Still he felt no pang of gratitude, for if in these things his life was made easier and more luxurious, he repaid it amply by the work he did. In a surprisingly short space of time the management of the estate devolved itself on to his broad shoulders. My lord was no longer young, and the late campaign had taxed his strength, even though he would not admit it. He lost some of his untiring energy, and he was content to put the reins of government into Simon's hands, since his son would have none of them.

So life drifted onwards for a time, placidly enough, with but one incident to disturb its even tenor. And this was the coming of Malvallet to Montlice.

He rode up to the castle, late one afternoon in September, attended by his page. One of Montlice's varlets, astonished at his advent, was sent to advise my lord of this visit.

Fulk was with his lady, and when he heard the news, he screwed up his eyes and frowned.

"Simon," he said succinctly. "Plague be on him!"

"But Malvallet in our domain!" cried my lady.

"Curse his impudence," growled Fulk, and went out with his rolling gait to receive this unwelcome guest.

Malvallet was standing before the fire-place, his hands behind him, and one spurred foot tapping the ground. He did not move a step to meet Fulk, but merely inclined his head haughtily. Midway across the hall Fulk paused, and returned the faint bow every mite as stiffly.

"My lord?" he rumbled.

"I regret the necessity which compels me to intrude

on your land, my Lord of Montlice," said Malvallet icily. "I desire to see my son, Sir Simon of—Beauvallet."

"To what purpose?" A red gleam appeared at the back of Fulk's eyes, sure sign of danger.

"Your pardon——" Malvallet gazed back at him unflinchingly—"That is mine affair."

"Nay it is mine, my lord. Simon of Beauvallet is in my service."

A little pulse started to throb on Malvallet's temple. Fulk regarded it, pleased.

"That is an error which I will rectify," Malvallet said. Under the calm of his voice anger sounded.

"Will you so, my lord? And what if Simon wills otherwise?"

"Sir Simon is my son, sir."

"Good lack, have ye but just discovered it?" Fulk jeered.

Malvallet bit his lip.

"Just, Lord Fulk."

"Hey, hey! And he has squired me these three years!" Fulk said, and watched the barb go home.

"That would not have been had I known, my lord."

Fulk gave a great laugh.

"Well, I suppose ye knew of the existence of a child, Lord Geoffrey. Methinks your efforts at paternal authority are a thought belated."

Malvallet was silent for a moment, curbing his anger. Presently he looked up again.

"My lord, will ye have the goodness to summon my son?"

"To what avail?" Fulk asked politely. "Three years since he came to me of his own free will, in preference to you. I do not think he is like to change."

Again Malvallet battled with himself. But his voice trembled a little with passion when he spoke.

"Nevertheless, my lord, I demand to have speech with him."

"Demand, demand! And by what right do ye 'demand' in my domain, my lord?"

"I have told you. Simon is my son."

"Simon is my servant," Fulk retorted quickly. He saw Malvallet's jaws clench.

"This bandying of words is useless!" Malvallet said. "We but waste time."

"Why, so I think," bowed Montlice. "I will e'en summon your horse."

Malvallet tapped the table between them with his riding whip. He leaned forward, glaring at Fulk.

"Lord Fulk, I do not stir from this spot until I have seen Sir Simon!"

Then, ere Fulk could reply in kind, a deep, cold voice spoke from the doorway.

"Who is it desires speech with Simon of Beauvallet?" it said. "I am here."

Malvallet swung round. Just within the hall stood Simon, a very giant of a man, regarding him fixedly from under lowering brows.

For a moment no one spoke. Then Malvallet strode forward.

"So thou art my son," he said slowly.

"Am I?" Simon answered. "I have forgotten."

With their eyes they measured one another. Malvallet spoke quietly.

"I come to offer thee the shelter of my roof, Simon."

"I need it not, my lord."

"A place at my table," Malvallet insisted, "next thy brother, a place at my side as my acknowledged son."

Simon's lip curled, sneering.

"Oh, brave, my lord! Thy bastard son, forsooth!"

Malvallet flushed.

"I will make thee great in the land; ay, and I will give thee fair estates."

"I need them not, my lord."

Again there was a silence.

"Ye defy me, Simon? Ye have hate of me in your heart?"

"Nay."

"Then return with me to Malvallet, and bear thine own name."

"No name is mine save the one I have chosen."

"An insult to me, that name!"

"Is it so, my lord?" He looked upward at Malvallet, without any feeling in his glance.

Malvallet stretched out his hands.

"Simon, to what avail, this coldness of thine? Am I not thy father?"

"So I am told," Simon replied.

"Have I no right to thee? Has Montlice my right?"

"No man has a right to me, save it be the King. The law gives thee none. I am what I am."

"Thou shalt be something more than what thou art."

"I doubt it not."

"Through my contriving."

"Nay."

"Simon," Malvallet cried, "is there no blood-tie betwixt us?"

"It has never been thy pleasure to acknowledge it," Simon answered coldly.

"I knew not of thine existence!"

Simon looked him over.

"Thou didst know that a child would be born to thee by Jehanne, my mother. Thou didst make no effort to provide for it, nor to discover even whether it were boy or girl."

Malvallet's hands dropped to his sides.

"It is resentment then, that makes thee churlish now?"

"I feel none."

"Then what moves thee to this coldness, Simon?"

Simon waited for a moment before replying.

"If I do seem cold to thee, my lord, it is not from hatred or soreness of spirit. Thou art a stranger to me. How should I bear thee affection who have never shown me any?"

Malvallet winced.

"All this will I make right betwixt us, my son. Let the past be buried, for indeed there is love for thee in me now. Canst not forget the harm I have done thee by mine indifference?"

"Thou hast worked no harm on me. The past is naught, as shall be the present."

"Simon, Simon, thou art unjust and cruel! Hadst thou come to me, three years ago, I would have taken thee to my bosom!"

The green-blue eyes narrowed.

"In me, my lord, is Malvallet blood. A Malvallet asks no favours. Hadst thou come to *me* three years ago, then indeed might things have been different. It was not then convenient to thee, or mayhap thou hadst forgotten that a base-born child of thine was living. In those days I did fend for myself because it was not thy pleasure to seek me out. Now, when my need of help is dead, it has become thy pleasure. It is not mine."

Malvallet heard him out in silence. He answered very low.

"Mayhap I do deserve thy scorn and thy hatred. But is thy hatred so great that it denies me the means to make amends?"

"I have told thee, my lord, that I feel no hatred for thee."

"I had rather that than thine indifference!"

"If I cause thee pain, I do crave thy pardon. What else but indifference can I feel for one with whom I have never exchanged a word until today?"

Malvallet went nearer to him.

"Come with me now, Simon, and I will teach thee to care for me! Come away from the land of Montlice! Thou—my son!—canst not remain here!"

"Ay, that is what irks thee," Simon answered. "I serve thine enemy, Montlice. Were I an hundred leagues from here thou hadst not come to me today, or ever. Thy pride is hurt."

"I swear it is not so!"

Simon jerked his shoulder.

"No matter. Whate'er thy motive, mine answer remains the same. I owe my Lord Fulk allegiance, and I will break my word for no man."

Then there fell another long silence. Malvallet made a hopeless gesture with his hands. He spoke dully.

"No argument will prevail with thee?"

"None."

"Then we must part—foes?"

"I bear no malice to thee or thine, my lord, and between thy son and me is friendship. But whiles I serve Montlice his enemies are mine. Tell Geoffrey he was ill-advised to send thee to me, but tell him also that one day he and I will meet again when there shall be naught of enmity betwixt us."

"And betwixt thou and me?" Malvallet cried eagerly.

"Again naught. Neither love nor hatred. The past is dead and with it our kinship, but if ever we two shall meet again it will not be as foes."

"Thou art—generous," Malvallet said slowly. "Think well before ye say me nay! Much can I do for thee, and very powerful can I make thee. Do these things count for naught?"

"My lord, it is my set purpose that I will take no honour, no power, no wealth, no title, that I have not earned by mine own endeavour. I like not thine easy road, but all these things will I acquire, either by toil, by skill, or by valour. I do thank thee for thine offer, but mine answer is nay."

"Ay, thou art a man," Malvallet sighed, "and my blood runs hot in thee. This is farewell, but before I go, wilt thou not lay thy hand in mine and tell me that my past neglect of thee is indeed forgiven?" He held out his hand, looking almost wistfully at his son.

Simon put his into it deliberately, and for a moment their fingers gripped.

"If wrong has been done to me I do readily forgive it, for thy neglect has made me what I am, and no cossetted stripling of the court."

Malvallet still held his hand firmly.

"Promise me one thing, Simon! If ever thou shouldst have need of me, if ever thou shouldst wish to undo this day's work, thou wilt put thy pride aside and come to me, for that will be thy condescension, not mine."

Simon frowned.

" 'If ever I have need of thee'—I can stand alone. 'If ever I should wish to unsay my nay'—that will be never. I will promise, my lord."

Malvallet almost crushed his hand. Then quickly he released it, and looked at Simon with a queer, twisted smile.

"Thou son after mine own heart!" he said softly, and strode forth with never a word to Fulk, and never a backward glance.

There was silence for a long minute when he had gone. Fulk was looking at Simon with wonderment in his eyes.

"Is it to please thyself or me that thou hast said Malvallet nay?" he asked.

"Both, maybe," Simon answered briefly, and swung out of the door.

V

How he rescued a fair damsel, and discovered a plot

The rest of the year passed quietly for those at Montlice, and once Simon's grip was tight upon his men so that they durst not annoy him, be he at home or abroad, he began to ride out around the neighbouring country. Sometimes he took young Alan with him, but more often he was accompanied by his squire, a sturdy youth, who worshipped, in awe and fear, the ground on which his master walked. Occasionally Simon would go still farther afield so that he was absent from Montlice for days together. Fulk grumbled a little, and was curious to know the reason for these escapades. Simon would not tell him, nor did anyone know why he rode about the country, lynx-eyed, surveying every estate to which he came with a speculative glance that was sure sign of some scheme afoot within him.

At first Fulk's grumblings were loud and insistent, but when he found that they had no effect upon his obstinate captain, and that in consequence of his absence no harm nor laxity in discipline came upon his men, they abated somewhat, and he bore with Simon's vagaries with as good a will as possible.

Simon rode out one morning in the year 1404, bearing to the south-east. With him went Roger, his squire, in a gloomy mood, for he had fallen foul of Simon that very day and had received a severe reprimand, accompanied by a searching, flaming glance which he had learned to dread. Therefore there was no conversation on the journey, and Roger, feeling both sore in spirit and nervous, trotted as far behind his master as he dared. Simon paid no heed to him and felt no desire to talk. Now as ever he was frugal of words, and spoke rarely, but to the point. A little after ten he paused at a wayside tavern and dismounted. Roger rode up to receive his horse, and was bidden tend it and get his own dinner. Simon strode into the tavern and made a right hearty meal. Out he went again and pushed on towards the county of Suffolk. On the road they passed a large area of cultivated land, with a small castle raised on a slope, overlooking the domain. The place seemed well populated, but about the castle itself and the surrounding fields was an air almost of desolation.

Simon reined in his horse, and rose in his stirrups, the better to survey the land. There was pasture land in plenty, good grazing-ground, as Simon knew; away in the distance lay orchards and woodland, while through the estate ran a sluggish stream that wound about the castle, and kept moist the land. It appeared to be a prosperous domain, but little movement was afoot, and little care seemed to have been spent upon it for some months at least. In the distance men were working on the fields in a desultory fashion, but for the most part the peasants were lounging by their doors, exchanging idle talk. Simon beckoned to one of these, and the man came running, and knelt beside Simon's horse.

"Whose land is this?" Simon asked.

The man shook his head.

"Lord, we have no master now, save the King. It is crown land, I do think, but there is no one to rule here."

"How so?"

"My lord went with Lord Hotspur 'gainst the King, sir. He died." The man crossed himself.

"By steel or by rope?"

He answered in a hushed voice.

"By rope, my lord." The peasant glanced up at him. "So perish all traitors!" he said quickly.

Simon paid no heed.

"His name?"

"John of Barminster, good my lord."

"There is no heir?"

"Nay, my lord, and the land is confiscate."

"What call you it?"

"It is known as Fair Pastures, my lord."

Simon turned in his saddle to look about him.

"How many leagues girdle it?"

"Four, my lord. It is a fair barony."

"What cattle have ye?"

"Six herds, my lord, and all good beasts, save one which died yesternight of a colic. It is as my lord left it, with some two score swine in all, and many of the sows in litter. The stable is full, but the horses grow fat and lazy with little usage. Three falcons hath my lord's steward, in ward, fine birds, sir, and fleet of wing. The hounds run wild, and the sheep stray, for there is none over us to command we do this or that, so that little land is ploughed, and much sack is drunk."

"What force do ye number? Of archers, men-at-arms?"

The man shook his head sadly.

"But few, my lord. My lord took eight score with him in all. Some returned to royster here and abuse us. The rest are gone I know not where. Some slain, mayhap, others with the rebel Owen. All is waste here, till the King sends one to rule over us and subdue these accursed soldiers." He waved his hands excitedly. "Naught is safe from them, sir, naught sacred to them! There is no priest on the estate, and no master at the castle. The men-at-arms carouse there, and the steward waxes fat on my lord's larder. Little enough is left now in the cellars, and everywhere there is drunkenness and rioting!"

Simon made no comment, but the peasant saw his eyes grow hard. Still he stared about him, while his squire watched curiously. Then Simon gathered up his slack rein and tossed a groat to the kneeling man.

"Peace be with ye!" he said curtly, and set his horse at a brisk trot. Roger fell in behind, and for a long time they proceeded in silence.

When they stopped again it was close on four in the evening, and Roger's resentment had grown considerably. He was hungry, he was thirsty, he was stiff and tired from the long hours in the saddle, he was very bored, and he wished to heaven his master would find some other amusement than this wandering about the country.

As he dismounted, Simon cast the squire a quick, shrewd glance. He had worked him hard this week, and Roger's eyes were black-ringed from fatigue, his movements slow.

"We rest here tonight," Simon said. "Take the horses to the stable and wait to see them tended."

"Yes, sir," Roger answered, devoutly thankful for this respite.

Simon strode into the tavern and calling for the host, demanded a room for himself and another for his squire.

The landlord inspected him covertly. Evidently this was not one to be denied. He bowed, spreading out his hands.

"Alack, fair sir, woe is me, I have but one room to offer, save that in which sleep the common people! If your good lordship would take that one room, and let me find space somewhere for your squire—? But an hour since one came riding from Essex and I have given him my great front room. Alack, that I did not know of my lord's coming, for this man is not gentle, I think, yet I durst not say him nay now, for he is a brawny fellow and hot of temper!" He looked up at Simon with a comical expression of despair.

"Let be," Simon answered. "I will take the other room and my squire shall sleep with me. See to it that supper be prepared for us."

The little man bowed till his forehead seemed in danger of touching his knees.

"My lord is generous! The chamber is not so ill, sir, and I will see to it that you are made comfortable. As to supper, I have a haunch of venison roasting, as you

59

see. In one little half-hour, sir, I will have all ready, if your lordship will deign to wait."

Simon nodded.

"Ay, it will do. Fetch me a tankard of ale, mine host, and let one be brought for my squire."

"Ah, my lord, at once, at once!" the landlord cried, and scuttled away to his cellar. He reappeared in an amazingly short time with two brimming tankards. One he set upon the table, the other he presented to Simon, watching him drain it, with an anxious eye.

"Is it to my lord's taste? Will my lord have me fetch him more?"

"Nay, not now." Simon set down the pewter vessel. "I will drink it at supper, good host. See to it that my squire gets his tankard when he comes from the stables." He strolled out of the hot kitchen by the door at the back, and went to stretch his legs in the wood that lay beyond the small garden.

He went slowly, his hands behind his back and his brows drawn close together. Some project he seemed to be turning round in his brain, for his keen eyes had a far-away look in them, somewhat ruminating. He walked on through the wood, treading heavily and noiselessly crushing the tiny spring flowers 'neath his feet. Somewhere near at hand was a brook which burbled and sang, and towards that sound Simon bent his steps, intending to lave his face in the fresh water. Then, of a sudden, the air was rent by a shriek, followed by yet another, and a cry for help.

Simon paused, listening. The voice belonged to a woman and to one in distress. Simon was no knight-errant, but he went forward quickly, cat-like, so that not a twig squeaked.

He went softly round a corner of the beaten track, and found himself in sight of the brook he had heard. An overturned bucket lay across his path, and not six paces before him a serving wench was struggling wildly to be free of a great muscular fellow who had her in his arms and leered down into her frightened face.

Simon came upon him like a tornado. No sound had betrayed his approach, so that when he sprang it was like an unsuspected cannon-shot. He caught the man by the neck, and putting forward all his great strength, wrenched him staggering back. The girl gave a little glad cry and fell upon her knees with intent to kiss Simon's hand.

"Oh, sir! Oh, my lord! Oh, sir!" she sobbed incoherently. "I came to draw water, and—and——"

Simon paid no heed to her wailing. Setting his feet squarely he awaited the other man's rush. The fellow had fallen, but he picked himself up, purple with rage, and with a roar came upon Simon, head down, and fists doubled. Simon stepped lightly aside and delivered a crashing blow as the man passed him. The tousled head was shaken, like that of some wounded bull, and the man wheeled about and rushed on Simon yet again. This time Simon stood firm and closed with him.

To and fro they swayed on the moss carpet, arms locked tight about each other, straining and panting, and trampling the moss underfoot. Beads of sweat stood out on either forehead, teeth were clenched, and lips parted. His opponent was older and bulkier than Simon, but his muscles were not in such splendid fettle. Time after time he made a supreme effort to throw Simon, and time after time he failed. Simon's arms seemed to grow tighter and tighter about him till the breath was almost crushed out of his body. He realized that he could not throw this fair young giant and he twisted suddenly and cunningly so that he broke away. But in so doing his jerkin was rent open across his chest, and a leathern wallet fell to the ground and bounced to Simon's feet.

The bully lost his head, seeing it, and his eyes started in wide apprehension. A strangled cry he gave, and sprang forward to retrieve the wallet. Before he could come upon it Simon's sixth sense, ever acute, had warned him that here was something more than a lewd fellow waylaying a serving-wench. He stepped swiftly forward, over the wallet, and braced himself for the shock of meeting. The ruffian crashed into him so that he had to fall back a step. Yet he contrived to close with the man again, and held him in a bear-like embrace.

Then began a struggle in comparison with which the former one was as nothing. Plainly Simon's opponent was desperate, filled with a great fear lest Simon should gain possession of that wallet. He fought like one possessed, and Simon's muscles cracked under his crushing hold. Once the man tripped over a projecting root, and fell, dragging Simon with him. For a time they rolled and struggled on the ground, breathing in great gasps, sweat pouring down their faces, each one striving to get uppermost. At last Simon had his man under, and wrenching free, sprang up and back. In a flash the fellow was on his feet, and as he rushed on Simon yet again, Simon caught the glint of steel. And seeing it, his eyes narrowed to brilliant points of anger, and his stern mouth shut tightly. He did not wait for his attacker to fall upon him, but sprang to meet him, catching him about the waist with one arm, and with his free hand gripping that treacherous dagger-arm above the wrist. So swiftly had he acted that the man had no time to stab, but was well-nigh carried backward by the weight of Simon's leopard-spring.

Simon had pinned the fellow's left arm to his side, nor did his hold slacken for one moment, while with his iron right hand he gripped the other arm until the bully's mouth was awry with agony as he struggled to get away. Then Simon gave a quick turn of his wrist and the dagger fell to earth with a thud. A groan burst from the man's lips, and as Simon released him his right arm fell useless. Despite the pain of his broken bone he was game still, remembering that precious wallet, and came charging forward, only to be met by a shattering blow upon the jaw. He flung up his unhurt arm, and reeling, fell heavily to the ground. Simon was upon him instantly, one knee upon his chest, pinning him to the ground. Again the bully groaned, and made a convulsive effort to shake Simon off. But an iron hand held him down by the throat, and, shifting his position, Simon knelt across him so that with his knees pressed to the fallen man's sides he held him powerless. With his free hand he pulled a whistle from the neck of his tunic, and placing it between his lips, blew thrice upon it, shrilly. He glanced over his shoulder at the girl, who crouched by her bucket, hiding her face in her hands and weeping.

"Cease thy lamentations, wench!" he commanded, "and bring me the wallet that lies yonder."

She rocked herself, wailing.

"Oh, sir! oh, sir! Have—oh, have ye slain him?"

"Nay, thou foolish child. Do as I bid thee."

But still she crouched where she was, and would not look up. Simon's eyes grew a little colder, and his voice a little softer.

"Thou didst hear me, wench?" Had his squire been at hand, he would have shivered at the note which sounded through the softness.

The girl dragged herself up and went with lagging steps to where the wallet lay. She brought it to Simon, trembling, and having given it into his hand, retreated quickly.

The prostrate man made one great effort to be free, but his strength was gone, and one arm hung useless. Simon controlled his struggle with his right hand alone, and with the other thrust the wallet into his belt.

Through the wood came footsteps running. Roger shouted from somewhere near-by.

"Which way, sir? Which way?"

"Hither," Simon called. "By the path that leads towards the brook."

The footsteps grew louder, and Roger came racing round the bend to his master's assistance. He paused when he saw what was toward, and gazed at Simon wonderingly.

"Go fetch the rope from thy saddle holster," Simon ordered calmly. "Hasten, and say naught to anyone."

With another astonished glance at the weeping girl, Roger turned and ran back through the wood. When he reappeared it was with a coil of stout rope which was one of the things that Simon always carried with him in case he should come upon robbers on the road. He went with it to Simon, and between them they trussed the swearing, groaning man, deftly and securely.

Simon pulled the last knot tight and stood up. He

took the wallet from his belt, unfastening the strap that bound it.

A choking cry came from the bound man.

"My lord, my lord, there is naught of import therein, I swear! Some letters from my lass at home—that is all! For the love of God, sir, do not look!"

Simon paid no heed, but drew from the pouch some three or four packets. Each one was sealed, and as he examined the seal, Simon's eyes narrowed to slits, and he cast a searching glance at the man at his feet. For the seal was to all appearance that of the dead King, Richard the Second, for whose sake Glyndourdy fought, and Hotspur had died. The first packet was addressed to a baron who lived not ten miles from Montlice, and whom Simon knew well. The others were all to nobles living either in Norfolk or Cambridge.

Without the faintest hesitation Simon slit open one and spread out the crackling sheets. The letter was couched in fair terms, and it assured my lord the Baron of Crowburg, faithful adherent to the true king, Richard by the Grace of God, lately escaped into Scotland, that despite the lying reports of his death, set about by the usurper, Henry Bolinbroke, called the Fourth of England, King Richard lived, and was shortly to show himself, when he would call all his faithfuls to his side to depose the monster Bolinbroke, and his son, Henry of Monmouth. And to all of this he, the writer, could testify, as he had seen and had speech with the blessed King, and who should know him better than himself who had been gentleman of the bedchamber during his reign? And if my lord still was wary of believing this truth, let him closely inspect the seal upon this parchment when he would surely recognize it as King Richard's own. There was much more in this vein, and the letter was signed "Serle," and dated a month earlier. Under the signature there was yet another, and examining it closely Simon saw that the scrawl was "Richard R."

He folded the letter carefully, and together with the others put it back into the pouch, tucking the whole away into his own tunic. In his journeyings here and there some faint rumours had come to his ears of the late King's being still alive, in Scotland, with a great force of French and Scots waiting to cross the border. He had paid no attention to the tale, thinking it but a fantastic belief of the common folk, but this letter warned him that there was more in it than that. He realized that he had surprised a pretty plot, and his eyes kindled a little at the knowledge. He turned and beckoned to Roger, who was trying to comfort the girl.

"Here, lad! Thou must help me to carry yon fellow back to the tavern. Leave the silly wench to dry her tears. No harm has been done to her."

Roger came, rather sulkily, and laid hold of the now unconscious man's legs. Simon took his head, and they set off towards the tavern, the girl bringing up the rear and sobbing loudly all the way.

They set their burden down without the kitchen door, and Simon went in to seek the landlord. He took him aside, and questioned him sharply.

"When came that fellow ye spoke of?" he asked.

The landlord gazed at him.

"W-which fellow, lord?——Ah, your pardon! But an hour before your noble self."

"What know you of him?"

The landlord began to look alarmed.

"I—I have never set eyes on him before, good my lord!" To his horror he found that Simon was looking at him piercingly. Flustered, he stared back in bewilderment.

Simon nodded.

"That is the truth, I think."

"God's truth, sir! Why——"

"I have that fellow bound without," Simon said grimly. "Thou hast harboured a traitor, unawares, maybe."

The man's eyes seemed like to pop out of his head.

"A—a *traitor*, lord? Now, by my troth, lord, I knew of naught 'gainst this man! I swear it by the Rood, sir! and the neighbours will tell ye that there is no more loyal servant to the King——"

"Ay, that will do," Simon interrupted. "Provided ye obey my commands in this matter I will hold ye blameless, but if ye refuse to obey—why, then 'twill be my duty to report ye for a dangerous fellow."

Mine host wrung his little fat hands.

"Oh, my lord, my lord, I will do aught you please! For my respectable house to harbour a traitor! Oh, woe is me, that I was born under an unlucky star! At my birth they foretold——"

"Hold thy tongue! Have you a strong place wherein I can imprison this man?"

The little man clapped his hands to his head.

"Have I? Have I? Ah, yes, above the stable, in the loft! Only reached by the trap-door, and the roof sound as can be, good my lord!"

"Then lead me thither," ordered Simon, and went out again to his prisoner, the twittering landlord at his heels. They bore the victim in the wake of mine host, and with difficulty mounted the ladder leading into the loft. There they deposited the man, and leaving Roger to stand guard, Simon departed with the landlord, and bade him fetch ink and parchment. When these were brought him he sat down at a table and proceeded to write to my lord of Montlice, tersely, and with none of the customary embellishments of style.

"My Lord,

"I am bound for London, having taken a man prisoner here who bears traitorous dispatches concerning the late King. Send me Gregory with six men of his choosing who shall relieve me here. And this with all speed tomorrow.

"SIMON OF BEAUVALLET.

"Written at Salpetres at the tavern of the Ox."

He folded this document and sealed it; then he went out again, and calling Roger down from the loft, gave him the letter.

"Look ye, Roger, thou must ride back to Montlice at once, and deliver this into my lord's own hands. Then change thy horse for another—Sultan or Rover—and bring with thee my mare, Fleet-foot. Gregory will come back with thee, and thou shalt take my horse

66

Cedric to Montlice again. We ride to London on the morrow."

Roger stared.

"To London, sir?"

"Have I not said so? Keep thy prating tongue still to all save my lord. Now go."

Roger heaved a sullen, weary sigh. He turned away, unenthusiastically.

"Stop!"

Roger jumped, and paused. He looked over his shoulder at Simon.

"Stay thou at Montlice," said Simon evenly. "Send me Malcolm in thy stead. He will maybe stand the journey better than thou, and spare me these black looks. Go."

Roger flushed to the roots of his curly hair. He came back to stand before his master.

"Nay, sir, I—I—shall stand the journey—very well. Bid me not send Malcolm!"

Simon looked down at him sternly.

"Malcolm will serve me better, and with a readier will," he said cruelly.

Roger swallowed hard and sent a fleeting glance upwards.

"Indeed, sir—I—I am sorry, that—that I have angered thee. Take me with thee, sir! Not that—that dolt Malcolm! *He* would not serve you as willingly as would I." He gave a contemptuous sniff, for between him and Malcolm was a heated rivalry for Simon's favours.

"Very well," Simon said. "Take the short road home, not the route by which we came. Thou'lt return to-morrow. See to it that ye go at once to bed on your arrival. It is understood?"

Roger's spirits revived miraculously.

"Ay, sir. I will do as ye bid me!" He caught Simon's hand, kissed it, and went gaily off to the stables.

Simon went back to the tavern, where he collected linen and some wood which he fashioned into a rough splint. With these and a bottle of Rhenish and a loaf of bread, he went to see his prisoner.

This worthy had come out of his swoon, but he lay quiet and weak upon the floor of the loft. Simon un-

tied his bonds, and ripping up the sleeve of his leathern
jerkin, set the bone of his broken arm and bound it to
the splint. The man groaned a little, and winced, for
Simon's surgery was crude, but he offered no resistance. Simon gave him the wine and bread and stood
silently over him while he ate and drank his fill. Then
he rebound him, leaving his useless arm free, and
made him a comfortable bed of straw. After that he
departed, without having said one word, and bolted
the trap-door on the outside. He went back to the
tavern for supper, and the landlord marvelled at his
appetite. But he was more than shocked that Simon
should elect to sleep in the stable under the loft when
he had three men who might guard the prisoner during the night. Simon refused the offer of these men
curtly. He was never one to shift responsibility.

VI

How he rode hot-foot to London

Simon had hardly finished his breakfast next morning
when Roger returned, leading his own mare, and accompanied by Gregory, Simon's lieutenant, and six of
his most trustworthy men.

At sight of this troop the landlord was thrown into a
flutter. It was bad enough to have a prisoner in his
loft, but seven great men to house was too much for
him. Simon had told him what was expected of him,
and although he dared not expostulate, the little man
wrung his hands despairingly and screwed up his face
into a hundred worried wrinkles. He had had experi-
ence of men-at-arms and their ways, and he feared for
the peace of his household and the well-being of his
cellar. He hinted at these qualms to the impervious
Simon, who waved him aside with the curt promise

that for any damage these men of Montlice did he should be paid in full. That was all very well, thought the landlord, but it would not recompense him for the loss of his good name and that of his house. However, he was something of a philosopher, and finding that there was no help for it, he trotted away to arrange for the soldiers' accommodation.

Simon went out to meet his men, and was greeted by a smart salute from every one. Roger slipped from the saddle and presented him with a packet from Montlice which Simon reserved for future perusal. He turned to Gregory, who stood respectfully awaiting his orders.

"Send thy men to stable their horses, Gregory, and come with me."

Gregory gave the order, and leaving the flustered landlord to guide the men to the stables, followed Simon to the back of the house. Together they paced the little garden while Simon told him briefly of what had happened.

"Ye will quarter your men here, Gregory, and look to it that there be no laxity of discipline, for which ye will answer to me. There must be a guard over the prisoner all the time. Ye will arrange for that. And no one is to have speech with him save yourselves. Nay, nor sight of him. Ye will deliver him to whoever shall come from London with orders from the King, or from me. And when ye have delivered him up ye will return at once to Montlice. It is understood?"

"Exactly, sir."

"Keep the prisoner in the loft. It is safer. I start for London as soon as Roger of Maitland has broken his fast."

Gregory bowed.

"Shall I take command at once, Sir Simon?"

"At once. Remember that I will have no carousing among the men."

As soon as Gregory had departed, Simon broke the seal of his lord's letter, and started to decipher the wild scrawl.

"To Sir Simon of Beauvallet.

"What in Hell ails thee, lad, that thou must poke

and pry into plots and other such treasonable matters? Let well alone, and for God's sake do not implicate thyself to thine own undoing! Thy letter has started my gout again. If thou must ride to London because thou hast waylaid a traitor on the road, thou mightest at least write me the full sum of it! The few lines I do receive from thy hand would enrage a saint, nor could thy rascally squire tell of aught beyond thy fight in the wood over a wench or some such fandangle. And I tell thee, Simon, that I had thought more of thee than that thou'dst embroil thyself in a quarrel over some silly maid. Natheless I say naught for I do suppose that thou wilt ever go thine own headstrong road, plague be upon thee for thine obstinacy!

"Were it not for this accursed gout which, as thou dost know, hath me fast by the leg, and is an hundred times worse from thine unreasonable behaviour, I would be up and after thee to learn the whole tale from thine own tongue, and see for myself what maggot has entered into thy head. And a pretty welcome thou wilt have at Westminster, thou silly boy, carrying a cock and bull story of a trumped up plot! Were it not that I know what a headstrong, impudent determination is thine, I should say thou wouldst never gain access to the King. But I do suppose that thou wilt, and by the front door, as thou didst come to me when thou wert but a babe. I do conjure thee not to break the heads of his guards, for that would surely land thee in gaol, which I do trust will happen if it might tame thy hot blood. And furthermore thou must know that I am considerably incensed with thee and would have come with Gregory had I not had this accursed gout, if only to break my stick across thy shoulders. And if thou art slain by footpads on the road, or clapped into prison for an importunate fool, it will be but thy just deserts, and I shall not grieve nor move a finger to aid thee.

"I send thee twenty guineas by Roger, against thy needs, and if thou stand in need of a friend, or a lodging, repair to my cousin, Charles of Granmere, who hath a goodly establishment in the Strand, which is in London, and show him this letter. He will maybe keep thee from running thy silly pate into a halter.

"God be with thee, my dear lad, and bring thee safe home again. If thou dost stand in need of more money, ask it of my cousin in my name. And bear a courteous tongue in thy mouth, and spare the King that fiery glance of thine, else he will surely account thee mad and be not wrong neither. I would I might go with thee, dear lad, but I know that thou art wise enough for ten.

"I send thee my love and blessing, lion-cub.
"FULK OF MONTLICE.

"Written at Montlice."

Simon smiled a little as he finished this remarkable epistle, and turning, found that Roger was by his side with a purse in his hand.

"Sir, my lord sent this. I forgot to give it thee with the letter."

Simon took the purse.

"Hast thou breakfasted, Roger?"

"Ay, sir. I am ready, and your mare hath the devil himself in her." He spoke feelingly, and grinned a little as Simon smiled.

"Bring her to the door, lad." He went into the tavern to speak again to the landlord, and left five of my lord's golden sovereigns on account. Thus it was that the landlord's spirits rose considerably, and he was able to bow his guest out in his best manner.

Side by side Simon and his squire rode south-west towards Royston, at a brisk, steady pace. There they dined and rested, and again set off down the old Roman road to London. They lay that night at a village near Hertford, and were up betimes on the morrow to complete the journey. The horses were tired, so that they did not reach Bishopsgate until after dusk, when Simon at once set about finding a lodging for the night.

He had heard that the city abounded with ruffians and footpads, but none sought to rob him, nor did he meet with any rudeness when he paused to inquire the way. He asked for a tavern as near to Westminster as possible, and an interested mercer directed him to the Lamb and Saracen's Head, or, if he found it full, to the Rose, near-by. Simon thanked him gravely, and with Roger riding sedately behind him went at a respectable pace to this hostelry. They had no difficulty in securing a room, and the supper laid before them was plentiful enough to satisfy even their hungry appetites. Roger, in a twitter of excitement, implored Simon to let him walk out after supper to see the town, but this Simon would not allow, sending him peremptorily to bed, well-knowing that he would not dare to disobey. He himself sallied forth, armed with a dagger and his trusty quarter-staff. It may have been this stout weapon which kept him immune from assault, or it may have been his formidable bearing. At all events he wandered in perfect safety about Westminster, returning early to the tavern to rest.

On the next morning he set about the making of his plans. He had not a doubt but that, if he willed it so, he could gain access to the palace during an Audience with the utmost ease, but he was wise enough to realize that this would be of very little use to him. In all probability he would have no opportunity of speaking privately to the King. Nor did he consider that this would be a proper way of approaching Henry. Accosted by a strange knight in the midst of a reception, he might very well feel annoyance and wave Simon and his news aside. And once that had happened Simon knew that he would never gain a hearing. Had the Prince of Wales been at Westminster he might have risked a rebuff, for he knew that the young Henry would remember him. But the Prince, having wintered in London, was now back on the Marches.

Simon decided at length to write to the King, and accordingly he called for quills, ink, and parchment, and sat himself down to compose a suitable note. It proved to be no easy task, for his epistolary style was naturally curt. He had wit enough to see that curtness would not tend to make easier his mission, and he spent the best part of the morning writing and rewriting. In the end it was, for him, a very fair letter.

"My very dread and Sovereign Lord the King,

"Your Gracious Lordship may perchance remember

one Simon of Beauvallet whom you knighted at Shrewsbury after the battle in last July. This same Simon of Beauvallet doth now write to your Majesty with intent to beg an audience of you, or of one of your Majesty's Council. The matter I would disclose to your Majesty is of great import, as I do judge, and should be attended to with all speed lest it lead to more serious harm. But three days since, I did chance upon one whom I found to bear documents in his possession addressed to various lords of the counties of Cambridge and Bedford, purporting to come from the late King, and seemingly fastened with his seal. These papers I would deliver up to your Lordship, or to those whom your Lordship shall appoint to receive them. The messenger I hold under lock and key and well guarded by the men of my Lord of Montlice.

"If it be your Majesty's pleasure to search further into this matter, I do beseech you to give me a hearing, when I will tell all that I know, and disclose the whereabouts of this messenger.

"In humble obedience to your Majesty's gracious wishes,

"SIMON OF BEAUVALLET.

"Written at the sign of the Lamb and Saracen's Head."

Simon dusted the finished letter and carefully sealed it. Then a new difficulty presented itself, to wit: how he should assure himself of this letter reaching the King. He thought of Fulk's cousin, Charles of Granmere, and, much as he disliked asking for aid, he decided to repair to his house in the Strand and demand his assistance.

He called Roger to him, who sat kicking his heels by the window, and bade him fetch their horses. Delighted at the prospect of seeing more of the town Roger ran to do his bidding, wreathed in smiles.

Together they rode towards London and proceeded down the Strand, past the greater palaces till they came upon one that was less magnificent, and bore the name Granmere Hall. They rode into the courtyard, and on a lackey's demanding their business,

Simon asked for my Lord of Granmere in no uncertain tones.

"Tell my lord that Sir Simon Beauvallet comes from my Lord of Montlice!" he said peremptorily, and, dismounting, signed to Roger to stay with the horses.

He followed the lackey into the central hall of the palace, and waited there whiles the man bore his message to my lord. Presently he returned, and bowing to Simon, begged him to follow him to my lord's apartment.

Simon was ushered into a long low room where sat my Lord of Granmere, a man of middle age with a kindly rugged countenance, in which his eyes twinkled humorously. He came forward as Simon entered.

"Give you good den, sir. Do ye come from my cousin?"

"My Lord Fulk directed me to seek you out, my Lord of Granmere, in case I should need assistance. And lest ye should doubt that I do indeed come from Montlice he bade me show you this letter which he did write to me."

Charles of Granmere took the scrawled sheets and read them through. When he came to the end, he smiled, and gave Fulk's letter back to Simon.

"Ay, that is my cousin's fist," he said. "Methinks his words to you give me insight into your nature." His eyes twinkled more than ever. "What is this plot, if it be not an impertinent question, and what may I do for you?"

Briefly Simon gave him the outline, and showed him his letter to the King.

"It is not my way, sir, to seek assistance, but although I think I might succeed in this, unaided, the thing will be quicker done if you, my lord, will consent to bear my letter to the King."

"Well, that is good sense, Sir Simon. Hast a hard head on thy shoulders. Where art thou staying?"

"At the Lamb and Saracen's Head, my lord, with my squire."

Granmere's eyes twinkled anew.

"It seems that I should be defying my cousin's behests an I allowed thee to remain there. Wilt thou honour my poor house, Sir Simon?"

Simon flushed.

"Ye are more than kind, my lord, but all I ask is that ye will bear my letter to the King."

"Why, this is churlish!" Granmere chided. "It would be my pleasure to house thee. I do beg that thou wilt send thy squire back to the inn to pay thy reckoning and to bring thine appurtenances hither."

Simon considered for a moment, and shot my lord a swift, piercing glance. Then he bowed.

"I thank you, sir."

And that was how he first met Charles of Granmere.

My lord went to Westminster on the following day, and when he returned it was with a message from the King commanding Simon to a private audience that evening at six o'clock.

"He remembers thee," Granmere said. "He says that thou wert the thirteenth knight, and when I described thee he said at once that thou wert the man recommended for knighthood by the Prince. He is anxious to learn of thy plot. There are too many such afoot for his liking."

"And while the French Court pretends to lend credence to these tales of Richard being in Scotland, there will be a-many more," Simon said grimly.

"But Henry is a man," Granmere answered. "He will triumph throughout."

"It is the young Henry who is a man," Simon said.

When he presented himself at Westminster Palace that evening he was led at once to the King's chamber, where he found Henry and the old Duke of York.

Simon paused on the threshold as his name was announced, and went stiffly down upon his knee. The King nodded to him, observing him with shrewd, deep-set eyes.

"Come forward, Sir Simon of Beauvallet," he said. "We have to thank you for your courtesy and dispatch in informing us of this treacherous plot."

Simon advanced, and standing before the King's chair, told at his request, the story of Serle's messenger and his fight with him in the wood. It was not a graphic account that he gave, but it was concise, and devoid of embellishments or exaggerations. While he spoke the King watched him, chin in hand, marking every changing expression of Simon's face, and every little movement of his strong, well-shaped hands. He listened carefully, several times interrupting to put a gently-spoken question. Yet for all Henry's kind way and courteous manner, Simon knew that he was under cross-examination, for the questions came thick and fast as his tale proceeded, and it would have been very difficult to have avoided a slip had his story been false. The searching queries, and the steady scrutiny might well have discomposed Simon and have caused him to stumble or lose the thread of his narration. But he was not flustered and not a whit ruffled by these questions, which seemed to indicate that the King disbelieved him. He respected Henry for his lack of credulity and answered him firmly and patiently.

"And the documents?" Henry said at last.

Simon presented them, and waited in silence while the King and the Duke slit them open one after the other and perused them. The Duke muttered angrily as he read, and once or twice his eyes flashed, and he thumped his fist on his knee, but Henry read on calmly and almost detachedly. When he had come to the end he struck a small gong that stood on the table at his elbow, and on his secretary's coming, ordered him quietly to bring the papers captured in Scotland in December. These were fetched, and the King compared them with those Simon had brought, the Duke of York looking over his shoulder.

Presently Henry looked up and at Simon. His sunken eyes rested on him kindly for a moment before he spoke.

"Ye have done well, Sir Simon. Of how great an import these papers are, or what people this Serle has cozened to his side, we do not know. That we will find from the messenger. At all events it is a cunning plot, for I could not myself tell this seal from that of the late King, and the signatures do indeed bear a resemblance to his hand. The common folk might naturally be deluded into thinking Richard alive. How the gentle-people have received the false news we cannot know as yet."

"No man of culture, of education, could believe so empty a tale," the Duke said hotly.

"Oh, I find that the nobles believe in most empty tales, if they are like to bring them greater wealth, or greater rank!" Henry said tranquilly. "Have you, Sir Simon, heard talk of the late King?"

"Vague rumours I have heard, sire," Simon answered. "Also talk of certain gold and silver hearts which King Richard was wont to give his knights, and which are now seen in Essex. I gave the rumours no credit, sir, thinking them but peasants' tales, but it now seems to me that they are the fruits of this plot."

"Perhaps," Henry said. He gave a short, half-stifled sigh. "I suppose there will be plots until my death—and after." He glanced up at Simon. "King Richard is indeed dead," he said.

"I never doubted it, sire," Simon replied. "But he will come to life many times yet."

The Duke laughed a little at that, and even the King smiled.

"Ay, that is so. Where lies this messenger from Serle?"

"At Saltpetres, my liege, in the tavern of the Ox. Six men guard him under one Gregory for whom I will vouch."

"He must be conducted hither," Henry said. "We will send to fetch him. Ye had best write to this Gregory, commanding him, lest he refuse to give up the prisoner without word from you." Again he struck the gong. Simon noted that although his movements were languid, and his voice so gentle and tired, he went expeditiously about his business, and was not one to put off till tomorrow what might well be done today. When the secretary came he spoke without turning his head. "Bring writing materials." As soon as his command had been obeyed, he nodded to Simon. "Will you write now, Sir Simon?"

Simon went to the table, and seating himself at it, drew the parchment sheets towards him. Henry watched him, liking the decisive way in which he set about his task and the entire lack of hesitation in choosing his words that he displayed.

"To Gregory Arnold of Saint Dormans," Simon wrote.

"Deliver your prisoner unto the King's men who shall come for him bearing this my command, and repair at once to Montlice as I bade you.

"SIMON OF BEAUVALLET.

"Written at Westminster."

He sprinkled sand over the sheets to dry the ink, then, shaking it off, rose and gave his note to the King.

Henry read it, and smiled.

"I think ye are a man of action, Sir Simon," he said, "not of letters."

Simon smiled, too, and bowed.

"I trust that that is so, my liege."

Henry laid the parchment down.

"Until the prisoner is brought safe to London, that is all, sir. It is our pleasure that ye remain with my Lord of Granmere until we send for you. We have to thank you again for your care of our person and our realm." He struck the gong twice, and this time a page came who conducted Simon out.

VII

How King Henry thanked him

There followed a fortnight of forced inactivity for Simon, but although he could do nothing further concerning the plot, he was not altogether idle. Much time he spent in exploring the city, and my Lord of Granmere contrived to keep him occupied by inviting many guests to his house, to all of whom he presented Simon. And if some of these gentlemen did not like the silent, direct young man whom they met, at least they were not in danger of easily forgetting his strangely forceful personality.

It did not occur to Simon that he might write to his lord at Montlice, assuring him of his well-being, and when Granmere offered to send a messenger with any letter that he might wish to send, he was rather surprised, and refused the offer.

"But mayhap my cousin Fulk is worried at thy long absence!" Granmere pointed out.

"That is not very likely," Simon said.

"He may think thee dead, or lost!"

Simon smiled a little.

"He knows me too well to think that, my lord."

Granmere waved his hands.

"But at least write him that thou hast arrived in London!"

"That he knows."

"That thou hast seen the King!"

"That also doth he know."

Granmere looked at him hopelessly.

"My good boy, how can he know?"

Simon smiled again, sweetly.

"Because he doth know me, my lord. What I set out to do, I do."

Granmere sat down.

"One cannot always be sure of success, Simon."

Simon looked inscrutable.

"Why, boy, surely thou dost know that!"

"No, my lord, that is what I will not know."

My lord laughed at him, but he leaned forward, interested.

"Simon, suppose that thou didst engage on an impossible emprise—something in which thou couldst not succeed?"

"That were the action of a fool, my lord, and I do not think I am one."

"Nor I!" Granmere laughed again. "Thou wouldst never set out to do the impossible?"

Simon reflected.

"Nay, I think not, sir. Yet I believe that there is very little that is impossible. There is always a way."

"So if ye find not that way, ye will let be? Suppose that thy greatest friend lay imprisoned, and it was seemingly impossible to rescue him, because thou hadst discovered no way? Would ye then let be?"

Simon thought it out carefully.

"Ay, my lord. But I think that I should find a way," he said gravely.

Granmere looked him over.

"By God, I believe that thou wouldst!" he said.

At the end of the fortnight came a second summons from the King, and in obedience Simon presented himself at the Palace early one morning. As before, he was conducted to the King's closet, but this time he found some six or seven gentlemen of the Council there beside the King. Henry gave him his hand to kiss.

"We do rejoice to see you again, Sir Simon. Methinks some apology we do owe you for the long days ye have been kept waiting."

Simon rose from his knees.

"If during these days, sire, information has been yielded, then are they not wasted," he said in his deep, deliberate voice.

One of the gentlemen seated about the long table, smiled. Henry saw it, and the smile was reflected in his eyes.

"Ye speak sooth, Sir Simon, and that is better than a courtier's soft, flattering answer." His glance flickered a shade reprovingly to the gentleman who had smiled. "Will ye not be seated, sir?"

Simon thanked him, and sat down in a vacant chair. Henry folded his hands in his sleeves.

"Ye will like to know, Sir Simon, that full inquiry has been made into this matter of Serle's plot, and much has been discovered. The messenger whom ye waylaid came safely to London, but methinks he was something stiff of limb, and sore in every part of his worthless carcase." He looked quizzically at Simon as he said this, and Simon gave his short laugh.

"That is possible, my liege."

Henry ran his eyes down Simon's large, muscular person.

"I think it was inevitable, sir," he said solemnly. "But that is not what we would say. This man has been put to the question, and he disclosed all that he knew. I will not weary you with the details of this traitorous affair, but it will interest you to know that the tale of Richard's living still has gained the seeming credence of many of my unfaithful nobles in the eastern counties, and even so far indeed as your Cambridge. Thus your vigilance and your promptitude have not been for little cause. Rather they are of great service and import to the realm, for because that ye have brought the news of this plot thus early to our ears, we are enabled to deal with it at once, and to crush the seeds of rebellion ere they have had time to sprout and multiply." The gentle voice paused, then, as Simon said nothing: "This is not a little thing to have done, Sir Simon," Henry said.

There was silence for a moment. Simon looked up.

"The deed itself was little, sire, and easy. It is only the fruits of the deed that are great. To me is small honour due, for by chance alone did I discover the plot, without toil, and without intent."

"Some of the greatest issues in the history of this world have had birth from Chance," Henry answered, "yet to him whom the finger of Chance guided to the vital spot has honour ever been due."

Simon did not answer. He hoped that Henry would continue to talk, for the soft voice pleased him, and he was interested in what the King had to say.

Henry resumed after another pause.

"I see, Sir Simon, that ye do think your share in this matter but trifling, since it was not done with pain and travail, and of intent. But a measure of intent there was, for having discovered this plot what easier than to take no action, or to send the messenger on his way with those documents?"

Simon's eyes narrowed.

"That were treachery, sire, or indolence and lack of

care for your Majesty's person and the safety of the realm."

Henry slid one hand along the arm of his chair.

"It were indeed so, Sir Simon. None of these faults was yours."

"Nay."

"Rather was zeal yours, and loyalty, and firmness of purpose. It was not chance alone which brought you safe to London, and which has brought your prisoner, too. It was determination brought you, sir, and strength both of body and mind which kept you safe from robbers, and brought you thus surely to my presence. Ye frown. Is it not as I say?"

"It is true that mine own wit and strength brought *me* here, sire," Simon said, who had no false modesty. "But it was your Majesty's men who brought my prisoner."

Henry's lips quivered. Two or three of the gentlemen of the Council chuckled a little.

"That is so," Henry agreed, "but by whose contriving was the prisoner safely delivered into their hands?"

"By my lieutenant Gregory's contriving, sire," Simon answered seriously.

Henry bent his brows upon him, but his eyes twinkled.

"Sir Simon of Beauvallet, are ye determined to foil me at every turn?"

"Nay, my liege," Simon said. "But it seems that your Majesty would give honour to me where it is due unto another."

"Under whose orders acted this Gregory?" Henry asked.

"Under mine, sire."

"Then ye will agree, Sir Simon, that his part was but to obey, asking no questions."

"Ay, that is so, my liege."

Henry nodded.

"Will ye also agree, sir, that honour is due to him whose brain planned the whole emprise so well that it was carried through with no hitch or stoppage?"

Simon considered this.

"It seems just, sire."

"It is just," Henry assured him. "I sent for you hither that I might reward you for your services, but it hath taken me all this while to convince you that ye are deserving of a reward. Nor am I sure that I have done it even now. Are you convinced, Sir Simon?"

Simon smiled.

"Your Majesty's reasoning is so full of wit that it were insolent of me to dispute your judgment. And indeed as your Majesty has put the matter, it seems reasonable enough. Yet it was in all truth a very little thing that I did, sire."

"Sir Simon, are you content to let me judge of the magnitude of the service ye have rendered me?"

Simon's rare humour peeped out.

"Ay, my liege, since that promises to be more to my advantage."

"And to your advancement," Henry said in amusement. "Tell me, Sir Simon, what may I do for you? Is there something that ye do desire, and that I can give you? Advancement in rank? Gold? Land? Tell me!"

Simon rose to his feet, swiftly turning a certain cherished project round in his mind. He looked down at Henry, hardly knowing that he did so, and Henry saw his eyes keen and shrewd, and knew that something was he weighing in his brain. He leaned back in his chair, waiting.

After a short pause Simon spoke.

"My lord the King, one thing is there that I desire."

"If it be within my power to give it you, it is yours."

"It is in your power, sire, but it may not be pleasing to your Majesty to accord it me."

"What is it?" Henry asked. "It would not have been pleasing to me to have had a rebellion thrumming about my ears."

"Sire, in Cambridge, to the south and east of Montlice, is a fair barony of little size, but, as I judge, of passing great wealth. It is named Fair Pastures, and it was once the property of one John of Barminster, who joined with Percy against your Majesty, and was fitly hanged for his pains. The land is confiscate unto the Crown, sire, but your Majesty has neither set one to rule over it in your name, nor given it to some noble

83

about your person. It is in disorder now, and the serfs are masterless, while lawless men ravage the place. Give this land to me, sire, and I will bring law and order into it, and hold it as mine own, myself owning allegiance to you!"

"It seems not much to ask," Henry said slowly. He looked at one of his Council. "What know ye of this place?"

"I remember it, sire. It is as Sir Simon says, not large, but fertile. Naught has been done with it as yet."

Henry brought his eyes back to Simon.

"Is this indeed your desire? There are larger, more orderly lands I might bestow on you."

"Nay, sire, I need them not. It is this barony I desire."

"Why?"

"There are several reasons, sire, but the greatest of all is that its name is very like to mine."

"Fair Pastures—Beau Vallet. Ay, that is a good omen. Ye shall have that land, Sir Simon, and ye shall call it Beauvallet and be yourself Lord of Beauvallet. The deed of gift shall be sent to you at Granmere Hall, and ye shall subdue your turbulent subjects. Can ye do that, I wonder?"

Simon smiled grimly.

"I can do that, sire."

("I make no doubt he can!" whispered one of the Council to his neighbour.)

"Then the land is yours, and I have paid my debt to you. Ye shall not wait long for my mandate, I promise." He held out his hand, and Simon knelt.

"I do thank you, sire," he said sincerely.

"Nay, 'tis I thank you," Henry answered. "I need have little fear of risings near Beauvallet now. This gift is to mine own advantage, for ye will hold the peace under me in your barony. May you prosper, my Lord of Beauvallet."

When Simon told Charles of Granmere what had befallen him, Granmere clapped him heartily upon the back, delighted at his protégé's good fortune.

"Why, it is excellent, Simon! The King must have conceived as great a liking for thee as have I!"

"Have you a liking for me?" inquired Simon, rather taken aback.

"That have I! Have I been so cold in my bearing that thou shouldst doubt it?"

"Nay, but kindness may mean naught. It is curious how many people call me friend, who call friend so few."

"Well, I do trust I merit that title," Granmere said.

"Oh, yes," Simon answered. "Thou and my half-brother, Geoffrey of Malvallet, and my Lord of Montlice. Alan, too, I suppose, although he would rather be my slave."

"Thou hast not many," Granmere commented.

"Nay, for I can find few whom I desire to call friend."

"Yet you count my cousin amongst these few? He is not most men's choice."

"My Lord Fulk and I have dwelt amicably enough together for three years and more. Were there not friendship between us we had not done that."

"I do not think so indeed!" Granmere said, and laughed. "What will he have to say concerning thy sudden elevation?"

"He is like to say much," Simon answered placidly. "He knows that I go mine own road."

"Holy Virgin, what fights thou must have had!"

"Oh, no," said Simon. "We understand each other very fairly."

"Do ye so? Well, ye are a fitting pair!" Then he burst out laughing again. "Thou and Fulk!" he gasped. "I would give much to see it!"

"Well, so thou mayst," Simon said, watching him gravely. "Come with me to Montlice, and pay my lord a visit."

Granmere checked his mirth.

"By God, I believe I will come! Why it is seven years since I set eyes on Fulk! We will ride together, Lord of Beauvallet."

VIII

How he returned to Montlice

A week later, Charles of Granmere and Simon of Beauvallet rode through Montlice towards the castle, their squires behind them. Word flew round that Sir Simon was back, and all along the road men came out to cheer him, and women dropped him shy curtseys. He acknowledged all with his curt nod, and sometimes he hailed a man by name and asked after his wife or his children.

"Why, thou art beloved here!" Granmere exclaimed. "What hast done to make them cheer thee so?"

"I know them, and they know me. Some fought at Shrewsbury with me. That makes a bond."

They arrived at the drawbridge and went over, saluted by some half-dozen men-at-arms, who one and all gave Simon welcome. And so they rode up to the castle door, and dismounted there. A lackey saw them from an upper window and cried the news abroad. Out came Alan, full tilt, with Fulk hobbling after him.

"Simon, Simon, thou art alive and safe! Ah, God be thanked! We knew not what to think! Simon, I swear thou hast grown!" Impetuously Alan flung himself upon Simon, only to be put gently aside, as Simon stepped forward to meet my lord.

Fulk came roaring.

"Hey, Simon lad! Hey, thou rascally, turbulent, naughty knave! How darest thou stay away all these weeks! Hast no regard for me at all, cub? Praise be to God, no harm has come to thee! Holy Virgin, I would they had clapped thee up for a mad rogue! I might have known thou'dst return to enrage me further, small thanks to thee for doing it! Lord, Lord, thou'rt broader still! And had no one the sense to break thy head?" For once Fulk's reserve deserted him. He discarded his stick and caught Simon in a large embrace, kissing him loudly on both cheeks. "Thou self-willed puppy! I thought I was rid of thee at last! But no! Back thou comest, with not a hair out of place, as cool as ever thou wert! Now as God's my life, I've a mind to send thee about thy business! We do well enough without thee, Master Stiff-Neck. Think not that we missed thee, thou conceited boy! Oh, Simon, Simon, let me get hold on thy hands!" And thereupon he seized both Simon's hands in his, and gripped them as though he would never let go.

Simon was a little flushed at this excited welcome, and his voice was deeper than ever as he answered Fulk, and strangely moved.

"Thou couldst not shake me off, my lord. And glad I am to be here again with thee. Thy gout is no better?"

"Better! How should it be better when I have to take thy place here and work myself to a shred all for a silly boy's whim? Hey, hey, who's here?"

Granmere, who had been an amused spectator, came forward.

"Hast also a welcome for me, cousin?"

Fulk released Simon and surged to meet his kinsman.

"Ay, that have I! God's Body, it's a dozen years since I set eyes on thy countenance, Charles! Didst bring my rascal Simon home?" He proceeded to embrace Granmere.

"Nay, he brought me," Granmere answered.

"Ay, ay, he would!" chuckled Fulk. "Come within, lad, come within! Simon, Simon! Where goest thou, pray?"

Simon paused. He was walking away from the castle with Alan at his side.

"I go to look to my men, my lord. Hast need of me?"

Fulk exploded into a mighty bellow.

"He goes to look to his men! Beshrew me, was there ever such another? Come thou here, sirrah, this instant! Have I need of thee, forsooth! Thou quittest my side for a month, wandering God knows where, and as soon as thou art back, thou dost go to 'look to my men'! Come thou here, I say, ere I lose my temper with thee!"

Simon came back to them, and seizing him by one arm and Granmere by the other, Fulk bore them into the great hall and shouted in stentorian tones for sack and ale to be brought. Then he sank down into a chair, and puffed.

Granmere withdrew his hands from his ears.

"Cousin, I rejoice that the passing of years has not affected your lungs," he said. "Methinks they could hear thy voice in London."

"Ay, I can shout with the best of them," Fulk answered complacently. His unwonted display of feeling over, he turned to Simon and addressed him more or less quietly.

"Well, didst thou see the King, my Simon?"

"Twice, my lord."

"Well, well, I guessed as much! What of thy silly plot?"

Granmere answered him.

"A great deal. One Serle hath a buffoon coached to counterfeit King Richard in Scotland, and half the country would have risen for him, had it not been for Simon here."

Fulk opened his little round eyes as wide as they would stretch.

"So, so! Tell me the whole tale from the very beginning, Simon, and see thou tellst it better than in thy letter. By Our Lady! My blood boils anew when I bethink me of that letter! Three or four bald words, and there was I a-fret to know the whole story! Well, go on, lad, go on!"

"There's not much to tell," Simon said. He took a long drink of sack. "I rode out one morning, as ye know, and came to Saltpetres in time for supper, where I chanced upon a fellow in the wood behind the inn and discovered that he bore treasonable papers, so——"

"Hark to the boy!" Fulk cried. "How didst chance on this fellow, numskull?"

Simon sighed.

"I was walking in the wood, sir, and heard a woman

scream. I went to see what was toward and found this ruffian with her in his arms. So I came upon him unawares and flung him backwards from her."

"Of what like was this woman?" demanded Fulk suspiciously.

Simon stared.

"Of what like, sir?"

"Ay! Was she dark or fair, comely or plain?"

"Faith, I know not, my lord. She—she was just a woman. Plain, I think."

Fulk grunted.

"Go on!"

"The fellow came upon me and I closed with him. No, first I hit him, I think."

"Where?"

"Over the ear. Then we wrestled awhile, and he broke away. Then a wallet fell from the bosom of his tunic, and for fear lest I should seize it, he came at me again. And when he found he could not throw me, he drew his dagger and rushed to stab me."

"Cur!" roared Fulk. "Drew steel, eh? Dastardly cur! And what didst thou do?"

"I broke his arm," Simon said simply.

"Well done, well done! What next?"

"Next I called Roger to me and we bound him. The rest is nothing."

"Tell it!" Fulk ordered, and accordingly Simon recited the tale of his adventures up to his second interview with the King. Then, as he paused, Roger came into the hall, and on Fulk's hailing him good-naturedly, doffed his cap, blushing.

"So thou hast brought Sir Simon safe home, eh?" Fulk said jovially.

Roger, already bursting with pride over his master's new honour, and agog to tell the news to someone, answered primly:

"My lord took no hurt, sir."

Simon looked up frowning; Granmere smiled at the boy's suppressed excitement; Fulk stared.

"What's this? Who now art thou 'my lording'?"

The boy drew himself up.

"My Lord of Beauvallet, sir."

"Roger, get thee hence!" said Simon sharply. "Thy tongue runs away with thee."

Roger retired, somewhat crestfallen.

"Lord of Beauvallet, Lord of Beauvallet! What means the boy?"

Granmere spoke.

"For his services the King made Simon Baron of Beauvallet, and gave him a land called Fair Pastures, which was once the estate of John of Barminster."

"Simon!" Alan was out of his chair in a flash, catching his friend by the shoulders. "A lord? Thine own estate! Oh, Simon, I am so glad! Father, is't not marvellous?"

Fulk collected himself with an effort. He rolled out a huge oath, which seemed slightly to relieve him. Then he stared at Simon afresh.

"A lord! God's my life, what next? John of Barminster's estate? Christ's Wounds, wert thou my page but three years since?"

"Ay. Else had I not now been lord, sir."

"Come thou here!" Fulk commanded, and when Simon knelt before him, smote him on the shoulder, and embraced him again. "It is great news, lad, and I am glad for thy sake. But it means that I must lose thee, and I like it not."

"I must have gone one day, my lord, and as it chances I go not far."

"Ay, but who's to take thy place here, my lion-cub?"

"Alan is of an age now, my lord."

"Bah!" growled Fulk. "Alan to take thy place! As if he could do one tittle of what thou canst do!"

"He must," Simon said.

"I hope I shall live to see the day! Simon, I shall miss thee sorely."

"And I you, my lord. Yet I shall be but a few miles distant."

"H'm!" Fulk let him go. "In what condition are thine estates?"

"In bad condition, my lord. There has been no master there since last July."

"Good lack! Thou'lt have work enough even for thee!"

"So I think, my lord, but it is work I like."

"Ay, ay. And thou shalt have as many men from here to help thee as thou askest of me. My Lord of Beauvallet, forsooth! Little did I think that thou'dst come to this, three years ago! And by the straight road, God wot! as thou didst say thou wouldst ever go! Ah, what an obstinate babe thou wert then! Charles, dost thou know that I have borne with this headstrong boy for three years?"

"I do wonder that ye are both alive," Granmere replied.

"I'll not deny he has enraged me a-many times, but can one fight a block of ice? Well, well, come ye in to supper! This is a glad and a sad day for me." He heaved himself up, and leaning heavily on Simon's shoulder, led the way into his chamber, where supper lay ready for them.

They rode out next day, Fulk and Granmere, Alan and Simon, to survey Simon's lands. Not even Fulk's swollen foot would induce him to remain behind. He was assisted into the saddle, groaning and cursing, by three of his varlets, and rode abreast with his cousin, while Alan and Simon fell in behind.

"Will there be a place for me in thy castle, Simon?" Alan asked.

"Ay, whenever thou wilt," Simon answered. "And when I have set the place in order."

"I suppose thou wilt do that well enough. But it will be no easy task."

"I have never wanted that," Simon said.

Presently Alan shot him a mischievous glance.

"Who shall be mistress of Beauvallet, Simon?"

"None."

Alan laughed.

"So thou sayest, so thou sayest, but love comes to all men one day."

"I do pray it will pass me by."

"Ah, no, thou wilt fall, Simon! I shall see thee at some gentle maid's feet, I know!"

"Wilt thou?" Simon said grimly. "I doubt it, lad."

But Alan shook his head wisely and laughed again.

They rode rather silently through Fair Pastures,

looking about them with appraising eyes. Occasionally Fulk turned in his saddle to make some remark to Simon.

"There has been no work done here for months, lad. See that field yonder."

"I do know it," Simon answered.

Then as they passed a group of loiterers on the road:

"Too little toil, too much sack," Fulk growled. "Thou hast a hard time before thee, Simon. When wilt thou come here?"

"At once, my lord."

"Ay, ay. And how many men wilt thou take with thee?"

"None, my lord, save Roger, my squire, and little Arnold, my page. And that only if it be thy pleasure."

"Much use would they be to me always pining to be with thee," grunted Fulk. "Thou shalt take Malcolm also for thy squire, then may Roger still have with whom to fight for thy favours. Art thou wise to refuse my men-at-arms? Will ye not take a man from Montlice to be thy Marshal?"

"Nay, I will bring no strangers into Beauvallet. For the nonce I will make shift without a Marshal, but when I do better know my men, then will I promote some of them to rule under me."

"There speaks a sage man," Granmere remarked. "I shall look to see thee master in a month."

Simon smiled a little.

"In three months there shall be no lawlessness here," he promised.

IX

How he took possession of his estates

In a small chamber by the kitchens at the Castle of
Fair Pastures, now known as Beauvallet, sat Master
Hubert, the steward, with James, called the Short-
Leg, on account of his limp, and Bernard of Talmayne,
the late John of Barminster's secretary. They sat about
an oaken table on which stood three brimming tankards of sack and a jug full of that liquid for when the
tankards should need replenishing. Master Hubert, a
little, pot-bellied man with an inflamed countenance
and a large voice, fruity in *timbre,* was speaking,
aggrievedly and as one to whom some sore injury has
been done. Ever and anon he smote the table with his
fat hand, and his voice throbbed with a righteous
indignation.

"Now I do say it is not to be borne!" he swore, "and
by my troth, it shall not be borne! Are we to cringe
under this tyrant's heel? What is he to us, I ask of ye?
Whose men are we? Why, we were John of Barminster's! But he being hanged for a rogue, whose
men shall we be? Why, our own, say I, and rightly so!"
He paused in his harangue and glared belligerently at
his friends. "Who shall gainsay it?" Then as neither
James nor Bernard seemed inclined to gainsay it, he
continued. "We were very well before this beetle-
browed deathshead came upon us. There was good
food in plenty, much sack and strong ale, a rich land
to call our own, and a life of ease and peace for us.
What have we now? Why, what but a heavy-jowled
youth, who comes upon us like a tyrant and an op-
pressor? Not a word of warning, not a moment's respite to think on the matter at our leisure! Down he

comes with his pert squires and tramps into the castle, willy-nilly, with his devil's eyes like stones, and his thundering voice like a death-knell!"

"Nay," Bernard interposed. "Ye mistake, Master Hubert. He spake softly enough, though with a note of danger creeping through the softness."

Master Hubert thumped the table anew.

"What matters it how he spake, Master Secretary? His words were a death-knell!"

"Ay, that is so," Short-Leg agreed. "Death-knell indeed, and as full of proud arrogance as an egg is full of meat." He picked up his tankard and sought to drown his troubles in the comforting sack.

The steward crossed his fat legs and loosened his doublet.

"Arrogance indeed! What did he, I ask? To what lengths did his pert haughtiness carry him? Why, to call me to him in the hall! Me! As though I had been a scullion for the kitchens instead of the steward of Fair Pastures. He sent a varlet to fetch me—me! I ask myself today, why was I fool enough to go to him? Can ye tell me? Was it not because I am a courteous man, and peace-loving? What else should——"

"I did hear that it was because he sent his squire with yet another message when ye did tarry," Bernard said drily. "And I did hear that the message ran shortly and sweetly: 'Tell Hubert the steward that he knows not me, but that I know him.' Then ye did go."

Master Hubert's full-blooded face grew purple. Before he could answer the secretary he had recourse to his sack. Then, wiping his flaccid lips on the back of his hand, he said in a voice half-choked with rage and drink:

"Take heed how ye listen to scullions' gossip, Master Secretary! It is true that he did send that curt message, but could he intimidate me? I was of a mind to show him what manner of man am I, but I bethought myself—is it befitting for this coxcomb to stamp about the castle over which I am lord since Barminster died? I did go to him, constrained by courtesy, and when I came to the hall what found I? What but a mountain of a fellow with a damned flaxen head crammed full of haughty tyranny? A springald with not a hair to his lip, but great brows that 'most hid his wicked eyes, and a nose like to my hawk's beak yonder."

"A jaw like a mastiff's, a frame like a giant's, eyes like two daggers, a smile like a tiger's snarl," Bernard murmured.

"Ay, he is all that!" Master Hubert said. "A murrain be on him! And when I came to him, what did I do? I did bow in all politeness, yet stiffly withal, to show him that I'd not brook his surliness."

"I did hear that ye did bow so low that your head came below your knees," Bernard said.

"Ye heard! Ye heard! Ye will hear next that I kissed his feet!" Hubert cried angrily. "Little truth will ye learn from the scullions' talk, Master Secretary! I bowed, as I have said, welcoming him with pleasant words, and demanding, as is my right, to learn of his business."

"Ay, and thou didst continue speaking, and continue speaking, whiles he stood there as quiet as the statue of King Richard Lion-Heart that is in Saltpetres, and spake never a word, nor seemed to breathe," piped Short-Leg suddenly. "And one hand he had on his hip, and the other he laid on his sword-hilt. And he interrupted thee not, nor seemed to grow out of patience, yet looked so great and formidable that even I was afeared!"

"Hold thy babble!" Master Hubert ordered, "though true it is that such was his discourtesy that he had no answer to my greetings, nor gave any sign of having hearkened to my discourse! Then when I held my peace, seeing that he was dumb and deaf, what did he but shoot at me a sudden glance the very thought of which makes——"

"The blood freeze in your veins," Bernard said gently.

Master Hubert snapped at him.

"Ay, with anger, Master Bernard! On my life, I grew pale and trembling with choler at the fellow's impudence! I could scarce speak, so great was mine ire!"

"Yet still thou wert courteous," James said eagerly.

95

"Thou didst speak him fair, saying, 'Lord, what may be your pl——' "

"I do know very well what I did say without thy senseless reminder!" Hubert rounded on his tactless friend. "I spake him fair, for, thought I, is it befitting for one in my high position to bandy words with a ruffianly tyrant? 'What may be your pleasure?' I said. Then, with an effrontery at which I still gasp, 'I am lord of this estate,' he said, and handed me a parchment roll. And there I found it set down in many words that the King had given Fair Pastures to Sir Simon of Beauvallet, who was now to be baron, and call the land after himself. Beshrew me, I suffocate, at the thought of it! Give me air!" As though to prove his words he tore his doublet open still further, and rolled his eyes alarmingly. The obsequious James hastened to replenish his tankard, but the secretary paid little heed to Master Hubert's sufferings. He leaned back in his chair, a smile hovering over his thin lips. After another draught of sack, Master Hubert resumed his harangue.

"Then, ere I had time fully to grasp the import of that infamous document, he spake again, demanding that I should bring to him the accounts of the barony since last July! By Our Lady! I was so taken aback, so affronted, and so enraged, that I could find no words with which to express myself. And when I would have spoken reasonably to him, he turned on his heel saying: 'See ye have them for my inspection in the morning.' Oh, I burn, I rage! All night was I at work striving to remember this payment and that, and setting all down in the book. And on the morrow I did go to the late lord's chamber where sat this coxcomb, with you, Master Secretary, nor had we reached an end by ten of the clock. There he sat, and questioned me till my poor head reeled, and ever and anon he shot me that evil look from out his strange eyes, whereat I choked with passion. All the accounts of last year and the year before did he read, up to July, and knew to a farthing what sums were collected yearly, how many heads of cattle we numbered, how——"

"Ay," James interrupted, "and he summoned Nicholas

of the Guards to give an account of his men. Rare it was to see great Nicholas stammer, and strive to bluster and over-rule my lord's queries."

"And all the while," said Bernard dreamily, "he did sit as still as carven stone, with only the glitter in his eyes to show that he lived. And when the bully Nicholas would have shouted and blustered more, than of a sudden he sprang to life. Methinks I shiver still."

"They told me," James said, "that he scarce raised his voice above the usual, yet so great and cold was his passion, so menacing his look, that Nicholas was silenced, and stood sulkily enough whiles my lord cut him in twain with his tongue. I would I had been there to see it," he sighed regretfully.

"But that is not all!" Master Hubert cried. "He had the audacity to summon also Edmund, the Marshal, that aged fool! What said he to Edmund, Master Secretary?"

"Not much," Bernard answered. "I think he is not wont to waste his words. He spake the Marshal courteously enough for his years' sake, but he asked him this question and that, till the Marshal was nigh to weeping with mingled fear, and shame for his negligence. My lord had the full sum from him, and at the end he said with great gentleness, 'Edmund of Fenton, it seems that ye grow too old for your task, since rogues thrive under your rule and ye are either too weary or too fearful to check their arrogance. It were better that ye should retire now with the pension that I will give you.' And not another word would he vouchsafe, for all the Marshal's pleading and argument. It is in my mind that my lord knoweth a rogue when he doth see one, nor will he bear with incompetence."

"How now, Master Secretary!" the steward exclaimed. "This is pretty hearing indeed! Master Fenton is a worthy man, and not one to be prying into another man's affairs! Now is he gone, and God alone knows what will come to this poor land!"

"Nay, not God alone," the secretary said. "My lord knows also."

Master Hubert flung up his chubby hands in horror. "Oh, blasphemous man!" he cried virtuously. "To speak thus lightly! Oh, that I should live to hear thee!"

James the Short-Leg took this opportunity of filling his tankard. Master Hubert caught sight of him, and heaved a gusty sigh.

"Ay, drink, James, drink! 'Tis little ale or sack will flow in the future. Verily this new lord hath lynx-eyes! I shudder to think of the things he threatened to do unto me if I gave more than he commanded to any man in the castle! Oh, an evil fate hath befallen us! He is everywhere at once, so that I have ta'en to starting at every sound! And what doth he purpose? No man can tell, for he goes softly and saith little. He doth ride forth all this week about the estate, and I learn from Robert the Herd that already he knoweth each man by name and how many children he hath, or what is his fortune. Plague be upon it, the peasants cheer him and hasten to do his bidding. They are all upon the fields again, and tending the cattle."

"Ay, but the guards murmur against him," James remarked. "And the men-at-arms would rise against him at any moment."

"Small wonder!" Master Hubert said. "For what hath he done? Why, within a week of his coming he had laid strict rules on all the men-at-arms and archers that are here, so that they fret and grumble. And as for Maurice of Gountray who commands them, it needs but a spark to set him blazing. Would that I had died before this fate had come upon us! We were happy before, but now no man may call his soul his own. Back hath come Father Jocelyn, and we have Masses and penances enough to make a poor man's flesh shrink. Woe is me! Oh, woe is me!" Overcome by grief and sack, the steward beat feebly at his breast and moaned. "If he would but make known his vile intentions!" he cried. "My teeth are all on edge because that I know not from one hour to the next when he will fall upon me!"

Someone knocked upon the door and the steward started upright, pulling his doublet together. His little eyes shifted uneasily.

"En—en—enter!" he said.

A page thrust his head into the room.

"My lord hath need of Master Bernard," he said importantly.

The steward drew himself up.

"Ho!" he grunted. "Is it for this you disturb me, boy? A murrain seize your impudence!"

The boy grinned.

"Shall I bear that message to my lord?" he asked tauntingly. "Is it not convenient for Master Bernard to come to him?"

Bernard rose.

"If it is convenient for my lord, then is it convenient for his secretary," he said with some dignity.

The steward blew out his flabby cheeks.

"I wonder that ye go so humbly! I wonder at it!"

Bernard went to the door.

"I go because I dare not tarry," he said.

Master Hubert laughed jeeringly.

"Oh, brave! Oh, brave! Ye will tell me next that ye love this new lord, craven!"

"I think I do," the secretary said, and closed the door softly behind him.

The page, a child of ten or twelve years, danced a few paces in front of him adown the corridor.

"Oh, and I do love this lord!" he said. "He lets not the bullies beat us and ill-treat us, and though he is cold to us and stern, he is kind withal, and just. And though he flies not into a passion over a little thing, yet we durst not disobey his commands. Nor does he strike one down when one comes late to do his bidding, as the old lord was wont to do, but looks at one so that one is afraid, and shamed. Indeed, I am glad that he is come, for it was an ill time for us pages when the Marshal ruled."

"Where is my lord?" Bernard asked.

"In the chamber looking south where he doth sit so often. He sent me for you, yet I do not think he is angered with you!"

The secretary smiled faintly, and leaving the page to join his fellows, went to Simon's room.

Simon was seated at a table, his arms resting upon it, and his brows frowning. He glanced up as Bernard entered, and then the heavy frown lifted a little.

"Sit ye down, Master Bernard," he said. "There is much I would say to thee."

The secretary looked at him in momentary surprise, for this was the first time that Simon had made use of the familiar "thou" in speaking to him. He drew up a chair and sank into it, his gentle, tired eyes resting on Simon's face.

"I have been in this land a fortnight," Simon said, "and much have I seen. Mayhap ye think that I have been strangely inactive?"

"Nay," Bernard answered. "Your lordship hath done much already. The peasants cleave to you. I have thought that ye but hold your hand until all things be clear to you."

"That is so," Simon said. "And until I should know what men I might trust."

The secretary bowed his head.

"I do now wish to take counsel with thee," Simon said evenly.

The secretary looked up, a sudden gleam in his eyes.

"Ye trust me, my lord?"

"Ay."

The tired shoulders straightened.

"Your trust shall not be misplaced, sir," he said earnestly.

"That I do know. I am seldom out in my reckoning of mankind."

"Yet I have done little to bring order into Fair Beauvallet."

Simon glanced at him enigmatically.

"All men were not born to fight," he said. "Why didst thou stay here?"

Bernard made a hopeless gesture with his hands.

"For three reasons, my lord. Lack of money, love of this land, and—indolence."

"So I judged. Money thou shalt have, indolence thou must lose, love of this land I trust thou wilt retain. Tell me now, what knowest thou of the Captain, Maurice of Gountray?"

Bernard hesitated.

100

"He—he is a dour man, sir, and—and not easily won over."

"So much the better. I have looked well into the records of the estate, and the mentions I find of him lead me to think him honest and stiff-necked, obstinate, yet a ruler."

Bernard looked admiringly across at him.

"That is so, my lord. But he loves not you, for ye have taken command of his men, and shown him that ye think him worthless. He curses your name, for all that he was at fault in allowing drunkenness and strife to come upon his men. He—he is slow to wrath, sir, but when his wrath flares up, it makes him blind and careless of what shall befall him. I think he will fly out upon you, and mayhap he may seek to do you an injury."

Simon nodded.

"He is easily dealt with. What of Nicholas of the Guards?"

"Like all bullies, sir, he is a coward at heart."

"That also I know. What friends hath he?"

"But few, my lord. He is too harsh in his dealings with the guards, for them to love him."

"So I thought. What record hath Basil of Mordaunt?"

The secretary was at a loss for a moment.

"I do not think I know him, my lord," he said hesitantly.

"No? He is a quiet fellow of some thirty-five summers, with broad shoulders and a square head set close upon them. He looks one between the eyes."

Recollection came to Bernard.

"Ah, yes, my lord! I know but little of him, save that he is peaceable in his ways, and orderly. The men like him, I believe."

"It is in my mind to promote him to Nicholas's room," Simon said.

"Ye will degrade Nicholas, sir?"

"Nay, I will banish him. If I read him aright he is a sly fellow and I want none such here."

"You are wise, my lord. I had thought ye would put a stranger in command."

Simon smiled, a different smile from the deadly snarl Bernard had seen before.

"Yet ye call me wise," he said.

"I had not realized how wise, my lord," Bernard riposted.

"Nay? How read ye Walter of Santoy?"

"Do ye know every man in Beauvallet, sir?" asked Bernard wonderingly.

"I have need," Simon said. "Dost thou?"

"Nay, my lord, to my shame. But I know this man, and I would call him good. Also he is beloved of the men-at-arms."

"That will suit my purpose well," Simon nodded, but he did not disclose what was his purpose. "I think to make Harold the Smooth-Tongued steward in Hubert's room."

"Then ye will do wisely, sir, for he is an honest man, and sober. What comes to Hubert?"

"Naught," Simon answered. "He goes."

"Thus ye will be rid of a very pretty mischief-brewer, sir. He is full of indignation at your coming, and although he durst not go openly against you, he might do much harm by his talk."

"Ay." Simon rose. He pointed to the sheets of parchment that lay scattered over the table. "Have the goodness to make me fair copies of these, Master Talmayne. I go now to send for Maurice of Gountray."

Bernard stood up.

"My lord, if he comes not be not too enraged, for he——"

Simon glanced over his shoulder, smiling rather grimly.

"Dost thou think I shall bungle my affairs, Master Talmayne?"

Bernard looked him in the eyes.

"Nay, my lord. Your pardon."

Simon gave his short laugh and went out.

He sent his squire to summon Maurice, but Roger returned alone.

"My lord, he will not come!" he said, wide-eyed. "He—he bade me tell you he—he comes not at any—any—any——"

"Well?"

"C-coxcomb's call, my lord!"

"So?" Simon smiled unpleasantly. "Then I will e'en go to him."

Roger put himself in front of him.

"Sir, take me with you!"

Simon looked down at him.

"Wherefore?"

"I—indeed, I mislike his looks, sir!"

Simon laughed, and taking his squire by the shoulders put him aside.

"I need not thy protection, lad. Go thou to Malcolm, and bid him be ready to accompany me forth in an hour."

"Oh!" Roger ran after him. "Sir, let me ride with you! I am not weary, and Malcolm——"

"Thou didst hear me, Roger?" Simon said softly.

Roger sighed and fell back.

"Ay, my lord."

Simon strode out into the sunlight. He crossed the courtyard to the men-at-arms' quarters, and went in quietly. He walked through the hall, past staring, whispering soldiers, and made his way to the room which he knew to be Gountray's.

He entered with his noiseless step, and found Maurice up with an oath and stood as if at bay.

Simon walked forward unhurriedly. He favoured Maurice with a long look before he spoke.

"This time I have come to you," he said abruptly. "Another time I shall not do that."

"I care not for your threats!" Gountray cried.

"I never threaten," Simon answered composedly. He went to the table and lifted two wine bottles from it. These he flung out of the window with unerring aim.

"Now, by God——!" Gountray roared, and sprang forward.

Simon's cold voice checked him.

"Do ye think it no shame, Maurice of Gountray, for a strong man to become a drunken sot?" he said.

Maurice flushed to the ears.

"I'll not be answerable to you for my actions!" he snapped.

"Ay, that will you," Simon said, "or leave this my land. I care not which ye choose, but an end will I have to your carousing and your rebellious insolence."

"Rebellious insolence, forsooth!" Maurice cried. "Ye have yet to prove yourself strong enough to be my master! Think ye I will bend the knee to a pert boy not out of his teens?"

"Ay," Simon answered.

"Then know that it is not so! I will fight ye for as long as ye remain here, and my men will refuse to do your bidding! One and all will stand by me! Ye have chosen to slight me, but I will show you of what stuff Maurice of Gountray is made!"

"Ye have shown me," Simon said deliberately. "Within a week of my coming hither I knew you for a drunken knave who proves himself trustless in the absence of a master. I see you now, a common, brawling malcontent whose muscles are weak for want of training, whose temper is soured by the lawless, pleasure-seeking life ye have led during these past months. I have little use for such, Maurice of Gountray. I want true men about me, not worthless braggarts who bluster and shout, yet who have not honour enough or strength to keep their men in order when the master is away."

Livid with rage, Maurice sprang forward again. His passion enveloped him, so that all semblance of sanity was gone. Simon had supplied the spark that was needed to set his rancour in a blaze. In a flash he had whipped his dagger from its sheath and had rushed upon Simon, blindly.

There was a moment's wild struggle, and then Simon's hands were about his wrists like iron clamps, bearing them downwards. Panting, Maurice glared into the green-blue eyes, and saw them passionless.

"Twice in my life hath a man sought to slay me foully," Simon said. "This is the second time. The first was when a base cur, a traitor little above the swine, could not worst me in a fight. Then, being base, he drew steel and would have stabbed me." He paused, staring grimly into Maurice's eyes, until they sank, and the dark head with them. Then, with a quick, scornful movement he released Gountray's wrists, and turned away, presenting his back, fair mark for an assassin's dagger.

The tinkle of steel falling on the stone floor sounded behind him, and a man's laboured breathing. He went quietly to a chair, and sat down, not even looking at Gountray.

Maurice spoke unsteadily.

"I have—never—done that—before."

Simon said not a word. Maurice turned, flung out his hands.

"You goaded me to it! I would never have drawn steel had you not taunted me so!"

Simon turned his head and looked at him. Maurice went to the window, leaden-footed, and stood with his face averted. After a moment he came back into the room, his mouth set as though in pain.

"Well . . . Kill me!" he said. "My honour's dead."

Still Simon said nothing. Maurice stood before him, twisting his hands, his head bowed. Suddenly he looked up, and his voice quivered.

"Ah, can you not speak?" he cried. "Are you made of ice? I have sought to stab you foully, like a—cur! What will you do with me? Death would be welcome!"

"I seek not your death," Simon answered sternly. "But by this one foul act have you placed your life and your fortune in my hands."

Maurice straightened himself a little, but his head was bowed still, his fingers twitching.

"Well," Simon said slowly, "I will make you my Marshal."

For one whirling second Maurice was dazed. He took a hesitating step forward, staring in blank amazement. Then he recoiled.

"Ah, you mock at me!" he cried.

"I do not mock."

Maurice opened his mouth to speak, but only passed his tongue between his dry lips. He was trembling, and sweat stood on his brow.

"Will—will you not—explain——?" he said hoarsely.

"Sit down," Simon ordered him, and waited to see him sink limply into a chair. "What I have said, I have said. I will make you my Marshal, but I will have obedience from you."

"But—but——" Gountray's hand flew to his head as one in wild bewilderment "——I sought to kill you! In that moment I could have done it, ay, and would have done it!"

"I know."

"Then——My lord, you torture me! What punishment will you inflict?"

"None."

"None!" Gountray came to his feet. "You—you—— *forgive*?"

"I forget," Simon said.

"But why, why? What have I done to deserve your mercy?"

"Naught. It is my pleasure. Sit ye down again, and listen. When I came hither I did find your men disorderly and drunken, yourself no better. Yet I do know a man when I see one, and I do know that ye are one, if ye will it so. And I do also know a ruler of men and a fighter. Therefore I say that I will make ye Marshal in Edmund's room, where ye shall prove yourself worthy of my trust. But I will have obedience and no black looks. So if ye hate me and wish me dead, get thee gone from Beauvallet, for thou art of no use to me."

There fell a long silence. Then as Simon's words sank well into his soul, Maurice came to his knees before him, sobbing drily in overwrought gasps.

"Ye cannot mean what ye say! What trust could ye place in me?—a cur who is like to stab you in the back when ye are unarmed!"

Simon smiled a little at that, but he said nothing.

"Hanging is my desert! Ye have said that ye found all in disorder here, and myself a drunken sot! True it is—God pity me! What use have you for me now?"

"I have told you."

Then Maurice caught his hand and kissed it.

"My lord, I swear that since ye are pleased to forget my treachery and to elevate me thus undeservedly, I will never—give you just cause to—regret it—so help me, God!"

"That I know," Simon said calmly, and laid his hand on Gountray's shoulder, gripping it.

Maurice raised his head and looked full into the compelling eyes.

"My lord—forgive!" he whispered.

"It is as nothing," Simon answered, and rose. "Come thou to me this even, for there is much I would ask of you, and I think ye can fitly advise me." He held out his hand, and after a moment's shamed hesitation Maurice laid his own in it. In that long grip was his allegiance to Simon sealed.

X

How he brought order into his lands

The next thing Simon did was to dismiss Nicholas of the Guards. At the same time he made it known that Basil of Mordaunt was to succeed him. Thus he did away with almost all opposition, for Basil was an easy-going, generous fellow, liked by his peers, and respected. Nicholas did not take his dismissal quietly. As soon as he was out of Simon's hearing he fell to shouting his grievance over the estate, vowing that he would pay no heed to the new, upstart lord, but would hold his place and his men in Simon's very teeth. In this he had little support, for the guards were weary of his hectoring and blustering. They listened to him in silence, but when he had gone they conferred amongst themselves, and for the most part agreed that they would be well rid of him. Yet for very fear of him and because they did not know their lord's temper, they remained obedient to Nicholas until they should see which way the wind would blow. Some few declared openly that they would stand by Nicholas, but these were his friends and their number was small.

Nicholas went roaring to the men-at-arms with intent to stir up rebellion. Gountray was no friend of his, but among the men he counted some six or seven allies. He found them murmurous and ill-at-ease, for they had a new captain in Walter of Santoy who was busily employed in disciplining them. Nicholas knew better than to approach him.

"Maurice of Gountray will stand my friend," said he loudly. "If Maurice is dismissed he will be at one with me. He and I will smash this fellow!"

"It is rumoured that Maurice of Gountray is Marshal in Edmund's room," one of his friends said uneasily.

Nicholas laughed gustily.

"A likely tale! Why, he hath sworn how he will meet this lord, and hath cursed his name! I warrant ye I shall find a friend in him." He swaggered across the courtyard, and came most opportunely upon Gountray who emerged from a door leading into the castle.

"Ha, good Maurice!" Nicholas cried, past enmity forgotten. "Come hither, man! There is somewhat I would say to thee."

Maurice paused a moment and waited till Nicholas came up to him.

"I have orders to see ye leave this place within the space of seven hours," he said coldly. "Look to it that ye are gone."

Nicholas lost a little of his colour, but he strove to laugh as at a joke.

"Why, this is pretty hearing, beshrew me! From whom do ye take your orders, Maurice of Gountray?"

Maurice looked him steadily between the eyes.

"From my lord of Beauvallet, sirrah."

"Ho-ho! Do you tell me that, Master Gountray? But yesterday ye did speak brave words against him!"

"Much hath happened since yesterday, Nicholas Conrad, and for what I have said against my lord am I heartily ashamed. Ye will leave this land today." He strode on, and as he passed him Nicholas noticed the chain about his neck that bespoke his marshal's office.

Back he went to the guard-room to find Basil of Mordaunt in his place. Then his rage knew no bounds, but he had little support now that the men saw that my lord's word was not idly spoken. The end of it was that Nicholas departed from Beauvallet in an hour, calling down curses on Simon's head.

In the week that followed strange and strenuous changes were wrought in Beauvallet. Malefactors were brought to judgment and Simon's hand was heavy upon them. When they sought to rebel, the men found that his yoke was securely round their necks, and his new officers implicitly obedient to him. The week passed in grumbling and petty mutinies, but at the end of the week men knew Simon for master. Regulations were formed, irksome at first, but sound, as the wiser fellows realized; Simon was found to be ruthlessly just, and if his rule was stern, at least he was not above knowing his men individually. He had ever a nod and a curt word of greeting for all who crossed his path, and he mingled freely amongst them, saying little, but making himself familiar to them. The peasants were set to work again, and laboured with a will, because work meant fair wages. Walter of Santoy had orders to drill his men, and although they groaned under it, they submitted, and very soon put some life into their labours, for no one knew when Simon would appear upon the scene, watching closely from under his jutting brows, chary of praise, but giving it where it was due.

Disgust was felt when he ordained that archery was to be practised, and some of the peasants who were compelled to enter into this sport grumbled loudly, and declared that Simon worked them to a shred. But when he came himself with his great bow, and shot with them they ceased their lamentations to admire his skill. And when he declared that to the man who could shoot an arrow farther than his own he would award a prize of a grant of land, competition became keen, and day after day saw the serfs fitting arrows to bow till they could almost rival the archers themselves.

Within the castle all was quiet. Master Hubert had departed, wailing, and the new steward slipped into his place. There was plenty of work and plenty of good food, a fair dole of ale or sack, and sports to occupy spare hours. In a surprisingly short time the men of Beauvallet settled down under the new régime, and were content.

It was not until the end of the month that Montlice rode over to see Simon. He came without warning one day, and appeared before the castle just before ten, accompanied by his son and his cousin. Simon was shooting with his men, so Gountray, who received the guests, dispatched Arnold, Simon's page, to fetch him.

Arnold sped out across the country, clad in the new green and russet livery. He came upon Simon among the archers, in the act of loosing an arrow from his bow.

Simon watched the arrow's flight, and without turning his head, spoke to his page.

"Well, Arnold?"

This was an uncanny trick he had, and which greatly bewildered and discomposed his men. No matter how softly one might creep up to him, he always knew of the approach, and needed not to see who it was who drew near. Arnold was accustomed to the trick, so he showed no surprise.

"My lord, there are guests at the castle! My Lord of Montlice, Sir Alan, and my Lord of Granmere. Master Gountray sent me to fetch you."

Simon rose from his knee.

"I will come," he said. He stayed but to speak with Santoy a moment and followed Arnold to the castle. Arnold would have taken his bow, but Simon shook his head, smiling.

"How far wouldst thou bear it, child?"

Arnold drew himself up till he stood half as high as the bow.

"I could carry it, my lord, indeed!"

"I doubt not thy good will," Simon said, but he would not relinquish the bow.

Arnold walked demurely behind him then. It was a curious turn of character in Simon that he liked children. His pages fell over one another to serve him and were perfectly happy if he but nodded to them, while the littlest one of all's pride when Simon lifted him over a broad ditch one day, knew no bounds. He was Gountray's son, a dark, curly-headed boy of eight named Cedric, who owed his office to his own impertinence. When he found that his father would not speak for him to Simon, he determined to speak for himself. So up he went to the castle, a chubby little fellow with merry eyes, and waylaid Simon on his way out.

Simon, remembering his own coming to Fulk of Montlice, was amused. He made Cedric page with Gountray's consent, and the child seemed to walk straight into his rather dormant heart. He was the one person in all Beauvallet who would openly defy Simon, and once when he burst into tears of rage at being thwarted, his father and the Secretary were struck dumb by the sight of him seated on Simon's knee in the great hall.

He it was who now entertained Simon's visitors with engaging and solemn conversation.

"And who art thou, young hop o' my thumb?" Fulk asked him.

Cedric answered importantly.

"I am my lord's page. I made him take me."

Fulk burst into a roar of laughter.

"Oh, tit for Simon's tat!" he cried. "How didst thou make him, prithee?"

"I said that I *would* be his page. And I am. He calls me the little one."

Alan smiled, drawing the small person to him.

"That sounds not like Simon," he remarked. "Dost thou like thy lord?"

"Ay, I love him dearly. As much as my father." Cedric paused to give weight to his next statement. "I have sat upon his knee," he announced with due solemnity.

"Holy Virgin!" Fulk said. "What comes to our Simon?"

Simon entered at this moment, and Cedric, wriggling free of Alan's hold, skipped towards him.

"My lord, I received these guests with my father, and I gave them chairs, but I have not done your bidding!" He chuckled mischievously and danced before Simon.

Simon gave him his arrows.

"Put these away then, little miscreant—and see thou dost not play with them!" he added as Cedric trotted off. He came forward and grasped Fulk's hand.

"My lord, ye are more than welcome, and you, Lord of Granmere. Well, Alan?"

"Never saw I so great a change in any land!" Fulk assured him. "We came to pry upon thee and to see how thou wert progressing, and behold! the place is as orderly as a monastery! As we passed we saw on all sides good work on hand, while as for thy household, it is as quiet as the grave! What hast done, lion-cub?"

"It was very easy," Simon answered. "I struck at the heads of the disorder. How fares Montlice?"

"We miss thy strict hand," Fulk grimaced. "But Alan doth what he can. God's my life, when I think that scarce a month ago this land was peopled by drunken rogues, and the crops going to ruin for want of care, and look at it now, I can scarce believe mine eyes!"

"I am not surprised," Granmere remarked. "From what I had seen of thee, I had thought to see thee conquer within the month. Who was yon chubby page?"

Simon smiled a little.

"That is my Marshal's son."

"Who sits upon thy knee," Alan teased.

Simon looked up.

"Did he say that? 'Twas but once, when he cried because that I chid him for some fault."

"Simon," Fulk interrupted, "I demand that ye loose thy tongue and tell me all that thou hast performed here!"

"Well, sir, if ye must have the full tale, will ye come out whiles my varlets lay dinner?"

"Ay, that will we," Fulk nodded, and rose. "Alan would stay with thee, if thou'lt permit him."

Alan locked his arm in Simon's affectionately.

"I shall stay whether thou likst it or no."

"Why, of course thou canst stay!" Simon said, and led them forth into the sunlight.

They returned presently to dinner, when Simon presented his marshal, his captain, and all his other officers. It was nearly three hours later when they came away from the table, and Fulk took Simon aside.

"Simon lad, thou art now come to manhood," he began, by way of preamble. "There is a proposition I would set before thee."

"My lord?"

Fulk tapped him on the shoulder.

"Look ye, boy, thy land should have a mistress, ay, and an heir! Now it is in my mind to give thee my daughter Elaine, though I had intended her for John of Balfry's son. What dost thou say to that?"

Simon compressed his lips.

"Why, sir, I say that albeit I do thank thee for the honour ye would do me, yet were it best that ye should give the lady to Robert of Balfry."

"Thou'lt none of her?" Fulk was incredulous. "Bethink you, silly boy, she is comely and gentle, and fair-dowered!"

"Ay, sir, but she loves not me, and I love not her."

Fulk was inclined to be offended.

"Mayhap thou dost look higher for thy bride?"

"Nay. I look nowhere for a bride. I have no love for women, and I think to remain a bachelor."

"But that is folly, lad!" Fulk cried, a little appeased. "A docile wife is a great thing to have!"

"Is it, sir?" Simon said drily. "Methinks I admire not gentleness, nor docility."

"But, thou dost love children, Simon!"

"Do I?" Simon considered the point. "Nay, I think not."

"Thou dost, lad! What of thy little page?"

"Cedric? Yes, I do care for him, yet I want him not for mine own."

"Simon, Simon, thou quibblest! Since I have been in Beauvallet I have seen more pages than thou canst possibly have need of! What made thee take them—children that they are?"

"They—they are useful to me," Simon answered, rather lamely. "They run mine errands."

"How many hast thou?" Fulk demanded sternly.

"Six," Simon said gruffly.

"And what does one man want with six pages?" Fulk persisted.

"I—I find employment for them."

"Tush!" said Fulk. "Thou dost like to have them follow thee about."

"Nay! I send them from me—when they plague me."

"Simon, thou canst not deceive me," Fulk told him. "Thou hast a love for children, and shouldst breed thine own."

Simon flushed a little.

"Nay."

"And I say, ay!"

"My lord, it is to no avail that ye seek to persuade me. I will take no woman to wife."

Fulk grunted, but he knew Simon too well to argue any further.

"Well, please thyself. But one day ye will know that I was right, and a man must take a wife unto himself."

"I will tell you when that day comes," Simon promised.

Alan remained at Beauvallet a week, and Simon was rather glad of his companionship. He organized a chase for Alan's amusement, and hired mummers from a neighbouring town. But Alan was quite content to dispense with these forms of entertainment, and to please Simon he went with him to practise archery. When he came away from this tedious sport, he shot Simon a sidelong glance. Simon was aware of it without seeing it.

"Well?"

"How hast thou contrived to endear these men to thee, Simon?"

"Have I? Some of them like me not."

"But most do like thee. What is it they do find to love in thee? What do any of us find? Thou art stern, and cold, and hast no love for any man."

"Alan, if thou dost wish to prate of love, go do so to thy lady-love. I know nothing of it."

"Why do thy men love thee?" Alan insisted.

"I know not. Perchance because I bend them to my will."

"That may be so," Alan mused. "But why do the children so dote on thee?"

"Because I pay but little heed to them."

"Nay, that cannot be so. In truth, Simon, long as I have known thee, I still know thee not. Something there is 'neath thy coldness of which I wot not."

"There is hunger," Simon said, thereby closing the conversation.

When Alan had returned to Montlice, Simon set about reforming his men-at-arms, and archers, with so much success that within the space of six months he had a very fair army at his beck and call, composed of peasants' sons, and some wandering soldiers. Walter of Santoy proved himself an admirable captain; so that Simon relaxed some of his vigilance, and turned his attention to the cultivation of his land. In Gountray he had full confidence, and Maurice would have worked himself to death to please his lord.

And so the year rolled placidly by and the New Year came. Then, when Simon had begun to look about him in search of fresh emprises, came Geoffrey of Malvallet, his father, one damp morning, to visit him.

When word was brought of his coming, Simon went swiftly out to meet him, and knelt to receive his guest.

"My lord, ye do me great honour," he said gravely.

Geoffrey raised him.

"I hardly dared come to thee, Simon, but now I have an excuse for this visit which perhaps thou dost think importunate."

Simon led him to his private room.

"Nay, sir, I am honoured."

Geoffrey glanced around.

"Well, thou hast estates, after all. Of thine own endeavour."

"As I did say I would have them," Simon answered, and sent a page to bring ale. "What is your will of me, sir?"

"I am the bearer of a letter to thee from thy half-brother," Malvallet answered. "Will ye read it?"

"From Geoffrey? Ay, that will I, and gladly! Will ye not be seated, sir?"

Malvallet chose a chair by the window, and watched Simon break the seals of Geoffrey's letter.

"To Simon, Lord of Beauvallet.

"Dear and entirely well-beloved, I greet thee well, and send messages of joy and congratulation on thy new good fortune. I do know thy land and like it well. May thou prosper exceedingly as thou deservest!

"My brother, I do write to urge thee that thou shouldst come hither with what force thou mayst muster to join again with the Prince in quelling that most naughty rebel, Owen de Glyndourdy, whose followers are rife in this ill-fated land. Despite the fair promises of His Majesty's Council, made in August, saying that he should have men and provisions enough to march boldly out against the rebels, naught hath been forthcoming, and at this date at which I write our force numbers little over five score men-at-arms and twelve score archers. Now that thou art thine own master wilt thou come not again to fight at my side as thou didst promise? Matters grow serious here in Wales, for thou must know that in December of last year fell Cardiff, and Harlech, and Llampadarn, our most cherished fortresses. The rebel Owen hath not been so great before, and indeed, if we are to conquer him we must set out against him, and that as soon as spring shall have come. And with the spring, come thou, my brother, and I will promise thee as goodly a battle as that of Shrewsbury which thou didst so much enjoy.

"I send thee my love and greetings.

"GEOFFREY OF MALVALLET.

"Written at Shrewsbury."

Simon folded the parchment slowly.

"Wilt thou go?" Malvallet asked abruptly.

Simon seemed to consider. His eyes wandered to the window and stared out across the quiet fields. He brought them back to his father, and smiled.

"It seems likely, my lord," he said.

*   *   *

He rode next day to Montlice to take counsel of Fulk. To my lord's surprise Alan sprang up, vehement.

"If thou dost go, Simon, then so will I!" he exclaimed. "Too long have I rested at home! I will lead our men to Wales, and I too, will taste the joys of battle!"

When he had recovered from his amazement, Fulk scoffed.

"Little joy wilt thou find in battle."

Alan turned sharply.

"If thou dost say me nay, my lord, then will I go in Simon's train. Alone!"

"No need for such heat," Fulk grunted. "Thou shalt go if thou dost wish it. When dost thou think to depart, Simon?"

"Next month, my lord, towards the end, so that I shall come to Wales in March."

"And leave thy land masterless?"

"Nay. Maurice of Gountray shall rule in my stead."

"As he ruled when Barminster died?" Fulk inquired with heavy sarcasm.

"I am not Barminster," Simon said.

XI

How he won his gilded armour

March saw him in Wales at his brother's side, engaged in hard fighting and hard generalship. April brought him back to Shrewsbury unscathed, but May saw him marching south to Usk, one of the Prince's trusted officers, and the Prince's friend. And at Usk, where they fought the rebels fifteen hundred strong, he engaged with Glyndourdy's son Griffith, and fought him in single combat till he had him worsted from sheer fatigue. Then took he Griffith prisoner and surrendered him to the Prince.

Henry was enthusiastic over his prize, and smote Simon on the back.

"Ah, Beauvallet! Would that I had thee ever by my side! What wilt thou of thy prisoner?"

"His armour, sir," Simon answered. "His ransom, if ransomed he be, is yours. But, if it please your Highness, I would have his gilded armour."

"That is a strange wish!" Henry said. "Wherefore? Dost like the golden tint so much?"

"Ay, and the workmanship, sir."

"Thou shalt have it, then," Henry promised. "Simon of the Gilded Armour!" He laughed, linking his arm in Simon's. "Verily, I do believe it is a new title thou seekest! Already have I heard tell of Simon the Lynx-Eyed, Simon the Cold-Heart, Simon the Lion, Simon the Soft-Footed, and I know not what beside! Whence come these names, lad?"

"From foolish men's tongues, my lord," Simon answered.

"Then shall I be foolish," Henry said, "for I shall call thee Simon the Silent."

The middle of July saw Simon home again, with Geoffrey and Alan riding one on either side of him. Between these two enmity was dead, for when Geoffrey had clasped Simon's hands on his coming to Wales, Alan had stood aloof and ill-at-ease, seeing which Geoffrey had gone to him with his charming smile.

"Our sires dispute, Sir Alan, but what shall we do?"

"For my part I would we might agree!" Alan had answered instantly, and grasped Malvallet's hand.

When Simon rode into Beauvallet he found all quiet and in good order, and a glint of satisfaction came to his eyes. At the castle door his household stood to welcome him. But one there was who forgot decorum and ran forward, arms outstretched.

"My lord! my lord! Lift me? Oh, lift me!" Cedric cried, almost sobbing with excitement and heedless of his father's shocked protest.

Then Simon the Coldheart bent in his saddle and hoisted his page up with one strong hand, and held him against his shoulder. One little arm encircled his neck, the other plump hand gripped Simon's doublet tightly; Cedric gave a wriggle of content, and buried his face on Simon's shoulder.

Simon looked down at the curly head with a curious smile on his lips.

"Thou hast missed me, Cedric?"

The arm tightened about his neck; Cedric nodded.

"Methought thou'dst have forgot thy lord."

Up came the dark head, indignant.

"I am not a babe—to forget thee so soon!"

"Cedric!" exclaimed Gountray, coming forward. "Thou must not speak so to my lord! To say 'thee'—thus pertly!"

"I will!" Cedric announced stoutly. "My lord cares not!"

"My lord, forgive his rudeness!" Gountray said in concern. "Indeed, I can do naught with him since ye are gone. He minds me not. I doubt I am too soft with him, but I have no other son, and—and perchance I spoil him with indulgence."

"Let be!" Simon said shortly. "Loose thy grip, little one; I would dismount." He handed Cedric to Gountray, and swung lightly down from the saddle. He had a word of greeting for all who stood there, and many were the inquiries after his welfare. He answered each man in kind, and passed into the castle, Cedric dancing at his side, and his other pages following him like a troop of puppies, so that when he stopped to speak with his secretary he stood in the midst of a small band of green and russet clad boys, towering above them, while they swarmed about him, relieving him of first this, and then that, and squabbling amongst themselves for the supreme honour of bearing his sword away. One flew to unbuckle it, three others laid hold of the scabbard, glaring at one another belligerently, and two more knelt to unfasten Simon's spurs. He seemed quite unaware of these somewhat noisy ministrations, but talked calmly over the pages' heads to his amused secretary. Being smaller by far than the rest, Cedric found himself with naught to carry away. Not to be outdone, he climbed upon a chair and removed Simon's cap from his head. He also tried to remove the surcoat from Simon's shoulders, and his fat little fingers tugged busily at the clasps until Simon became aware of his efforts. Then he put them all from him.

"Have done, have done! Would ye have me quite unrobed? Go put my cap away, Cedric! Roger, take my sword from that babe; he will fall over it. Edmund, fight not over my spurs! Thou'lt scratch thyself. Take heed! And be ye all gone till I send for you, turbulent brats!" He nodded to Gountray. "I will speak with thee after supper, Maurice, and thee also, Bernard." He strode away to the staircase, and went swiftly up to his chamber, followed only by Malcolm, his squire.

Walter of Santoy cast a laughing glance at Gountray.

"This place will soon be over-run with pages," he remarked. "Surely I did see three more than when we left Beauvallet?"

"Ay," Gountray replied. "My lord had given orders they were to be enrolled. One falls over them at every step, but it is my lord's pleasure. And since my lord did strike Patrick of Kildare senseless for beating little Edmund, two days before he set out on his travels, never have children been more indulged in this land! As for mine own son, he is grown so defiant and mischievous that only my lord can check him."

"Things have come to a pretty pass," the steward sighed, for he was weak with children and they plagued him unmercifully.

"Pretty indeed," Bernard said softly. "Methinks it is a sweet thing to see the iron lord with these babes about him like flies around a honey-jar."

"They are very importunate," Roger complained. "They cluster about my lord so that there is naught for us poor squires to do. And he will not say them nay. And—and when I did push Donald so that he fell—I meant not that he should, but I was angered—he would not have me near him for three whole days! So that *Malcolm* waited upon him!" At the thought of this past injury his eyes flashed, and he withdrew to dwell upon it darkly.

After supper, Maurice of Gountray came to Simon's

room to render an account of his stewardship. Simon listened intently to all that he said, and read over the accounts. Maurice spoke hesitantly, anxious lest he should have failed to satisfy his lord. Just at the end of his recital he looked at Simon almost shyly.

"There—there is one other matter, my lord, in which ye may perhaps think I have exceeded my duty. In your absence I—I did what seemed best to me." He paused, unaccountably nervous before this man who was full fifteen years his junior. Simon said nothing so Maurice continued, squaring his shoulders: "I did discover three lewd fellows, sir, among your guard, who were friends of Nicholas. They were set upon stirring the men to rebellion in your absence, the which Basil reported to me. So I did summon them to—to judgment, sir, and Edwin of Palmer, whom I saw to be the leader, I banished in your name. The other two I did punish—and they are quiet now." He looked up again, diffident, and in his eyes was a look of fidelity such as is seen in the eyes of a dog.

"Thou hast done well," Simon said. "In all things thou hast acted as I should have acted had I been here."

At the sound of that cool voice, Gountray sat straighter in his chair, and one or two worried lines upon his brow were smoothed away.

"If—if I have pleased you, sir, I—can be easier in mine own mind."

"I am pleased, but it is no less than I expected."

"My lord—I have but one ambition in life, and that is to merit your trust, so that I may—in time—wipe out the black memory of what I—sought to do to you."

Simon brought his fist down upon the table between them.

"A year ago I said three words to thee, Maurice of Goungray: 'I have forgotten.' "

"Ye have not yet said: 'I have—forgiven,' my lord," Gountray answered low.

"Then I say it now. I have forgiven. Though why thou shouldst want forgiveness from any man, I know not. The past is dead."

"My lord, I—I thank you! And for all that you have

121

done for me, upholding mine authority, and permitting my son to tease you, I thank you."

"Thank me not for pleasing myself," Simon answered. He rose, and Maurice with him, and as Gountray would have left the room, he spoke again, more lightly. "Thou wilt think me careless, Maurice. Before I went to supper I walked out to cast a look on my lands, and Cedric followed me. He ran a sharp thorn into his hand, and it bled grievously before he showed me what had happened." Then as Maurice looked rather anxious. "I pulled the thorn out and bound his hand. I think it will be well tomorrow."

"Sir, it is kind indeed of you to take such pains with Cedric! I will go look to him." His hand was on the latch of the door when Simon spoke again.

"I could not but hurt him, but he shed not one tear."

He rode to Malvallet a week later, and was royally entertained by his father. When he had gone again, Malvallet turned to his son Geoffrey who still remained at home.

"Geoffrey, I do love that boy," he said abruptly.

"And I, sir."

Malvallet spoke bitterly.

"I shall never be more to him than a friend."

Geoffrey said nothing to that, and there fell a silence. Then he looked across at his father, smiling.

"Thou wouldst have liked to see him when he took Owen's son prisoner, sir. On my word, he was here, there and everywhere, vying with the Prince himself in spurring our men onward. Then he came upon Griffith in one part of the field, and engaged him to single combat. Methought they never would have done, for Griffith is no weakling, sir, and he tilted and hacked at Simon until my heart was in my mouth. But Simon is untiring, and at last Griffith's arm sank, and he yielded himself prisoner. Simon haled him to the Prince, and demanded naught from him but his armour, a curious set, gilded over, and so delicately fashioned that when on it hath scarcely any weight at all. And when next we fought, he wore that armour so that he was a mark for all eyes. Seeing him so much to the fore, his men did press onward to join him, inspiring the others. That victory the Prince vows is due to Simon's valour alone. Henry hath a great liking for him, sir, and would have kept him at his side had Simon willed it so."

Malvallet nodded slowly.

"Ay. He will be great one day—if he wills it so."

"And if no woman comes into his life to divert his thoughts," Geoffrey said.

"There is no woman as yet?"

Geoffrey laughed.

"Holy Virgin, sir, if thou couldst but see Simon with a maid! He pays no heed to them, nor seems to notice their presence! I tell him he will fall one day, and Alan tells him, too, but in truth, sir, I think he never will!"

"I wonder," Malvallet said.

"Or if he doth, 'twill be before some timid, pale-faced wench who will make of herself a carpet for his disdainful feet!"

"I—wonder," Malvallet said again.

PART TWO

I

How he came to Normandy

He stood upon a hill by Alençon, looking out over France, and the wind blew his fair hair all about his face, and whipped his surcoat round his mailed form. He was past thirty now, and ten years had gone by since he became Lord of Beauvallet.

Behind him, sprawling on the soft grass, was his squire, a handsome youth with black curls and merry eyes. They were thoughtful now and admiring, for they rested on Simon, pondering him.

Simon stood motionless, half-turned away; he had not moved or spoken for some minutes, but was frowning over the fair land stretched at his feet. His squire watched the grim profile respectfully, glancing from the massive, projecting brow with the deep-set eyes shining from beneath it, to the strong jaw-bone, outlined clearly in the bronzed, lean cheek. One of Simon's hands hung listless at his side, and presently clenched a little; the spurred feet were well apart and firmly planted. The squire reflected idly that the pose stood for all the strength and purpose that were Simon's. He rolled over on to his side, supporting his head on one slim hand, still watching Simon.

This was not the first time that Simon had set foot on French soil. Twice before had he marched into this land; once under the King's brother, Thomas, Duke of Clarence, and again under Henry himself, when they had fought at Agincourt. He was famous now for his generalship; his name was linked with that of Clarence, or of Umfraville; he was spoken of as the Fifth Henry's friend, and the Iron Lord. Of some he was beloved, of others hated, but no man ignored him or thought him of little count. He had become great, and this by his own wit and strength. He had no equal save the King himself in generalship; no commander was so instantly obeyed, and no commander was so greatly respected by his men. He had power and wealth, a splendid body, fit for any hardship or endurance, a not unpleasing countenance, and a quick, cool brain. Yet something he seemed to lack, for with all his assets and attainments, he was cold as stone, almost as though some humanizing part of him had been left out in his fashioning. There were those who said that a softer side of love and passion was not in him, but Henry the King, wiser than these, would point to some frolicking page in the Beauvallet green and russet when he heard this criticism.

"What! Do ye think Beauvallet hath no tenderness within him? Fool, what of the children?"

The critics were silenced then, for Simon's love of children was well-known.

"It sleeps," Henry said once to Simon's half-brother. "It will awaken one day."

Geoffrey turned his head.

"Of what speak you, sir?"

Henry's eyes were upon the distant Simon.

"Of the passion that lies in Simon."

"There is none, sire. Once I thought as you think, but I have known him for fifteen years, and never once have I seen him melt, or lose one jot of his coldness. Save with the children."

"Ay, save with the children. By that sign, Geoffrey, I do know that there is that in him that will spring to life one day."

"There is icy rage, sir," Geoffrey answered, smiling. "What manner of woman will it be before whom Simon will fall? How many fair maids hath he passed by? And now he is past thirty. He is not like to love. It is too late."

Henry smiled, laying his hand on Malvallet's arm.

"Geoffrey, Geoffrey, sometimes thou art a fool! Alan is wiser."

"Alan is very wise in all matters of the heart, sir," Geoffrey retorted. He cast a laughing glance to where sat the young Montlice, chin in hand and soft eyes dreaming.

Henry followed his look, echoed his laugh.

"What a trio have I about me!" he said. "My Soldier, my Knight, and my Poet."

And as such they were known, close friends all three, and each one unlike the other. Clarence once named them Iron, Flame, and Silver, and marvelled at their friendship, but the King's name for them was more apt. Simon was all a soldier, dauntless and cool, born to rule and to lead; Geoffrey, the Knight, had a hot courage, a courtier's tongue, and an impetuous spirit; Alan, the Poet, was a dreamer, unfit for wars, yet partaking in them much as some troubadour of a hundred years before, born to love, perhaps not greatly, but often and sweetly. He followed where Simon led, but Geoffrey would sometimes leap ahead with characteristic blindness, only to be dragged back by Simon's inflexible will. They had been together now, this ill-assorted trio, for many years. Geoffrey and Alan had watched Simon's gradual conquest of his lands with amused yet admiring eyes; they saw him rise to fame without feeling a spark of jealousy stir within them; they looked on Simon as master, but they thought him a child in everything that had to do with the heart. Time and again had they watched him with some fair lady, breathlessly waiting to observe a change in him. Each time disappointment came, for although he had met the greatest and most lovely ladies of the time not one of them had ever stirred the sleeping passion within him. He was not, as some strong men, timid of the gentler sex; in a maiden's presence his tongue did not stumble, nor did his tanned cheeks flush. It was simply that he had no room for women in his life, and no liking for them in his heart.

Cedric, the squire, plucked a blade of grass and began to suck it meditatively. His eyes were upon Simon's broad shoulders, and he was wondering if his would ever match them in breadth or straightness. He sighed a little, for he was a slim youth, not square-set as was his lord, and without the iron muscle that had been Simon's long before he had attained Cedric's age. His eyes travelled down Simon's tapering flanks, to the arched, spurred feet, and then up again to that stern, rugged face. He had not been told why they had tramped out of Alençon this afternoon, and he knew better than to ask, privileged though he was. He had followed Simon to this hill, silent all the way, for Simon was deep in thought. Cedric guessed that he was puzzling over some weighty problem, by the frown on his brow, and the grimness about his mouth. They had been stationary upon this hill for a long time now, and Cedric rather wished that his lord would say or do something to relieve the tedium, instead of gazing far away at the distant horizon.

Then Simon spoke in his deep, grave voice, without turning his head.

"Canst find naught better to do than stare at thy lord, child?"

Accustomed as he was to Simon's unexpected ways, Cedric was startled. He had thought that Simon had forgotten his presence, nor been aware of the fixed scrutiny behind him.

"Nay, my lord, I think not."

Simon smiled a little.

"I am so pleasing to thine eye?"

"Yes, sir," Cedric answered simply.

Simon moved at last, and looked down at his sprawling squire. There was a note of feeling in his voice now.

"Thou lazy pup!" he said, still smiling. "Take that grass out of thy mouth."

Cedric ejected it, laughing up at Simon. He made no effort to rise, for well he knew that he was privileged in his lord's eyes. Other pages had come and gone, but for none had Simon cherished the same affection that he felt for Cedric of Gountray, who, long years ago, had forced himself upon his notice.

"Lord, when do we move from Alençon?" he asked presently. "Are we to remain here for aye?"

"When the time comes ye will know," Simon answered curtly.

Cedric was in no way abashed. He sat up, hugging his knees.

"It is soon, I think," he said shrewdly, and cast a glance upward at Simon's impassive countenance. "I wonder, do we march with the King, or with the Duke?" He paused a moment, "Or alone?" he added softly.

Simon vouchsafed no reply, but jerked his head, as a sign that they were going. He set off with striding steps towards the town, Cedric trotting along beside him.

Within the gates they came upon Sir Alan, whereupon Cedric fell discreetly to the rear.

Alan slipped his arm in Simon's, looking up at him with the subservient affection that not all the years had tempered. He was very little changed from the youth Simon had met without the castle of Montlice. His face had retained its girlish curves, his figure its slender grace. He was attired in silks and velvets, for he scorned a soldier's garb save when it was necessary.

"Simon," he said in an undertone, "whence comes this talk of sending thee to Belrémy?"

"From idle men's tongues belike," answered Simon shortly.

"It is not true?"

"True enough, but prate not of it, Alan."

"Thou art indeed to pit thy strength against the Lady Margaret of Belrémy?"

"Ay."

"Where Umfraville hath failed thou art to conquer. Shalt thou take the town, Simon?"

"God willing."

Alan chuckled softly, whistling "Deo Gratias" below his breath.

"I too shall come, of course," he remarked dreamily. "I have a mind to see this Lady Margaret."

Then Simon smiled.

"There will be no love-making while thou art with me, Alan."

"Will there not? Thou shouldst bear the Lady Margaret off thyself, lad. That indeed would be a conquest."

"Um!" Simon grunted. "A spitfire to wife? I thank thee."

They were nearing the King's quarters, and passed several kinghts who waved a greeting, or asked a question of Simon.

"I came in search of thee," Alan said. "The King would speak with thee. Where hast been?"

"Over yonder, upon the hill."

"Wherefore?"

"To think, and to breathe. The town chokes me. Dost thou come with me to the King?"

"Ay. Geoffrey is there, and swears he will go with thee to Belrémy. So we fare forth together once more."

They entered the house and made their way up the staircase to the King's apartments. Henry was there, with Geoffrey of Malvallet, and Gilbert of Umfraville. He looked up as Simon entered, and smiled.

"Hither, my Soldier. I did send for Gilbert."

Umfraville came forward to grip Simon's hand.

"Unlike me, thou'lt be like unto Caesar, Simon," he said. "To Belrémy wilt thou go, and where I saw, thou wilt also conquer."

"Thou wouldst have conquered but for the short space of time accorded thee," Simon answered slowly.

Henry laughed, signing a sheet of parchment that was spread out before him.

"Hark to my soldier! He blames me for Umfraville's defeat."

"Nay, sire!" Geoffrey interposed swiftly. "He is not so ungallant."

"He is not gallant at all," responded Henry. He pushed the parchment from him, and turned to look at Simon. "He is honest. Tell me, Simon, was it my fault that we took not Belrémy?"

"Ay, sir," Simon replied imperturbably. "Ye did underrate the enemy. The task had been too easy before."

"That is so," nodded the King. "And now a woman baulks me. So I send her Simon the Coldheart."

Geoffrey laughed out.

"Nay, nay, your generals feel no love for her, sir! She is a very Amazon. Is it not so, Gilbert?"

"Ay, so I believe. I have not seen her, nor any of my men."

"They say she is garbed in armour and fights at the head of her men."

"Whether that be true or not, her men are wildcats," Gilbert said ruefully. "I met them but once when a body marched out upon us by night. Thou wilt do well to have a care, Simon. The town is so strongly fortified that 'twould take thee months to batter down the walls. Provisions they seem to have in plenty."

"By the gleam in Simon's eye, I know it to be a task after his heart's desire," Henry said quizzically.

Simon gave his short laugh.

"Ay, sir. I will hand you the keys of Belrémy."

"And I will write a canzonet to music on it," Alan said. "Save that our King be not with us, it will be another Agincourt."

"What, dost thou go with Simon, my Poet?" Henry asked. "Who then will charm mine ears with song?"

Alan blushed, shaking back his curls.

"So please your Majesty, I must e'en stay by Simon lest he lose his heart to Margaret the Amazon," he bowed.

"Nay, the woman Simon will wed must be some puling lass with a timid tongue," Henry retorted. "It is always thus."

"Twould be to mate an eagle with a dove, sir," Gilbert said. "Simon will return to you an enslaved creature, having prostrated himself at the Amazon's proud feet."

"Well, she is a fair maid, so I hear," Henry said. "Dost thou covet her, Simon?"

"Nay, sire. Her lands rather. Alan shall charm her into submission."

Henry laughed.

"Is that thy reason for taking my Poet from me?"

"What else, sir?" Simon answered, smiling. "A soldier he is not, nor a leader."

"And what shall Geoffrey do?"

"Oh, there is work enough for Geoffrey," said Simon tranquilly. "Whither do ye go, sir, when ye quit this town?"

Henry looked up at him gravely.

"Back to Falaise, my Soldier."

Simon nodded.

"Ay, take that town, sir. It is worthy of the endeavour."

"So if the King take Falaise, Simon shall take Belrémy," Gilbert remarked. "Who shall say which task be the harder?"

"I shall say." Alan had seated himself by the window, apart from them, but now he turned his head, smiling sweetly upon Sir Gilbert of Umfraville.

"Speak, Sage," Henry invited.

Alan crossed his legs.

"Belrémy is the harder task, sire, saving your presence."

Geoffrey frowned.

"Wherefore, Alan?"

"Because the Sire de Mauny rules Falaise, and the Lady Margaret rules Belrémy."

Geoffrey shook his head.

"What dost thou mean?"

"Ay, propound me this riddle," Henry said.

" 'Tis very simple, sir. A man holds Falaise, and a woman, Belrémy. I would sooner fight a man than a woman."

"This woman," Gilbert corrected. "Alan is right. When a woman guards her own she is more dangerous than a man. Yet this lady knows not Simon."

"And Simon knows not her," Alan answered gently.

II

How he encamped before Belrémy

Midway through October in that year of grace, 1417, Simon appeared before the town of Belrémy, with an army fifteen hundred strong, Geoffrey of Malvallet leading the van, John Holland, Earl of Huntingdon, the left wing, and himself the right, Alan of Montlice with him, acting Master of Simon's Horse. Two squires came in Simon's train, Cedric of Gountray and Edmund Marnet. In the rear, with the ordnance and provisions, were the surgeons, the priest, and one John Tarbury, with his officers, as Master of Works.

Belrémy stood upon a slight incline, with its castle frowning down upon this force, and its grey walls sullen and forbidding.

"God's my life! I like not this place!" murmured Alan, at Simon's side.

Simon looked out from under his heavy brows, surveying the town, and Alan saw him smile. It was his tiger-snarl, and Montlice shivered a little, pitying Belrémy.

Simon turned, glancing along his halted army. He spoke over his shoulder to his squires.

"Fetch me John of Tarbury. Alan, bid Huntingdon march on to cover the western side. He knows."

Within an hour the army was at work, under Simon's direction. His men were set to build wooden huts, for Simon anticipated a prolonged siege, and winter was drawing on. Trenches were dug, and palisades erected for the protection of the army, and until these were finished, some ten days later, the camp was hard at work, both officers and men.

Simon sent a herald to the town, bidding them surrender, but the Lady Margaret returned a hot answer, that he should enter Belrémy over her dead body. Simon had no taste for heroics, and he received this answer indifferently.

And so he began his blockade, hearing occasionally some tidings from the King. He had learned the art of war under Henry, and he followed his precepts strictly, with the result that he lost no men, save by sickness, during all that weary siege. Nor did he once lose patience, although Geoffrey of Malvallet was nigh to weeping from boredom and inactivity.

"Simon, Simon, art thou grown timorous?" he cried one night, standing by Simon without his tent.

"Nay," Simon answered placidly. "Nor am I of a sudden foolhardy, Geoffrey."

Geoffrey jerked his shoulder in impatience.

"Shall we sit down before this town for ever?" he demanded. "To what avail your bombardment? The walls of Belrémy seem made of granite! They laugh at thy guns! I tell thee, Simon, this is waste of time!"

Simon deigned no answer, nor looked at his half-brother.

"To what avail?" Geoffrey asked peevishly.

"So that I may weaken their fortifications, and, by hunger, weaken the soldiers."

"And thy mines? Dost thou hope to enter the town under ground?"

"Maybe," Simon answered.

"Were I in thy place I would storm it now in full force!" Geoffrey exclaimed.

A little smile flitted across Simon's face.

"That I know. Yet I am wiser than thou."

Geoffrey laughed at that, and slipped his arm in Simon's.

"Ay, I know. How much longer, Coldheart?"

"Thou shalt feast at Christmas within those walls," Simon said, pointing. "I pledge thee my word."

"A month hence!"

"Nay, three weeks only. Fret not, Geoffrey. I do indeed know my strength."

"Oh, I doubt it not!" Geoffrey heaved a sharp sigh. "My men grow troublesome, and murmur."

"Check their murmuring, then. 'Twere to more avail than this whining in mine ear."

Geoffrey flushed.

"I have not thy power over them. I can lead them into fight, but I cannot hold them in leash."

"Ay, but thou canst; none better." Simon spoke slowly, not looking at Malvallet. "Quell thine own complaining, Geoffrey, and thou mayst then rebuke thy men."

"Even as thou dost now rebuke me?"

"Even as I do now rebuke thee."

There fell a silence upon them, until Geoffrey spoke again.

"Thou art right, Simon. I will mend my ways. Thy pardon."

Simon turned, hand outstretched. Some of the severity went out of his face.

"What is this fiery blood that runs in thy veins?" he asked, and gripped Geoffrey's fingers till the bones cracked. "Is it Malvallet blood?"

"Nay, for it is not in thee. Give ye good night, Simon. I'll school myself. Even as Alan," he added, as the young Montlice came towards them. "What dost thou, pretty poet, out of thy bed at this hour?"

Alan came to Simon's side, and laid a hand on his shoulder, leaning on it. His head was bare, and he was wrapped about in a great velvet cloak, unlike the other two, who wore their armour. His dark eyes shone in the light of the fire at their feet, and he spoke softly.

"The night was so still," he said. "Thy voices woke me. What is toward?"

"Naught," Simon answered. "Geoffrey pants to scale yonder walls."

"Geoffrey must always fight," Alan nodded. "I think I would we might remain here for ever. There is peace in the air, and an ode in my head."

"There is frost in the air," Geoffrey shivered. "If Simon will not march in, I could find it in my heart to wish they would march out upon us, so we might have action at last. Simon hath pledged me his word we shall feast in Belrémy on Christmas Day, Alan."

"He must always be boasting," Alan replied. "I pray God we may enter together and whole."

"That will not be if thou dost forget thine armour," Simon said. His deep voice cut through the stillness like a knife. A sentry, hearing it, peered through the darkness to see where stood his lord.

"I wonder, do they starve within?" Alan said, looking towards the black shadow that reared itself before them, and was Belrémy. "No help came to them."

"When Umfraville drew off to Alençon they revictualled the town, belike," Geoffrey said.

"The New Year should see their skins stretched across fleshless bones," Alan insisted. "In the winter starvation and sickness come swiftly. Thou couldst hold the siege, Simon, and waste no lives."

"I will not."

Alan looked up at him under his lashes.

"What is thy motive, Simon? In an assault ye must lose men; in a blockade 'tis but the enemy who dies."

Simon gripped his arm above the wrist, and held it so, as in a vice.

"Fool! Were I to hold this town till starvation came, I should enter it over children's bodies. I war not with babes."

Alan was silent, abashed. From Simon's other side spoke Geoffrey.

"It is for this, then, that thou'lt risk an assault, Simon?"

"Ay, but I risk naught. I strike not until the proper time. Go thou to bed, Geoffrey; it is past midnight."

Geoffrey stretched himself.

"I am aweary," he sighed. "Thy great mine reaches almost to the walls now."

"It must reach farther," Simon said grimly, and laughed to himself.

Alan and Geoffrey strolled away together.

"What doth he purpose?" Alan wondered. "Some plan he hath, I'll swear."

"Ay, but he says naught. Mayhap we are to enter Belrémy through this mine he digs so hard."

"What! And be caught like rats in a trap? That is not Simon's way."

"Who knows? When the time comes he will tell us his will. If I read him aright he is as yet undecided. One thing I know."

Alan yawned.

"And I. That I must sleep or die. What is thy knowledge?"

"That we enter Belrémy by Christmastide. What Simon says, he means."

"He speaks not until he is sure," Alan said. "If he told me he would march into Hell by Christmas and enslave the Devil, I would follow him."

Geoffrey crossed himself.

"So would we all. Belrémy will be hell enough, God wot!"

"And the Lady Margaret, the Devil," Alan chuckled.

III

How he took Belrémy

He struck a week before the promised date, and the manner of his striking was typical of his policy throughout his career. His mine ran from the camp beneath the town-walls to a corner of waste ground within the town. He had made his calculations exactly, a rough plan of Belrémy as his guide. Two hours' work would make an outlet from this subterranean passage.

Simon called a council of his captains on the day before his attack, and laid his last commands upon them. Holland was there, a youngster, unskilled in wars, but brave as a lion, and eager; Geoffrey, dark and tall, peerless in attack, and Alan, dreamy and nonchalant, yet ready to obey any order, blessed with the Montlice dash and verve whenever necessity called. They gathered together in Simon's tent, unwontedly grave. Huntingdon was clad in leather, his armour laid by, and sat upon a rude bench, leaning forward the better to keep his eyes on Simon. Geoffrey stood before the table, fully equipped, but Alan had drawn a stool near to the entrance of the tent, and was dressed in soft cloth and silks. He rested his head in his hand, and his eyes were upon Simon, wide-open, and shining with a child-like innocence. Simon himself sat at the table, plans before him, in such a way that he might look easily from one to the other of his captains. His hands were loosely clasped upon the rough wood; he frowned, but his voice was passionless and even.

"You, Huntingdon, at the sounding of the horn at seven in the morning, shall fall upon the western gate with all your force, using your three towers of archers, and your breaching-tower. The wall hath crumbled 'neath your cannon. Ye should breach it easily now, and ye must set about the task with much to-do and noise, so that the garrison may think I seek to enter there in full force. Thus ye draw their fire. It will be easy enough, for it is at the western gate that they are most vigilant. There they expect assault. Twelve men will creep along my mine at five o'clock, to break away the earthcrust within the town. When the signal is heard and the townsfolk are thrown into a turmoil by Huntingdon's sudden attack, those twelve will run swiftly to the southern gates which I now front, and open them. You, Malvallet, with Montlice, shall charge then, and enter. There will be fighting enough to satisfy ye all, but the greater part of the garrison will have flown to defeat Holland. Malvallet, your task then is to ride westward through the town to Holland's assistance. Montlice will press forward to the centre, where stands the castle. I shall be with you by then." He paused, and shot a keen glance round. "Ye do understand?"

"Ay," Huntingdon nodded.

"Well enough," Alan sighed.

"But one thing," Malvallet said.

Simon's eyes were upon him.

"And that?"

"I do understand mine own part, for 'tis child's play. What part do you play, sir?"

"I lead those who enter the town by the mine. I am the twelfth man," Simon answered quietly.

On the word there was an outcry.

"You have assigned to yourself the most difficult task!" Huntingdon exclaimed.

"Nay, Simon, it is not fitting," Alan said softly.

"At least ye will take me with you!" Geoffrey cried.

"Nay." The word fell heavily, enforcing silence. "It shall be as I have said."

"But, Simon!" Geoffrey threw out his hands impulsively. "What comes to us if ye fall?"

"Then shall ye be commander in my room. I fall not."

Huntingdon smote his knee.

"Beauvallet, take my place, and let me take thine! Indeed, indeed——"

"Silence, Holland. What I have said I have said."

Alan rose, stretching himself like a cat. His eyes seemed more childlike than before, his pose more indolent.

"Simon, for the love that lies betwixt us two assign thy task to me."

Simon came to his feet, and laid his hands on Alan's shoulders.

"Thou love-sick child! Then were we indeed lost. Be content to do my bidding."

Alan clasped his hands on Simon's arm.

"Simon, I beg of thee!"

"And I." Malvallet clanked forward, and smote Simon upon the shoulder. "Lad, there is too much danger in thy task. We need thee for other things, and if thou art slain we fall to pieces."

Simon shook his head indomitably.

"Thou wilt meet me within the gates of Belrémy, Geoffrey. My hand on it."

Malvallet wrung his hand.

"Simon, if so be they slay thee before thou hast flung open the gates, Belrémy shall have no quarter. That I swear."

A gleam came into the curious eyes.

"Beauvallet dies not with his task unaccomplished, Geoffrey. Now listen to me, and cease thy plainings. Lie safe and still behind yonder palisade until the gates swing back, and the bridge is down. Then charge swiftly over. Let no movement be seen in my camp that thou canst avoid. Thyself lead the van, and let Alan follow. And come quickly, Geoffrey, for it may be that I shall need thy help."

"By God!" Malvallet swore, "if I come not at once, may I be damned eternally!"

Simon nodded briefly, and turned to address them all.

"And further, let this my command be given out: If any man strike down a woman or child in the fight, or offer injury where none is courted, his life will I take, and that right speedily. I will have no burning or pillaging, but order and chivalry. Ye do understand?"

"Ay."

"Then that is all. Fare ye well, Huntingdon. I shall not fail you."

The young Earl gripped his hand for a moment, smiling.

"We meet within Belrémy, Beauvallet. God be with you and keep you in His care."

"And you." Simon watched him swing out of the tent, and turned to his two friends. There was a little warmth in his voice now, and his eyes rested kindly upon them.

"If this be my last fight, my lands go to the King, by this my Will." He picked up a sealed parchment. "My wealth I have divided equally between you, saving only that which I have left to my Marshal, Maurice of Gountray, and mine other men. I leave this packet with Bernard of Talmayne. One of you will care for Cedric and Edmund for my sake?"

"I will," Alan answered and turned away, lifting one flap of the tent and gazing out.

But Geoffrey put his hand on Simon's shoulder.

"Simon, ye have never spoken thus before. Not in all our fights. What ill-omen dost thou feel, my brother?"

"None." Simon smiled into the anxious eyes. "Yet

141

this will be a stern fight, and I would leave all in order."

"If thou shouldst be slain," Geoffrey began, and broke off. "Well, thou dost know."

"Ay."

"If thou shouldst be slain," Alan said slowly, "then shall the vixen Margaret die."

"Nay. That is folly. I die not. But if any one of us be missing tomorrow, when all is done, those that are left will have lost the most faithful and the dearest friend. Go now, Geoffrey, and sleep whilst thou may."

Geoffrey lingered still.

"And thou?"

"I have to see my captain, Walter of Santoy, and I must attend to some other matters. Remember, Geoffrey, if I fall tomorrow, thou art in command. Subdue Belrémy and invest it under Huntingdon. Then repair at once to the King. I can tell thee no more."

"If thou dost fall before thou canst open the gates——?"

Simon smiled grimly.

"That may not be. Fare thee well, my brother." He watched Geoffrey walk to the entrance. "Tell thy men to follow the Gilded Armour. I shall wear it."

Geoffrey nodded. He paused by Alan and spoke to him.

"Thou wilt be ready, Alan?"

"Ay. I will come to thee when Simon goes, to hear thine orders."

Geoffrey nodded again and went out. Simon's secretary entered from the inner tent, and Alan waited until Simon had finished with him. Bernard went softly out to summon Walter of Santoy.

"It grows late," Alan remarked. "Six of the clock. Thou wilt rest, Simon?"

"Presently."

"Who goes with thee into the town?"

"Mine own people. Eleven men."

"Well, they would die for thee," Alan said, as though he found therein some grain of comfort. "Cedric also?"

"Nay, he is too young. Take the boy with thee, Alan, for he will not be left behind. He is enraged

already that I will not take him with me. Have a care
to him."

"I will. I'll see thee again, lad, when thou art ready."
Alan smiled over his shoulder, and sauntered out to
his own quarters.

The night was very still and calm, the silence broken only within the camp where men moved stealthily about in preparation. The palisade had been
undermined so that it would fall as soon as the sup-
ports were withdrawn. Away to the left Huntingdon
was moving, with less stealth and more noise.

Simon stood at the entrance to his mine, tall and
square, girt in his gilded armour, which glinted in the
light of the fires. His great sword hung at his side, but
his lance and shield he had discarded to be brought to
him in Malvallet's charge. He was wrapped about in a
great cloak, as was each of his men, and he carried his
green-plumed helm beneath his arm. Alan stood by
his side, while he called the names of each of his
followers. Every man answered promptly but softly.
Dimly they were outlined against the black sky. Simon
cast a quick glance over them, and turned to bid Alan
farewell. He wasted no time, but held Alan's hand a
moment in his mailed clasp.

"God be with thee, Alan. Follow the Gilded Armour,
remember, and have a care to thyself. Give me the
torch."

It was handed to him and he bent, entering the
mine, sword in hand. One by one his men crept in
behind him, and presently were hidden from Alan's
sight in the gloomy tunnel. Even the glow of the
torch-light faded; it was as though the earth had
swallowed one and all.

Treading softly, and bent almost double, the line of
men went steadily along the dank, earth-smelling passage, following the torch, and trusting implicitly to
their leader. And so at length they came to the end of
the mine, where they could stand upright. For a moment they stood listening, and then, quietly, Simon
gave the order to begin to break upwards. Concealing
cloaks were laid aside, and arms bared. Each man was

furnished with either a pick or a spade, and with these they set to work, digging upwards as steeply as was possible. Simon himself flung down his cloak and helm, and hampered as he was by his armour, fell to hacking away the earth, his torch stuck in a niche in the earthen wall. There was no word spoken for a long time, but when Simon turned to pick up a spade his eyes fell on the eleventh man, shovelling the earth away with a will. A curly black head met his eye, and a young, strained face down which the sweat rolled in great beads. The boy raised his head at that moment and saw Simon's stern glance upon him. He paused in his work to send his lord a look of piteous apology, not unmixed with triumph.

"You and I shall have a reckoning to settle for this, Cedric," Simon said softly.

Cedric nodded, flushing.

"Ay, my lord. That I know. I could not let ye come without me. If—if aught befall us—you—you will have—forgiven?"

Simon's hard mouth twitched.

"It would seem so. Go to now."

Cedric threw him a grateful smile and returned to his digging with renewed vigour. Not another word was spoken; the work was done as silently as possible, and no man shirked his full share of this arduous task, although the tunnel was dank and airless, and the roof seemed to close down upon them. These picked men of Beauvallet would cheerfully have died sooner than fail their lord, or grumble at his strictness in a time of stress.

At last the foremost, one Malcolm Clayton, glanced back over his shoulder, and spoke in a hushed voice.

"Lord, my pick went through."

Simon scrambled up the crumbling slope of loose earth.

"Then silence now, as you value your lives. Stand back, the others."

He was obeyed instantly; the panting, sweating men rested on their tools, watching Simon and Malcolm break through the thin crust. It was slowly done, and carefully, but at length a wave of frosty air came down to them, and they drank it in gladly. Still Simon worked, making a hole just large enough to admit a man. Then he set down his pick, and raising himself on Malcolm's shoulders, peered cautiously above the opening. Down he came again, springing lightly, and nodded.

"Bank the earth to form a step. You, John and Peter. The dawn is upon us."

Again they set to work, and soon had fulfilled his behest. A pale grey light filtered down into the tunnel, but overhead the sky seemed still dark and frowning.

Simon gave the order to stack the tools. Wine had been brought in small leathern bottles; they drank deeply of it before they donned their helms and cloaks. Cedric picked up the golden helm and shook its waving plumes free of the dirt. He buckled it on to Simon's neck-plate, and clasped the long green surcoat upon his shoulders. Then Simon wrapped the dark cloak over all and picked up his great sword. It gleamed wickedly in the torchlight, and the golden helm seemed to glow with an inward fire. Beneath its peak Simon's eyes looked calmly forth and the green of his plumes seemed to steal into them, so that he appeared as some huge knight all gold and green. His men were nervous through anticipation, but his measured voice quieted them.

"Extinguish the torch."

It was done, and the golden figure faded to a black silhouette against the faint light. Each man stood very still, and breathed rather fast. Again the cool voice spoke.

"Silence now until I speak. The time should be soon. Follow me close, but keep your swords hidden and show no fight until ye see me draw. Cedric, stay by me throughout."

A low murmur of assent came and then all was eerily silent. Yet through the chilling darkness and the tense period of waiting Simon's magnetic personality seemed to spread over his men so that their jagged nerves were soothed. Not one amongst them but

145

placed his whole trust in Simon, believing implicitly that he would lead them to victory.

Time crept by on leaden feet, and bit by bit the grey light grew stronger. Above, all was quiet as the grave, so that the very silence seemed to din in the waiting men's ears.

Presently one fidgeted unconsciously, and drew a deep, sobbing breath. Against the light they saw Simon raise his hand, and once more there was quiet.

Then, as from a long way off, a horn sounded, wailing across the land. Thrice came the call, and something like a gasp of relief broke from eleven tense throats. Away in the camp, Geoffrey of Malvallet had given the signal for attack. Still Simon moved not, but stood rock-like, waiting.

Faintly came the noise of a great shout. Holland had obeyed the signal. Eleven men fixed their eyes upon their lord, muscles taut, to move at his least command. He stood immobile, his head slightly tilted, listening.

Gradually, the noise grew, though it came muffled into the mine. An explosion rent the air; Holland had trained his one cannon on to the western wall the better to attract attention.

Nearer at hand turmoil sounded, subdued at first, but increasing in volume. The town was awake, and plunged into sudden and desperate activity.

At last Simon moved, and spoke one word.

"Follow." He mounted the rude step and scrambled through the hole with surprising agility. Quickly his men followed, and found themselves on a patch of waste ground behind some rude houses, amidst rubbish and garbage. They closed up behind Simon and strode after him across the uneven ground.

"Remember, ye are soldiers of Belrémy," he reminded them. "Spread a little, but follow me."

On they went, and broke into a trot as they emerged upon a narrow street. It was thronged with hurrying men, and from the windows and doors of the houses women called, some hysterical, others calm. Soldiers were running towards the western ramparts, buckling on their swords or mailed gloves. Simon's little band separated quickly and ran after him, to the south, pushing and jostling the excited townsfolk. From behind came the roar of Holland's attack, but they tarried not to listen. On they sped, out into the main street and down it towards the gates, always keeping the green plumes in sight, and gradually drawing near to Simon again.

Through the rapidly filling street the gates loomed large ahead, and from them came part of the garrison, mounted, and galloping to save the western walls, heedless of the scattered humanity flying from before the plunging hoofs.

They were upon the gates now, and Simon's voice rang out, clarion-like above the din.

"To me, and do what I do!"

Full upon the startled sentries he rushed, and cried: "The Seneschal! The Seneschal!"

They fell back instantly, thinking he came from the Marshal, and he swept on, his men at his heels, to the gate-tower. There again they were accosted, but this time the sentry but asked for news.

"They are through on the western side!" Simon shouted, and thundered up the stairs, sword drawn. At the top some fifteen men were fretting, trying to hear or see what was toward. They fell upon Simon.

"What news? What news? Are they through? Bring ye commands?"

Before they had realized he was a stranger, he had struck, and with a quick movement, had flung his cloak about the foremost, muffling and blinding him. The room was suddenly full of armed men, and they hacked down the tiny garrison with deadly precision. Swords were wrenched from scabbards, daggers drawn; all was confusion in that desperate fight. Then again Simon's voice rang out, and they saw him wrench at the lever which let down the bridge.

"John Malcolm, Frank, guard me this!" he called, and was lost again amid the scuffling fight.

A cry went up for help; someone reached the great bellrope, and set the iron bell clanging a wild alarm; dead and wounded lay upon the floor, but Simon's eleven men were whole, three of them guarding the drawbridge lever as he had commanded. Simon plunged forward to the door, waving a huge key.

"The rest follow me!" he cried, and was gone down the winding stairs. Out they raced, pell-mell, to the barred gate.

The bell had stirred the garrison station nearby to action. From a little way off came shouts from the oncoming soldiers.

"Guard my back!" Simon gasped, and struck down a man who sought to stand against him. He leapt over the body and fumbled with the key. Cedric was at his side; behind them, his men were engaging with the startled enemy. Slowly, slowly the bolts were pushed back, and the iron bars removed. The gates swung back.

Simon swerved round on his heel to meet the attackers. Some dozen men-at-arms were striving desperately to reach the gate, but Simon's men had the advantage of them and could hold them in check till Geoffrey came. Simon hacked a way through for himself and Cedric, intent on reaching the gate-tower before the soldiers, who were even now in sight, some mounted, and charging down the narrow street. He was just in time, for a small body of men rushed to the tower to draw up the bridge before it should be too late. They came upon a great knight in golden armour, who stood within the doorway, and met their charge like a rock. His sword slashed and thrust mercilessly, his brow was lowering.

Then a welcome sound fell upon Simon's ears, a roar and the thunder of hoofs on the wooden bridge. He heaved a short sigh of relief, for the men who guarded the gate for him were hard-pressed, and could hold out no longer. His voice rang out above the medley of sound.

"Stand aside! Stand aside! Let Malvallet finish!"

Even as he shouted to them they had sprung away from the gateway, pressing back against the walls to let Malvallet through.

Plunging into Belrémy came the English, Malvallet at their head, unmistakable by his black plumes and surcoat. He held his lance in one hand, his shield in the other, with the bridle of his own horse, and that of Simon's huge black charger. Behind him came his own men, and such was the force of their charge that they bore the French backwards into the town, so that they broke, and fled in confusion. In that brief respite Geoffrey wheeled about and came back to the gate. He saw Simon at the entrance of the tower, and charged down upon his assailants, scattering them.

"All safe?" he cried.

Simon caught his horse's bridle, and the shield from the saddle.

"Ay. I wait to see all in. Ride to the western ramparts now."

Geoffrey turned again, and galloped back into the open street. An order was shouted, and the vanguard closed in behind him, horse and foot, orderly in an instant, the archers with their cross-bows held ready. The cavalcade streamed down a side street, making for the western gate.

Again the bridge shook, this time beneath the weight of Alan's onslaught. In he came, red plumes waving, and his brilliant surcoat stretched out behind him by the wind. Close behind him, riding three abreast, were his horse-archers, skilled warriors every one, mounted on trained chargers. As Alan rode past, Simon shouted to him above the clatter of hoofs on the cobblestones.

"On to the market-place! I join thee there! 'Ware men from the right!"

Alan glanced quickly over his shoulder, and waved his sword gaily in token that he had heard; then he was gone down the main-street to where the French had gathered, ready to defend their own.

In silence Simon watched his soldiers come running through the gateway, pikes levelled, and every foot striking the ground as one. His eyes glinted as he observed their shining armour and their disciplined appearance. There was no semblance of riot in their attack; they came swiftly and orderly, fine men all of them, and well equipped.

At last came Walter of Santoy, in green-and-russet, Beauvallet colours, riding at the head of the rear-guard, some score and a half men-at-arms mounted.

They halted within the town, and spread quickly to guard the bridge at a sharp command from Santoy. Eleven of them rode on to where Simon stood, and saluted, dismounting, and holding their steeds in readiness for the men who had entered the town with Simon. It was all done as if by machinery, without fluster.

Then at last Simon moved. He turned, and called up the stairs of the gate tower.

"All in! Down now to me!"

Down the stairs clattered the three men he had left aloft, wounded every one, but dauntless. Six of Santoy's men went up to hold the tower in their place, and the three tired warriors mounted their waiting chargers, for they were to form Simon's bodyguard. One man of the eleven was too badly wounded to move, but the others swung themselves into their saddles. Simon looked them over.

"It was well done," he said, and from him that was praise enough to set them blushing. He glanced towards the one who was wounded, and raised his hand to his helm in stiff salute. "God be with you, Malcolm."

"And with you, lord!" Malcolm gasped, and fell back into the arms of the surgeon who had come with Santoy.

Simon mounted his coal-black horse, and watched Cedric fling himself into the nearest horse's saddle.

"Onward!" he said, and spurred forward down the street in Alan's wake.

The English had pressed on to the wide market-place, but there the French were gathered, soldiers and townspeople, and there they made a determined stand.

"Way for Beauvallet!" Simon roared, and pressed through to the fore. A hundred voices took up the cry; a wave of relief seemed to sweep through the English ranks.

"Way for Beauvallet! Follow the Gilded Armour! The Lion, the Lion! Follow the Gilded Armour!"

The market-place was a medley of fighting men, a blaze of colour, with here and there the red-and-gold of Montlice showing, fighting shoulder to shoulder with the Malvallet black. Green-and-russet men were scattered all over, and away to the right, the King's men hacked and hewed with Alan at their head.

Simon pressed on towards one of his captains, rapped out a sharp command, and rode to the left. The captain wheeled about to the right, shouting Simon's order as he went. In a moment it seemed the English fell into two divisions, and the left flank charged after the great golden figure ahead, bearing down upon the enemy like a battering ram. Back and back fell the French till the market-place was left behind, and the mad fight swept on into the narrow streets beyond.

Women shrieked from doors and windows, hysterical at the sight of blood, and the sound of steel on steel and the roar of voices. Children who had slipped out into the road, fled hither and thither, terrified at this sudden invasion of fighting men. One babe ran right out into the road almost beneath the plunging hoofs of Simon's horse. He wrenched the animal back upon its haunches and swung it deftly to one side, stooping to hoist the child up by its mud-spattered skirts.

An agonized, sobbing scream came from the side of the road, where the mother had flattened herself against the wall. Simon cut his way towards her, the babe held safe behind his shield, its face buried in the folds of his surcoat. He handed it down to the woman.

"Get ye within doors," he told her sternly, and was gone again into the mêlée.

From the other end of the street enemy reinforcements came running, and the French retreat was checked and the English fell back a little.

Simon rose in his stirrups; his voice blared forth, and at the sound of it his men rallied round him again, and put new zest into their blows.

"For St George and the King!" Simon cried, and someone behind him started to roar out the song of Agincourt.

A score of voices took it up, and again the English pressed forward.

A burly fellow at Simon's side smote down one

Frenchman who would have hamstrung his horse, and as he did so he sang jovially.

" 'Our King went forth to Normandy'—have at ye now! 'With grace and might of chivalry'——So, so! That for thy pains! 'The God for him'——Would ye, would ye? 'Ware, lord! 'ware!—'wrought marv'lously' ——Oh, brave, brave, my lord! On, on! 'Wherefore England'——Hey, John Dawlish, Peter Westmere, take it up!—'may call and cry: De-o Gratias! De-o Gratias!' "

"Deo Gratias, Deo Gratias!" came the roar from all around, and on the words the English swept the French backwards, pressing on and on, down the street.

For fully an hour the fight lasted, all over the town, but at length, first in one place, and then in another, the French cried for quarter. In a little while the truce was called, and comparative silence fell, the battle-yells dying away. Quarter was granted everywhere, and soon the sheriff sent to Simon, who had pushed his way back to the market-place, surrendering the keys of the town.

Dead and wounded lay upon the ground, but already the women and the non-combatants were out, tending the wounded, whether they were French or English.

Simon found one of his captains in the crowd, and delivered his orders. Most of the French soldiery, it seemed, had fled north to the castle, which still held firm, and wherein lay the Lady Margaret.

Across the square came Malvallet, his armour dented and battered, his surcoat torn.

"God be thanked! Thou art alive!" he cried, and reined in beside Simon. "Huntingdon is in long since. Where is Alan?"

"I have not seen him. To the right, I think, down the street. Holland hath his men in hand?"

"Ay. They tend the wounded, some of them. We hold each gate. I'll go seek Alan." He turned, and picked his way across the square.

When he came back it was full half-an-hour later, and the market-place was almost cleared.

"Simon, Simon!" Malvallet cried, and Simon turned

sharply, waiting for Geoffrey to come up to him. "Alan is taken! Taken by that she-devil, and carried into her stronghold!"

"What!" Simon glared into Malvallet's haggard face. For a moment he was silent, and then his upper lip curled back, showing his teeth in that famous tiger-snarl.

"If I have not Alan by nightfall, may my soul wither in hell!" he said softly.

IV

How he saw the Lady Margaret

By noon he had brought some semblance of order into Belrémy and had held a long parley with the sheriff. The usual proclamations were posted up, in the King's name, promising fair treatment and protection to all who would swear allegiance to Henry. For the most part the townsfolk availed themselves of this clemency, for they were tired of the long siege, and anxious to re-victual the town. Simon's men were stationed round the town and in it, and at length he had leisure to consider Alan's predicament. It was rumoured that Montlice was first wounded, and then overcome by the Lady Margaret's men-at-arms.

"Simon, thou'lt rescue him?" Geoffrey said anxiously. They were in the justice-house, which Simon had made his temporary headquarters.

"Ay," Simon answered. "She will look to hold him as hostage, but I have her in a vice. I hold her uncle prisoner."

"Her uncle? He fought this morning?"

"He is her Marshal. The Sire de Galledemaine. Huntingdon took him. Bernard, bring thy quill, and parchment."

The secretary collected them, and sat waiting for further orders.

"Write," Simon said slowly. " 'To the Lady Margaret of Belrémy. In the name of His Most Gracious Majesty, King Henry the Fifth of England and France, I, Simon of Beauvallet, command that ye surrender the keys of the Castle of Belrémy within the hour, swearing fealty to His Majesty King Henry, and delivering the knight, Sir Alan of Montlice, into my hands.' Thou hast that?"

"Ay, my lord."

"Dispatch it by my herald at once, then, and bid him await the lady's answer."

"What folly is this?" Malvallet asked, when Talmayne had withdrawn. "She will laugh at thy message."

"Perchance. It is my formal command. If she laughs now, she will weep later."

The herald returned within the hour, and knelt to give Simon the Lady Margaret's packet.

Simon broke the seals and spread the crackling parchment sheets before him. Over his shoulder Geoffrey read:

"To Simon of Beauvallet.

"If ye depart not from this my city within the space of twelve hours, surrendering the keys unto Ferdinand de Valmé, my Sheriff, the knight, Sir Alan of Montlice, swings from the ramparts in thy sight.

"Written at my Castle of Belrémy this twenty-first day of December."

Geoffrey let fly a great oath, and clapped his hand to his sword-hilt.

"Thou wilt storm the place, Simon?"

Simon smiled.

"Nay. That would surely bring death to Alan, thou hothead. Write again, Bernard: "If my commands be not obeyed, I, Simon of Beauvallet, do swear by the Rood and by all the blessed Saints that the Marshal, Jean de Galledemaine, dies before the Castle of Belrémy with the other prisoners in my hold, and every third breadwinner of this town. And further if any harm be done unto the knight, Sir Alan of Montlice, I do swear by God that I will raze this city to the ground, slaying all who dwell therein and sparing neither woman nor child. And that ye may see that I swear it not idly, six of the children will I slay before the castle if ye surrender not at once.' "

Malvallet laughed.

"Oh, ay! With thine own hand, belike!"

"It will not come to that," Simon answered. He waited until Bernard had sealed the parchment and given it to him. He handed it to the herald. "If the Lady Margaret should speak with thee, asking what manner of man I may be, thou wilt tell her that what I say I will do, I do. Thou didst deliver mine other message into her hands?"

"Ay, my lord."

"She spake not?"

"Nay, sir. She withdrew with her gentlemen, and was closely veiled."

Simon nodded.

"Go then."

When the herald returned again it was with a verbal message.

" 'Tell my lord of Beauvallet,' " he recited, " 'that the Lady Margaret, Countess of Belrémy, will treat with him within her castle of Belrémy if he comes alone, and under the laws of truce.' "

"Thou'lt not go alone into that trap!" Geoffrey exclaimed.

"No trap is it," Simon said.

"What! Thou wilt trust to a woman's honour?"

"Nay." Simon smiled unpleasantly. "She dare not harm me, or detain me. If I return not within the hour lead out the Sire de Galledemaine, and slay him before the castle. Then if I still make no sign, thou mayst sack the town, to show that I lied not, and storm the castle, for I shall be dead."

"What does thou purpose?" Geoffrey asked curiously. "Once within her stronghold thou art lost."

Simon laughed.

"Am I so? Once within the castle, and I may crush the she-devil at will." He rose. "Thou art lord in mine absence, Geoffrey, but look to it that ye obey mine orders." He went out to his own quarters, where he found Cedric resting on his pallet, relating his glorious adventures to Edmund, who listened curiously, drinking in every word. When Simon came in, they both started up.

Simon looked Cedric over keenly.

"Thou wert wounded?"

"It is naught, sir," Cedric blushed. His arm lay in a sling.

"The surgeon hath seen to it?"

The boy fidgeted.

"Nay, my lord. I asked him not, for he was busy with others, and indeed my wound is trifling."

Simon went to him and unbound his arm. An ugly flesh wound met his eye, which still bled sluggishly.

"Fetch me water and clean linen," Simon ordered briefly, and Edmund ran out. He came back with the water, and watched his lord wash Cedric's wound quickly and deftly. Simon bound it up again, and Cedric's teeth slowly unclenched. He was rather pale, for Simon's methods were rough and ready.

"Get thee to bed," Simon said, "and stay there. Edmund, bring mine armour. Ye have cleaned it?"

"Ay, my lord."

"Fetch it then, and get thee ready. I go to the castle."

Cedric, who had retired to his pallet, raised himself on one elbow.

"My lord!"

The hard eyes looked down upon him coldly.

"Well?"

"Take—take me!"

"Edmund goes with me. Lie thou still."

"But, sir!——"

"It shall be thy punishment for defying me today," Simon said inexorably.

"Oh, my lord, no! I cannot let ye go to the castle without——"

"Let? Let? What is this talk? Thou wilt be silent, Cedric, an ye desire not my displeasure."

Cedric's eyes filled with tears.

"My lord, punish me how you will, but take me with you now! If—if aught should befall you——"

"What help could ye give me?" Simon said scathingly.

Cedric plucked at his blanket with trembling fingers.

"I—I should—at least be—with you. If—if ye should be slain, I—I——"

"Ye will have learned a lesson. I am not lightly defied, Cedric."

The boy turned his face to the wall without another word. Not until Simon was fully clad in his shining armour, did he speak again, and then it was to Edmund, who stood preening himself in his green and russet dress.

"If harm comes to my lord, I will beat thee senseless!" he whispered savagely.

Simon strode out, an amused glint in his eyes.

He rode through the town with Edmund close behind him, and came quickly to the castle. The bridge was let down for them, and they went across at a walkpace. In the courtyard Simon dismounted and gave his horse into Edmund's charge. Unattended, he followed the steward into the castle.

The great hall was empty, and the steward led Simon across it, to the Countess's audience-chamber. He swung back the curtain, and sonorously announced, "My Lord of Beauvallet!"

Simon entered, stepping firmly, yet panther-like. Within the room he paused, hand upon his sword-hilt, and sent a swift glance round.

Upon a dais, seated on a throne-like chair, was the Lady Margaret, like a pillar of ice. Her regal head, crowned by a cloud of black locks, and a great horned head-dress, from which hung a veil of gold net, pearl embroidered, was held high. Not a muscle in her long white throat quivered; her face was mask-like, oval and pale, with thin, disdainful lips, and black eyes that shone between lowered lids. The lashes, long and curling, seemed to cast a shadow on the perfect skin beneath them. Her nose was short and straight, the nostrils finely carved, and slightly pinched. She was clad in a gown of wine-red silk, which moulded itself to her superb form, showing the swell of her breasts, and the long line to her hips. It fell about her feet in a great train, hiding them, and clung close to her rounded arms till it widened at the wrists in huge sleeves which brushed the ground as she walked. Her white hands lay along the arms of her chair, the nervous fingers gripping the carved wood tensely. On her bosom a great ruby glowed, the only living thing about her.

Beside her stood a dark gentleman, foppishly clad, who regarded Simon with a faint sneer upon his full lips. He twirled a rose between his fingers, and raised it to his nose now and again. Other gentlemen were scattered about the room, all in court-dress, and all watching Simon curiously. Behind the Countess stood three of her ladies, still as was their mistress.

Simon walked forward deliberately. He seemed to tower above the men present, an incongruous figure in the midst of this elegant assembly, Saxon-fair, and all in gold save for his waving plumes, and long green surcoat. Before the dais he halted, and glanced calmly at the Countess from beneath his helm.

"Madame," he said in blunt French, "I am here to receive your submission."

The haughty lips curved in a pitying smile. The Countess made a gesture with her right hand, and the foppish gentleman stepped forward. He answered Simon in lisping English.

"You are a leetle brusque, milor', is it not so? Madame my cousin desires to make terms with you."

The Countess moved slightly, and Simon saw her eyes flash.

"My terms are these," Simon said, addressing her. "If ye do surrender unto me the keys of this castle, and do swear fealty to my master, King Henry"—he raised his hand to his helm a moment—"I can offer you his gracious protection and clemency."

A pulse on her temple throbbed angrily.

"My cousin," she said, also in English, "tell him that it is for me to make terms." Her voice was clear and cold. She did not look at Simon.

The dapper gentleman seemed to deprecate this harshness.

"Ah, *oui!* You will agree, milor', that Madame la

Comtesse is in a more fit position to treat than are you."

Simon's mouth was grim.

"Nay, sir. I cannot agree. I hold Madame and you all in a vice."

The Frenchman smiled.

"Aha?" He raised the rose gracefully. "One man against—shall we say five score?"

Simon shot him that rapier-glance, and despite his effrontery, the Frenchman involuntarily stepped back.

"I came under the laws of truce," Simon said harshly.

The Chevalier de Fleurival recovered himself. He raised his shoulders nonchalantly.

"In times of stress, milor' . . . *eh bien!* You walked in so—so—without guile, is it not so?"

"And if I walk not out within the hour, the Sire de Galledemaine dies before your gates."

The Chavelier paled a little, but still he smiled.

"So you think, milor', to take this castle single-handed?"

"Within the hour."

"Est-ce possible?" The Chevalier laughed gently. "My father, the Sire de Galledemaine, is old, milor'. Death comes easily to the old."

"And to the young." The words fell heavily, and again the Countess stirred in her chair.

"That foolish threat!" The Chevalier shook with supercilious merriment. "We are not fools, milor'."

"If ye surrender not this castle, and Sir Alan of Montlice, then will ye indeed be fools," Simon said calmly. "Ye will see my soldiers burn Belrémy to the ground, and slay all those who dwell therein. I threaten not."

The Chevalier smelt his rose delicately. Over it, his eyes never left Simon's face.

"But if, milor', you are dead, to what avail? I have heard such threats before."

Simon smiled.

"Ye know not me, sir, if ye think my captains obey not my word, whether I am quick or dead."

"Yes? But ye grow discourteous, milor'. Be sure the Comtesse desires not your life. Her terms are that if ye will withdraw your men from Belrémy, swearing never to return, she will deliver Sir Alan of Montlice into your care as soon as ye have left the town."

"I thank Madame la Comtesse!" Simon's voice grated. "But she is over-proud, methinks."

"In a word, milor', you refuse?"

"I ignore."

The clear voice from the throne spoke again.

"Tell him, my cousin, to consider well. If he refuse my terms, then will I send to dispatch Sir Alan of Montlice right speedily, and will send him the same road."

Simon stood silent, and a gleam of triumph came into the Chevalier's eyes.

"That gives food for thought, milor'?"

Simon heeded him not, but looked at the Lady Margaret.

"That is your last word, Madame?"

"My last word," she answered.

Then Simon moved. In a flash he had torn his sword from the scabbard and was upon the dais, holding the weapon shortened, the point touching the Countess's white breast.

There was a horrified cry; the men sprang forward, but stopped short as Simon drew his arm back to thrust. His left hand gripped the Countess's wrist; he looked over his shoulder at the room.

"One step more, and your mistress dies," he said softly. "The truce is at an end."

The Countess sat rigid, braving Simon with her dark eyes. The Chevalier had dropped his rose. He spoke uncertainly, ashen-cheeked.

"Milor', milor'! One does not offer violence to a lady."

"But a she-devil one burns," Simon barked, "as I will burn this Amazon if I find not Sir Alan, alive and unhurt."

A shudder went through the Chevalier; one of the ladies-in-waiting started to sob wildly.

Simon looked down into the proud face that defied him so bravely.

"Those six children, madame, my captain holds in safe custody," he said. "Ye shall see them die."

Her eyelids flickered uncontrollably, and he saw the muscles of her throat contract.

"You would not dare!"

Simon laughed.

"An ye fail to order your men to submit, madame, ye will see how much I dare."

"Cur!" She spat the word at him, breathing short and fast. "Ye would kill babes? Cur that ye are!"

"Nay, 'tis you who will kill them, madame."

Her fingers clenched together.

"I will first kill Sir Alan of Montlice!" she flashed, and turned her head. "Go, Henri de Malincourt! Slay me this English Alan!"

"Ay, go," Simon said, and brought his sword to her breast. Under its point a tiny red speck appeared, but the Countess flinched not. Only she stamped her foot.

"Go, I say!"

One man stepped forward a pace.

"Madame, I dare not," he said humbly.

"Craven! Will not one of you do my bidding? Call me not mistress again if ye defy me now!"

The Chevalier raised one shaking hand.

"Let no man stir. Milor', this is between men. Release my cousin."

Simon's hold on the lady's wrist tightened till she bit her lip with the pain of it.

"Bid thy men swear before God to submit themselves," he said.

Her teeth were tightly clenched.

"Thou shalt slay me first!"

Tighter and tighter grew his hold on her arm.

"And thy people?—the children of Belrémy?"

For a long minute she glared up into his strange eyes, but try as she might she could not read his mind.

"Ye seek to force me to yield through pity!"

"God wot, not I! Hast thou any, thou breaker of truces?"

Again she spoke to the men who stood rooted to the ground before her.

"Ye are ten to his one! Think ye he would dare to slay me? On to him, I command!"

A little deeper pressed the sword, and the red speck grew. Simon smiled grimly down upon his foes.

The Chevalier's eyes shifted from face to face; all the smiling insolence had gone out of them. They came at last to his cousin. His mouth worked a little.

"Cousin, thou must yield! I implore thee, be not foolhardy!"

"Yield! I? To this English boor? Bah!"

"Ye would be wise to listen to your cousin," Simon said. "I will give ye one minute, and then I will strike home."

"Thus you seal your own doom!" she cried. "Once I am sped, there are ten men ready to fall upon thee!"

"It matters not," Simon said. "If I die no Frenchman will live in this town by sunrise tomorrow. The minute passes, madame. Think well."

The Chavelier flung up his hand.

"Cousin, thou art distraught! I stand as regent during thy madness. Is there a man here will refuse to recognize me as lord?"

A low murmur of approval went up.

"Then I submit, milor', in the name of the Countess Margaret."

The Countess lashed round in her chair.

"Ah, never!" she cried, and would have flung herself upon Simon's sword, had he not drawn it swiftly back. He bowed slightly to the Chevalier.

"Ye do swear before God to offer no violence nor obstruction either now, or later?"

The Chevalier was biting his nails, seeking feverishly for some outlet. He sent Simon a look of hatred.

"I swear before God to offer no violence nor obstruction now or later."

"And for thy men?"

"And for my men."

"Good." Simon jerked the Countess to her feet. "Ye will lead me now, madame, to Sir Alan of Montlice. These gentlemen will go before."

"Milor'!" The Chevalier was livid with rage. "Is that necessary? Unhand my cousin! You have mine oath!"

"I would sooner have thy cousin, for thus shall I also have thine oath," Simon answered.

The Chevalier quivered with outraged dignity.

"It seems ye trust us not, sir!"

The green-blue eyes narrowed.

"Fair sir, were I a fool, then should I trust to your word. I am not a fool."

The Chevalier's hands flew to his sword-hilt.

"Ye shall answer to me for that insult!" he choked.

Simon spoke sternly.

"When I entered this place, sir, I entered it alone, as the Countess desired, under the laws of truce. Those were her words. But once within these portals it pleased the Countess, and ye all, to forget the laws of truce. Ye did threaten me with violence, who had come to treat. I fight clean, sir, when I may, but I choose my foe's weapons, and when the foe seeks to fight me foully, why, then, the time for chivalry is past. Lead on, Sir Chevalier."

The Chevalier went blindly to the door, and the courtiers followed him, one by one. Last of all came Simon, holding the Countess a little before him. She struggled once, striking up at his face with her free hand, but Simon forced her onward. She went proudly then, her head held high, carrying herself with queenly dignity, her skirts sweeping behind her.

Out into the great hall they went, past startled menials, to the narrow stairway. The Countess went forward, for two could not walk abreast, and Simon had released her. Up they went to a room in the tower. There Simon took her wrist in his hold again, and as she winced, loosened his clasp a little.

Alan lay upon a couch beneath the narrow window; he was resting on his elbow, and his head was supported to his hand. A bandage crossed his forehead, and one arm was in a sling. He glanced up as the cavalcade came in, and his lips set firmly.

"So my Lord of Beauvallet would not yield?" he said faintly. "Ye were all so certain!" He laughed, and withal his weakness there was a ring of pride in his voice. "Beauvallet is made of sterner stuff, and well he knows that life to me, under thy conditions, is disgrace!"

Then Simon clanked in, and Alan gave a great start.

"Simon!" A look of horror came into his wan face. "Ah, no, Simon! Not thou! Death were easier!"

"Didst thou think that I would leave thee to die?" Simon asked him gently. "I hold this castle—alone."

Alan sank back against his pillows. A laugh shook him.

"Oh, thou indomitable one!" he chuckled. "I doubted thee not until this moment! Geoffrey is safe?"

"Ay. I came but to see that thou wert alive, and well-tended. I go now, and the Lady Margaret goes with me, as hostage for thy safety."

"Ah no, by God!" the Chevalier exploded. "Would ye put my cousin to this shame?"

"Oh, brave to war on women!" the Countess snapped. "Do with me as ye will, but take heed lest I strike thee one day when thou art grown careless! Thou shalt pay in full, I swear!"

"Whither go ye, Simon lad?" Alan asked.

"To Malvallet. If I return not, he will sack the town. I shall come again with my men, never fear. Thou art safe, for if harm befall thee, the Lady Margaret dies by my sword."

The Countess drew herself up. Her bosom rose and fell quickly. Full into Simon's eyes she looked, her own blazing with anger.

"I will not rest until I have avenged myself," she said very quietly. "Thou English beast!"

V

How he brought the Lady Margaret to the justice-house

Through the streets of Belrémy, past staring townsfolk and saluting men-at-arms, Simon rode, a veiled and cloaked lady on a white palfrey beside him, sitting very upright in her saddle. Behind came Edmund with another lady, veiled also, and speaking never a word. To the justice-house they went, walking sedately, and there dismounted.

Out came Malvallet, armour-clad but bareheaded, his dark eyes eager.

"God be thanked, Simon!" he said fervently. Then he saw the tall woman beside Simon, and stepped back a pace. "What's to do now, lad?"

Simon did not answer him, for the guard-men were eyeing him curiously. He bowed stiffly to his charge.

"Enter, madame."

Marvelling, and all perplexed, Malvallet stood aside to let the lady pass. She swept by him, into the lofty hall where Simon transacted all his affairs, and where sat Bernard of Talmayne, busily writing. Bernard stood up, astonished at the sudden entrance of two ladies in the company of his lord.

With a quick, impatient movement the Lady Margaret flung back her veil. Geoffrey caught his breath at the sight of her proud beauty. Her companion also unveiled. She was a little lady with brown curls and big blue eyes. Just now those eyes were exceedingly haughty, but at the back of them Geoffrey thought he discerned a twinkle.

"My captain, madame," said Simon. "Sir Geoffrey of Malvallet. The Countess Margaret, Geoffrey."

Geoffrey started, and threw Simon an amazed glance. But in a moment he had hidden his surprise and pulled forward a chair.

"Pray, madame, will you not be seated?" he bowed, all his courtier instincts to the fore.

The Countess hesitated a moment, looking at Simon. Then she sat down, allowing her cloak to fall away from her gleaming shoulders. Her foot tapped the ground imperiously.

"Well, sir? What now?"

The little lady went to her and stood behind her chair. She smiled upon Geoffrey graciously, as if to thank him for his consideration.

Simon clanked to the table behind which Bernard stood, spell-bound.

"Go prepare me two rooms above," he said. "Let Walter of Santoy set a guard of mine own men upon them, so that not a mouse may creep out unseen. Hasten."

Bernard stammered something unintelligible and hurried out. Simon turned again to his prisoner.

"Madame, rest assured that I shall look well to your housing, that ye may suffer no discomfort during your sojourn here. Alan is safe, Geoffrey."

Geoffrey nodded. He clapped his hands vigorously, and when a lackey appeared, ordered wine to be brought. This he offered to the Countess, on one knee.

"I need naught," she said coldly.

Her companion rustled forward, taking the horn from Geoffrey's hand.

"Nay, madame, but taste a little!" she coaxed, and whispered something in the Countess's ear.

The Lady Margaret smiled faintly and took the horn. Geoffrey made haste to fill another for her lady, and was rewarded by a smile, and a curtsey.

"I thank you, m'sieur."

"My Lord of Beauvallet," said the Countess coldly, "for how long do ye seek to detain me?"

"Ye shall be within your castle by noon tomorrow, madame," Simon answered shortly.

The smouldering eyes challenged him.

"As mistress or prisoner, sir?"

"The decision rests with you, madame. Mistress shall ye be if ye will swear allegiance to King Henry."

"I bend not so easily, milor'," she sneered.

Simon's lips tightened.

"Mayhap ye will break then, madame."

She laughed at him, but her little teeth were clenched.

"Ye know not Margaret of Belrémy, sir!"

"I think it is you who know not Simon of Beauvallet," Simon said, with the glimmering of a smile.

Bernard came back into the room.

"It is done, my lord. Santoy was here."

The Countess rose, drawing her cloak about her. She addressed Simon softly.

"Let there be an understanding between us, sir."

"I desire naught better, lady."

"Then mark well what I say. I give no parole, I swear no allegiance. It is war between us to the death, for I am not vanquished yet, nor will be! Ye would do well to beware my vengeance, Lord of Beauvallet!"

"I thank ye for that warning," Simon retorted. He held back a curtain at the end of the hall. "Go before me, madame."

When he returned to the hall it was some time later, and he had shed his armour for a long green tunic which fell below his knees and was slit at the sides to give him greater freedom in walking. Heavy spurred boots were upon his feet, but his head was bare, the light hair still clubbed at neck and brow, brushed and smooth. He was frowning, but when he met Geoffrey's quizzical glance, the shadows went out of his eyes, and they twinkled responsively.

"Oh, Simon, Simon, thou dog!" Geoffrey teased him. "What have ye done?"

The corners of Simon's mouth turned down ruefully.

"I have brought a wild-cat into our midst," he answered. "Belrémy is not wholly mine yet, though I hold the town and the castle."

Geoffrey seized him by the shoulders, pushing him backwards to a chair.

"Sit, thou squire of dames, and tell me what passed within the castle."

"Little enough. I entered alone, and was led to my lady's audience-chamber, where she sat amidst her court, with her cousin beside her."

"Cousin?"

"Ay. Him I expected, for his father, the Sire de Galledemaine, spoke of him. A puny creature with a rose. Faugh! So soon as I had set eyes on him I knew what manner of man I had to treat with. They had thought to frighten me with threats, deeming me a fool to walk thus coolly into their trap."

"Said I not that it was a trap!"

"Nay, but I knew the workings of it. They would have taken me prisoner, mayhap slain me. I know not."

"What!" Geoffrey started up. "But it was truce!"

"So I thought. Yet I suspected treachery, so was I not taken unawares. There was some parley at first. My lady was proud enough, and high in her talk. Then they flung veiled threats at me, and I made an end."

"Simon, thou art like an oyster! How made ye this end?"

"I drew my sword upon the Lady Margaret, and thus held her men at bay."

"Ye—ye——Oh, *preux chevalier!*" Geoffrey broke into a long laugh. "They would not think of that, the Frenchmen!"

"Nay. Not that dainty court. After that it was simple. They led me to Alan who lay in a fair chamber in the tower. He is wounded, but I think not badly. Then came I here, with my lady as hostage. The Chevalier hath sworn an oath of submission, but I trust him not. Now I will invest the castle. It shall be my quarters, and thine. The town is quiet?"

"Ay. The people are amazed at thy clemency. All France thinks King Hal an ogre."

Simon rose.

"I must see Huntingdon. Where is he?"

"By the southern gate. His men bring the baggage into the town. Where wilt thou quarter thy men, Simon?"

"Some here. I make provision for the others this

168

day. Geoffrey, summon a score of thine own men-at-arms, and a score of the men of Beauvallet. I will have thee ride into the castle and make all ready. They will not offer ye resistance, for fear lest I should slay the Countess."

Geoffrey picked up his cap.

"Thou'lt not ride in thyself?"

"Nay, there is work for me here. Take what arms ye find, Geoffrey, and keep the court under close surveillance. I would confine the Chevalier, but that he submitted. Watch him. I will come later. Take Master Hubert for Alan," he added. "I trust not their French leech."

Geoffrey lounged out, yawning.

"Heigh-ho! When shall we be quit of this troublesome town, I wonder?" At the door he paused, and looked back at Simon.

"She is lovely enow, lad, but I like not that termagant beauty."

Simon drew the ink-horn towards him.

"Lovely? Oh, ay!"

"Thou hadst not remarked it?" An impish smile danced across Geoffrey's mouth. "Take heed lest she slight thee for Alan."

Simon's hand travelled slowly across the paper. He laughed.

"Holy Virgin! She would kill Alan with but a look. She will kill me an I watch her not."

"And dost thou admire the tigress, my brother?"

"Not I." He paused in his writing. "She is very brave," he added reflectively.

"She would have slain thee foully," Geoffrey said solemnly.

"Ay. She is a woman. Get thee gone, Geoffrey, and summon thy men."

"Oh, I go, I go! I leave thee to dream of thine Amazon."

Simon smiled.

"Ye leave me to quarter my men," he said.

VI

How the Lady Margaret could not stab him

The Lady Margaret sat on a raised dais, looking out of the window on to the bleak gardens of her castle. A fire burned at the far end of the chamber, and by it were gathered some four or five of her ladies, chattering together, and stitching at a length of canvas. The Lady Margaret sat with head averted and resting on her slender hand. She was dressed all in dull yellow, and her black hair lay over her shoulders in two great braids. A gold net covered her head and hung down to below her knees. Presently she sighed, and turned impatiently.

"Get thee gone, get thee gone!" she commanded petulantly. "Thy silly chattering goes through my head. Jeanne, stay with me."

The ladies departed softly, taking their work with them. The little lady who had smiled upon Geoffrey that day in the justice-house seated herself by the table, and looked up at her mistress gravely.

Margaret plucked nervously at her gown with fingers that quivered. Her delicate nostrils were a little dilated, and the long black eyes were troubled.

"Ay, thou art calm!" she said suddenly, and turned fiercely upon her companion. "Tell me how I may defeat this English bully!"

Jeanne folded her hands. A smile hovered about her mouth as she answered.

"Why, Margot, it seems that he is—a man."

"What mean you? A man! Ay, and an uncouth boor!"

"But still a man," nodded Jeanne de Faucourt. "He hath thy measure, Margot *chérie*."

"Ye think he will vanquish me? Ye think that?"

"Why, I know not! Perchance. For till now thou hast known no man."

Margaret sprang up and came down from the dais.

"Oh, ay, ay! Thou art at one with this bully! Geoffrey of Malvallet hath bewitched thee!"

Jeanne went a rosy red.

"Nay, madame!"

The Countess laughed angrily.

"Think ye I have no eyes? An Englishman! Thou!"

"He—he is very courtly, Margot," Jeanne pleaded.

"Very courtly! To march into my domain, disarming my servants, wassailing in my hall at Christmastide! Oh, he charms thine ears with compliments, I make no doubt! Soon ye will desert me entirely!"

"Madame!" Jeanne rose, trembling.

Margaret ran to her, and caught her in her arms.

"Nay, I meant it not! I—I am distraught with trouble! Jeanne, I did not say it! It was not me!"

Jeanne thrust her gently into a chair, bending over her and stroking her hands.

"Poor Margot! Poor Margot!" she crooned and drew the proud head to rest on her shoulder.

Margaret clung to her, sobbing for a space, but soon she disengaged herself and dashed her hand across her eyes.

"Cry! I! I—I have seldom done that, Jeannette."

"Thou art too war-like," Jeanne chided her, and knelt by the chair. "Margot, Margot, make thy submission! To what avail this tilting against Lord Simon? He hath the advantage of thee in that he is a man, and holds thy lands beyond recall. Be wise, mignonne! Be wise!"

"If I could but escape!" Margaret fretted. "If I could but reach Turincel!"

"Turincel! Why, *chérie*, it is ten leagues distant!"

"What matter? If I could reach it, Fernand de Turincel would aid me! Aid me to throw this Beauvallet out of my land!"

"Yes, Margot, yes, but thou canst not escape, and thou canst not journey ten leagues alone."

Up went the dark head.

"Ay, but that could I! Why, Jeanne, hast forgotten my strength?"

"But thou art a woman, *chérie*," Jeanne said gently.

"An Amazon!" Margaret came to her feet, eyes flashing. "He calls me that, the English tyrant! Well, I will show him what an Amazon can do!"

Jeanne sat back on her heels, staring meditatively into the fire.

"He is a strange man, this Lord of Beauvallet," she remarked. "His men do worship him, yet he is stern and silent. And he is tender with the children."

"Tender with the children? He would have slain them!"

"Sir Geoffrey told me, no. He is half-brother to Lord Simon, and he says that if any man maltreat a child, Lord Simon's hand is heavy upon that man."

"Lies, lies! He is cruel, I tell thee! Cruel!"

"Nay, he hath treated thee fairly, Margot."

The Countess swung round to face her, bosom heaving.

"Thou dost think that? What of this scar I bear upon my breast? Thou didst see him press his sword into my flesh! What of this bruise on my wrist? It is three weeks now since he gripped my arm, but still I bear the marks of his fingers!"

Jeanne looked up at her mistress.

"I think that scar will always remain," she said pensively.

"Ay! And so shall I always remember! I will not rest until I have avenged myself! Jeanne, Jeanne, have ye forgotten how he used me, under the eyes of mine own people? Have ye forgotten how he put me to shame in the open street?"

"Nay, none knew thee, and he said naught."

Up and down the room paced my lady, lashing herself into a fury.

"Would that I had slain his Alan! Thus should I have hurt him! Ay, to the quick! Ah, why did I seek to treat with him?"

"Ye could not have slain Sir Alan. Ye do know that, Margot."

"That could I! It was his threat that persuaded me!

An empty threat; thou sayst! I would I had laughed at it."

"He would have found another way," Jeanne said slowly. "He is not easily worsted, Margot."

"We will see!" The black eyes narrowed. "She-devil, he called me!"

A soft knock fell on the door. Jeanne rose to admit the Chevalier. Instantly Margaret's passion left her. The colour died out of her cheeks, and her mouth took on its haughty curve.

The Chevalier came bowing into the room.

"Sweet cousin, thou art well?"

"Well enough. What want ye, Victor?"

"Always so cold!" he languished. He watched Jeanne withdraw to the window, and came closer to his cousin. "The English bear grows careless, methinks. He sits writing in the hall with none to guard his back. For once his faithful squire is absent."

She was indifferent, moving away from him.

"I brought thee this, Margot," the Chevalier said softly. Into her hand he slid a dagger with a jewelled hilt.

Her lip curled.

"What would ye have me do with it?" She tossed it on to the table.

"Make thyself mistress yet again," he answered, watching her.

"Stab him in the back? Pah!"

The Chevalier shrugged, spreading out his hands.

"A woman 'gainst a man. What matter?"

She drew herself up, looking scorn upon him.

"Ye grow noisome, Victor. Stab him thyself, if thou wilt."

"Oh, I have submitted!" the Chevalier said nonchalantly. "Else would I surely stab him, and rid this land of his tyranny." He paused, and shot her a sidelong look. "Thou were not always so nice, sweet Margot. Perchance thou durst not essay this venture?"

That stung her.

"Durst not! Do ye think I fear Simon of Beauvallet?"

"He is very ruthless," the Chevalier answered. "But a quick stroke from behind. . . ."

"Ah, you sicken me!" she cried. "If I slay him 'twill not be from behind! Get thee gone from my room!"

The Chevalier walked mincingly to the door. He paused by the table as if to pick up the dagger.

"Leave it!" Margaret said sharply.

When he had gone, she swept to the table and hid the dagger in the bosom of her dress.

"I would be alone, Jeanne."

Jeanne rose, and without a word left the room. The door closed behind her, and once again the Lady Margaret fell to pacing the floor. At length she stopped, and drew the dagger from its hiding-place. Then, gathering her skirts close about her, so that they made no sound, she went to the door, and opened it. Before her the stone stairs led down to the great hall. Tiptoeing she approached them, and slowly descended.

In the middle of the hall Simon sat, his back turned towards her, writing. The scratching of his quill on the parchment was the only sound to be heard. He wore no armour, and his back was fair mark for an assassin's dagger.

The Lady Margaret paused on the bottom step, hardly daring to breathe. Cautiously she stepped down, her little, soft-slippered foot making no sound on the stone floor. Inch by inch she went forward, never taking her eyes from that fair head, her dagger held ready. She meant to creep up to him and to strike him above the heart before he could save himself. Her lips were slightly parted, but her hand was steady, despite the wild beating of her heart. Nearer and nearer she approached until she was but three paces from him.

Simon's hand travelled to and fro across the parchment. He did not lift his head. The silence seemed to grow, and still the Lady Margaret crept on. Then Simon spoke, his voice deep and calm.

"Strike where the neck joins the shoulder, my lady," he said, and went on writing.

The Lady Margaret started back, letting fall her skirts. Her hand flew to her cheek, and now it was trembling. Her face went white, and her eyes dilated. Of a sudden she had grown cold, and her knees threatened to give way.

Simon signed his name elaborately, and sprinkled sand over the parchment. Then, and then only, did he rise and face the Countess.

"Well, why do ye not strike?" he asked her. "I wear no shirt of mail, and I have told ye how to stab. Art thou afraid?" Then, as she did not answer, nor move, he strode forward under her petrified gaze, and folded his arms. "Strike, Margaret of Belrémy."

With a great effort she pulled herself together, setting her teeth. She lifted her dagger, her eyes riveted on his, but still she did not strike.

"Thy hand trembles," Simon jibed. He stretched out his arm, and closed his fingers round her wrist. "Here," he said, and brought her hand to his neck, so that the dagger pricked his tunic. "Push home, my lady."

"Loose me!" she whispered. "Loose me!"

Simon laughed, releasing her hand. Quickly she stepped back, stumbling over her train. The dagger tinkled to the ground.

"I—I—oh, one day I will do it!"

"Thou wilt never do it now, lady. The time is past, and thy courage forsook thee."

"No!"

"What then?"

"Oh, ye are a devil! a devil! How heard ye mine approach?"

Again he laughed.

"I heard ye not."

She stared, hands clasped at her breast. Simon looked her over.

"Think ye I would sit alone and unguarded in this place had I not the sense that warns me of danger? I have tested thine honour before, madame, and I take no risks."

She winced.

"Mine honour? What of thine own, Simon of Beauvallet? What honour has thou who will threaten a woman?"

"No threat, madame. The scar on thy breast shows whether I lie or not."

"I will pay ye for that, tenfold!" she cried. "Ye hold me captive, but ye shall see of what stuff Margaret of

Belrémy is made! Dearly shall ye rue the day ye sought to pit your strength 'gainst mine!"

Simon stirred the dagger with his foot.

"The means lies there, madame. Take up that plaything and sate your vengeance."

"Nay, I will meet thee on equal terms, milor'! At the head of mine army!"

"Ay, I have heard that ye lead your men into battle. Ye were better occupied in your stitchery, madame."

She laughed then, and came a step nearer to him.

"Were I so, my lord? Yet I did defeat Umfraville, and would have defeated you, had you not taken Belrémy by a trick!"

"It was thy wits against mine, madame, and my wits won the day."

"A coward's trick!"

"A ruse, madame, and one that beat you. I could have starved you into submission, but I chose the quickest road as always."

She flung back her head.

"Not yet have I submitted, Lord of Beauvallet!"

"Thou wilt submit."

"Ye know me not! Ye may do what ye will with me, but ye will kill me before I bend to you!"

"We shall see, madame. There are many things I can do to you, but I think ye are not worth it."

Colour flew into her cheeks.

"Thou insolent! Out of my way!" She caught up her train and would have gone up the stairway had not Alan blocked her path, coming slowly down. His arm still lay in a sling, but the bandage had been removed from his head. He wore his hair long to conceal the scar upon his temple.

"Your pardon, madame." He came down into the hall, and bowed to her.

Her eyes rested on his wounded arm for a moment, and travelled from there to his forehead.

"My men strike hard, Sir Alan, is it not so? They leave their mark. A little deeper, and that scar that mars thy beauty would have dispatched thee!"

A swift tread sounded behind her. Simon's hand

descended on her shoulder, pulling her round to face him.

"By the Rood, madame, I am minded to have thine arrogance whipped out of thee! Get thee gone to thine apartment, and let me see you no more today!"

"Simon, Simon!" Alan remonstrated.

Margaret laughed at him.

"The gentle knight would protect me from the English boor's wrath! I need no protection, Sir Alan! Had I that dagger now, ye were dead a minute since, Lord of Beauvallet! Take thy hand from my shoulder! I go when I will, and how I will, I'll have you know!"

"Ye go now," Simon said grimly. "Away with you, or I call my men to carry you to your apartments!"

"Oh, you—you——!" Margaret struck him furiously, on his stern mouth. Then she broke free, and ran quickly up the winding stairway to her chamber.

Alan drew a deep breath, looking at Simon.

"The termagant! Simon, what will you do with her?"

"Conquer her," Simon answered, and led him to a chair. "Sit, lad. The vixen, to taunt thee so!"

Alan smiled.

"I would not be alone with her for untold gold. Yesterday she braved Geoffrey so that he was trembling when he came to me, with anger and fear. He said she would have killed him had she a weapon to hand. She is like a tigress in her fierceness."

"She hath never met her master—until now. But I will school her."

Alan looked at him through half-closed eyes. He said nothing, but his smile grew.

Upstairs, Margaret had cast herself into Jeanne's arms in a fit of wild weeping.

"I could not slay him! I could not slay him! Oh, he is a devil, a devil! He knew that I was there, yet he heard me not! Oh, that I had had the strength to strike home. His fingers on my wrist—ah, was ever a woman so beset?"

"I knew thou couldst not slay him," Jeanne said calmly. "I saw thee creep down the stairway, but I feared not."

Margaret sprang away.

"Wait! Wait! I will do it yet, I swear! I will escape—I——" She stopped. "Ah, no! Thou wilt tell Sir Geoffrey. I had forget."

"Oh, my dear, my dear!" Jeanne cried, and flung her arms about her. "Would I betray thee? Not for an hundred Sir Geoffreys."

"He—deems me a creature of no account!" Margaret said tensely. "He scorns me because I am a woman. I will show him what a woman can do!"

VII

How he found Geoffrey and Jeanne on the terrace

On the broad terrace Jeanne sat sewing, a fur cloak about her plump form, for although the sun was shining it was but a wintry sun, and the day was frosty. To her came Malvallet, bedight in crimson velvet and gold lacing. Mademoiselle looked up, surveying him.

"Oh, fie!" she murmured and turned her head to gaze pensively at a robin. "The soldier turned popinjay, i' faith. He shames the sun." She picked up her needle again.

"This is cruelty," Geoffrey said mournfully, and sat down upon the parapet, facing her.

"Doubtless he will take a chill," Mademoiselle sighed. "Such cold stone!" She sent a fleeting glance towards the damp parapet.

"I wonder, will she be sorry?" Geoffrey asked the sky.

"He dreams of his English love," Mademoiselle nodded sagely.

"In truth, she is unkind today," Geoffrey said. "She doth not look at me."

"Oh, she hath no mind to be blinded!"

"Yet every time I do look into her eyes I am blinded and so bemused that I can see naught else for ever after."

"She must be very beautiful," Mademoiselle said. "This English maid."

"Not English yet," Geoffrey answered. "Please God I will make her so ere long."

Mademoiselle bit her thread.

"The gentleman is courageous indeed," she said, and bent again over her work.

For a time there was silence.

"Jeanne," Geoffrey said pleadingly.

Mademoiselle started.

"Oh, are ye here still?" she asked in innocent surprise.

Geoffrey came to her side and knelt. He stole one arm about her trim waist.

"Nay, Jeanne!"

"He will certainly be pricked," Jeanne said, plying her needle faster still.

His right hand imprisoned hers.

"Sweet, thou shalt not torment me. Listen, and I will tell thee of my lady-love."

Mademoiselle gazed blankly before her. A provocative smile lingered about her lips.

"I might call for help," she mused.

"Nay, I need none," Geoffrey answered promptly. "This lady, sweet, is little and lovely. So little that I might hide her in my pocket and forget that she was there."

"This is English gallantry," sighed Jeanne. "Poor lady!"

"Not 'poor', Jeanne, for she hath all a man's heart."

"Which is so little," quoth she, "that she slipped it into her bag and forgot that it was there. Hey-day!"

"But even though she forgot, being cruel, it still remained, braving her coldness and her tauntings, and waiting very humbly till she should grow kind."

"A craven, cringing heart, wasting its life."

"Nay, for although it was humble, it kept a close watch on the lady. And even though she scorned and flouted it, it made solemn oath unto itself that it would devote its whole life to guarding her welfare and her happiness."

"Why, then, it was a busy heart, for doubtless it had sworn that oath many a time before."

"Not so, Jeanne, for before it was asleep."

"Oh, grammercy, was this its calf-love then?"

"All its love, lady. It knew none before it beheld the little lady with the big blue eyes and the pretty dimples. A French maid, Jeanne, with brown curls and a cruel tongue."

"A spitfire, forsooth!"

"Just a wilful maid."

"And French." Jeanne nodded dreamily. "An enemy. Indeed, I am sorry for this heart."

Geoffrey's arm tightened about her.

"The heart is happy enough, Jeanne, but what of its owner! It left him to serve the lady, and now he hath none."

"It was so little that he would scarce notice its absence," Jeanne said.

"But he does indeed notice it, and though he would not have it return to him, he would fain have the lady's heart in its place."

"Oh, it would freeze him, sir!"

"He might warm it, sweet."

"Nay, for he is English, and the lady's foe. And mayhap the lady's heart has been given elsewhere."

Geoffrey rose.

"Now I know why she is cold," he said. "Her heart was gone already, so that she had none to give this Englishman. So he left her—with his heart."

Jeanne inspected her stitchery.

"Perhaps, after all—it was still a virgin heart," she said softly. "The—the lady's, I mean."

Geoffrey came back.

"And might it be won, Jeanne?" he asked.

She bent lower still over her work, and the long lashes veiled her eyes.

"By an English foe, sir?"

"By an English lover, Jeanne."

She poised her needle, looking at it intently.

"Nay. It could not be won."

"Never?"

"Never. You see, sir, it was a cold, cruel heart, and it repulsed all its suitors. And—and it was a shy heart—but true. So—so one day—it left the lady—very secretly, so that at first she did not know that it had gone, and—and slipped into a man's pocket. And—when the lady—tried to recall it—it would not come, but nestled down in its hiding place. But—but it was such a timid little heart, that the man—he was a great, stupid Englishman—never knew that it was in his pocket, but besought the lady to give it to him. He was so blinded, you see—and just an English conqueror."

"An English slave," Geoffrey said, and knelt again, his arms about her. "A suppliant at the little lady's feet."

"But he was very strong and masterful withal," Jeanne murmured, and let her stitchery fall. "And—and clad in crimson velvet which he knew became him well. A conceited popinjay, sir."

Geoffrey drew her to rest against his shoulder.

"Nay, for he doffed his work-a-day clothes and donned the crimson velvet only to do his lady honour."

"A peacock preening himself to dazzle the hen," Jeanne replied, and smoothed her russet gown.

"She was such a pretty hen that he decked himself in velvet so not to show himself a drab fellow beside her loveliness."

"Oh, I do not think he was very drab," Jeanne said into his ear. "In his steel armour with the black plumes in his helm, and the black surcoat floating from his shoulders, and his great sword in hand—he—he was a fine figure."

"When saw ye me thus, Jeanne?"

"From the tower window, sir. And I hated you. You and your leader, the icy Lord of Beauvallet."

"And Alan?"

"Alan? Oh—well, he was my lady's prisoner—and one does not hate a helpless man. And—and indeed he makes pretty love to a maid." Unseen, she smiled.

"Doth he so?" Geoffrey turned her face up, a hand

181

beneath her chin. "I will speak with Master Alan. Is his love-making so pretty as mine?" He kissed her red lips.

"Prettier by far," Jeanne retorted, when she could. "For he did not squeeze me brutally, nor take advantage of my loneliness."

"Why he is but half a man, then," Geoffrey answered, and kissed her again.

Her bosom rose and fell quickly; she returned his kisses for a while, then struggled to be free of him, her neck and cheeks a rosy red.

"Oh, but we are traitors, both!" she cried, and set her hands on his breast, thrusting him away.

"Traitors, sweet? Why?"

"Thou to the Lord of Beauvallet, I to the Lady Margaret! While these two stay at enmity I must cleave to the one, and thou to the other."

"The Lady Margaret will make her submission," Geoffrey said.

"Ah, you do not know her! She hath never bent the knee yet. I have been with her since childhood, and—and I know how strong is her will."

"Fifteen years have I known Simon," Geoffrey answered, "and I have yet to see him beaten."

"But now he is pitted 'gainst a woman, and therefore is defenceless, for what weapons can he use? I tell thee, Geoffrey, ever since my lady's father died, she hath ruled supreme. She will never bend, least of all before an Englishman."

"In truth, the Lady Margaret is an Amazon," Geoffrey said ruefully. "I mislike these tigress-women."

"That is not true!" Jeanne cried hotly. "She is the sweetest, dearest lady! She shows herself tigerish to you, because you seek to conquer her!"

"Not I!" Geoffrey grimaced. "I do not willingly cross her path."

"She is brave and proud! But to her own people she is, oh, so kind and just!"

"Beshrew me, I am glad that I am not of her people."

"Sir," said Jeanne coldly, "loose me!"

Geoffrey kissed her averted cheek.

"Nay, I meant not to anger thee, my dear. The Lady Margaret is what you will. I care not. No woman is aught to me save one."

Jeanne pushed him away.

"Geoffrey, loose me! Here comes thy lord! Oh, rise, thou great stupid!"

Along the terrace Simon was coming, capless, and Jeanne glanced from his face to Geoffrey's.

"In truth ye are much alike," she said. "But the one is 'beau' and the other is 'mal'."

"We are half-brothers," Geoffrey told her. He turned to greet Simon. "Hast need of me, lad?"

Simon bowed awkwardly to Mademoiselle.

"Nay. I thought Alan was here. I ask your pardon for my intrusion."

In the depths of his strange eyes Jeanne saw a twinkle. She blushed, sewing quicker than ever.

"I have seen not Alan. What's amiss?"

"He bears the title, Master of the Horse," Simon said with heavy sarcasm. "I would have him attend to his affairs."

Jeanne spoke demurely.

"Methinks Sir Alan is in the western hall, milor'."

Geoffrey chuckled, for the Lady Margaret's ladies often sat there.

"Who is the charmer, my Jeanne?" he asked.

A frown reproved him.

"I believe it is Mademoiselle Yvonne de Vertimaine," Jeanne answered.

"Wilt fetch him for me, Geoffrey?" Simon said. "Ye will find me here."

Geoffrey smiled.

"Simon, do ye fear to enter the ladies' bower?"

"I would not rob you of that sweet delight," Simon answered. "Go, Geoffrey. I will bear Mademoiselle company."

"Thank you!" Geoffrey bowed ironically, and sauntered away down the terrace.

Jeanne found her heart beating rather fast. She had been present when Simon had captured her mistress, and she had accompanied Margaret to the English camp. Both of these experiences left her very nervous

183

of Simon. Now he sat down upon the parapet, looking at her.

"So ye have captured my captain's heart, mademoiselle," he said slowly.

Jeanne looked at him. He was smiling down at her pleasantly, and she plucked up her courage.

"No, sir. He gave it to me."

"It is all one. I take it you and he will walk to the altar soon?"

Jeanne shook her head.

"It cannot be, milor'."

"Ah?"

"I serve the Countess."

"I see," said Simon. "Yet when I have quelled this turbulent lady, what then?"

"Ye will not do it, milor'," she said confidently.

"Shall I not? I might ask thine aid."

She paused in her stitching, and looked him steadily between the eyes.

"Ye would be ill-advised, sir."

"Oh?" He raised his brows. "Like mistress like maid, is it?"

"Ay, sir."

"Not all Malvallet's pleadings will make thee change thy mind?"

"Sir Geoffrey, milor', would be the last to have me turn traitor."

"I but ask thy persuasion, lady."

"You ask in vain, sir."

"So? Then let me tell thee, mademoiselle, that if the Lady Margaret cannot be persuaded, she may yet be coerced."

"Oh, brave!" Jeanne exclaimed scornfully.

"It is in my power," Simon said imperturbably, "to execute the Countess. Hast thou thought of that, I wonder?"

"Ye would have all Belrémy about your ears, like hornets," she answered.

"It would not worry me. If I have not the Lady Margaret's submission soon, I shall be forced to take stronger measures. Let her take heed, for I mean what I say."

"I doubt it not." Jeanne eyed him for a moment. "Yet would ye not slay the Countess, for ye are English, and I have heard that their justice is great."

"As ye shall see," Simon answered grimly.

"And—and do ye war on women?" Jeanne asked.

"Ay, if need be."

"It is very sad," she sighed.

VIII

How the Lady Margaret plotted

The Lady Margaret sat with some of her ladies in her audience-chamber. A dark-eyed page was at her feet, playing on a small harp, and Jeanne sat beside her. Margaret lay back at her ease, a splendid figure against the fur-skin that covered her chair. At the far end of the room some gentlemen stood, conversing together; the Chevalier leaned over the back of his cousin's chair, whispering occasionally in her ear. She paid little heed to his sallies, but now and then jerked her shoulder impatiently, and frowned.

"Art cold today, sweet cousin," the Chevalier whispered.

"I have not changed, Victor," she answered curtly. "You weary me."

"But one day, fairest, you will change? Shall I never find the way to thy heart?"

"At a distance I might like you better," she said.

"Cruel, cruel! Ah, Margot, if ye would but smile upon me, what might not we do to oust this English boor?"

Her lip curled.

"I need no help from you, Victor."

His voice sank lower.

"No, *ma belle*? Yet thou didst not slay him when I gave thee the chance."

She flushed, tapping her foot on the floor.

"I told you that I would not."

"And thou didst not essay it?" he purred. "How then came my dagger upon the floor in the great hall?"

"Oh, go, go!" she said quickly. "I would not kill him, because—because—I will—find a surer way."

He drew himself upright, still smiling.

"Is it indeed so, Margot? Now I had thought. . . . Ah, well!" Sighing, he strolled out, and the Countess gave a little shiver.

Slowly the colour died from her cheeks. She turned to her page, laying a caressing hand on his shoulder.

"Thy song is joyous today, Léon."

He looked up at her, eyes a-sparkle.

"Yes, madame. I am gay because the English lord hath granted me a pass out of the castle. I go to see my father, without the town."

The long fingers on his shoulder gripped suddenly. Surprised, he looked up again, into the beautiful face bent over him, and saw it pale, lips slightly parted, and eyes shining.

"Is—no pass needed to leave the town?" Margaret asked softly.

"Nay, madame, for the town hath submitted."

He heard the quick intake of her breath, and wondered.

"Léon, when wilt thou go?"

"Tomorrow, madame, if it please you."

"And—and where is thy—pass?"

He patted his tunic.

"Safe here, madame. My lord signed it today."

"Léon——" Margaret spoke in a whisper—"Thou dost love me, is it not so?"

"But yes, madame! I would die——"

"Then come to my room presently—with—with thy pass. And say naught, Léon! Say naught!"

"Yes, madame," he answered obediently, but his eyes searched her face in mystification.

She leaned back, and in a moment had called one of the courtiers to her side, laughing gaily, and chattering with him, so that Jeanne glanced at her shrewdly more than once. Presently she rose, brushing her hand across her eyes.

"Ah, now I am tired, and have the migraine! Come with me, Jeanne." She went out slowly, leaning on Jeanne's arm. Never a word spake Mademoiselle until the door of my lady's chamber was closed behind them. Then she turned to Margaret, taking her hand.

"Margot, what dost thou purpose?" she asked anxiously.

Tense fingers clutched at her wrists.

"Jeanne, you swear—you swear to stand my friend?"

"But *chérie!* Can you ask?"

"This Geoffrey——" Jealous, suspicious eyes glared into hers—"you would not betray me to him? You would not?"

"Never! Margot, what ails thee? Tell me, please! What said you to Léon?"

"Jeanne—I—I *trust* thee!"

"And so thou mayst."

"Then listen!" Margaret dragged her to a seat. "Léon hath a pass! To go from the castle tomorrow. You see? Tell me now, am I not a little like him?" With a quick movement she was at her looking-glass, gazing close upon herself. "Black eyes, the nose—well, no. Mine is more straight. Lips? Too haughty, Margot dear. No matter. Let us essay a glad smile. Ay, it will suffice. Enough for this Simon. A cap pulled low over my brow. Height?" She drew herself up. "I will measure me 'gainst Léon." She swept about, clasping her hands, eyes a-brim with triumphant laughter. "Jeanne, shall I not make a pretty page?"

Jeanne started up.

"Margot, what wouldst thou be at?"

"I would go to Fernand de Turincel. Nay, but listen! A page-boy excites no suspicion. Ten leagues. I might find a horse. It shall be given out here that I am sick a-bed. Even an I walk to Turincel I can reach it within three days. Yes, yes, I can! Oh, Jeanne, shake not thy head!"

"*Chérie*, thou art distraught! Bethink ye, it is all too

perilous an emprise for a maid. I could not let thee try it. Ah, *mignonne, mignonne,* I could not!"

"Thou shalt come with me then! As—as—my sister! Smile, Jeannette! It means escape, and help!"

"But the danger——"

"Pho! Have I not my dagger? If thou art afraid, I'll not take thee, but go alone. Thou hast sworn to stand my friend."

"Margot, thou canst not do it!" Jeanne cried. "Would you don boy's raiment? Margot!"

"That would I!" laughed the Countess, and drew back her skirts to show her tapering foot. Smiling she regarded first it, and then her lady. "Too small, you think? But long, Jeanne. And—and a shapely leg."

"Margot!" almost wailed Jeanne. "Thou—thou art mad!"

"I was never more sane!——There is Léon! Open, child!"

Jeanne crept to the door, and admitted the handsome page.

"Ah, the good Léon!" Margaret gave him her hand to kiss. "Léon, thou wilt help me?"

"Yes, madame, of course. But I do not understand——"

"Am I not about to tell thee? Léon, swear not to divulge what I shall say to any living soul! Not even my cousin. Swear!"

"I swear, madame."

"Thou sweet boy! I want thy pass. Quick, let me see it!"

He gave it to her, staring. The Countess spread it out.

"The secretary writes plain," she remarked. " 'Léon de Margrute. . . . This is mine order, Simon Beauvallet.' *Dieu,* what a flourish! Léon, I want this pass! I escape from the castle tomorrow. Thou art in my plot now!"

"But, madame, you cannot——"

"And a suit of thine apparel. Hose, tunic——Oh, I'll spare thy blushes, Jeannette! Bring me them secretly, Léon, tonight. Ah, Léon, thou wilt do it? I *ask* thy help!"

He bowed.

"Madame, I must obey. But indeed, indeed——"

She covered her ears.

"I will not listen! Keep close tomorrow, my Léon, so that they shall not wonder at thy presence here. And—and see ye choose me a plain, dark dress, with a cap to set on my head. Go now and fetch it, dear boy! I'll reward thee for thy pains. Oh, and thou shalt have another pass when I return! No need of it then, perhaps."

The astonished page retreated. Jeanne sank down on to a chair.

"Margot," she began weakly, and stopped. "Oh, Margot!"

The Countess picked up a quill and dipped it in the ink.

"See, Jeanne, there is room to add 'and sister'. Think you I can copy this fist? Give me parchment!"

Jeanne brought it, and watched her mistress practise writing on it. At length Margaret wrote upon the pass, and sat back surveying her handiwork.

" 'Tis marvellous. Let it dry, Jeanne, my sister. Aha, Simon of Beauvallet, how now?"

"We are not yet escaped," Jeanne said drily.

"But we shall escape, very early. Look out thine oldest dress, *petite*, and wear a hood and cloak. Oh, I should have written 'brother', and we could have been boys together."

"Heaven forbid!" Jeanne shuddered.

The black eyes sparkled.

"Conceive Malvallet's face of horror! Oh, la, la! In truth, thou art too small for the part, and all a woman. Now I"—she glanced down herself—"I am a thin creature—well, thin enough, and tall. I shall make a comely lad. . . . Enter, Léon! Enter!"

Back into the room came the page. Blushing, he laid a neat bundle on the table.

"I—think—I have forgot naught," he stammered.

"Thou dear boy!" Margaret kissed him on both cheeks. "There! Keep my secret well, Léon, and thank you, thank you, thank you!"

No sooner had he left the room than she untied the bundle, holding up each garment in turn.

"Oh, the brave hose! See, Jeanne! . . . A cap—the tunic, the—oh, the trunks!" She went off into a peal of laughter, and let them fall. "Go away, Jeannette, into my closet! And—and come when I call!"

Jeanne crawled away into the outer chamber. There followed a long pause, punctuated by gurgles of merriment from within my lady's chamber. At last Margaret called to her, and she went back into the room.

Before the looking-glass stood a slim stripling in a short brown tunic, a dagger in his belt, and a cap crammed down over his eyes. Long shapely legs were cased in brown hose, and set well apart. Margaret swaggered forward.

"Am I not brave? Sister, I salute thee! These clothes make me smaller, but 'tis no matter. Jeanne, Jeanne, look not so horrified!"

"Margot, for God's sake!" implored Jeanne. "Thy—thy *legs!*"

Margaret inspected them, and cut a caper.

"Said I not that they were shapely? See what a fine calf I have! I must stuff the shoes a little to make them fit, but otherwise it is perfect. The high collar hides my throat, too, which is well. Would it be well to cut my hair, think ye?"

"No!" gasped Jeanne. "A thousand times, no!"

Margaret pulled off her cap, revealing the dark braids bound round and round her shapely little head.

"It might be safer," she reflected. "I cannot wear my cap always, and perhaps it might give rise to suspicion. What was it my father said?—'See thou dost always set about thine affairs thoroughly, and do not the half only of a thing.' Give me the scissors!"

"Margot, I implore thee, do not! Thy lovely hair! I—I *will* not countenance it."

The Countess stood irresolute.

"It—it is—very nice hair," she said undecidedly. "I doubt it would grow but slowly."

"Half thy beauty goes with it!" Jeanne said vehemently.

Margaret looked at her seriously.

"Thou dost indeed think that, Jeannette?"

"Yes, yes! Margot, it would be wicked to cut it off!"

"It is to my knees almost. Well, perhaps I will leave it." On went the cap again. "Wouldst thou know me, Jeanne? Speak truly!"

"Scarcely." Jeanne walked round her, inspecting. "Thou art suddenly so little. I had thought thee tall."

"So am I, but this raiment dwarfs me. The face, Jeanne! the face!"

Jeanne stepped back, looking into the Countess's face with narrowed eyes.

"I should know thee, of course. But mayhap I should need to look twice."

"Would Simon of Beauvallet know me?"

"They call him the Lynx-Eyed," Jeanne said dubiously. "And yet—without thy horned head-dress, or thy long braids and veil—yes, thou art different."

"Summon Hélène," commanded my lady. "I can trust her, and we will see if she knows me at once."

Jeanne departed, presently returning with Mademoiselle de Courvonne. Margaret was standing before the fire, arms akimbo, and the long point of her cap drawn down over her shoulder, so that it hid the right side of her face a little.

Mademoiselle cast her a fleeting glance, and on encountering a wicked wink, blushed hotly, and turned her back.

"Where is Madame?" she asked Jeanne. "What does the page here?"

Margaret walked forward, striding nobly, and put her arm about Mademoiselle's waist. The girl recoiled.

"Sirrah!"

"Speak me fair, speak me fair!" Margaret adjured her.

"Madame!" Mademoiselle fell back a pace, hands clasped at her breast. *"Madame!"*

Margaret swept her a bow.

"Am I not a pretty page, sweet chuck?" she smiled.

"Mon Dieu!" gasped Hélène. "But—but wherefore?"

Margaret told her, and the lady in waiting's eyes grew rounder and rounder. Before she could exclaim or expostulate, however, a knock fell on the door of the adjoining closet.

"Who——? That is not my cousin's knock, but a . . . Go, Jeanne!"

Jeanne slipped softly away, closing the door behind her. Margaret tiptoed to it, listening. There came the sound of voices, one deep and forceful.

"Beauvallet!" Margaret slid away from the door. "What can he want?"

Back came Jeanne, and whispered:

"I have told him that you are abed. Get thee between sheets, madame, quickly!"

"But what doth he want?"

"Naught, I think. He hath not seen you this day."

Margaret pulled her hair down, and skipped into bed, drawing the clothes up under her chin.

"Tell him I am aweary. Why should he wish to see me?"

"I wonder?" said Jeanne, who had her suspicions. She went out again to Simon. "Madame will see you if it is necessary, milor', but she bids me say that she is aweary."

"I am sorry to trouble madame," Simon answered, "but there is that I would say to her."

"*Eh bien!*" Jeanne shrugged daintily, and allowed him to pass into the Countess's chamber.

From the great bed Margaret regarded him haughtily.

"Am I to have no privacy, sir?" she inquired.

Simon, strangely ill-at-ease in these unaccustomed surroundings, bowed, and answered awkwardly.

"I cry your pardon, madame, but I may not see ye tomorrow. I go out to Sal-de-lac, where I shall rest three days. I am come now to say that during mine absence ye will please to keep your rooms. Ye will pardon my discourtesy, but a guard will be set upon these rooms from noon tomorrow, when I depart."

The Lady Margaret's eyes flashed dangerously.

"Your insolence passes all bounds, sir!"

Simon smiled.

"Mayhap, madame. Your ladies may come to you, but you may not go out."

"A prisoner in mine own castle! Get thee hence, Lord of Beauvallet!"

But when Simon had gone, she sprang up, flushed and excited.

"It could not be better! It could not be better! Malvallet will command in his absence, and he would not dare to force himself upon me! None will notice mine escape, and all but Hélène here, and—and—Amélie, or Isabelle, must think that I am sick. Oh, it is marvellous, marvellous! We will leave this place at four in the morning, Jeannette, thou and I!"

"God pity me!" Jeanne sighed, and turned her eyes away from the Lady Margaret's attire with a shudder.

IX

How the Lady Margaret escaped

The Lady Margaret tramped blithely along the high road, a knapsack slung over her shoulder, and a staff in her hand. Beside her trudged Mademoiselle Jeanne, very weary, and very nervous. She wore a kerchief over her curls, and a cloak wrapped round her form. She, too, carried a staff, but whereas the Lady Margaret swung hers boldly and stepped out with a will, Jeanne's little feet stumbled often over the stones, and she leaned heavily on her staff.

"Sister," said the Lady Margaret, "how many leagues think ye we have covered?"

"An hundred," Jeanne answered with feeling.

"Nay, I think not. Let me see. We did leave Belrémy at half after four—Jeanne, was it not easy? Not one of those great oafs of English guards suspected, and Lord Simon was nowhere to be seen! Then we walked to Balderin, which is two and a half leagues distant from Belrémy, and it was eight of the clock. How long did we spend at the tavern where we breakfasted?"

"Five minutes," sighed Jeanne.

"Nay, I think it was half-an-hour. Jeanne, did I not swagger well? And—and kissed the wench who served us!"

Jeanne shivered.

"My heart was in my mouth. Thou wert—thou wert—*terrible!*"

Margaret laughed.

"I was wonderful. Just a pert page-boy. Well, when we left Balderin we went onward to Razincourt. And then it was a little after eleven, was it not?"

"That village! Ugh! The tavern! Oh, *mon Dieu!*"

"And the drunken peasant who would have clouted me for a saucy knave had he not stumbled over the chair." Margaret gave a little skip, chuckling light-heartedly. "We ate dinner there, and I drank sack," she grimaced. "Some of it I managed to spill," she added pensively. "I think we remained there an hour. The dinner was not—very nice, was it?"

Jeanne closed her eyes for a moment.

"The meat . . ." she moaned.

"I know. Well, after that we did walk on and on—on——"

"And on and on and on."

"Thou silly Jeannette!—till we came to the brook. And there we rested a while. And now we are here, and I wonder where it may be?"

"Where what may be?"

"Here," said the Lady Margaret, embracing the whole countryside. "I had planned to rest the night at Tourdelonne. It is a tiny village, my poor Jeanne, and mayhap we shall sleep in the stable. What is the time, I wonder? It must be after three."

"Long after three. We have been walking for hours."

"It has not seemed so to me. But if we have, then Tourdelonne must be near. And when we are there we shall have covered five leagues, Jeannette, and another day will see us at Turincel."

Jeanne wilted.

"We—we must walk tomorrow—as much as today?" she asked.

"It is wiser," nodded the Lady Margaret firmly. "Oh,

194

Simon of Beauvallet, ye shall rue the day ye sought to quell Margaret of Belrémy!"

"I do trust we shall not rue the day we sought to escape from Simon of Beauvallet," Jeanne said peevishly. "My feet are raw and blistered."

"Thou poor little one!" Margaret slipped an arm in hers. "Lean on me, Jeannette. I should not have brought thee. It was thoughtless and cruel! Thou hast not my strength!"

Jeanne pulled herself together.

"Nay, I am well enough, Margot. Shall—shall we have to sleep—in the common room, think you?"

"I do not know. Perhaps we may find two rooms. One for you, at least."

Jeanne clutched her arm.

"Margot, we must not be separated!" she implored.

Margaret drew her arched brows together.

"I must see what I can do," she said. "Perhaps if I say that thou art sick, they would give thee a chamber, and I could steal into it when none is watching. It is too cold to sleep in the woods, alack!"

"Sleep in the woods!" Jeanne almost shrieked. "Margot!"

"But it is impossible in this weather," Margaret assured her. "Ah, look ahead! I see houses!"

"Hovels!"

"Tourdelonne!"

"I could welcome my Geoffrey," sighed Jeanne. "Even though he were in a rage with me." Her face brightened. "I wonder, is he very terrible when he is angered?" For a time she pondered this question deeply. "I think he might be," she said at length, and nodded, pleased.

"If ever ye take him to husband he will assuredly beat thee," Margaret remarked. "Because he is English."

"Oh, dost thou think so?" Jeanne stepped out more briskly. "He might, of course, and yet . . . no, I think he is too gentle and kind. But very masterful. I wonder what he will say when he finds me gone?" She dimpled a little.

"I wonder what he will say when I bring Turincel about his ears?" Margaret said viciously.

"Ah no, Margot! You—you must not! Kill—Lord Simon, if you will—but—but not Geoffrey!"

"Never fear." Margaret patted her shoulder. "Thou shalt have him as thy prisoner."

"Then I shall not like it at all," said Jeanne decidedly.

"What! Dost thou like to be his prisoner?"

"Yes, I do," Jeanne said.

Margaret's lip curled.

"An English tyrant's prisoner! *Mon Dieu*, where is thy spirit?"

"It went when I fell in love with Geoffrey," Jeanne answered. "One day thou wilt understand."

"God grant that day be long in coming!" Margaret cried.

They were come now to the straggling hamlet, and they halted before the rude tavern. From within came the sound of men's voices, laughing noisily. Jeanne shrank a little closer to the Countess.

"Margot—must we——!"

"We must," Margaret said resolutely, and drew a deep breath. She knocked loudly on the door, and took a firm hold on her staff.

Presently the door was opened, and the landlord faced them, clad in a soiled leather jerkin.

"Good sir," began Margaret, as deeply as she was able, "my sister and I journey to Joulinceaulx for the festival. Have ye room for the night?"

"No," said the landlord uncompromisingly, and would have shut the door, but that Margaret set her foot within.

"But listen, good host, my—my father gave me a little money for the journey, and I can pay for our lodging."

The landlord seemed undecided, but Jeanne, plucking up courage, clinched the matter.

"Oh, sir, do not turn us away! Indeed, I am weary, and hungry. Could ye let us sleep in the loft above the stable, perhaps?" She smiled wistfully upon him.

"Well, come within," he grunted. "But I'll see thy money first!" he added, turning truculently upon Margaret.

She pulled out a gold piece, and gave it him. His

eyes shone greedily, and he pocketed it, beckoning them in.

The kitchen was very hot, and smelt of sack. Some half-a-dozen men were sprawled about a large table, upon which supper was laid. When they saw Jeanne one or two of them sat up, smirking, but for the most part they paid no heed to the newcomers.

As unobtrusively as possible the two girls slipped into their places at the table. Margaret pushed her shrinking companion on to a stool at the end of the table, and seated herself beside her, in between Jeanne and a burly fellow with a ferocious red beard. The landlord thrust two wooden platters of salt-beef before them, and some coarse bread. Hungry as she was, Jeanne's dainty palate turned from the unappetizing, ill-cooked and badly served food, but she made shift to eat, choking down her repulsion. Margaret, who was made of sterner stuff, betrayed no disgust at the rude fare, but fell to with a will. One of the men sitting opposite eyed Jeanne curiously, so that she blushed, and kept her eyes lowered.

"Yon wench picks at her food," remarked her tormentor. "A dainty maid!"

"My sister is not strong," Margaret said quickly. "She hath no appetite."

"The food is good enough," growled their host. "If it is not to thy liking——"

"It is good indeed," Margaret made haste to assure him. "Is it not, Jeanne?"

"Yes, Léon. Very good," Jeanne answered in a small voice.

"Perchance thy sister is used to richly cooked meats?" sneered the landlord, unconvinced that his guests were not slighting his culinary efforts.

Margaret nodded.

"My sister is serving-maid to the Lady Margaret of Belrémy," she said daringly, and heard Jeanne gasp beside her.

There was a guffaw of laughter.

"That for a tale!" jeered the man opposite. "Thou pert youngster!"

Margaret's neighbour leaned across her to stare at Jeanne, whose hands began to tremble.

"Well, she is pale enough," he rumbled. "Thy hands are too white, lass. Thou dost not labour on the fields, i' faith."

"She is my lady's tiring-woman," Margaret said.

A little stir went round the table.

"And what art thou, springald?" asked one. "Page, belike, with thy grand tunic?"

"Page indeed," nodded Margaret. "My lady hath given us leave of absence to—to journey to Joulinceaulx for the festival."

"And what may be thy name?" inquired the red-bearded man.

"Léon Margrute," Margaret answered promptly.

The landlord came to the table.

"The accursed English are in Belrémy, is it not so?" he asked.

"Ay." Margaret's eyes flashed.

"What does thy lady?"

"She is prisoner."

"Ho-ho!" The man opposite Jeanne clapped his hands to his sides. "The proud countess prisoner! Ho-ho! There's for her and her hot blood!"

Jeanne laid an imploring hand on Margaret's arm, for the Countess had grown suddenly stiff. She recovered herself, and forced a laugh.

"Hast seen my lady, then?" she asked.

"Once, when she rode out with her fine court. A haughty maid, indeed! Men say that she leads her men into battle. There's a shrew!"

"She—she did so once," Margaret admitted. "And well they fought!"

"Riding astride her horse, clad in armour! A forward, masterless wench!"

Someone cracked a lewd joke, and Margaret's cheeks became scarlet with fury. The red-bearded man grinned.

"See the young turkey-cock! Perchance thou dost love thy lady, Léon Margrute?"

"That do I!"

"And is she kind to thee?"

The colour died out of Margaret's face. She laughed.

198

"Oh, she is sometimes kind, and sometimes cruel."

He nodded sympathetically.

"Ay, ay! 'Tis ever thus with these noble dames. But surely thou art over-young, lad?"

Certainly she looked it in her boy's gear, though in reality she numbered twenty-five summers.

"I—oh, I am—seventeen," she stammered.

"And thy pretty sister?" asked the man before Jeanne, leaning over the table to leer into her face.

Jeanne shrank back, gripping her fingers together.

"Eighteen," Margaret answered. "Be good enough to sit back, sir. Ye discommode my sister."

"Thou saucy knave! Is thy sister so nice then, that an honest man——"

"Let be, let be!" growled Margaret's burly neighbour. "The maid is tired."

"Too tired to kiss?" the tormentor grinned, and lurched forward across the table.

Jeanne gave a tiny cry, but Margaret was on her feet in a trice, dagger in hand.

"Keep off, sirrah!" she commanded. "My dagger is sharp."

On the instant there was an outcry, and three men scrambled up and would have come at Margaret had not the red-bearded giant interposed his huge frame.

"Tush! Sit ye down, Jacques and Louis! 'Tis but a lad. Let the girl be, Founard!"

"I would teach the pert knave to speak his elders fair," grumbled one, but he sat down again. "Thou art too soft, Ranaud."

Ranaud thrust Margaret into her seat.

"Put up thy dagger, foolish pup, else I will let them at thee."

"I'll have no brawling here!" the landlord cried. "Out ye go, young sir, and your sister with ye! Thy pretty ways and mincing tongue!"

Ranaud brought his great fist down on the table so that the platters jumped.

"Let be, I say!" he roared. "God's Wounds, what is this pother? If the wench is modest, why, the better for her! I'll crack thy skull for thee, fat host!"

The landlord drew back muttering, for Ranaud was

too formidable for his taste. The discontent subsided gradually, and in a little while Margaret took Jeanne's hand and rose.

"Good sir," she said, addressing the landlord. "Wilt show us the way to the stable-loft?"

"I have no room. Hast eaten. Go now."

"Nay, I prithee——"

Up got Ranaud, his little eyes blazing fiercely.

"Have I to teach thee a lesson in manners?" he thundered, and the landlord retreated.

"I will show thee, I will show thee!" he said hastily.

"And I will come too," said Ranaud.

Out they went into the fast-gathering gloom, the landlord hurrying nervously before them, Jeanne clinging to Margaret's hand, and Ranaud striding along beside them, towering over all. So they came to the tumble-down stable, and with a muttered word that they would find the ladder into the barn in place, the landlord went away.

Margaret turned to the kindly giant.

"I have to thank thee, sir, for thy protection," she began. "Indeed——"

"It is naught. Up with ye into the loft, and bolt the trap, youngster. Mayhap I will accompany thee part of the way to Joulinceaulx. All ways are one to me."

"Why, it is—it is very kind," Margaret said nervously, "but——"

"It is not your goal, belike?" Ranaud asked shrewdly.

"I—of course it is—I mean——"

"Oh, I am not curious!" he answered. "Go thy way if ye will, but I am a masterless man, and I have taken a fancy to thee. Art over-young to go wandering over the country alone with thy sister."

"You—would come with us?" Margaret asked uncertainly.

"Ay, if ye will. There are a-many rogues about, and mayhap ye will be robbed or killed. If we join company I can guard thee from such. Ye can trust me."

"Indeed, I think so," Margaret said, and put out her hand. "May—may we speak more of this in the morning?"

"Ay, if ye will." Margaret's hand was lost in a gigantic paw. "Get thee to rest now. And bolt the trap."

"I will," she promised. "I thank you, sir."

She and Jeanne climbed cautiously up the worm-eaten ladder into the loft.

"Oh, how dark!" quavered Jeanne. "Was—was that a rat?"

From below came Ranaud's deep voice.

"If the lass is affrighted I will fetch a lantern."

"Oh, thank you!" Jeanne said fervently.

Heavy footsteps were heard retreating. After a short pause they came back again, and Ranaud mounted the ladder, bearing a lantern.

"It will last the night if ye burn it low," he told Margaret.

By its feeble light they saw a heap of straw in one corner.

"Soft enough," grunted Ranaud, and clambered down again. "Pleasant dreams to thee."

"And to thee," Margaret called after him, and closed the trap-door, bolting it securely. "Oh, Jeanne! Did—did you really see—a rat?"

"I heard a scuffle," Jeanne answered tearfully. "Shall you take this Ranaud with us?"

"I know not. Think ye he is honest?"

"He is large," Jeanne said, as if that were more to the point.

"That is true. And withal his fierceness I think he is gentle enough, and chivalrous. Mayhap I will take him as far as Turincel. I hope he is not a rogue, cozening us so that he may the more easily rob us."

"I do not think so at all," Jeanne said, and sank gingerly down upon the straw. "God be thanked, it is soft and clean!"

Margaret stretched herself down beside her.

"Ah, how soft! Indeed, I am weary unto death."

"Lewd fellows, dirty food, and rats," Jeanne sighed. "Perhaps Geoffrey will have discovered our absence by now," she added hopefully.

"Never! Thou dost speak as though didst want him to come in pursuit!"

"I do want him."

Margaret raised herself on her elbow.

"Faint heart! His coming means my death! Art turned traitor, Jeanne? Think ye Simon of Beauvallet would hesitate to kill me for this?"

"I would entreat Geoffrey to intercede for thee."

"Geoffrey! Beauvallet would heed him not! If I read him aright, he follows his own road in all things. He is the leader, and thy Geoffrey hath but to obey his commands."

"Geoffrey is no weakling!"

"He is not the man Beauvallet is. Beauvallet counts no cost."

"Art very interested in the Iron Lord," Jeanne said snappishly.

"Interested! I hate him! Do I not go to summon aid against him?"

"I have a feeling that this stupid, mad emprise is hopeless," Jeanne remarked. "Geoffrey will come."

"Nay, I will succeed! If any come it will be Beauvallet, but he will come too late! He shall see of what make is Margaret of Belrémy."

"And when he comes, Margaret of Belrémy will see of what make he is. And when Geoffrey comes——"

"Oh, cease thy prating of Geoffrey!"

"Then cease *thy* prating of Beauvallet," flamed Jeanne, and turned her back.

X

How the Lady Margaret came to Turincel

By a brook which gurgled joyously over the pebbles at its bed, surrounded by gaunt, leafless trees, three travellers sat, eating their mid-day meal. The air was frosty, the ground hard, and the three sat close together for warmth, and were wrapped in great cloaks.

In the middle, munching a crust of bread and meat, was the Lady Margaret, and on one side of her Jeanne crouched, on the other Ranaud, who was humming to himself.

"How many leagues to Turincel?" inquired Margaret, between bites. "Dost thou know, Gaston?"

"Two, belike," he answered, and produced a bottle of wine. "Will ye drink, lassie?" he asked Jeanne. " 'Twill warm thee."

"Where got ye that?" demanded Margaret, round-eyed.

Ranaud chuckled.

"From the landlord's cellar while ye slept last night."

"Did—did you steal it?" Jeanne asked, shocked.

"Hard words, hard words."

Margaret uncorked it and drank a little.

"Stolen or no, 'tis grateful and warming," she said. "I could have paid, Gaston."

"No need," he grunted. "Best keep thy gold pieces close. What do ye at Turincel?"

Margaret hesitated.

"I—I would fain trust thee, Gaston, but——"

"Ye may well do so. I give away no secrets."

Jeanne tugged at Margaret's sleeve.

"Nay, nay, *chérie!*" she whispered. "Have a care!"

"Why should I not tell him? He is honest, I know, and he hath befriended us! Gaston, I—I seek Fernand de Turincel."

"So I thought," said Ranaud calmly.

"You thought—? But how—why——!"

"Belike ye bear a message from the Lady Margaret?"

Margaret drew her cloak more about her legs.

"I—I am—the Lady Margaret," she said.

"Well, I know that," Ranaud said composedly, and took a pull at the wine-bottle.

"You—know it?" Margaret stared at him in amazement. "How? When didst thou guess?"

"When ye pulled out your dagger at yonder inn," Ranaud answered. "I was once at Belrémy, and I saw you oft-times. But the disguise is good," he added. "Go ye to seek help 'gainst the English?"

"Ay! To throw them out of Belrémy. Ye too will stand my friend?"

Ranaud nodded, his mouth being too full for speech. Margaret laid her hand on his arm.

"Thou art a good fellow," she said gently. "When I am come into mine own again, shalt ask me for what ye will."

"Bah, I want no reward," he said. "I am Ranaud, and I go where I please, and do what I please."

"Ye call no man master?"

"Nay, I am a masterless man. Lord, Lord, but none will take me for a rogue."

"I will take thee," Margaret said. "Shalt be my bodyguard, as thou wilt."

"I will think on it," Ranaud answered. "The lass is not thy sister?"

"Nay, but my dear friend."

"Ay, so I thought. It will serve best for me to call thee Léon, madame."

"Ah, please! I am not 'madame' now. In—in this gear." She blushed a little, but Gaston's glance was impersonal enough.

Presently they arose from their frugal repast, and proceeded on towards Turincel, arriving there shortly before three in the afternoon. The gates of the town were open, nor did anyone challenge their entrance. They walked soberly along the narrow streets towards the castle, which stood in the middle of the town.

The drawbridge was down, and some men-at-arms were lounging upon it. Margaret walked up to them boldly, and accosted one of them.

"Is my Lord Fernand within?" she asked.

The man stared at her, then nudged his companion, and laughed.

"Ye should have given warning of your coming, Highness," he said with mock solemnity. "Then my lord would surely have stayed at home."

Margaret curbed her quick temper.

"He is away?"

"Oh, yes, Highness, he is away!"

She looked at him sharply.

"It would be well for you to speak truthfully, my

friend. My lord will punish any insolence offered to me."

The man laughed.

"Will he so? My lord is perhaps a friend of thine, whelp?"

"A friend indeed," Margaret answered. "I will inquire at the castle for him, since ye are so ignorant." She made as if to pass on, but the soldier barred her way.

"Nay, nay, it will not suffice. I have mine orders, and I will obey them. Get thee hence, saucy puppy!"

Margaret flung up her head.

"Knave, ye know not to whom ye speak! I am the Lady Margaret, Countess of Belrémy."

The soldier shook with laughter.

"Is it indeed so? I am Fernand, Duke of Turincel, at your service, Countess."

"Ye do not believe me? Summon your captain hither, and ye shall see!"

"The lad is foolish," said another man, tapping his forehead.

"I know. I had thrown him off the bridge, else."

"Shall I cut thee a way?" Ranaud asked, surging forward.

In an instant pikes were levelled.

"How now! Brawling and roystering, eh? Away with ye, all!"

Margaret thrust forward, checking her turbulent henchman.

"Put up, put up! Tell me, good fellow, is it true that my lord is in Paris?"

One of them, more good-natured than the rest, answered her.

"Nay, he is gone to present his submission to King Henry, lad."

For a moment all reeled before Margaret's eyes. Then she sprang forward.

"Ye lie! Ye lie!" she cried furiously.

"Gently, gently! 'Tis true enough. We want no ravaging of our land. My lord hath promised allegiance to the English King, and hath promised to aid none in withstanding him. Why, what ails the lad?"

It was Jeanne who flung her arms about the Countess.

"*Chérie, chérie!*" she whispered. "Come away! Perchance it is not true. Come!"

Margaret suffered herself to be led away, stunned by the shock. Ranaud took command of the party, and conducted them to a small hostelry near the gates of the town. In the deserted parlour, Jeanne knelt before her mistress, chafing her hands and crooning to her.

"*Ma belle, ma mignonne! Petite chérie,* lift thy head!"

A big tear rolled down Margaret's cheek, and at the sight of it Jeanne drew her head to rest on her bosom, and Ranaud discreetly retired.

"In vain! all in vain!" Margaret whispered. "Fernand turned traitor. . . . What shall I do? What can I do?"

"Why, sweeting, we will find a way, never fear! Thou—thou wilt not return to Belrémy and—and make thy submission?"

The slim form quivered.

"Never! Never while I live! Go back, vanquished, humble, broken? Ah, not that! Rather would I stab myself!"

"But, *chérie*, what canst thou do? At least Belrémy spells safety for thee, and thou canst not wander over the countryside at will. Beauvallet will treat thee fair, I know. Smother thy pride, sweet, and go back. Indeed, indeed it is wisest!"

Margaret sat up, brushing away the tears.

"Shall I be unfaithful to the name I bear? What says my motto?—'Conquest or death'—well, I will conquer. Would my father turn back? Nay, nay! Why, what ails me? There is a boulder in my path, and I lose heart! Body o' me, I will go on!"

"But where, *mignonne*? Thy father was a man, thou art but a woman."

"No woman I. In man's clothes I stand, and a man will I be. He called me the Amazon. Full well will I merit that title. Let me think! Let me think!" She flung off her cap, running her fingers up through the thick masses of her hair, eyes narrowed and keen, elbows on her knees.

Jeanne rose silently, and went to the window. Presently Margaret spoke.

"Jeanne, perhaps our good Gaston would conduct thee back to Belrémy, if I asked him."

"I go with thee," Jeanne said shortly.

"But thy feet, little one! Thou canst do no more."

"What thou canst do, I will do."

"Thy heart is at home, with Malvallet."

"My heart is here with thee."

"I may tramp many leagues, and I must march quickly."

"Then march I too, till I drop."

"Oh, Jeannette, Jeannette, thou art too brave and sweet! Thou dost deserve a better, kinder mistress! Not—not a turbulent—Amazon. God help me! Where is Gaston?"

"I know not. He went out a while back. I think he leaves us here."

"Ay." Margaret's head sank back into her hands, and for a long time there was silence.

Back into the little room came Ranaud, seeming to fill it with his great bulk and height.

"Supper comes," he said gruffly to Jeanne, and jerked his thumb towards the still figure by the fire, with an inquiring lift of his red brows. Jeanne shrugged, and Ranaud seemed to understand, for he gave a grunt, and sat down by the table.

The landlord entered presently, bringing supper, and when it was set out upon the table Jeanne went to her mistress, and laid a hand on her shoulder.

"Come, sweet; supper."

Margaret roused herself.

"Supper? Ah, yes I must eat, I suppose. Why, the good Gaston has returned! Gaston, heard ye aught in the streets?"

"Ay. 'Tis true enough, what they told you on the bridge."

Margaret heaved a little sigh.

"Well; I doubted it not. What have we here? Bacon, as I live, and fresh beef! Gaston, how should we fare without thee?"

"Well enough," he said, and fell to carving the meat.

For some time Margaret ate in silence, frowning, and seeming not to hear the desultory conversation of her two companions. But after a while she spoke, looking at Ranaud.

"Gaston, how many leagues onward lies Vazincourt?"

His little eyes widened in a momentary surprise.

"Some thirteen leagues or more, to the east."

"No nearer?"

"That is the quickest, lady. And the way runs through the lands of Raoul the Terrible."

"Ah!" She caught her breath. "And if one went not that way?"

"Sixteen—twenty leagues. I know not."

Margaret relapsed into thought, and did not speak again until supper was over. Then she pushed her stool back from the table, and Jeanne saw that her mouth was tightly set.

"I will go there."

"Go where?" Jeanne asked her.

"To Vazincourt. To the Sieur de Larousie."

"Through Raoul's lands? Humph!"

"Margot, ye rave!" Jeanne cried. "It is impossible!"

"Nay." The pointed chin was determined. "Naught is impossible. I will go to Arnaud de Larousie. Thou dost know, Jeannette, that he will do—what I wish."

"At a price, perhaps," Jeanne said meaningly.

Margaret's face quivered, and was still again.

"I would pay that price. He is a good man."

"All to sate thy vengeance?"

"To set my land free from the English tyrant."

"Thou wouldst never, never reach Vazincourt."

"That will I. But, Jeanne, *petite* Jeanne, if thou dost indeed love me, thou wilt return to Belrémy."

"If thou art determined to go, naught shall part us. I swear it."

Ranaud picked up his tankard.

"Here's to thine emprise, lady!" he said, and drank deeply.

A soft light came into Margaret's eyes.

"Thou good fellow! I owe thee more than I can hope to pay, Gaston, but one day, when I rule again in Belrémy, come to me, and thou shalt have all that I can give thee."

"A murrain on what ye can give me!" growled Ranaud. "Ye have given me adventure, and I am ever one for that." He chuckled, and slapped his thigh.

"I have brought thee out of thy way, good fellow. But here we part company, and I shall not forget."

He drank again, and passed the back of his hand across his mouth.

"I come with ye," he announced doggedly. "A pretty thing it would be for ye to travel through Raoul's lands alone."

"Ah!" Margaret caught his hand impulsively. "No, no, my friend! I could not permit it! I'll not have your blood on my head. But I thank you! Oh, I thank you a thousand times!"

"My blood be upon mine own head. I am no puny weakling. I ask but a little fighting, and I am satisfied. I come, willy-nilly."

"My friend, I—I cannot take thee." Margaret flushed. "I brought—could bring—but little money, and—and—I have not enough——"

"I've money enough, and what I cannot buy I steal. The reckoning shall come later. Come with ye I will. . . . And that is my last word!" he roared suddenly.

Margaret laughed, and a sparkle came into her eyes. Up she sprang, and seized the tankard.

"Then here's to our emprise, our glorious emprise!" she cried, and drank deep.

"And here's to a right brave lady," Ranaud said, and stood to drink his toast.

XI

How the Lady Margaret fell into the hands of Raoul the Terrible

They plodded valiantly on, over fields and through woods, and to help their tired feet onward, they sang a little, cheerily, Ranaud in a deep bass which seemed to come from a bottomless cavern within him, Margaret in a full contralto, and Jeanne in a small, weary soprano, which made itself heard spasmodically. They eschewed high roads, for they were in Raoul's land, and the fame of his infamy had spread far and wide. Two days since they had left Turincel, but they went slower now, and sometimes Ranaud carried Jeanne in his great arms. The spring had gone out of Margaret's step, and her feet were blistered and raw. Yet she made no complaint, but bit her lips when they walked over rough ground, so that her companions should not suspect. They visited no inns, but had furnished themselves with provisions at Turincel. The first night they had sheltered in a disused hut, but the second night had found them sleeping out in the open, wrapped about in their cloaks, and thanking God for the milder weather. Stiff and sore had the two girls been in the morning, but Ranaud showed no signs of fatigue or discomfort. Now they were tramping steadily eastward, hoping to leave Raoul the Terrible's land behind them by nightfall.

"Bad land," Ranaud remarked presently, breaking off in the middle of his song. "Drunken roysterers. Like master, like man. All goes to ruin while Raoul feeds his pleasure. Pah!"

"Hast ever seen him?" Jeanne asked.

"Ay, once. A pig of a man, with flabby cheeks. A frog, a toad, a rat, a spider! Vermin!"

"Why, thou art very bitter!" Margaret said, and looked up to see him scowl.

"I've reason."

"What was thy reason, Gaston?"

"A girl," he growled. "My girl. Lascivious beast! May his bones rot in hell!"

"Amen," said Margaret. "Ah, a stream! Needs must I bathe my feet."

"Oh, water!" Jeanne limped forward thankfully.

They stayed by the stream awhile, resting, but presently Jeanne saw red berries growing near-by, and went to pluck some, singing softly to herself. Margaret stayed by the stream, lying flat upon the ground, arms crooked behind her head, half-dozing. Jeanne's voice came to them.

"Oh, such pretty, pretty berries! See!"

Margaret raised herself upon her elbow, smiling, for Jeanne had made herself a wreath of berries, and entwined them in her long plaits. In her russet dress, berry-hung, and her red mouth laughing, she was very beautiful, like some woodland elf. Margaret clapped her hands lightly, applauding her.

"Wait, I will fetch thee some!" Jeanne cried, and dived into the bushes.

Again Margaret fell to drowsing, lulled to sleep by the sound of Gaston's low humming. How long she stayed thus she did not know, but suddenly she was roused by the sound of horses' hoofs, and a scream. In a flash she was on her feet, and Ranaud too. Once more the scream rang out, and it was Jeanne's voice.

Ranaud crashed into the bushes through which Jeanne had gone, Margaret at his heels, dagger in hand. They came out upon a clearing, and away to the right, down a cutting saw men and horses.

Quarter-staff gripped firmly, Ranaud thundered down upon this group, and as they drew near to it, panted over his shoulder to Margaret.

"Raoul! Raoul! The devil hunts!"

Into the midst of the group they rushed, striking right and left. A squat man with a white face and loose

211

cheeks sat upon a black mare, and held Jeanne before him, across his saddle-bow. He gave a quick order, and some half-a-dozen men closed in upon Ranaud, swords drawn. Someone from behind her wrenched her quarter-staff from the Countess, and flung steel-like arms about her, bearing her backwards. She turned her head to see Ranaud down, and three men lashing his wrists and ankles together.

"Toad, toad!" Ranaud roared. "Misshapen toad! God's curse be upon thee!" He spat at Raoul, writhing still, and struggling.

"Truss him," Raoul purred, and let his small, heavy-lidded eyes travel slowly over Margaret, who was seeking madly to free herself. "These be none of my people," he said, and looked down at Jeanne. "A sweet slut, i' faith. Take her, one of you." He tossed her to the man whose horse stood beside his. "Spies, belike. Armagnac spies. Bear them after me." He wheeled his horse about and set it at a canter, through the wood.

Her captor threw Margaret face downwards over his saddlebow, and swung himself up. "Lie still, wild-cat!" he said, and rode on after his master.

Through the wood they cantered, and out on to the open country. For miles, it seemed to Margaret, they galloped along in Raoul's wake, the hunt all about them, and somewhere near, Gaston, roaring out defiance. When at last they halted, she was bruised and shaken from her jolting ride, and for a moment, when she was set upon her feet, she could see nothing for the dancing specks before her eyes. Then the mist cleared, and she found herself within the courtyard of Raoul's palatial hunting-lodge. A great rambling house of stone, it was, with turrets at each corner, standing upon a fair space of land and backing upon a slight incline. One minute had she in which to take in her surroundings, before she was jerked forward into the big hall. There Raoul stood, and Margaret shuddered a little. He was short and broad with a great paunch, and bloodshot, lashless eyes. The skin about his face and jowl hung in white folds, and his mouth was wide, the lower lip sagging to show pointed yellow teeth.

Gaston was carried in, cursing, and flung down by

his sweating, staggering bearers. Raoul's wicked eyes ran over the huge form, and his grin grew.

"Cut the bonds. Methinks I do know this fellow."

One of the men released Ranaud, and he struggled up. He would have come at Raoul, had they not hemmed him in with swords.

"Yes, I do know him." Raoul laughed a little, very softly. "You did seek to kill me once, good giant, long years ago. I remember."

"And I will kill thee yet!" Ranaud bellowed. "Fat, shapeless spider!"

"Gently, my giant. I will make you sing small presently!" Raoul said sweetly.

Margaret twisted free of her captors, and ran to where Jeanne crouched upon the floor. She fell on her knees beside her, drawing her into her arms. Raoul smiled wider still.

"The pretty cooing doves," he said, and Margaret grew cold at the sound of his purring voice. "Lock them up together, the doves," he commanded. "Who shall say I am not merciful? A last night in each other's arms." Again he chuckled, so that his fat body shook like a jelly. "Pray that ye may find favour in mine eyes, sweet chuck. Alack, I have no time to waste on thee now. Away with them!"

A guard tossed Margaret over his shoulder, another caught Jeanne up. They were borne across the hall and along a passage. A flight of narrow steps ended this passage, and down it they went to a bare chamber whose only window was a narrow slit cut in the stones.

"Sleep well, my beauties!" Margaret's bearer laughed, and set her down. He went out with his companion, and the key grated in the lock.

"Margot! Margot!" Jeanne stumbled towards her, white-faced and trembling. "Margot!"

Margaret flung her arms about her, holding her close, and pressing the berry-wreathed head to her shoulder.

"Ah, my dear, my dear, what have I done? Into what den have I dragged thee? God forgive me!"

Jeanne clung to her sobbing.

"His face, his face! He kissed me! Ah, the feel of his foul lips!" She broke off, weeping bitterly.

For a while Margaret soothed and petted her, stroking the brown curls with gentle, motherly hands.

"Thy Geoffrey will come," she said desperately. "Beauvallet is in pursuit now. Please God he will come!"

"Too late, too late!" Jeanne moaned, and feeling the berries against her cheek, tore them off, and cast them from her. "How could he come? How could he know?"

"He will come," Margaret repeated. "He will come."

"Thou dost not believe it! Thou dost not!"

Margaret was silent for a moment, and Jeanne looked wistfully up into her face.

"Margot—Margot, thy dagger? Thou wilt lend it me?"

Margaret bowed her head.

"Lost," she said bitterly. "But I will find a way. I must. If the worst—befall us—I will tell this Raoul who I am. He—he cannot then—harm us. I—I think he cannot."

"Tell him not!" Jeanne gripped her arms. "What cares the Terrible for thy rank? Or—or he might— seek to make thee wed him, to gain thy rich lands. Margot, promise that thou wilt not tell him! It would break my heart! Thou wouldst not hurt me so?"

"God knows," Margaret said, and cast herself down upon a wooden bench. "What have they done with Gaston? His and thy blood on my head! Ah, why did I let thee come? Selfish, headstrong shrew that I am!"

"Nay!" Jeanne was at her side in an instant. "Thou couldst not have prevented my coming! I would have followed thee barefoot!" She caught up Margaret's hand and kissed it passionately. "Ah, my dear, my dear!" she crooned, and clung to the Countess.

The night passed on leaden feet, and dawn found them fitfully asleep, arms locked about each other. Slowly the grey light grew, and awakened Margaret. She opened heavy eyes and looked about her at the grim stone walls that cased her round. Very pale she was, and tight-lipped. Courage shone out of her dark eyes, but at the back was fear. She glanced down into Jeanne's face, and shivered a little. Jeanne smiled in her sleep and murmured something. Margaret knew that she was dreaming of her lover, and a tiny sob shook her. She sat very still, waiting for Jeanne to awaken. And in a little while Jeanne stirred, throwing out her arm, and looked up into her mistress's face.

"Margot *chérie*. . . ." she murmured drowsily, and suddenly remembered where she was. She struggled up, eyes wide, and looked round, shuddering. "It—it is—tomorrow," she said. "I—I pray God—it will soon be over."

Margaret rose, stretching her aching limbs.

"I will not lose hope!" she said vehemently. "If I had but my dagger! Ah, to plunge it into his black heart!" Her hands clenched.

"Oh!" Jeanne covered her face with her hands. "Thou—thou couldst not!"

"Could I not? That could I, and blithely too! Hark!"

Jeanne started up, hands clasped at her breast, for down the stone stairs without heavy footsteps were coming.

"Bear a brave front!" Margaret implored, and pulled her down on to the bench. "Let them not see thy fear!"

The key grated in the lock, and the door swung back. A soldier came in, bearing bread and wine.

"See how kind is my lord!" he said, and set down his burden. "In a little ye shall come before him, pretty pigeon." He patted Jeanne's cheek, which flamed under his hand. "Thou and thy sweet lover. Fare thee well!" He went out, and her rigidity left Jeanne. She started to tremble, gripping her fingers together.

Margaret picked up the wine, coaxing her to drink, and crumbled a little of the bread.

"It chokes me!" Jeanne cried. "I—cannot!"

Margaret left her then, and went to the narrow window, tip-toeing that she might peep out. The country stretched away beneath her, dotted here and there with houses. Sighing she came back into the room, and sat down beside Jeanne, to wait.

Hours crept by, but at length footsteps sounded again

on the stairs, and again the door was thrown open. Two men entered, and beckoned to them.

"My lord waits," one said, and laughed. "Do ye shrink, little dove? Nay, but he hath ta'en a fancy to thee. Fret not."

"I—cannot!" Jeanne whispered, and shrank back.

But Margaret took her hand and led her forward. Up the stairs they were led, along a corridor, up more stairs, through large rooms until they came to one which was carpeted with skins of wild animals, and at one end of which was a dais with a carved chair thereon. In that chair Raoul sat, a gorgeous figure clad in scarlet and gold, his bowed legs crossed, and one hand stroking his hairless face. Some four or five of his courtiers were in the room, and at the door through which the girls had come an armed guard stood.

Raoul smiled gently upon his prisoners and motioned them to stand before him. A great noise sounded without, and Ranaud was brought in, roaring out curses. His guards kept a firm hold on him, but he spat at Raoul yet again.

"Silence him," Raoul sighed, and one of his men struck Gaston across the mouth so that the blood sprang up.

"If ye are noisy, ye will be gagged," Raoul said, and turned again to the pair before him. For a long time he gazed at them.

"The white dove trembles," he remarked presently, and turned his eyes to Margaret, surveying her long and closely. He leaned forward in his chair, and under his scrutiny Margaret felt the red colour flood her cheeks. Desperately she sought to stop this betraying blush, and stared back into the little eyes defiantly.

"Ah!" Raoul breathed, and rose. He came down from the dais and stood before her. He looked her over closely, and passed his hands over her taut body. His smile broadened. "Well, ye make a pretty boy, my dear," he said, and removed her cap. Down tumbled the thick braids, over her shoulders, reaching almost to her knees. "But ye make a prettier woman," Raoul said. "Now, I wonder. . . ?" Again he caressed his chin.

"I had thought thy companion lovely," he remarked. "But thou art stronger meat."

Margaret closed her eyes for a moment, holding fast to her courage. Beside her she could hear Jeanne's quick, sobbing breaths.

"No peasant wench thou," Raoul went on. "So what do ye in my land? Methinks I have somewhere seen thy face before. Thy name?"

Margaret shut her teeth.

"No name? Some great lady art thou? Escaping belike.... From whom...? From the English, perchance. Now I made my submission a long time ago, and it may be that the English would give much to have thee back again." He looked at her sharply, chuckling. "And yet thou art very beautiful. I think I have a mind to thee myself. What is thy name?"

Margaret's hands were clenched hard at her sides. From behind her came Ranaud's voice.

"Tell him not! Tell him not!"

Raoul wheeled about with something like a hiss.

"I shall not tell," Margaret said quietly. "Save at a price."

"I bargain not," Raoul smiled. "Thou wilt tell."

"Trust him not! Make no terms!" Ranaud cried.

"He desires no terms," Raoul said, and came closer to Margaret, placing his hand beneath her chin. "Think well, sweet chuck. I have means to make thee tell at my disposal. Fire, rope, and the sword."

"I fear not death."

"Death!" Again he chuckled. "Nay, I am more subtle, pretty. A rope about thy wrists, fire between thy thumbs.... Be wise, sweeting. How wilt thou like to see thy companions die before thine eyes? Slowly, ah, but slowly!"

At last Margaret shrank.

"If I tell you, will ye swear to let my friends go safely hence?"

"We will see," Raoul smiled. "Thy lewd fellow there once sought to slay me. Well. Now it is my turn. For the wench——" he shrugged. "Thou hast killed my want of her. Let her go."

217

"Ah, no!" Jeanne cast herself upon Margaret. "Not that, not that! Margot, Margot!"

Margaret put her gently from her.

"What matter? I am the Lady Margaret of Belrémy, Lord Raoul."

He betrayed no surprise, but nodded.

"Belrémy, eh? Now I have an old, old score to settle 'gainst thy land. Methinks I have found a way. Would it hurt the proud burghers of thy land to see thee my chattel, I wonder? Or I might wed thee. . . . It doth not please thee, that prospect? Thy land 'neath my heel, and thy beauty 'neath my hand. A sweet thought, i' faith."

"My land is under English rule!" Margaret flashed.

"Is it so indeed? Then I will keep thee for as long as thou shalt please me. I weary soon, but thou hast spirit and it should be amusing to tame thee. Thou shalt lie willingly in my arms, Margaret of Belrémy, before many days have passed."

A shudder went through her, and quick as thought she drove her clenched fist into his grinning face. Her guard seized her, pinning her arms to her sides. Panting she glared at Raoul, whose smile had grown more evil.

"Thou wilt not do that again, wench," he said, and struck her lightly on the cheek. "A blow for thy blow, but next time it shall be a kiss."

She sneered, eyes aflame.

"Thou puny spider!" she said bitingly. "Thou poor, misshapen wretch!" She saw his lips curl back, showing his red gums, and knew that she had touched him on the raw. "Poor dwarf!" She laughed exultantly, and braced herself, for he had come up to her again.

"Let be," he told her guard, and took her in his long arms, crushing her against his fat body. "Dwarf, but strong, Margaret of Belrémy. Spider who has caught a silly fly in his web." Then he kissed her, and she struggled madly to free herself, straining away from him. "Lie still, little fly," he said softly, and kissed her again.

XII

How Simon set forth in pursuit

He left Belrémy at noon on the day of the Lady
Margaret's flight, having set a vigilant guard about
her cage. He had no suspicion that the bird had flown,
so he went to Sal-de-lac in ignorance of how he had
been tricked. Geoffrey was left in command of the
castle, and there was much to be done, for which
reason he did not, on that first day, miss Mademoiselle Jeanne. But when, on the second day, she neither emerged from Margaret's chamber, nor received
Geoffrey in the anteroom when he entered on his
round of inspection, he felt aggrieved and ill-used.
The Countess's other ladies were there, chattering
and sewing; one of them, Mademoiselle Hélène, who
was a grave-eyed lady and in Margaret's confidence,
came forward to curtsey to him.

"The Lady Margaret, mademoiselle?" Geoffrey asked
politely.

"Monsieur desires to speak with her?" Hélène said
composedly. "Madame is suffering from a headache,
but doubtless——"

"No, no!" Geoffrey made haste to say. "I will not
disturb my lady." He lingered a moment. "Mademoiselle Jeanne is—is with her?"

Knowing glances were exchanged, and one girl
tittered. Geoffrey turned a dull red.

"Yes, monsieur," Hélène answered.

Geoffrey withdrew, too shy to ask to see Jeanne.
Not until the following day were his suspicions stirred,
and then but slightly. It appeared that the Countess
was still indisposed, and could not spare Jeanne from
her side. Geoffrey retired, a little puzzled, and closely

questioned the guards. Their answers were satisfactory, and he knew them to be honest, for they were Simon's own men. Still his suspicions were not quite lulled to rest, and he determined, much as he dreaded the task, to see the Lady Margaret when he went again to her apartments that evening, whether she were abed or not. Simon, he knew, would feel no qualms at entering her bed-chamber thus unceremoniously, but he was not fashioned of such stern and uncompromising stuff, and his chivalrous soul shrank from such unchivalrous behaviour.

He had just risen from dinner, some time before three in the afternoon, when Simon strode in, most unexpectedly.

"Why, lad!" Geoffrey cried. "I did not think to see thee before tomorrow!"

Simon tossed his cap on to the table.

"Nay. The business was speedily done. Something impelled me to return. I know not whether I am a fool or whether my instinct truly warned me of danger. Is aught amiss?"

"Naught. I—*think* there is naught amiss."

Swiftly the lowering brows met over Simon's hawk-nose. He shot Geoffrey his sudden, sword-like glance.

"Well?" The word was snapped, and Geoffrey laughed rather uneasily.

"I—Simon, I have felt restless in my mind all this day, but I think I am mistaken in my suspicions."

"The Lady Margaret?"

"I have not seen her," Geoffrey said reluctantly. "Yet she has not passed by thy guards. That I know. Her ladies say she hath the headache and keeps her chamber. That is all. Little enough, you'll say. Jeanne too I have not seen."

Simon threw off his cloak.

"Come with me now," he said briefly, and strode to the stairway.

Up they went to the Countess's apartments. Rigid guards presented arms, but Simon stayed not to question them. He knocked upon the door of the ante-chamber.

Hélène opened it, and cool-headed as she was, she

changed colour when she saw Simon, and her eyelids flickered. It was a very tiny sign of fear, but it did not escape Simon.

"The Lady Margaret is abed?" he asked.

"Yes, milor'," Hélène answered.

"What ails her?"

"A grievous pain in her head, milor'. She desires to be quiet."

"I shall not disturb her long," Simon said. "She should see a physician." He went into the room, and shot a quick glance around. Most of the ladies were unperturbed, for they knew nothing, but Amélie was white to the lips. It was enough for Simon. Without a word he stalked to the door which led into Margaret's bed-chamber.

There was a quick movement from behind him, and a rustle of skirts. Hélène slipped before the door, calm still, but pale.

"Milor', this is an intrusion," she said. "Madame cannot be disturbed thus."

"Mademoiselle," Simon answered harshly. "Your face betrays you. Stand aside."

But she would not, backing against the door, arms outflung to guard it.

"My orders are to let none in, milor'."

Simon laid a heavy hand on her shoulder.

"Your loyalty is worthy of praise, mademoiselle, but ye cannot fool me. I will lift you out of my way, if you do not this instant stand aside."

Hélène read the purpose in his eyes.

"Take your hand from my shoulder," she said freezingly, and stepped to one side.

Simon entered the chamber, took one look, and came back into the ante-room.

"So. Madame is ill," he said grimly.

Bewildered faces stared up at him, but Hélène stood proud and stiff, eyes cast down, and Amélie seemed to shrink into her chair. Unerringly Simon swooped upon these two.

"You, mademoiselle, and you, will follow me," he said, and to Amélie his words rang out as a death-knell. She crept out in his wake, Hélène at her side, and the horrified, bewildered Geoffrey bringing up the rear.

Simon led the way to the room where he conducted all his business, and sat himself down at the table, judge-like, motioning the two women to stand before him.

"Mademoiselle Amélie, ye will answer me truthfully," he said. "When, and how did the Lady Margaret escape from her room?"

Amélie sobbed and shrank against Hélène.

"I—I do not kn-know! I m-must not s-say!"

Simon's voice grew harder.

"Mademoiselle, you will be wise to answer me now, of your own free will," he warned her. "The Lady Margaret has escaped with Mademoiselle Jeanne. That I know, and that she escaped during mine absence. To leave this castle were impossible, unless she had a pass. Did she have one, or is she still within these walls?"

"I cannot, I cannot! Do not ask me! I—— Oh, Hélène, help me!"

Hélène stepped forward.

"Amélie knows naught, milor'. You frighten her to no purpose. And if she knew——The Lady Margaret's ladies do not easily betray their mistress."

"They have done so easily enough, if she has left Belrémy," Simon said. "Fool, do ye not know what perils lie in the path of two women, journeying over this country?"

Some strange note in his voice made Geoffrey look sharply at him. Simon heeded him not.

"I know what perils await her at your hands did I betray her," Hélène answered bravely.

"Think you I avenge myself on women?" Simon sneered. "Ye know not Beauvallet. Speak now, for, by the Rood, I swear I will wring thy knowledge from thee by torture if need be."

"And yet ye avenge not yourself on women."

"No vengeance, mademoiselle. A means, which I should be loth to take."

"Then know, sir, that my mistress is beyond the reach of your power."

"She is dead then," Simon replied. He turned again to Amélie. "Mademoiselle, there is as yet no need for thy tears, but if ye answer me not ye will weep tears of blood."

Amélie shrieked, and began to implore his mercy.

Simon held up his hand.

"Listen, both of you! By Christ's Wounds I do swear that no injury nor harshness shall befall the Lady Margaret at my hands. Now speak."

"I dare not! Oh, I dare not!"

Simon rose.

"Then follow me yet again, mademoiselle."

"Ah, no! Ah, no! I will speak! I promise I will speak the truth!" Amélie wailed, and would have fallen on her knees had not Geoffrey put her gently into a chair.

Simon sat down again.

"It is well for you, mademoiselle. When did the Lady Margaret escape?"

"The—the day—you went to Sal-de-lac. Before—very early in the morning."

Simon's eyes narrowed.

"I was still in the castle?"

"Yes—oh, yes! I—oh, God forgive me!"

"How passed she the guards without the castle?"

"It was Léon—his pass—she—oh, Hélène, Hélène!"

"Léon the page? Ay. I remember. How did she contrive to use his pass?"

"She—she went as a page. He gave—his clothes. And—and she wrote—'and s-sister' on the p-pass, so Jeanne—went with her."

A low whistle of admiration came from Geoffrey.

"Oh, the Amazon!" he chuckled.

"Where went she?"

"To—to Turincel—to—to bring—my Lord Fernand—to—fight you."

Simon smiled.

"Then that quest was vain. Turincel has submitted. Where next did she think to go?"

"I do not know. Indeed, indeed, I do not know!"

Simon was silent for a moment, frowning. Then he stood up.

"Ye may go. And Mademoiselle Hélène."

Hélène paused.

"Milor"—what will you do?"

"Do! I will fetch her back, silly girl. How could ye let her go thus? God and the Devil know what may have befallen her!" He waited until she had withdrawn, and then he turned to Geoffrey. "Send me Santoy, Geoffrey, and five men of Beauvallet. See them armed and mounted, with two horses to spare."

"Simon—think ye danger——"

Simon laughed shortly.

"I fear the worst. As I rode through this country I found it seething with rogues and footpads."

Geoffrey paled.

"God! And Jeanne—Simon, I come with thee on this quest. It is my right."

"As ye will. Wear thine armour. Send Alan to my room, he must rule here. The Chevalier is safe?"

"Aye. I think he knows naught." Geoffrey swung out.

Within the hour they were riding out of Belrémy, black plumes and green side by side, bearing for Turincel. They reached it in the evening, but Simon went at once to the Castle, only to be told that Fernand de Turincel was abroad. The Captain of the Guard received Simon, and eyed him curiously, for the fame of his name had spread over France.

"Tell me," Simon said curtly, "came there a page-boy to this castle within these last five days, with his sister, demanding to see Lord Fernand?"

"It may have been so, sir, but I know not. My men——"

"Will ye summon them, sir? The page was none other than my prisoner, the Countess of Belrémy."

The captain stared.

"The—the——God's my life! If ye will follow me, milor'——?"

Simon clanked after him to the guardroom, and in a very short space the guards were drawn up before him.

"Came there a page and his sister to this castle

lately?" the captain asked. "A page who desired to see my lord?"

The man who had rebuffed Margaret stepped forward.

"Ay, sir. A poor, bewitched lad, who said he was the Lady Margaret of Belrémy. There was a wench with him, and a roystering giant who would have offered violence when we denied them entrance."

"A man?" Simon addressed him. "Are you sure?"

"Ay, sir. A great burly fellow with a red beard."

Simon frowned.

"Know ye such an one, Geoffrey?"

Geoffrey shook his head.

"Not I. Tell me, good fellow, of what like was this page?"

"A pretty lad, sir, with black eyes and a hot temper."

"It is she, beyond doubt," Geoffrey said. "Saw ye which way they went?"

"Nay, sir. I—I did not think to look. I——"

"No matter." Simon turned on his heel. "Sir Captain, I thank you for your courtesy. I have heard enough."

"Milor' Beauvallet, I but regret I can tell you no more. Stay! At what hour came the page?"

The man looked at his fellows.

"It—it was late, I think, sir. Close on four. But I cannot swear to it."

"Then they slept in Turincel that night," Simon said. "Your servant, sir. Come, Geoffrey." He went out, the captain at his heels.

"Milor', my master would wish me to do all in my power——"

"I thank you. I have but to scour the taverns of this town and that I can best do myself."

"There are six, milor'. A guide——?"

Simon paused.

"You are very good, sir. A guide, if you please."

One was brought swiftly, and the cavalcade set out once more in the waning light.

"Art very surly," Geoffrey said. "They are surely in Turincel. Where else should they be?"

"The Lady Margaret is too obstinate to own herself vanquished so easily," Simon answered. "She will have gone on again. Plague take the woman!"

The insignificant tavern by the gates was the fourth at which they called, and by that time Geoffrey had grown uneasy. The landlord at the tavern was loth to disclose what he knew, until Geoffrey tossed him a gold piece. Then his tongue wagged freely, and it transpired that he was guilty of listening at keyholes.

"They rested the night here, sir. A parlour they had, and I did serve supper therein, for the lad was weary or ill. He crouched in a chair, and methought he looked very sick. I—I did—chance—to hear that they purposed journeying to Vazincourt. The—the red-bearded fellow—a bellowing, roaring bully, good sir!—did speak loud, and—and I did hear him say 'Raoul the Terrible'. Then there was some talk of danger in Raoul's land, and indeed, sir, no man will lightly enter it, for Raoul is the Devil himself. I—I think they did purpose going through his land, for it is the quickest way to Vazincourt."

"Raoul!" Geoffrey gripped Simon's arm. "Thou dost remember? That squat man with the loose speech and evil eyes! Into his lands! My Jeanne! Simon, to horse!"

"Thy Jeanne? She hath not the beauty of Margaret! If Raoul see the Countess—God's Death, what folly is hers?" He turned and would have gone out again to his horse, had not the guide put in a word.

"Sir, it were folly indeed to enter the Terrible's domain now! What good will ye do at night? Rest here till morning, sir!"

Simon stopped.

"Ay. I had forgot."

"Simon, Simon, do not waste time!" Geoffrey implored.

"We can do no good, as this man says. Pay him, Geoffrey; I will arrange with the landlord." He went into the tavern again.

Over supper they discussed the situation, Geoffrey in agitation but Simon calmly.

"If he has taken them prisoner he would not harm them. He is more like to sell them to me. He will not

226

offend us. Ye remember how he came to submit when first we landed? Faugh!"

"Simon, thou dost not know! Much have I heard of this man. Not for nothing is he called the Terrible, and women—women are his pastime."

"If he thinks to make a pastime of these women——" Simon broke off, but his eyes smouldered. "I will ride first to his castle. If they are not there—I will scour the land. It may be that they passed through unharmed. And yet—something warns me of danger. That red-bearded man . . . who could he be?"

"God knows. A rogue."

"Yet he went with them. Therefore he sought not to rob, for that could he have done here. The Lady Margaret commands men's loyalty and service, I think. God grant this one be true."

"Thou art very anxious for the Lady Margaret," Geoffrey remarked, but he was too worried to laugh or jibe at Simon.

"I am responsible for her to the King," Simon said shortly.

They rode next day into Raoul's lands, but although King Henry's warrant, which Simon bore with him, gained them fearful respect, they could discover nothing. Ranaud had been careful to eschew high-roads, and Raoul's domain was large. The tracks seemed lost, so Simon branched off to the north, deserting the route to Vazincourt, and riding towards Raoul's stronghold.

"If he hath not taken her, I must have his aid," Simon told Geoffrey. "Whiles we ride on to Vazincourt, Raoul must search within his own land. He dare not refuse me, for he is afraid for his peace. Ye remember his bearing when he came to the King?"

"Ay, and I would not trust him."

"In this I can trust him, for he is a coward, and he would sell his soul to keep King Henry away."

Raoul's castle lay some miles to the north, and so bad was the road that it was close on five in the evening when they came to it. A stir was caused by their arrival, but a cringing chamberlain assured them that his lord was away at his palace in the south, where he hunted that week.

An oath escaped Geoffrey, for this meant that they had ridden a day's journey out of their way. A storm was brewing, and they had not covered many miles on their return journey when it burst above their heads in such fury that Simon was forced to halt at the first village they came to, to take shelter for the night.

They were up betimes next morning, and rode on again in the calm weather that follows a storm. Shortly after eight they found themselves once more on the road that led to Vazincourt, and on inquiry of a peasant which was the way to Raoul's hunting-lodge, were bidden cut through the woods that flanked the road on one side, and to bear on to the south-west.

Picking their way, they pushed into the wood along the same path which Margaret and her companions had trodden the day before. Slowly they went, and carefully, for the low-hanging tree branches impeded their passage.

Suddenly Simon exclaimed, and reined in his horse. Startled, Geoffrey followed his gaze. By a clear stream lay a cloak, sodden with rain. Side by side he and Simon sped forward, and dismounted. Simon caught up the cloak, shaking it out. It was of a length to suit a boy, made of plain but rich stuff. Simon wheeled about, looking about him keenly.

"Ah!" Quickly he went forward to the bush through which Margaret and Ranaud had plunged when they raced to Jeanne's rescue. "That was not done by the storm!" Simon said, and pointed to the broken branches. "Some large body forced its way through. Did they not say the red-beard was a giant?"

"Through! Through!" Geoffrey said hoarsely, and dived in.

Simon followed him, and they came upon the cutting at the end of which Raoul had captured Jeanne. With one accord the two men strode down it, and presently came to where Margaret's dagger lay. Simon pounced upon it.

"There has been a struggle. See! Hoof marks!" He pointed to the trampled ground, and Geoffrey saw the muscles about his jaw stand out in anger. "Out on his hunt, belike, and found them. Two women. 'Twas good enough. By God, if harm has been done to either he will dearly rue the day! Come!"

"Simon, that devil with my Jeanne! My little, little Jeanne!" Geoffrey hurried after him, back to where their men waited.

Through the wood they went, and out on to the open. A rough track plainly showed the way to the palace, and they rode down it at a brisk canter.

"I command thee, Geoffrey, keep thy head! Raoul will give them up, but we are eight men to their hundreds, and we must go cautiously to work. I go as an envoy from King Henry. It should be simple."

"If he has hurt Jeanne——"

"If he hath discovered that the page is none other than Margaret of Belrémy, he will seek to sell her, methinks. He will not harm them, unless he is a fool."

Geoffrey said nothing, but he compressed his lips in a disbelief. Presently the palace came into view, and a few minutes later they halted before it. Simon turned to Walter of Santoy.

"Walter, Sir Geoffrey and I enter alone. Do you hold the horses here, in readiness. Stir not until I come. No danger awaits us, for I go as an envoy." He dismounted and gave his horse into Walter's care. Together he and Geoffrey went to the great door of the palace, and knocked upon it loudly.

A lackey opened it, but fell back when he saw the two armour-clad figures who stood there so menacingly.

Simon showed his warrant.

"I am Simon of Beauvallet, and I come with a message from King Henry to your master. Lead me to him, sirrah!"

"Lord Simon!" The man crossed himself. "My master is—is—occupied. I doubt——"

"Knave!" thundered Simon. "Do ye deny the King's messenger ingress? Lord Raoul knows that I come. Lead me to him!"

Too nervous and startled to reflect that his master had not warned his household of a messenger's advent, the lackey ushered them in, and called forward the

steward who thought it politic to placate this wrathful
man in golden armour. Accordingly he backed before
Simon, bowing low, and conducted him up the stairs
to the room where Raoul sat, with his three prisoners.
He flung wide the door and announced the Lord of
Beauvallet in the name of King Henry of England.

XIII

How he found the Lady Margaret

When Raoul pressed his flaccid lips to Margaret's mouth
a second time, she jerked her head back wildly, tear-
ing at his encircling arms like a tigress. Jeanne sprang
to her aid, eluding her guard, and was borne back
again before she had time to do more than strike at
the grinning face bent over Margaret. Slowly Raoul
controlled the frenzied struggling of Margaret's limbs.

"The dove shows fight indeed," he purred. "Well, I
like it better so."

Then was the door flung open, and then did the
steward call Simon's name. On the threshold two
knights stood; one all gold and green, the other black
and steel.

With an oath Raoul let Margaret go, pushing her
from him so that she fell on to the ground. This was
the worst that could befall Raoul, and as he passed his
tongue between his lips, he sought feverishly in his
mind for a plausible excuse wherewith to soften this
English devil. For of all things he most feared an
English invasion of his land.

But Simon had seen, and the sight of Margaret's
slim figure, fighting madly with this deformed, evil
creature, awoke some hitherto dormant emotion within
him. Rage surged up, and suddenly everything grew

red. For the first time in his life he forgot caution, and sprang forward.

"Dog!" he roared, and caught Raoul in his iron grip, forcing him backwards over his bent knee, down and down, hands tightening above the flabby throat, crushing out life. His lips were drawn back in a terrible snarl, and his eyes blazed. "Die, thou dog! Die!" he cried, and stabbed above the collarbone with Margaret's dagger, which he still held.

It was all over in a few seconds, but Raoul's men were upon Simon even as he stabbed. Up he sprang, throwing the dying man down, and tore his sword from the scabbard. After the first shock of surprise Geoffrey had acted quickly, dragging the steward into the room that he might not give the alarm, and slamming the door to. Out came his sword, and in a flash he was upon Simon's assailants, attacking them from the rear.

The two men who held Ranaud's arms, lost their heads, and released him to join in the fight. One only got to the struggling mass, for Ranaud seized the other, and dealt him such a blow upon the chin, that he lost consciousness. Then the giant rushed to aid Geoffrey, and kicking against one fallen man, stopped to wrench the sword from his dead grasp. With this he fell to work, using it like a quarter-staff, and causing considerable damage upon the armourless courtiers.

Margaret flew to where Raoul's crumpled body lay, and fell on her knees beside it, wrenching his light dress-sword from its scabbard. She thrust Jeanne back against the wall, and fought her way to Simon's side, stabbing and thrusting with all her might.

But although Simon and Geoffrey were armour-clad, they were badly outnumbered, and already the noise of this fierce battle had reached the ears of those below. Simon cast a quick glance behind him, to see how far away was the door that led into the room beside the dais. He started to back, and called to Geoffrey in English.

"At my side! Through the door behind me is our only chance. Guard thou Jeanne!"

"Ah, yes, yes!" Margaret panted, and made sign to

Ranaud, slightly jerking her head backwards. He nodded, bellowing out curses on his foes' heads, and wielding his sword like a maniac. Blood was dripping from a gash on his cheek, and from his left arm, but it seemed only to goad him to fresh endeavours.

Jeanne had heard Simon's command, and she slid along the wall, unnoticed in all this turmoil, and lifted the latch, ready to open the door at Simon's word.

The palace-guards were in the room now, but Simon had drawn right back into the corner, so that his little following was guarded on two sides by the wall. He spoke again, gasping.

"Back, Geoffrey! I will hold them. Get all through first. Open!"

Jeanne flung the door back and ran into the adjoining chamber, Margaret at her side. Ranaud followed and stood within—sword upraised. The French made a desperate effort to cut Simon and Geoffrey off from this means of escape, but they stood now in the opening, Geoffrey with his left hand clutching the latch.

Simon cut down the foremost guard, and leaped backwards. On the instant Geoffrey dragged the stout oak door shut, and between them they slammed the bolts home.

Simon wasted no words. He caught Margaret's hand and ran with her down the long, empty chamber to an archway at the far end. Through this they sped, Geoffrey with Jeanne in his arms, and Ranaud bringing up the rear, singing now, an exultant chant. Room after room they traversed, whither they knew not, while from behind came the sound of frenzied blows on the bolted door. At last they came to a large hall, leading from which were three doors, all shut. Margaret flew to one, opening it. A long corridor was revealed. Simon, who had gone to another, found that it led into yet another chamber.

"Here, here!" Margaret cried.

"On then!" Simon commanded, and flung the door he stood by wide. He hurried after Ranaud, who was rolling in Margaret's wake, down the corridor, and waited for Geoffrey to bear Jeanne through. Then he went himself, and stayed to shut the door.

"They should be through by now, but they will go by the door I left open," he panted.

From ahead Margaret's voice sounded.

"Stairs! Stairs!"

"Gently!" Simon hissed, and pushed by Geoffrey. "There may be men below. I go first." Sword in hand he went down the stairs, to find a scullion staring at him open-mouthed. They had come to the kitchens.

The scullion fled for his life, down yet another passage, calling for help.

"The window!" Geoffrey gasped.

"Nay, the door," Simon answered, pointing. "For your life!"

Ranaud tore it open, and out they tumbled into a narrow yard. At the end of it was a barred gate, and to this they ran.

Sounds betokening pursuit came from behind them, and it was with desperate fingers that Simon and Ranaud dragged back the bolts. The gates swung outward, and they found themselves upon greensward. To the right was Santoy, with his men. He saw them, and spurred forward, leading Simon's horse, and shouting to his men to follow.

Simon attempted no explanation, but flung Margaret up on to his horse. She clutched at the animal's mane, sitting astride, and gripping hard with her knees.

Geoffrey seized his own mount, and swung himself up, setting Jeanne on her feet before he did so.

"Hand her up!" he called, and Simon tossed her into his arms.

Ranaud clambered clumsily on to the back of one of the spare horses, grunting and cursing.

"God's my life, I've never sat a horse but once before."

Simon heaved himself into the saddle behind Margaret, his strong arms about her, lifting her across his saddle-bow.

"Cling tight," he said, and smiled down at her. "To the south, and spur them on!" he commanded his men, and on the word his horse sprang forward.

It was not a moment too soon, for through the gate

behind them came their pursuers, yelling in hideous discord. For a while they ran after the mounted men, but soon they realized the hopelessness of the chase, and turned back.

Simon looked over his shoulder.

"Gone to get horses, belike. Well, we are near the border, and a little while should see us out of this accursed land." He looked across at Geoffrey, and laughed. "Geoffrey, this is the first time—and the last, please God—that I have turned my back on the enemy."

"And the first time that thou hast lost thy head," Geoffrey retorted. "I was so taken aback—after thy warning to me, too, that I should keep a cool brain! God's my life, what will King Henry say?"

"He will say good riddance to a foul knave. Bear to the right, Santoy."

Raoul's palace stood but a league from the border, and soon they had crossed it, riding in close formation. Not until they were half a league into the neighbouring domain did Simon give the order to draw rein. Then they halted, while Simon slammed his sword home into the scabbard, and unstrapped his great green cloak from the saddle. This he threw over his shoulders, clasping it at the neck, and drew the heavy folds round him so that they covered the Lady Margaret, shielding her both from the cold wind and from curious eyes. He shifted her a little, so that she lay cradled in his left arm, held in an unyielding grip. Her late labours, the terror she had passed through, and the hardships she had endured during these last five days all told on her. While danger threatened and she had to take command of her emprise she bore up, shaking off fatigue, but now that Simon had come and swept all before him, the need for strength and watchfulness was gone. She lay limp in his arms, half-conscious, knowing herself safe at last. Too tired to realize—or, if she did realize, to care—that Simon was her hated foe, she nestled close against his hard armour, clutching his cloak with a little sigh of relief. Simon looked down at her, and saw that her eyes were shut. And something else he saw, which made the fierce light come into his eyes again. A red patch showed on the sleeve of her tunic. He turned his head, addressing Geoffrey, who was busy wrapping his Jeanne in a cloak.

"Geoffrey, she is wounded. I want linen."

Jeanne started.

"Wounded? Margot? Oh, sir, is—is it deep?"

"Nay, I think not. Give me thy kerchief."

Jeanne tore it away from her neck, handing it to him, and for a while Simon bent over his charge, slitting the sleeve of Margaret's tunic with his dagger. The wound was above the elbow, and slight, but Margaret gave a little cry when Simon started to bind it tightly round. He paid no heed, but tied the bandage, and drew his cloak round her once more, so that she was entirely hidden.

"Art ready, Geoffrey?"

Geoffrey was kissing Jeanne at the moment, but he nodded, and they trotted forward briskly. He drew away from Simon, and looked down into the big eyes that surveyed him.

"Art—art thou—angered with me, Geoffrey?" Jeanne asked him.

"No," he said simply. "I could not be."

The eyes grew rounder.

"I—I thought thou wouldst be furious," Jeanne said, just a little disappointed.

He shook his head.

"Nay, but I will take good care ye play me not such a trick again, sweetheart."

This was better. Jeanne sighed.

"But how wilt thou prevent me?" she asked.

"I will wed thee," Geoffrey said. "Then shalt thou see that I am a stern husband."

Jeanne's spirits were reviving fast. She dimpled.

"Thou wilt bear me, then, to the altar by force, sir."

"If need be," Geoffrey replied.

"Would—would you really?" she asked in keenest admiration.

"I would."

"Then I shall hate thee," Jeanne said severely.

He laughed.

"And make thy life a misery with my shrewish ways."

"Thou wilt be punished, then," Geoffrey said.

"How?"

He kissed her.

"Thus."

"It is very grievous," she said. "I do not think I could bear it."

"Then it is thy life which will be a misery," Geoffrey told her.

"In truth ye would make me your chattel," she sighed. "It is very sad and ungallant. But English, no doubt! A barbarous race."

"I will show thee how the English make love, sweet."

"Oh, I can guess, sir. With a club. As Beauvallet will woo my mistress."

"Beauvallet? Woo the Lady Margaret?" Geoffrey said incredulously. "Thy wits are wandering, Jeanne."

"It is you that are just a great stupid man," she replied scornfully. "I have seen it coming this many a day."

"But Simon doth not——"

"If Simon loves not my lady, why did he slay Raoul?"

"I do not know. I——"

"That is very true," Jeanne said firmly, and closed her eyes.

They rode on in silence then, but at noon they halted at a tavern. Both ladies were asleep, so their bearers carried them into the parlour. They did not wake until dinner was served, and even then Margaret was too worn-out to eat. She drank a little wine, but relapsed almost at once into heavy slumber.

An hour later they set out again, and rode steadily onward, not drawing rein again until dusk, when the gates of Belrémy loomed large ahead. They went through, and along the street to the castle. Jeanne woke then and stretched herself.

"Where are we?" she asked drowsily.

Geoffrey dismounted, holding her against his shoulder.

"Home, dear heart. See!"

"Ah, how good!" she exclaimed. "Set me down, Geoffrey. I will not be carried."

He put her on her feet, turning to Simon and holding out his arms.

"Let me take her, lad."

"Nay." Simon's arm tightened about Margaret's sleeping form. He dismounted carefully, and strode into the castle.

There were several people in the hall, Alan, the Chevalier, and a big man who sat back in the shadow. Hélène too was there, and she ran forward.

"Thou hast my lady?" she cried, and would have drawn back the folds of Simon's cloak.

He warded her off.

"Ay."

Alan hurried forward.

"Already! Both, lad? Ah, Geoffrey!"

The Chevalier minced forward.

"Milor', set my cousin down. It is not fitting that you should carry her thus. Her ladies will attend to her."

"Out of my way," Simon said curtly, and brushed past him to the stairs.

Margaret woke, pushing aside the cloak, and looking about her. She was flushed from sleep, and drowsy still.

"Home! Hélène!" She glanced up into Simon's rugged face, and her eyelids fluttered.

"If you please—I will walk," she said.

"I will carry thee to thy rooms," Simon answered. "Lie still, madame."

She remembered her boy's clothing, and obeyed. Simon swung quickly up the stairs, Jeanne and Hélène at his heels.

A bevy of ladies swarmed about him, but he pushed by to the Countess's chamber, laying her on the bed.

"Get her to bed," he commanded. "One of you fetch the surgeon for her wound." In his turn he was swept aside. The Lady Margaret's ladies gathered about her, exclaiming and fondling. Simon went out, back to the great hall.

A bluff voice smote his ears.

"Now by the Rood, is that my Simon? God's Body, what doth he with a maid in his arms? Ha, Simon, thou rogue! Come hither!" Fulk limped forward, hands outstretched.

"My lord!" Simon strode to meet him, and gripped his hands. "My dear lord!"

Fulk embraced him.

"My Simon—my lion-cub! I could not stay away. Fiend seize thee, thou hast grown again, or else I had forgotten thy great height. What a-God's Name do ye in all this golden armour? Thou popinjay! My lad, my lad, kneel not to me!" For Simon had dropped on his knee. Fulk pulled him up. "Give me thy hand again! I have heard of thy prowess, lion-cub. And thou wert once my pert squire! Glory, glory, I never thought I should live to be proud of thee!" He held Simon at arm's length, gazing at him. "Ay, ay, the same beetle-brows, and the same cold eyes. Turn to the light, silly boy! Now, by my troth, I do see a difference!"

Alan came to Simon's side.

"Wert thou surprised? My lord did come yesterday, straight from the King."

"I thought I dreamed," Simon said. "How come ye to these shores, my lord?"

"Faith, in a boat, lad. There was I at home, fretting for news of thee both, which came not, and could bear it no longer. Since my lady died and my daughters are both wed, I must e'en be near one or other of you. So off went I to London to my cousin Granmere. He did aid me, and I sailed for France with the mails. Then went I to the King, and he sent me here. And since yesterday I have heard of naught save thy prowess, and how thou didst capture this place. Simon, Simon, it was well done! Would that I had been with thee, lad, but I am old and this accursed gout—well, well! What hath come to mine Alan? He left Montlice a silly boy, sighing and singing for his lady-loves, and here I find him a man at last, which I never thought to see him. Hast made a soldier of him, lad?"

Simon led him to a chair.

"Nay. King Hal calls him his poet, but he can lead

an attack better than Geoffrey here, if he has a mind to it."

Fulk turned to look at Malvallet, who stood apart, watching them. Up he struggled once more and stumped forward.

"Needs must I take thy hand, Sir Geoffrey," he mumbled. "If thou wilt have it so. This is war-time, and there is no room for enmity between us two."

Geoffrey bent the knee gracefully.

"I am only too well pleased to have it so, my lord," he said. "For Simon, Alan and I are one."

So they clasped hands, and Fulk sat down again with all three about him. The Chevalier had minced away some time ago, and Santoy had taken the wounded and very much shaken Ranaud to find a surgeon, so that they were alone. Fulk blew out his cheeks, looking proudly from Alan to Simon, and smiled a little at the glory of Simon's armour.

"Well, I had heard of thy gilded armour, lad, but never till now have I seen thee in it. Thou coxcomb! And tell me, lion-cub, who was the lady whom ye bore in your arms?"

Simon rose, and glanced from one to the other of them. For a moment he was silent, and then the glimmering of a smile came into his green-blue eyes.

"That, my lord, is the lady whom I will one day take to wife," he said deliberately.

XIV

How he received the Lady Margaret's submission

My Lord of Montlice hobbled out on to the terrace. It was the day after Simon's return, and he was still in a state of incoherent surprise over the amazing announcement that Simon had made the night before. At the time, he had stared open-mouthed, and before he had in the smallest degree recovered from the first shock of surprise, Simon had gone. All the evening he had been busy, so there had been no more private conversation. This morning he was closeted with his secretary, so Fulk wandered out in search of his son, whom he found on the terrace, fitting a new string to his harp. Alan smiled when he saw his father, and his smile was very sweet, as always.

Fulk lowered himself on to the chair that Alan vacated.

"Fiend seize my foot!" he growled, and glared at it.

Alan sat down on the parapet, a gay figure against the dull stone. His father grunted.

"Still harping, silly lad?"

"Still," Alan answered.

"Hast naught better to do?"

"Simon would tell thee ay. But Simon hath no ear for music."

"He tells me that thou art Master of his Horse."

Alan laughed.

"It is true, alack!"

"He saith that thou art a good master, but I doubt he seeks to flatter thee to me."

"I think he doth," Alan said, and smiled again.

"Alan!" Fulk drove his stick on to the ground. "What meant the lad last night?"

Alan glanced up through his lashes.

"Last night?"

Fulk roared at him.

"Thou foolish boy! When he said that he would take the Lady Margaret to wife!"

"Well, sir——" Alan twanged his harp meditatively —"He is Simon of Beauvallet, so I suppose he did mean—just that."

"But thou didst tell me that the Lady Margaret hated him, and sought to slay him!" exploded Fulk.

"Ay, my lord."

"Then what maggot hath Simon is his silly head?"

Alan drew his hand across the strings so that they sang softly under his fingers.

240

"The maggot of love, my father."

"Love for a froward woman? Much have I heard of the lady on my way hither, and it seems to me that she is a bold, spiteful hussy."

"Bold, sir, and tigerish, but so is Simon. No milk-and-water maid could touch his heart. He must take a fitting mate unto himself. The Countess is such an one, and not soft speech will move her, but rugged strength, and maybe rough usage."

Fulk stared at him.

"Art very wise. I would fain meet this lady."

"Oh, sir, she will send thee from her side with a flea in thine ear."

"Oho!" said Fulk. "I am an old man." He stroked his grey hair ruefully.

Alan touched his hand affectionately.

"Yet the old man did come to France and is none the worse for his tedious journey," he said.

Fulk puffed, pleased at the compliment.

"Oh, there is life in the lion yet!" he nodded. "Who comes?"

Alan sprang up, for Jeanne was limping towards them.

"It is Mademoiselle Jeanne, who is soon to be Geoffrey's lady," he said, and kissed Jeanne's hand. "Mademoiselle, ye see here my father, Lord Fulk of Montlice."

Jeanne curtseyed in response to Fulk's bow, and went to sit beside him on the bench.

"Is it the gout?" Fulk asked, interested, pointing to her feet.

Jeanne dimpled charmingly.

"Nay, milor', it is—oh, it is blisters!"

"Ay, ay! Art a brave lass, I do hear."

"Not I, sir. 'Tis Margot who is brave."

"Mademoiselle," Alan interrupted, "what chanced in Raoul's palace? Simon says naught, and I have had no word with Geoffrey. Is it true that Simon slew Raoul?"

Jeanne closed her eyes.

"It was terrible," she said. "Raoul—Raoul had Margot in his arms. He—he kissed her, and she fought him.

241

Then—then, when I thought all was lost, there came the clank of armour, and Lord Simon stood in the doorway with Geoffrey beside him. Oh, sir, I thought mine eyes deceived me! So great they looked, the one all black and grey, and the other gold and green! Raoul pushed my lady away, but he was too late." Jeanne threw out her hand dramatically. "I saw my Lord of Beauvallet grow stiff all at once, and there came a light into his eyes such as I have never seen before. He smiled, and indeed, indeed, that smile drove terror into my heart. Just one moment he stood there, while I wondered what he would be at. And then he seemed to leap forward! In a second he was by us, and had seized up Raoul in his arms. He bent him over his knee, backwards, until methought Raoul's spine would snap. And he said"—Jeanne tried to imitate Simon's snarl—"'*Die* thou dog!' Then he stabbed suddenly, and the blood spurted up! It was horrible, horrible! After that it is all—a mist. They fought, all of them, even Margot, but they could not hope to conquer, so we fled through a door behind us, and ran, and ran, and ran! And at last we found a stairway, which led out of the castle. Raoul's men were hard on our heels, but we ran across a courtyard, and Ranaud wrenched the gate open. Then found we the horses, and fled for our lives."

"Simon ran away?" Fulk asked incredulously.

"What else could he do? I think—he lost his head. He meant not to kill Raoul, but when he saw my lady in his arms, he forgot caution, and only thought of vengeance."

"That is not like Simon!" Fulk said.

"It is like the new Simon," Alan answered.

To Simon came a French page, bowing low.

"Milor', I bear a message from madame."

"What is it?"

"Madame requests milor' to visit her. She hath that which she would say to milor'."

Simon rose.

"Lead me to madame."

The page conducted him to Margaret's rooms, and announced.

The Countess was alone, standing by the window. She was clad in a long red robe, and she wore a horned head-dress upon her head. She came forward a few steps, to meet Simon, and he saw that her hands were tightly clenched.

"Well, madame?"

Margaret moistened her lips. She began to speak jerkily, her eyes dark and troubled.

"Milor', there is much I must say to you. Ye have—placed me in your—debt." Her eyelids drooped a little, and the proud lips quivered.

Simon said nothing, watching her.

"I have first—to thank you—for—what you did—yesterday." The words stuck in her throat a little, but she went on bravely. "Had ye not come—to my rescue—I had been—what I will not think—today." Her eyes searched his face, but it was impassive. Simon's arms were folded across his great chest, and he stood very still before her. Again she moistened her lips. "Margaret of Belrémy—leaves not—her debts—unpaid. Had I not—fallen into Raoul's clutches—I would have—brought—an army to Belrémy—to fight you. But—I failed, and—you—rescued me. I—I desire now—to wipe away—the debt I owe you. So—so—I will—make my submission to you." Her voice had sunk, but it vibrated with her pride.

"I want more than that."

She started, clasping her hands nervously together.

"You—you seek—my life?" she asked, and squared her shoulders.

Simon came heavily up to her, and took her wrists in his hold.

"Thy life, ay. All of thee." Suddenly he bent forward, and kissed her, full on her red lips.

She sprang away, trembling and shaken, pressing her hands to her hot cheeks.

"You—oh, you insult me! I have not deserved—that! My God, I had—I had come to think you—a man of honour!"

"I insult thee not," Simon said calmly. "I want thy hand in marriage."

She stared at him, hardly comprehending. Then she recoiled, eyes aflame.

"You—you——For what do ye take me? Think ye I would wed—an English boor?" She spat the words at him, and her bosom heaved.

"I think that thou wilt wed me, madame. What I want, I take."

"Ye take not me! Mordieu, are ye mad? Wed me? I—I am Margaret of Belrémy!"

"Thou art my prisoner."

"No longer!" She stepped quickly up to him, her silken skirts brushing the ground. "I have made my submission!"

He looked down at her for a moment, in silence; then he drew a folded parchment from his belt, and spread it upon the table.

"It awaits thy signature, madame. Thy submission to my master."

Slowly she approached the table, and read the formal words. A little shiver ran through her, and she bit her lip. She sat down, and picked up her quill. For a long time she sat very still, but presently she dipped the quill in the ink, and quickly signed her name. She would have risen then, but Simon's hand was on her shoulder.

"There lies thy submission to the King my master," he said and she saw that his eyes gleamed. "But thy submission to me must come soon. Thy life is mine by right of conquest, and well dost thou know it. Willingly shalt thou come to me, and willingly give thy heart. For I will have all or nothing."

"Nothing, then!" she said hoarsely.

He smiled, and picked up the parchment.

" 'I have not, but still I hold'," he said, and laughed, swung round on his heel, and went out.

Margaret stumbled up, trying to control the wild leaping of her pulses. To her came Jeanne, and cast her a shrewd glance.

"Jeanne!" Margaret cried. "*He* has been here! He—he

kissed me. Oh, how I hate him!" Raging, she paced the floor, lashing herself to a fury.

"I have heard that hate is akin to love," Jeanne marked placidly.

"Love! I love that—that——" she choked for words. "He thinks to wed me! He! Ah, how I hate him!"

"Thou didst not hate him when he killed Raoul," Jeanne said.

Margaret paused, staring at her, wild-eyed.

"Did I not? Did I not? Oh, what ails me, Jeanne?" She sank down upon the floor beside her lady, sobbing.

"Pride dies hard," Jeanne said softly. "Thou art torn between love and hate."

"No, no! It is all hate, all hate!"

"Then why dost thou weep?"

"I—I do not know—I am distraught. It was his kiss, burning me! Shaming me! Ah, let me go!" She sprang up and away, rushing from the room straight into the arms of her cousin.

"Victor! You? What—do ye here?"

He twirled his scented kerchief, eyes running swiftly over her.

"I came to wait upon thee, sweet Margot, but yon yellow-haired Saxon was before me. Thou art strangely disordered, cousin." He bent forward, scrutinizing her. "Now what hath he done, I wonder?"

"Out, out of my way!" she cried, and swept past, down the corridor.

The Chevalier entered her room. Jeanne looked coldly at him, but he smiled.

"So the English oaf kissed my cousin?" he said gently, and showed his teeth a moment.

"Ye would appear to be in his confidence," Jeanne snapped.

He paid no heed.

"And she is all distraught. What does that betoken? . . ."

XV

How he came upon the Lady Margaret in the gallery

On a voyage of exploration through the castle, Fulk came to a wide gallery where the musicians were wont to play. Coming towards him, away from her rooms, was the Lady Margaret, tall and stately as ever in a cloth of gold, with her long hair braided, and a gold band about her forehead from which glowed a single sapphire stone. She paused when she saw Fulk, and looked him over, for he was a stranger to her.

Fulk looked back at her squarely, leaning on his stout ashplant. The Lady Margaret would have passed on, chin lifted, but he blocked her passage.

"Know ye the way back to the hall, madame?" he asked, in very fair French. "I have lost my path."

"The stairs are yonder, sir," she said, pointing.

Fulk sighed, and thought that he would be very cunning.

"Stairs, stairs, stairs! If there were chairs I should like it better. I have had the gout this many a day, lady, and it plagues me sorely."

The Countess hesitated, but Fulk's white hairs made her courteous.

"There are chairs behind you, sir," she said.

"Why then, madame, if you will be seated, so will I," he answered.

"I thank you, no." On swept my lady, but was arrested by Fulk's roar. He could never be patient for long.

"Come back, come back! God's Body, have I not been lonely enough? Come hither, whoever ye may be, and bear an old man company."

The Lady Margaret spoke coldly.

"I am the Countess of Belrémy," she said, and her tone should have crushed him.

"What care I for that?" he demanded. "If you wish to sing titles, I am the Earl of Montlice. Now sit ye down, a-God's sake!"

Margaret was somewhat taken aback.

"I—I do not know the Earl of Montlice, sir."

"That do ye. Sit thee down, I say!"

Margaret was inclined to be haughty, but when Fulk stamped his foot and swore at the pain, she laughed, and came to him, sitting down.

"I do not know why ye should desire to keep me with you," she said frankly. "I have no love for Englishmen."

Fulk lowered himself beside her.

"Now what hath been done to thee by an Englishman?" quoth he.

She flushed.

"Ye call it nothing that my land hath been ta'en by an Englishman?" she cried.

"Fortune o' war," he grunted. "Thou hadst a worthy foe."

"Sir?"

"Why I do hear that my boy Simon and thou do tilt at one another. Now Simon is a man, God wot!"

"Indeed, sir?"

"Did ye doubt it?" Fulk slewed round to face her. "A plague be on the lad, what hath he done? He was ever a pert, headstrong child, but I never heard that he did more harm to a maid than turn his back on her."

"Oh, he is very chivalrous!" she sneered. "See this scar on my breast! That did he with his sword!"

Fulk looked at it.

"Did he so? Wherefore should he do that?"

"Because I would not yield thy son to him, nor my castle!"

"Ah, well!" Fulk puffed out his cheeks. "Alan is dear to him. As for thy castle—what he had sworn to take he would take, willy-nilly. It is his way. Lord, Lord, I should know, for had I not to bear with him four long years? The lad was my squire, lady."

247

"Thy squire?" She was surprised, in spite of herself. "How could he be that?"

"Why, look ye, he was Malvallet's bastard, and Malvallet was my foe. When Simon's mother died he came to me, and bearded me in my lair." He chuckled. "I was a fierce fellow in those days, lady, but Holy Virgin, he was as fierce! A square-set whelp, some fourteen years old, and forced himself into my service. A pretty time I had with him, madame, and an obstinate, impudent cub he was. Many's the beating I've given him, but do ye think he cared? Not he! He'd e'en go his own road, say or do what I would. Cold as a stone, as strong as I was myself. Up he grew, like a young tree. The shoulders of him! He hath a blow which would fell an ox, lady, and the coolest brain ever I knew. Now hark while I tell thee how he came by his lands." Fulk settled himself more comfortably, and proceeded to recount the exploits of his beloved lion-cub. Margaret listened, eyes downcast, but once she raised them, and they were sparkling with sympathy for one of Simon's deeds. But at the end of the recital the colour died out of her cheeks, and she remembered that Simon was her enemy.

"Ye would seem to have a fondness for this Simon, milor'."

"Needs must I," Fulk grunted. "I do indeed love the boy. He cares for me a little, but he hath never asked a favour of me, and never will. What he wants, he will win himself. Never was there a prouder, more cock-sure lad!"

"It is praiseworthy, perhaps," Margaret said slowly, "but he cannot—always—win."

Fulk's eyes twinkled.

"So, so! And who shall teach him that, lady?"

She looked at him, and he saw her lips tight-shut.

"Aha! So ye think to bring Simon to heel, madame? I wonder if you will do it?"

"I desire only that he shall leave my land, never to return."

"Well, he is like to," Fulk announced. "He goes soon to join the King."

248

"I am glad," said the Lady Margaret primly. "I hope it will be very, very soon!"

"Here's a heat!" Fulk remarked. "Why dost thou hate him so?"

"I have told thee. Once I sought to kill him——" she spoke through clenched teeth—"and could not! Could not, though he would have let me! I was a coward, and now I do owe my life to him!"

"And didst fight at his side, if Malvallet and thy lady speak sooth. That was not done of hate, madame."

"I fought because—because I had to escape. Not to save him!"

Fulk grunted.

"And even now, had I the means to hand, I would slay him gladly! Ay, gladly!"

"Brave words," Fulk said. "Simon is not one to be worsted by a maid. What good would his death bring you? King Henry would fall upon thy land."

"I held out 'gainst Umfraville!"

"Ay, but the English are in now," Fulk said.

A soft yet heavy tread sounded. Along the gallery came Simon, and at sight of him the Lady Margaret rose, yet was too proud to seek refuge in flight.

Simon halted before her, looking gravely into her eyes. But all at once a smile came to disperse the gravity, and it was so unlike the smile she had seen on his lips before, that almost it drew from her an answering gleam. There was no grimness in it, but a species of amused understanding.

"So my lord hath found thee?" he said. "I dare swear he hath told thee that I was once the bane of his life."

"My lord is generous in his praise of you," she answered stiffly.

Simon glanced at Fulk with uplifted brows.

"Never said I one word of praise!" Fulk roared. "I praise thee? God's Body, I am not yet in my dotage! Praise—thou pert boy, what ails thee? My lady knows now thy stubborn temper. Praise, forsooth!"

Simon laughed.

"Wert ever chary of praise to my face, sir," he said mildly.

"And behind thy back!" Fulk averred. "A more worthless, blundering, silly-pated, obstinate lad never I saw! A pity is it that none ever thought to knock a little sense into thee."

"Nay, my lord, one did try, but it seemed he failed, although he had me in my youth to mould."

"A graceless, impudent coxcomb thou wert!"

"Indeed, I think I was so indeed," Simon reflected. "A sore trial to thee, sir."

"Thou art well enough," Fulk grunted. "Ye need not seek to cozen me."

"Why, sir, I do know it to be useless," Simon said.

Margaret glanced from one to the other. This new Simon was a stranger to her. The Simon she knew was a stern lord with little humour but great strength, not a smiling man who meekly listened to abuse of himself. She drew her skirts about her, preparing to depart, but Fulk struggled up, laying a hand on her shoulder.

"Now here is a right noble lady," he informed Simon bluffly. "Shouldst take a lesson from her, lad."

Simon's eyes were upon her face, and Margaret felt the colour rise to her cheeks.

"It boots not to sing my praise to Lord Simon of Beauvallet, sir," she said icily.

"Nay." It was Simon who answered. "I need no telling."

"Hadst best have a care to thyself," Fulk warned him jovially. "My lady will be satisfied with naught save thy life."

Margaret's cheeks were flaming now. She bit her lip, glaring at the well-meaning but tactless Fulk.

"My life is hers," Simon said quietly.

"I should have said thy death," Fulk chuckled.

Simon drew his dagger from its sheath and presented the hilt to Margaret.

"That also."

Margaret drew away from under Fulk's hand.

"The jest is no doubt amusing, sir. I will leave you to enjoy it."

Fulk conceived that this curious pair of lovers should now be left alone, so he stumped off towards the stairs, shaking his head over the incomprehensible ways of the younger generation.

Simon stood before Margaret, barring her passage. He was in a genial mood this morning, and strange forces were at work within him.

"Be pleased to let me pass," Margaret said imperiously.

He shook his head.

"In a little while, Margot."

"My name, sir?" Her eyes flamed.

"Thy name." He turned the naked dagger in his hand, looking down at it. "It was no jest, madame. If thou wouldst strike, strike now."

"Thou hast tied my hands," she answered bitterly. "I am not sunk so low. Thou hast told me that my life is thine by right of conquest. That is not so, but thou didst rescue me, in my dire peril, for which I must needs be grateful."

"I want not thy gratitude. That debt is paid, and the past is dead. If thou dost indeed hate me——"

"Ah, can you doubt that?" she cried.

He smiled a little.

"Thou hast assured me of thy hatred many a time, and of thine undying lust for vengeance. And yet. . . . Thou didst lie in mine arms once, content to be there, and it was not hate that prompted thee to feel thyself safe, and to sleep with thy head on my breast."

"You taunt me with that? I was weary, and beside myself with fear and—and everything!"

"Nay, I do not taunt thee. The memory of that ride is precious to me."

She was silent.

"Methinks," Simon went on, "I never knew thee until I saw thee clad in thy boy's clothes, fighting at my side."

She flushed.

"Not for nothing am I the Amazon," she said through her shut teeth.

"The Amazon? Nay, thou didst seem just a helpless child, grown suddenly small in thine unaccustomed raiment. It was that, I think, that awoke some devil within me, and made me slay Raoul."

She laughed harshly.

"I thank you, milor'! So it was with a child that thou didst—didst—fall in love—if love this be!"

"It must be love, Margot, but I know little of such matters. I only know that I want thee, and must have thee."

"Then know also, sir, that I will none of thy wooing! Now let me pass!"

He stood aside at once, and she almost ran down the gallery to her rooms, meeting Alan on the way, and brushing past him without a glance in his direction. Alan strolled up to Simon, half-smiling.

"One pair of lovers left I in the hall, and here I stumble upon yet another. And I—I the only real lover amongst you—am maid-less. It is a sad world."

"Alan," Simon said abruptly. "Tell me of love. What is it?"

"I can tell thee naught that thou dost not know already. Long, long ago I did say that the day would come when some maid should wake thy cold heart. Behold, it is here at last, and thou dost ask me to tell thee of love!"

"It is love, then, that stirs my blood? But—but—but——"

Alan laughed softly.

"It comes to all men once at least, and to some many times. To thee it came slowly, but to some it comes as a sudden shock."

Simon pondered gravely, and in a few moments Alan spoke again.

"I came in search of thee. I want to warn thee."

Instantly Simon was on the alert, and the softness went out of his face.

"Well?"

"I mislike the looks of yon Frenchman, the Chevalier. Of late there hath come a new gleam into his eyes, and I think he seeks to do thee harm."

"That little popinjay!"

"But he was first in the field," Alan said quietly.

"What mean ye?"

"Why, that he also loves the Lady Margaret, although she slights him."

"He—loves——!" Simon's hand clenched. "If I find——"

"Nay, listen, thou jealous lover! As I came hither I chanced on him, descending the stairway. Methinks he doth play the spy, and if it seems to him that thou art like to win the Countess, he will dispose of thee as best he can."

Simon shrugged.

"What can he do! He made his submission long since."

"And ye would trust to his honour, Simon?"

"I have as yet no reason—since his submission—for doubting it."

"Save his shifty eyes, and spying ways. I would like to see him safe under lock and key, lad."

"I cannot do that," Simon answered shortly. "Do ye think I fear him?"

"Not I, but the soft-spoken are the most dangerous of all foes. Look well to thyself, Simon."

"Ye think he will slay me?"

"Nay, I think he will try to," Alan riposted. "Or mayhap he will hire some rogue to do it for him, and thus in a little salve his conscience."

Simon smiled.

"I doubt that same rogue will find his task hard indeed," he remarked. "I have ears that hear that which makes no sound, and eyes that see in the dark."

"Still, be more watchful than ever," Alan warned him. "When do ye go to Bayeux?"

"Next week. I leave Geoffrey here, with thy father. Huntingdon must go with me."

"And I."

"And thou."

"When wilt thou return?"

"I know not." Simon sighed faintly. "The message that thy father brought told me that the King had need of me. He waits but to see Gloucester triumph, and Domfront fall to Warwick. Then he will march on Rouen."

"Whom will he leave to govern this land?"

"The Lady Margaret hath submitted. She will rule here."

"Some over-lord he will appoint."

"Perhaps Salisbury. Who knows?"

"Who indeed?" said Alan softly.

XVI

How he walked alone in the garden

Bareheaded he walked slowly through the garden that surrounded the castle, and the pale sunlight played about his fair hair, while the wind stirred it gently and blew it across his face. His sword hung at his side, but his hands were clasped listlessly behind him, and he bent his head, deep in thought.

It was four days since his talk with Margaret in the gallery and nothing further had passed between them since then. In two more days he would be gone from Belrémy, and for the first time in his life he was worried.

He paced slowly to and fro across the lawn before the castle, seemingly lost in his thoughts, frowning slightly. From an arbour close by the Lady Margaret watched him, hidden from his sight by the bushes through which she peeped. She had escaped from her ladies and come here to be alone, why, she knew not. Ever since the day when Simon had rescued her from Raoul she had been racked and torn by conflicting emotions. Not one of them could she recognize, but she knew that a strange misery had her in its hold, that would not let her rest, causing her sleepless nights and storm-tossed thoughts. She was hungry for an unknown something, and at times she would bite hard on her lip to hold back the rush of angry, heart-sick tears that sprang to her eyes. She was restless, too, and short with her ladies. Not even Jeanne would she have near her for long, but fled away by herself as now, fighting what she half-guessed to be a yearning for her mate. Try as she might she could not forget the feel of his arms about her on the ride from Raoul's land, or the touch of his lips on hers. Again and again she tried to lash her anger to fresh energy, remembering all Simon's iniquities, dwelling on them fiercely, pressing the scar on her bosom with nervous, trembling hands.

For a long time she sat motionless in the arbour, heedless of the cold, watching Simon's ceaseless, measured pacing with eyes that burned dark and troubled. Presently she saw him wheel to the left, and in a moment he had passed from her sight, through a gap in the yew hedge. Some of the rigidity left her then, and she fell to plucking at her gown, twisting the silk between her fingers, her mouth all awry with some inward pain. But in a little while she covered her face with her hands, and so remained for a long time, silent.

She did not know why she suddenly looked up, every nerve strained to attention. No one was in sight, but from somewhere near at hand had come the sound of brushing against leaves. It was a tiny sound; a bird might have caused it, or some small animal, and yet she leaned forward, peering through the bushes with eyes that were narrowed and keen. Again came the sound, and she rose, noiseless, her skirts gathered up in one tense hand.

To the left was the castle, to the right the hedge that bordered the bowling-green. Straight ahead, at the far end of the lawn was the gap through which Simon had gone. It led along an alley between high hedges, to her own garden, the pleasaunce, away from the castle. On the other side of the hedge that ran parallel to the castle were fields, leading down to the moat. It was towards this hedge that she looked, and presently, where the leaves were sparse, saw a shadow, moving stealthily beside it, on the other side. It was but a fleeting glimpse that she had, but her nerves sprang to a conclusion. Quickly she pushed through the tangled bush, and stepped on to the green. One moment she stood there, staring intently to the right, and again heard the faint rustle. The leaves seemed to quiver in one spot, and grew still again.

Every pulse was throbbing in her body, but she forced herself to walk calmly forward, outwardly careless and aimless. The blood sang in her ears, for she knew that there was one, perhaps more, behind the hedge, watching her intently. On she went, heart beating loud and unevenly, but walking slowly, looking about her. It seemed to her that the bowling-green had become of a sudden a vast desert which she could never span, but at last she came to the end, pretended to hesitate a moment, and then went through the gap. The path twisted almost at once, and so soon as she had rounded the bend, she caught up her skirts and ran as if for dear life along the tortuous alley.

Simon was in the pleasaunce gazing abstractedly down upon the sundial that stood in the centre. All about him were little walks and flower-beds, with snowdrops growing in them. The sound of light footsteps speeding towards him made him look up quickly, a hand to his sword-hilt. Into the pleasaunce came the Lady Margaret, panting for breath and running like one possessed. He started forward, brow lowering.

"What is it? Who hath dared——"

She almost fell into his arms, outstretched to receive her, clutching at his long tunic with desperate fingers.

"Come, come away—I implore thee! Give—give me—thine arm! Thy—thy—sword? Ah! Quickly, quickly! Away—from this—spot!"

Simon's hands were on her shoulders, his voice rang harshly in her ears.

"Who hath dared to molest thee? Answer!"

"None—none!" She tugged wildly at his tunic. "It—it is not that! Oh, come, come! Every moment you stay—may mean—death!"

He stared at her in surprise, then cast a quick look around.

"Death? What mean ye, child?"

"Oh, tarry not!" she implored. "I—take me to the castle—I beg of you! I—oh, come milor'! Come! Come! There is someone—lurking—behind the bushes! He—I saw him yonder, creeping in thy wake! Even now—he may be—upon us! For God's sake come away!"

But Simon had his arms about her and his voice was strangely moved.

"And thou didst come to warn me, Margot?"

In her frenzy she scarcely noticed his embrace, but beat her clenched fists against his breast.

"Oh, will you not come? Will you not come?"

"I fear no assassin that ever drew breath, child," he said gently, "but I will come if you will it so."

She brew a sobbing breath of relief, falling back.

"Then—then—walk on my right, milor', and—and—walk swiftly!"

Even as she spoke he had turned sharply round on his heel, staring into the bushes. Slowly he drew his sword, and went forward, panther-like. Margaret stayed by the sun-dial, trembling, but fearful of uttering a single cry lest it warn the prey he stalked of danger. She saw Simon leap forward, as if some spring within him had been loosed, and thrust with his sword through the hedge. A muffled shriek came, a scuffle, and the sound of thudding footsteps, retreating in haste. Simon turned, wiped his sword upon the grass, and sheathed it. Then he came back to Margaret and stood before her.

"Was it only out of gratitude that thou didst come to warn me?" he asked.

She started, gripping the edge of the sun-dial, and gazing up at him with wild, hungry eyes.

"Thine is a strange hatred," Simon went on, and held out his hands. "Is it hate indeed?"

Her knees shook under her; her breath came fast and uneven.

"Ay—hate—hate—hate! Ah, what ails me? What have I done? What—what—I am mad! Mad! I—it was gratitude! I—I have not changed! I yield me—never!" She shrank away, warding him off. "Touch me not! I could not let him slay thee—thus! I—I could not, but—I—I think—I am—like to—swoon!"

He caught her even as she swayed, sweeping her off her feet. One instant she struggled, crying out, and then crumpled up in his arms, her head falling back lifeless.

Swiftly Simon bore her to the castle, brushing past staring lackeys, and striding to the stairs. He came to the Countess's rooms, and there found Jeanne with Hélène.

"She hath swooned only," he said in answer to the startled outcry. "It was her wound, belike."

"Lay her down, lay her down!" Jeanne commanded, and spread cushions on the wooden settle.

Gently Simon laid his burden on them.

"She ran to warn me of danger from an assassin's knife," he said curtly. "She hath ta'en no hurt, nor I. Look to her, mademoiselle, and have a care."

Jeanne smiled a little at that.

"Yes, milor'," she said demurely, and with twinkling eyes watched him go out.

Sighing, the Lady Margaret came to her senses.

"Jeanne? Methought—ah, he is safe?" She struggled up, staring about her.

Jeanne pressed her back on to the cushions.

"Yes, *chérie*, quite safe. He brought thee here. *Mignonne, mignonne,* I would not lie to thee!"

The strained muscles relaxed. Margaret lay still, eyes closed. Presently she opened them, and looked wistfully up at her lady.

"I—I am mad, Jeanne," she said, and her lips quivered. "I—do not—really—care—whether he—is alive—or dead! I—my head—is reeling! Jeanne! I—I am—weeping! What—comes to me?"

"Love, *chérie*," Jeanne whispered, and kissed her softly.

XVII

How he left Belrémy, and how the Lady Margaret dealt with her cousin

Geoffrey burst in upon him, Alan following languidly at his heels.

"Simon, what is this I hear?" Geoffrey demanded. "Is it true that one sought to slay thee?"

"Ay." Simon smiled a little. "A creature in the Chevalier's pay." He nodded to Alan. "Thou wert right, O sage!"

"Of course I was right," Alan said placidly. "What wilt thou do now?"

"I go to Bayeux."

"Ay, but what of thy would-be assassin?" Geoffrey cried.

"Naught. I know not who he was, and I have no proof. Once I am gone the Chevalier will be happy enough."

Geoffrey was dissatisfied.

"I would clap him up!"

"I have not the power. He would deny the charge, and the Lady Margaret rules here now."

"Simon, it is not like thee to be magnamimous!" Geoffrey exclaimed. "What ails thee?"

"God knows. The Chevalier is too little for my vengeance, I think. I can punish him best by ignoring him. But when I am gone, do thou have a care, Geoffrey."

"I mislike the task of ruling this land," Geoffrey grumbled. "Leave Huntingdon, and take me with thee."

"He is too young. And thou wilt be content enough with thy Jeanne. She would never forgive me an I wrested thee from her now."

"What is that to thee?" Geoffrey stared. "Thou art changed indeed, Simon!"

Simon shrugged.

"Maybe," he said, and then was silent for a long time.

Later, Ranaud came to him, recovered now, and in high spirits. Simon received him unemotionally, but Ranaud tried to kiss his hand.

"Ah, lord, it was well done! I would it had been my hand that had slain the toad. By the Virgin, your grip was of iron on his fat neck!"

Simon smiled a little.

"Ye did well, Ranaud, though I slew Raoul. Art a brave man, methinks. What want ye of me?"

Ranaud smote his thigh.

"Thought I to myself, by God, this is a fit master for me! So please you, sir, I'll join your guards, or your archers. I have some training with a cross-bow."

Simon looked him over for a moment, and then nodded abruptly.

"If I am the master for thee, thou art the man for me, yet the Lady Countess doth command your loyalty."

"I am Ranaud, and I serve whom I please," the giant answered. "But it seems to me that the day is not far distant when I shall call ye both master, and own not two neither."

"That is as maybe," Simon said coldly, and drew pen and parchment forward to enrol Ranaud.

On the day of his departure he went to the Lady Margaret's bower where she reclined on a couch, pale and listless. He was clad in his armour, and at the sight of it her lips quivered.

"I come to bid thee farewell, Margot," he said quietly.

She rose, gazing at him.

"You—you are going—to Bayeux?"

"Ay. Thou art rid of me at last."

She winced at that, and her eyes filled with tears.

"You—return—not?"

"If God wills, I shall return. But if so be I fall in battle, think this of me, Margot, that if ever I harmed thee, or hurt thee, at least it was not of mine own desire. And remember also that I did love thee very dearly." He went down on his knee, most unexpectedly, and kissed her cold hand. "Plague not Malvallet," he said humorously. "He is no match for thy fierceness."

She smiled wanly.

"I have submitted."

"Ay." He rose and looked at her for a moment. "Farewell, Margot."

"Fare—well——" The whisper just reached him. He turned and went to the door.

The weights that held Margaret to the floor seemed to fall away. She stumbled forward, hands outstretched.

"Ah, thou wilt come back? Thou wilt!"

He caught her in his arms.

"I will come back. But when I come it will be to lead thee to the altar, if I am alive still." He bent his head and kissed her long and passionately, and although she did not return his kiss, she was passive under it. The next moment he had released her, and was gone through the door, away.

The Lady Margaret fell on her knees beside the table, clinging to it, while hard, dry sobs shook her. How long she remained there she did not know, but presently came the noise of horses' hoofs without, and the sound of voices. She pulled herself up, and dragged her feet to the window, kneeling on the high bench below it. Dry-eyed, she watched Simon clasp Geoffrey's hand in farewell, and kneel to receive Fulk's blessing. Then she saw him mount his horse, and ride towards the drawbridge, in the midst of his men. Once he looked up at her window and seeing her there, raised his mailed hand in salute. Then he was gone, and the clattering of the horses' hoofs died away in the distance.

Jeanne entered softly, and came to her mistress, passing an arm about her waist. So they stood for a time, silent, until Margaret disengaged herself. Her voice was calm, now, and cold.

"Jeanne, bid them fetch my cousin and his father."

"Yes, *chérie*. What will you do?"

"Fetch them, Jeanne," Margaret repeated gently.

When the Chevalier and her uncle came in they

found Margaret seated in a high-backed chair by the table, her hands folded in her lap, her stately head held high.

The Sire de Galledemaine bowed to her.

"You desired our presence, madame?"

"Yes, my uncle. I desire that ye shall hear what I have to say to your son."

The Sire looked surprised, glanced inquiringly at the Chevalier.

"Is it possible, madame, that Victor has annoyed thee?"

Her lips curled.

"Annoyed is a small word, sir. The Chevalier will understand, when I say that I think his own lands stand in need of him."

The Chevalier started, dropping the flower he held.

"Margot!"

"My name is not for such as you to use, sir!" she said haughtily. "Ye do know why I will no longer harbour you."

"Fair cousin, you are distraught," the Chevalier said silkily. "I know naught."

Her look was full of scorn.

"Ye desire that I should be more explicit?"

"Most certainly, madame, for I am in the dark."

"Then know, sir, that I was in the garden when you did send your bravo to slay my Lord of Beauvallet."

Her uncle gasped, falling away from his son.

"Victor! Madame, it cannot be true! My son——"

"Look at his face," she said disdainfully. "Is it not proof enough?"

The Chevalier was gnawing at his lip, livid, but he contrived to smile.

"You rave, cousin. I know naught of this affair."

"But ye will return to your own lands, sir, nevertheless."

The Sire came towards her, and his eyes were haggard all at once.

"Madame, it cannot be true! It were dishonour! I implore thee listen to Victor's defence!"

"Can he deny it?" she sneered.

The Sire turned to his son.

"Victor! My God, Victor, thou didst not do this thing?"

"Nay," the Chevalier muttered, but could not look at him.

His father started forward, seizing him by the shoulder.

"Look at me! Is it true?"

The Chavalier shot one glance at Margaret's rigid countenance, and laughed.

"You are over squeamish, *mon père*," he said carelessly.

The Sire's hands fell away from him as from a thing unclean.

"Thou craven cur!" he whispered, and turned again to the Countess. "Madame, I can say naught, save that this deed is as foul to me as it is to you."

She bent her head.

"That I know, sir. I do trust that thou wilt continue here, for I do value thy friendship. But thy son goes within forty-eight hours, or I will formally banish him from my domain. That is my last word."

"You are generous, madame," her uncle said, very low.

"For thy sake, my uncle," she answered, and stretched out her hand to him.

The Chevalier bowed.

"Then I take my leave of thee, fair cousin." He sneered at her. "When thou art miserable in yon Saxon's arms, think of me!"

"Go!" his father thundered. "Must you add to your vileness? Go!"

The Chevalier bowed again, ironically, and went out. His father picked up the flower he had dropped, and threw it into the fire.

"Madame, ye will excuse me. I am—not myself. This hath been a bitter blow. I would fain retire."

"Indeed, I am very sorry," Margaret said, her hand on his arm. "I could not do otherwise."

"Ye were too generous," he said shakily, and kissed her hand.

As soon as he was gone, Margaret turned to Jeanne, who all the time had stood silent behind her chair.

"*Chérie,* wilt thou request thy Geoffrey to wait on me here?"

Jeanne threw her arms about Margaret.

"Oh, Margot, Margot, it was well done. I will fetch Geoffrey at once!" She ran out, flushed and excited.

She found Geoffrey in the great hall, disconsolate at his friends' departure. When he saw her his brow cleared, and he held out his arms.

"Nay, I am come on an errand," she said demurely, and curtsied. "The Lady Countess doth request your presence in her chamber, milor'."

Geoffrey came to her, sweeping her off the ground in his embrace.

"What care I for the Lady Countess? Kiss me, thou rogue!"

Jeanne obeyed meekly, and was set down.

"This is very wrong," she reproved him. "It is no way to treat a herald. Follow me now, Geoffrey, at once!"

"What wants thy mistress?" he asked.

Jeanne led him up the stairs.

"No doubt she will tell thee," she said. "Geoffrey, it is not at all seemly to put thine arm about a herald's waist."

"Nay, but it is very seemly to put mine arm about my betrothed's waist," he retorted, and drew her protesting onward. Outside Margaret's door he paused. "Kiss me, or I will no further," he threatened.

"Thou art a sore trial," Jeanne sighed, and raised her bewitching little face. "No, that is enough, Geoffrey! What if someone were looking?" She opened the door. "Sir Geoffrey, madame!"

"Enter, enter!" Margaret said, and came forward to meet them. "Methinks thou wert gone a long time on thine errand, *chérie?*" Her eyes sparkled a little.

"That was not my fault, madame," Jeanne said. "Indeed, Sir Geoffrey is very—very—obstinate in the matter of—coming quickly."

"I doubt it not," Margaret smiled, and looked at Malvallet. "Sir, I did request your presence to tell you that I have banished my cousin from this land for—for setting his men to slay Lord Simon. I—I will have no such—dishonour on my head—so—so will ye please to—see to it that he is gone within—forty-eight hours? I—I do not desire that—anyone should be told—why he goes."

Geoffrey recovered from his amazement with difficulty.

"Madame! Ay, I will see to it. Let me say, madame, that I honour you—greatly."

She smiled rather sadly.

"It was—the least I could do," she said. "I—Sir Geoffrey, you and I—you and I—have fought in the past—and I have given ye—no cause to love me. But—but I am wiser now—a little—and I would wish to—live at peace with you."

Geoffrey knelt at once, kissing her hand.

"Madame, I thank you. Be assured that I will do all in my power to aid and uphold you in this land."

She pressed his fingers slightly.

"Thank you," she said. "When do ye steal my Jeanne from me?"

He rose.

"Why never, madame. I only seek to wed her. And that right soon."

"I—I wish you—happiness," she said unsteadily, and tried to smile.

Jeanne caught her hands.

"Ah, *chérie,* you too shall have happiness!"

Margaret's head was bowed.

"Maybe. I—I think I will be—alone for a while."

They left her then, her head held bravely and her lips smiling.

XVIII

How he came to Bayeux, to the King

He rode slowly into Bayeux, at the head of his men, Alan at his side, and Huntingdon some way behind, leading the rearguard. He had ridden north and west, past Falaise and Caen, for Belrémy was situated between Argentan and Falaise, commanding the centre of Lower Normandy some twenty-five leagues from Bayeux. On his arrival he went straight to where the King dwelt, taking Alan with him. Henry received him at once, and dispatched a page to conduct him to his room. He was there with his brother, the Duke of Clarence, who commanded one of the three divisions of the army, and whose task it was to prepare for the advance on Rouen.

When Simon entered Henry came quickly forward.

"Ah, my Soldier!" He would not permit Simon to kneel, but embraced him, and also Alan. "And my Poet! Where is my Knight?"

"At Belrémy, Sire," Simon answered. "Huntingdon came with me."

Henry was disappointed.

"I would you had brought Malvallet in his stead, Simon, but ye know best."

"Why, Sir," Alan said, "Simon left Geoffrey in a lady's arms. He is shortly to be wed."

"What?" Henry turned in astonishment. "Is it indeed so? Not—not the Amazon?"

"No!" It was Simon who answered, quickly. "One of her ladies."

"Is it so? I had suspected Alan of it, but not Malvallet. Sit down, Simon, and tell me all." He touched a pile of parchment sheets on the table. "Thy dispatches are very curt." He smiled, and picked one up. "Listen, Alan! 'My very dread and sovereign lord the King'—so we start, and all is well. But wait!—'I have the honour to inform your Majesty that the town of Belrémy did yesterday morning make submission after an attack from my forces. I have also the honour to inform your Majesty that the castle has ceded, save for the Lady Countess, who holds out against your Majesty. I am your Majesty's faithful servant, Simon of Beauvallet.' Well! My Majesty's faithful servant just whets mine appetite for news, and no more. Here again—'I am constrained to tell your Majesty that on Tuesday last the Lady Countess did escape from Belrémy, accompanied only by her lady, Mademoiselle Jeanne. I did set forth in pursuit, and finding madame in the hands of your Majesty's ally, Raoul, called the Terrible, did slay him for the treatment he did mete out to the Lady Countess. And so have rid Normandy of a very foul rogue.' I thank thee, Simon." Henry's eyes twinkled. "As you say in this lengthy dispatch, Raoul was mine ally. And a pretty time I have had, seeing his people who flocked here demanding thy head."

"What said your Majesty?"

"Why, I did say that I desired no further dealings with Raoul's men, but I would know why my allies are thus summarily slain, without trial or delay."

Simon stood up.

"Ay, Sir. I do owe you an apology, but in my place ye would have done the same."

"I doubt it not," Henry said. "But it was unlike thee to kill him without trial, vile though we guessed him to be."

"I did it in sudden, overwhelming anger, Sir." Curtly Simon told him all that happened in Raoul's palace.

Henry smote his hands together.

"By my troth, I would I had been there! The knave! I am well rid of him, indeed. But it has caused a deal of pother, Simon."

"The blame is mine alone, Sir."

"I'd not lay it on thy shoulders, my Simon. I must uphold my generals."

"Sire, if it please you, punish me for the deed, so the French shall not call you assassin."

"It is over now," Henry answered. "Clarence dealt with them."

Simon smiled across at the Duke, of whom he was very fond.

"Then I thank your Grace."

"I'd uphold thee through fire and water!" Clarence said. "But I was all amazed when I heard how Simon the Just had fallen."

Alan upraised his dreamy voice.

Nay, it was justice. Quick justice."

"The Poet hath spoken," Henry laughed. "Now, Simon, tell me from beginning to end, how you took Belrémy."

"By siege first, and then by storm, sir."

Henry clicked his tongue impatiently.

"And now I know," he remarked. "Alan, tell me!"

Alan crossed his legs.

"Certainly, Sire. We sat down before Belrémy until Christmas-tide, and lived in blissful peace. I composed an ode and Geoffrey kicked his heels. Simon likes not bliss, Sir, nor peace. He must always be at work. So he dug a mine into the town, under the southern ramparts, which seemed made of granite. Very pleased was he with the mine, Sire, and he set his brain to work out a plan. Huntingdon had sat down before the western ramparts, which were unstable and ready for assault. Simon bade him, at a certain hour of a certain day, train his cannon upon it for a while, and at a given signal, storm the walls, thus attracting the garrison. Geoffrey and I were in readiness with the rest of our army, for it was Simon's plan to go with eleven other men along his mine, to dig themselves out within the town, and, so soon as Geoffrey had given the signal for assault, and the town was in a turmoil, to speed to the southern gates and open them, letting down the drawbridge. The which he did, Sire, by some miracle, and in we rode, Geoffrey first, to hem Huntingdon's attackers in from the rear. I came second to lead my men into the town. With Simon in his gilded armour at our head, we swept all before us to the market-place, and there had a fierce battle. I was captured, Sire, and borne to the castle, whither fled most of the garrison. The town was Simon's then, but the Lady Margaret sent to tell him that if he withdrew not his men I should hang from the battlements." Alan paused, smiling.

"Go on!" Henry commanded. "What did Simon then?"

"He entered the castle, Sir, alone, as a herald. From all I can hear he did draw upon the Lady Margaret, who would have had him slain, and held his swordpoint against her breast, so that not one of her people dared move hand or foot, lest he should press home. She is a brave lady, Sir, and she would not have let Simon have his way, but that he threatened to sack the town and slay the children. Then, perforce, she yielded, and led him to me. Simon conceived that it would be well for him to enter the castle in force, so he left me where I was (I was wounded and could not rise) and took the Lady Margaret back to his quarters as hostage. And after that it was simple."

Henry drew a deep breath.

"By God, but thou art a Man!" he cried, and looked at Simon in admiration. "And the Amazon? Tell me of her!"

It was Alan who answered.

"She is the loveliest woman ever I saw, Sir, and the bravest. A tigress."

"But she submitted?"

"Ay," Simon said. "Because I did save her life. Give me leave, Sir. I would come out of this armour."

Henry nodded.

"Ay, go. And Alan too. I like not Alan in armour. Did my Lord of Montlice find thee? I sent him."

"He did arrive, roaring," Alan smiled. "We left him with Geoffrey."

"He is a man after mine own heart," Henry said, and dismissed them.

The very next day he called for Simon and was closeted with him for a long hour. When Simon emerged at last Alan was waiting for him, and took him apart.

"Well?"

A sigh escaped this new Simon.

"I am to go into the Côtentin. To join Gloucester. Huntingdon goes to Coutances. Thou art to remain here."

"For how long art thou to be away?"

Simon shrugged.

"Till the Côtentin is subdued. Gloucester plans to lay siege to Cherbourg as early in April as may be. Cherbourg will not fall easily."

"I see," Alan said, and said no more.

Simon left Bayeux the following week, but it was not until some ten days had passed that Henry, much occupied with the affairs of his conquered land, had time for private speech with Alan. Then, one day, when he was listening to Alan's harping, he roused himself, and spoke.

"Alan, what ails our Simon?"

Alan drew a last, sobbing wail from his strings, and laid the harp aside.

"Ah!"

"Dour he was always, but never did his mind wander as now it doth! Half the time he dreams, and once I heard him sigh. Simon! Then there is new light in his eyes, and methinks he is more gentle than of yore. What hath come to him? Is he sick?"

"Some call it sickness, Sire."

Henry turned sharply round in his chair to gaze at Alan.

"God's my life, he is not—he cannot be—in love?"

"Why, Sir, have you not always said, with me, that love would one day come to him?"

"Ay, but—Alan, I never suspected. Who is it?"

"It is the Lady Margaret of Belrémy, Sire."

The King's jaw dropped. In blank astonishment he stared at Alan.

"The Amazon? The Tigress? Alan, you jest!"

"No, Sir. True it is. I saw it coming slowly, but Simon knew not his own heart till he saw my lady in Raoul's arms."

"Then that was why he killed him!" Henry started up. "It was jealousy!"

"It was the lion in him, Sir, roused to awful rage."

Henry sank back.

" 'Fore God, I am glad I was not Raoul! And she? Doth she love him? Is there love in her?"

"Love there is, Sir, but also pride. She loves him, but she will not admit it, even to herself. They woo with daggers, Simon and his lady."

Henry smiled.

"I would give much to see it. She hates him, then?"

"So she says, Sir, but it is a strange hatred. She loves him, and when he returns to her, she will wed him."

"Return?" Henry frowned. "I had planned to have him at my side when I march on Rouen."

Alan said nothing.

"Speak, Alan!"

"If ye take Simon to Rouen, Sire, it is death to his happiness. That campaign may last a year."

Henry leaned his chin in his hand, thinking.

"What would ye have me do? If Simon loves indeed he must have his way. Geoffrey, too, I suppose. Yet I can ill spare them."

"He will follow your Majesty unquestioningly, Sir. It is not for me to advise you."

"He would sacrifice his love for his duty?"

"He is Simon of Beauvallet," Alan said quietly.

XIX

How they fared at Belrémy during his absence

The Lady Margaret walked upon the terrace of the castle alone. It was mid-March, and Simon had been absent for three long weeks. She had had news of him through Geoffrey, and knew that he was fighting in the Côtentin, away to the west, with King Henry's brother, the Duke of Gloucester. He did not write to Margaret, and he sent no messages. The letters that came from him came rarely, and were bald and unsatisfying.

The Lady Margaret glanced across the gardens wistfully. In the pleasaunce Geoffrey sat with his bride, she knew. She craved companionship, but she would not intrude into these two lovers' idyll. Her ladies wearied her, and she had sent them from her, to pace slowly up and down the terrace, her thoughts far away, and her black eyes sad and longing.

A rumble sounded behind her; Fulk was stumping after her, his little eyes twinkling good-humouredly.

"Hey, hey! Not so fast, lass!" he roared. "Come thou here, I say!"

He and she were close friends by now, and the haughty Lady Margaret came meekly to his side, to sit down on the stone seat. Fulk sank heavily beside her, puffing and blowing.

"What dost thou here, silly maid?" he demanded.

"I am not a silly maid," she answered mildly. "I am a woman-grown. So be not so rude, milor'."

"Ho—ho! And how old art thou? No more than twenty-eight, I'll swear."

"Twenty-eight?" Margaret sat up indignantly. "I am not yet twenty-six!"

Fulk laughed.

"A maid still! Now whence this fiery blush?"

"Do—do I look twenty-eight?" Margaret demanded.

"Nay, nay, twenty-one rather. What dost thou here, alone?"

"I was—taking the air."

"I'll warrant ye were sighing and pining for that lad of mine."

"Alan?" said the Lady Margaret coolly. "Nay, why should I?"

"Alan! Hark to the child! Simon, thou dull girl!"

"I—do not think of him at all! And—and I will not have ye—call me names!"

"Here's a heat! Art a pert, saucy lass, I say."

"Well, sir, and what else?"

"A wilful, headstrong baggage!" Fulk roared.

Margaret covered her ears with her hands.

"Do not shout at me!" she said. "I wonder you care to sit with a—a baggage!"

"So do I," Fulk grunted. "A fitting pair will ye make, you and Simon. Belike ye will scratch his eyes out before he hath time to school ye. Maids were more gentle when I was a lad."

"Milor' Fulk, I do not know why ye should couple my name with that of Lord——"

"There's enough, there's enough! Think ye I am come to listen to thy foolish chatter against Simon? Bah! Bah, I say!"

"I heard you," said the Lady Margaret.

"Thou and thy hate! Talk for babes! Empty lies!"

"Sir——"

"Now, will ye have done, Margot? Body o' me, do ye think to fool a man of my years? Thou froward maid!"

The Lady Margaret abandoned the struggle.

"Indeed, I have never been so set at naught and—and bullied in my life!"

"Better for thee if thou hadst," growled Fulk. "Thou dost need a master."

The Lady Margaret tilted her chin.

"And will have one. In Simon!" Fulk went on, louder. "Shake not thy head, I say!"

"He—Simon—will not return. Thou—thou must look for my master—elsewhere," she said, a tiny catch in her voice.

Fulk put his great arm about her waist.

"Said I not thou wert a silly lass? Did he tell thee that he would come back? Answer me, Margot!"

"I have forgotten."

"That for a tale! He said he would return, and he breaks not his word."

"I—I do not—care!"

"Ho—ho!" Fulk pinched her cheeks. "Canst look me in the face and say that, child!"

Margaret was silent, eyes downcast.

"Now here come a pretty pair," Fulk remarked, and looking up Margaret saw Geoffrey and Jeanne wending their way across the garden. Geoffrey's arm was about

Jeanne's waist, and his black head was bent over her brown one.

Margaret looked away, chin set firmly.

"Never fret!" Fulk said. "Simon will come. Hey, there!"

The absorbed couple below started, and looked up.

"Is this the way thou dost mind thine affairs?" Fulk bellowed jovially.

"Ay!" Geoffrey answered. "So please you, sir, this is mine affair."

"I am not at all," Jeanne said with dignity. "I shall warn all maids 'gainst marriage. Husbands are very ungallant persons." She looked up at Fulk. "Once I did think Geoffrey courtly and kind," she said plaintively.

"And thou thinkest it no longer?" Margaret asked, smiling.

Jeanne shook her head mournfully.

"He is a tyrant, madame. My life is misery."

"What hath Geoffrey to say?" Margaret inquired.

He laughed up at her.

"Why, madame, that maids are sweet, but wives are shrews."

"Oh!" Jeanne turned to pummel him.

Fulk's great laugh rang out.

"There's for you, Jeanne! God's Body, kissing again? Margot, let us hence! My stomach turns at all this billing and cooing. Give me thine arm, child." So they went away together.

"He—he—called me—the Amazon," Margaret said, as they crossed the hall.

"Simon? A murrain on him for a scurvy knave!"

She smiled faintly.

"And yet you love him."

"I? What ails the girl? I love that roystering, obstinate young hothead? Now, by my troth——"

"Who is lying now?" Margaret said softly.

Fulk squeezed her arm.

"Thou hast me there. He is a good lad, when all is said and done. I do wish to see him happy, Margot."

"Oh?"

"Ay. And think not that a pert, wilful lass who doth

274

not know her own heart shall gainsay my lion-cub! Think it not, Margot!"

"I—I—am not that—that wilful lass," she said, very low.

"Are ye not? Who——"

"For—for—I do know mine own heart well."

"Then what is it?"

"Ah, I—I shall not tell thee that."

"So long as ye do tell it to Simon, I care not," Fulk said gruffly.

XX

How he was sent for by the King

Early in April the King spoke again to Alan of Simon. He called him to his closet one evening, and smiled upon him, holding up a bulky packet of parchment sheets.

"Come hither, my Poet. These came today from my brother of Gloucester. Simon is alive and well."

"God be praised!" Alan said devoutly. "What says his Grace, Sire?"

"He says much," Henry answered. "On the first day of the month he came to Cherbourg, and sat down before it. Listen! 'But so well fortified and provisioned is the town that assault were folly. It but remains for me to lay siege to it, with your lordship's gracious leave, that in time I may starve it into submission. As I judge this task will prove long and arduous, I think not to enter Cherbourg until the summer, if I do enter it then. Your Majesty's well-beloved, Lord Simon of Beauvallet, whom I did send to aid Sir John Robsart in the taking of Carentan and St. Sauveur-le-Vicomte, did join me three days since with the news that the aforesaid towns have yielded to your Majesty. Beauvallet doth render good account of himself, and out of his whole force hath lost but seven men, three having died of sickness. I do beseech you, my dread Sovereign lord and brother, if you have need of Beauvallet, to send for him, for I have ample force, Huntingdon having come also to join me, from Coutances, which town did surrender to your puissant Majesty the Sixteenth day of March.' " Henry laid the parchment down. "This is good news, Alan."

"Very good, Sir, save that Cherbourg is so strong."

"Gloucester will reduce it. Mine answer to his dispatch is here." He touched a parchment-sheet. "I have sent to command Simon to join me, with his own men."

Alan bowed.

"What hath your lordship for him then, Sir?"

Henry seated himself at the table.

"I have thought deeply on it, my Poet, and at last I have seen how I may serve both mine own ends and his. I will make Simon warden of this land."

Alan's eyes widened.

"Sire!"

"Thou dost know that I have a Chancery in the making, Alan. Morgan is to hold the seal of the Duchy, Luttrell is to be Seneschal. But at the head of the military government I will have Simon, for he is all a soldier, and his grip on all matters military is of iron. Thus shall he remain in Normandy. Art thou satisfied?"

Alan knelt gracefully, and kissed the King's hand.

"Your Majesty is the kindest man alive," he said. "It is no wonder that your very name is beloved."

Henry pulled him up.

"Have done!" he said. "Malvallet and you shall be under Simon. Thus ye shall not be separated, and thus shall I know that my warden hath under him two men who will serve him faithfully, obeying his least command. I may march then upon Rouen with a quiet mind. Thank me not. If it please you, it doth also please me, save that I must lose my three Graces for a while."

"I cannot thank you, Sir," Alan said fervently.

"No words of mine could express what I do feel."

Henry laughed.

"I am glad of it," he said, and waved him away.

Ten days later Simon rode into Bayeux, the men of Beauvallet and some of Montlice behind him. As he came through the streets he was lustily cheered, and when he raised his hand in stiff salute, the cheers redoubled, and flowers were flung down before him, and caps tossed high in the air. So he came to Henry's quarters, and straightway went to where Alan lodged.

Alan sprang up as he entered, and clasped his hands for a long minute.

"My Simon!"

Simon smiled, and his fingers gripped Alan's. Then he released the slim hands in his.

"All is well with thee?"

"Very well. And with thee?" Alan asked affectionately.

"Gloucester carried all before him. Ye did hear that St Lo fell to Hungerford?"

"Ay. Gloucester sent word. Domfront holds firm against Warwick still."

"So I thought. But Domfront will fall before Cherbourg hath lost one stone from its walls. What doth the King want of me?"

"He told thee not?"

"Nay. His dispatch was as short as he says mine are wont to be." Simon drew it from the leathern pouch at his belt, smiling. " 'To our well-beloved servant, Simon of Beauvallet: It is our pleasure that you make all haste to join us here in our town of Bayeux, bringing with you the men of Beauvallet and Montlice. Henry R.' There is more, written on the back. 'And thus have I my revenge on thee, my Soldier. Have I stirred thy curiosity?' "

Alan laughed.

"Well? Hath he done so?"

Simon shrugged.

"I suppose I am to join Clarence. All ways are one to me. Alan, what ails the troops? As I rode hither they did cheer me as though I had accomplished some great emprise. What means it?"

"The King will tell thee," Alan answered. "Hast thou had word from Geoffrey?"

"Ay. Belrémy is at peace. The—the Lady Margaret did banish her cousin for seeking to slay me." His eyes gleamed suddenly.

"So I did hear. What does that betoken, think you?"

Simon did not answer.

"The Lady Margaret's hate is not so strong, perchance," Alan said gently.

"She hates me not. I'll go change my raiment before I see the King." He went out heavily.

Just before supper a page came to him, to command his attendance on the King. He went at once, and entering the audience chamber, found Henry seated on a dais, with his Council about him.

Simon paused on the threshold, and shot a quick look round. Then he went forward, and bowed low to Henry.

"Your lordship sent for me, Sir?"

"Ay." Henry held out his hand. "I have work for thee, Simon."

Simon kissed his hand and released it.

"That is good news, Sire."

"Arduous work, my Soldier," Henry warned him.

"I desire naught better, Sir."

"Give me the order, Philip," Henry said to Philip Morgan, standing beside him.

Morgan placed a long scroll in his hand, which Henry gave to Simon.

"Thou wert appointed to this office three days since, Simon, by vote of Council and my will."

Simon looked round again, slightly frowning. Then he bent his head over the parchment, and began to read. In grandiose terms it gave him to understand that it was the King's most gracious command that he be appointed Lieutenant and Warden of the Lands and Marches of Normandy,[1] to maintain the peace in

---

[1] As a matter of stern, Historical fact this post was held successively by the Earls of March and Salisbury. —*Author's note.*

the Duchy, and to have control over the troops that should be left therein, while the King went on to Rouen. Further, that it was the King's most gracious will that he should have under him the following knights: A list of names met Simon's eye, the first two of which were Sir Geoffrey of Malvallet and Sir Alan of Montlice. There was much more besides, and at the bottom of the scroll was Henry's seal and signature with the signatures of each one of his Council beneath.

Simon read on to the end. Then he looked up, straight into Henry's eyes. A long breath he drew, and there was a wondering look on his face.

"Is this—indeed your Majesty's pleasure?" he asked quietly.

Henry bowed his head.

"Sir——" Simon stopped, at a loss for words. "I—think I have done little to deserve this great honour."

A low murmur of dissent came from the Council. Henry nodded towards Luttrell, who rose. One by one the Council filed out, so that Simon was left alone with the King.

"Thou canst not refuse the task," Henry said, and came down from the dais. "It is sealed and done. A man must I leave behind me, so I leave thee."

"Refuse!" Simon laughed shortly. "I cannot tell you, Sir, what this means to me. If you do indeed think me worthy of this command, I can only thank you from the bottom of my heart."

Henry laid a hand on his arm.

"Thank me not. I serve myself. One thing I would suggest to thee."

"What is it, Sir?"

"That ye dispose your lieutenants how ye will, but that you yourself make some central spot your headquarters. Belrémy seems a right good town, and one that is large and of important standing. Get thee to it, my Soldier."

Simon looked sharply round at him, and his eyes narrowed.

"This is Alan's doing," he said.

Henry shook his head.

"Nay, nay, fear not that I seek to favour thee, thou proud lord! It is my will. Further it is my will that ye espouse the Lady Margaret with all speed. Simon, thou rogue! Never was I more amazed than when I heard that love had come to thee! Love for the tigress!"

"Nay, Sire!" Simon answered forcefully. "She is no tigress, but a brave lady!"

"An Amazon!"

"Nay, a babe, for all her years and stateliness."

Henry laughed at him.

"When I return from Rouen, I will see thy babe. Umfraville called her not that."

"He knew her not," Simon said, and smiled to himself.

Henry grasped his hand.

"God grant thee happiness, Simon. May thy lady be kind and gentle."

Again Simon laughed.

"Gentle she is not, Sire, kind I will make her. She is wilful and fierce, and swift with her dagger. It is a fighting maid that I will take to wife, not easily won. I would not have it otherwise."

"Thou must ever choose the hardest task," Henry said in amusement. "As soon as may be thou shalt go to Belrémy, but there is work yet to be done. May shall see thee in thy lady's arms. Wilt thou write to Geoffrey?"

"Nay, Sir. I will take them by surprise, so that my lady shall have no time to remember her stubborn pride. And, as your lordship doth know, mine is no able pen."

Henry's eyes twinkled.

"I have served thee out for thy curt dispatches, Simon."

"I was not curious at all, Sir," Simon replied. "I thought your dispatch to me long enough. It told me that ye had need of me. What more should I wish to know?"

"God's my life! Are ye turned courtier?" Henry exclaimed.

"Nay, I but spoke the truth," Simon said, rather surprised.

XXI

How he came to his own

The Lady Margaret stood by the sundial in her
pleasaunce, gazing wistfully down at it. It was May
now, and all about her flowers bloomed, while the
trees in the orchard, beyond the hedge, were laden
with blossom. The sun shone warmly down upon the
garden, and the birds sang, but the Lady Margaret
was sad.

For a long time she stood motionless, thinking of
one day in February when she had come running to
this spot to warn Simon of danger. And as she thought,
she smiled a little, drearily, and brushed her hand
across her eyes. Where Simon was she knew not,
whether dead or alive. No word had come from him
since March, and although Geoffrey made light of it,
saying that Simon would never write unless he were
forced to do so, Margaret felt the silence ominous, and
feared she knew not what.

Today she was strangely nervous, jumping at every
sound, as though she expected something to happen.
Even now she lifted her head, listening, for it seemed
to her that far away in the town some excitement was
on hand. The faint noise died, but it came again
presently, and she heard the echo of Fulk's great voice,
wafted to her by the gentle breeze. A deep breath she
drew, and stood very still, hands clenched at her sides
until the knuckles gleamed. She looked towards the
entrance to the pleasaunce, lips slightly parted, and
in her eyes were dread and hope.

And at length a soft tread reached her straining
ears, and her knees seemed suddenly to shake. Round
the bend in the alley that led to the pleasaunce, Simon

came, and paused some few yards away from her, looking at her from under his jutting brow.

The Lady Margaret stood very still; only her bosom rose and fell quickly, and her eyelids flickered. She gazed in dumb longing at the fair giant before her, but she could not speak.

Simon's deep voice reached her, and she quivered with a kind of fearful joy.

"Willingly shalt thou come to me, and willingly give thy heart," he said, and held out his arms.

The Lady Margaret took a faltering step forward, impelled by some invincible force. Her hands flew out, trembling.

"Milor'!" she whispered. "Thou hast—come back!"

"Ay, I have come as I swore I would. To lead thee to the altar."

A sob broke from her, but it was a glad sob. She came to him, swiftly, stumblingly, her eyes full of tears.

"My heart—was thine—long since!" she said brokenly. "Willingly—do I—come!"

Then she was caught in a great embrace, swept off her feet, and crushed against Simon's breast. She gripped the folds of his tunic with her slender hands, face upturned, half-crying and half-laughing.

"Thou art—with me again! Ah, Simon, Simon, I knew not what to think! I feared—Simon, milor'!"

His arms tightened ruthlessly about her. For one moment he looked down into her brimming eyes, his own ablaze with some new-born passion, then he bent and kissed her fiercely, on her eager mouth. And now, at last, the Lady Margaret returned his kisses, her pride dead, and all her fighting instincts flown.

So for a while they stayed thus, locked in each other's arms, till the grip about Margaret's shoulders slackened, and she was set upon her feet, breathless and quivering.

"My—queen!" Simon said huskily, and knelt suddenly to kiss the hem of her gown.

The Lady Margaret looked down at him, and in her face was all the wonder of love. Gently she laid a hand on the bent head, and put her other into his, drawing him to his feet.

"Simon, oh, milor', kneel not to me! It is I who am 'neath your heel!" She sank against his shoulder, and laughed unsteadily. "I swore vengeance on thee! Undying vengeance!" she whispered. "I said that I would make thee rue the day thou didst cross my path. Ah, Simon, Simon!"

His arms were round her once again, holding her close.

"Mayhap I shall live to rue that day," he said, and his rare humour peeped out. "Undying thy vengeance shall be, and on our marriage-day it will be complete."

"Oh, ungallant!" she cried, and put up her hand to touch his lean cheek. "Thou most cruel of lovers! Was—was ever a maid so harshly wooed?"

"Was ever a maid so hardly won?" he retorted, and carried her hand to his lips. "Thou tigress! Wilt thou stab me, I wonder, if ever I gainsay thee?"

"Never again!" she said softly. "I could not do it— that day in January, though I hated thee then. How should I stab thee now that my hate has turned to love? I would follow thee barefoot across the world!"

"Nay, for if I walked across the world, thou wouldst lie in mine arms, Margot. Never again shalt thou flee from me."

"Thy strong arms. . . !" she murmured. "Even as thou didst bear me from Raoul's palace. Stern, merciless conqueror! Simon, *mon maître et mon seigneur!*"

It was a long time before they left the pleasaunce, and then they went slowly, Simon's arm about his lady's waist, her head resting back against his shoulder, and her hand in his.

"I never thought to be so happy!" she sighed. "I never dreamed that I would bend to your will!"

"I must have loved thee from the moment I set eyes on thee," Simon answered.

Margaret smiled.

"What! Was it love then, that made thee mar my skin?" she pressed his hand to the scar on her breast.

"I know not. Thou wert a statue made of ice."

"An Amazon thou didst call me! But oh, thy sword hurt!"

He bent to kiss the scar.

"An Amazon thou wert, who flinched not nor cried out. How could I have treated thee so?"

"Ah, no, I am glad! I said that for as long as the scar remained I would remember thy cruelty, and so I will, and with it mine own attempted treachery. Simon, that shame will never die!"

"My shame is greater, Margot, for I threatened a woman, a child."

"No child am I, milor'. Just—just an Amazon."

He laughed down into her pleading eyes.

"That rankles still, my queen. I would not have thee aught but that. I did tell my King that the lady I love is a tigress, beautiful beyond words, swift with her dagger, proud and indomitable to her foes, but with a great heart, and a brave spirit."

Margaret blushed.

"Nay. I am not so fine. I have failed in all that I meant to do, and only succeeded in one thing. And that I did not mean to do. I stole what men thought was not there to steal. Thy cold heart, *monseigneur*. I swore to bring an army about your ears, and behold, I was foresworn. I tried to keep my hatred for thee alive, but it withered. See how thou hast humbled me!"

Simon drew her closer.

"One mistake didst thou make, dear heart. Thou didst set thy will against mine, for I had sworn to vanquish and to wed thee."

"How vain my fight hath been!" she sighed. "In everything was I beaten, till thou hadst me at thy feet. And even then I would not realize, though Jeanne knew, and my Lord Fulk roared at me for a pert, wilful baggage. A silly maid, he called me, and bade me know that Simon of Beauvallet was not one to be worsted by an obstinate woman."

Simon smiled.

"If my lord hath called thee names, then doth he love thee indeed."

"Oh, he hath not a good word to say for me, but

bellows at me until I tell him that he is wrongly named, and should be the Bull, not the Lion. There is only one Lion." She drew his hand to her cheek. "Thy King will let thee stay with me? Thou wilt not go forth again?"

"My King hath made me lieutenant of the troops he leaves in Normandy, Margot. Thou wilt never be rid of me again, but when he returns from his campaign I will show him a gentle, docile English wife."

"Nay, 'tis I who will show him a tamed husband. Thou shalt be Count of Belrémy, and rule my land—thy land now."

"And when I take thee to England thou shalt be the Lady Baroness of Beauvallet, for all I have is thine."

They had come now to the castle, and went into the great hall, hand in hand. Geoffrey and Jeanne were there, waiting for Simon to bring his lady in, and Fulk was standing by Alan, one arm flung round his son's shoulders. He and Jeanne came forward, Jeanne running to her friend, Fulk waving his stick at Simon.

"So there thou art!" he roared. "First it is Geoffrey and his Jeanne, kissing and fondling until I am made sick by the sight of it, and now thee, thou good-for-naught, and Margaret, the graceless lass! Hadst thou no more sense than to thrust thy head into the halter, thou silly lad? Let me get hold on thy hand, I say!" He wrung it vigorously, his little blue eyes twinkling ferociously. "Always thou must conquer! I could weep when I think how none hath ever withstood thee! Small wonder is it that thou art a conceited coxcomb. Margot, thou rogue, come to me!" He embraced her noisily, shaking her to and fro. "What did I tell thee? Did I not say that my lion-cub would master thee? I warrant he will tame thy hot blood, saucy maid!" He rounded on Simon again, smiting him fondly on the shoulder. "Now I do say that if she sticks her dagger into thee, it will be but thy just deserts, lad! We will see what a slip of a girl may do to thee! Oh, thou art well-matched! A pair of fools, by my troth!"

"Shouting and blustering again!" Margaret said severely. "Thy gout will plague thee more than ever, and that will be *thy* just deserts!"

Fulk laughed delightedly, never so pleased as when Margaret chided him.

"Oh, she will school thee, Simon! Never was there so determined a lass! God's Body, I never thought to get me a daughter so much after mine own heart!"

Margaret pushed him into a chair, dropping a kiss upon his brow.

"A Bull and a Lion," she said. "What will my life be betwixt you? What with thy passions and my lord's obstinacy—oh, Jeanne, am I not beset?"

Simon was kissing Jeanne's hand, in congratulation on her marriage. She dimpled, looking mischievously into his eyes.

"I shall warn Margot to have none of thee, milor'—I will tell her—oh, terrible things about a husband's tyranny!"

Geoffrey laid his hand on Simon's arm.

"Simon, mark well my words! Wives are the devil—and I know!"

"In truth," Alan sighed, "I am the only wise one amongst us all."

"Art a silly lad!" Fulk rumbled, and cast him an affectionate though fiery glance.

"Alan speaks sooth for once," Simon said, and placed his finger on Margaret's indignant lips. He had her in his arms again, and like a needle to the magnet, Jeanne had drawn near to her Geoffrey. "For Alan throughout hath known that needs must I fall, and at Margot's feet."

"Ah, and he knew that I love thee, even before I knew it myself," Margaret cried. "Methinks he hath worked very quietly to bring about our happiness. And yet he will not seek his own."

Alan smiled sweetly.

"I observe thy folly," he said, "and know mine own wisdom. That is happiness."

Jeanne looked at Geoffrey, and a smile passed between them, of boundless conceit. Margaret stole her hand into Simon's, smiling also. Not one of them answered Alan, and he laughed, leaning on his father's shoulder, and surveying his two friends with soft, satisfied eyes.

"Are my sage words beneath contempt?" he asked.

"Ay," Simon answered simply, and looked down into Margaret's face for a long moment. A deep breath he drew, and glanced again at Alan. "Beneath contempt," said Simon the Coldheart.

NEW FROM FAWCETT CREST

THE GLOW *Brooks Stanwood*	24333	$2.75
THE GHOST WRITER *Philip Roth*	24322	$2.75
LADIES IN WAITING *Gwen Davis*	24331	$2.50
DAMNATION REEF *Jill Tattersall*	24325	$2.25
SATAN IN GORAY		
Isaac Bashevis Singer	24326	$2.50
THE CATER STREET HANGMAN		
Anne Perry	24327	$2.25
DARK PIPER *Andre Norton*	24328	$1.95
SWEENY'S HONOR *Brian Garfield*	24330	$1.95

Buy them at your local bookstore or use this handy coupon for ordering.

COLUMBIA BOOK SERVICE (a CBS Publications Co.)
32275 Mally Road, P.O. Box FB, Madison Heights, MI 48071

Please send me the books I have checked above. Orders for less than 5 books must include 75¢ for the first book and 25¢ for each additional book to cover postage and handling. Orders for 5 books or more postage is FREE. Send check or money order only.

Cost $_____   Name _____

Sales tax*_____   Address _____

Postage_____   City _____

Total $_____   State_____ Zip _____

* The government requires us to collect sales tax in all states except AK, DE, MT, NH and OR.

This offer expires 1 June 81
8050